T0204318

The Chrome Suite

The Chrome Suite

SANDRA BIRDSELL

Published by VIRAGO PRESS Limited February 1994
42–43 Gloucester Crescent
London NW1 7PD

First published in Canada by McClelland & Stewart Inc., 1992
Copyright © Sandra Birdsell 1992

The right of Sandra Birdsell to be identified as the author of this
work has been asserted by her in accordance with the Copyright, Designs
and Patents Act 1988

*A CIP catalogue record for this book is
available from the British Library*

This is a work of fiction. The characters described are fictitious, as are
the events of the story. Any resemblance to persons living or dead is purely
coincidental.

An excerpt from the novel was published in slightly different form in the
summer 1991 fiction issue of *Quarry* magazine.

"Keeping Things Whole" by Mark Strand is reproduced by permission of the
author. The quotation from *The Sweet Second Summer of Kitty Malone* is
reproduced by permission of the author.

The words from Rilke are taken from *Duino Elegies*, translated by David Young
(W.W. Norton & Company, Inc., New York, 1978).

For my children
Roger, Angela, and Darcie Birdsell

ACKNOWLEDGMENTS

This is a work of fiction and I have taken certain liberties with dates of political events and with the year of publication of Matt Cohen's *The Sweet Second Summer of Kitty Malone*, which in reality first appeared in 1979.

I would like to acknowledge the assistance of the Manitoba Arts Council and the Canada Council, and to thank the universities of Alberta and Prince Edward Island for their support during my stay as writer in residence.

With thanks to Patricia Sanders, Armin Wiebe, Lynn Schellenberg, and, especially, Ellen Seligman.

The Chrome Suite

Keeping Things Whole

In a field
I am the absence
of field.
This is
always the case.
Wherever I am
I am what is missing.

When I walk
I part the air
and always
the air moves in
to fill the spaces
where my body's been.

We all have reasons
for moving.
I move
to keep things whole.

- Mark Strand

Part One

June 1992

"I can feel it," I tell the doctor, "right there." I press the spot just to the left of my breastbone where something swollen lies. Sometimes I imagine it to be thick and flat and the texture of liver, this thing that slides around inside my body, its presence felt in an almost imperceptible movement, a nudge against my bottom rib bone, my skeleton. At other times I envision the swollen thing to have the uncertain shape of an overripe tomato; hold it too tightly and your fingers will penetrate the thin membrane of taut skin and it will spill, a shapeless pulp, into the palm of your hand.

"Here?" The doctor's breath smells of mint tea. His fingers probe the area beneath my rib cage. Tanned hands, face. A recent vacation, I speculate, spent some place where the sun is stronger. Florida? Arizona? Perhaps Greece or the Caribbean. Perhaps one of the places Piotr and I had promised ourselves we would visit.

"There." I guide his cool hand. His fingers press down and the swelling shifts sideways, eluding his touch.

"Well," he says. "You see, it could be almost anything, and then it could be nothing at all."

"I see."

He turns away from the table and sits down at his desk and

3

slips my chart from its folder. "So how is your professional life these days?" he asks. "Still tramping off here and there?"

"Fine." I gather the paper gown closed and sit up. *Living With Hypertension, The Facts of High Blood Pressure*. I read the titles of the books jammed into a small bookcase beneath the window.

He squints at the chart. "You were here back in October before last," he says to himself. He glances up and smiles. Good teeth, I think. "I just happened to turn on the television the other night and caught part of that National Film Board series, the second episode, the one you wrote? Well, it was quite good, yes, quite, quite good, I think," he says.

"That's ancient. I can't believe they're still running it."

"Now then, you'll just have to get busy and write some new stuff, won't you?" His tanned forehead crinkles and he squints at the chart again as though the question he will ask next has only just come to mind. "And your domestic life? How's that going?" He sets the chart on his lap and riffles through it. "Weren't you – ?" he asks. "Wasn't there someone in your life fairly steady for a while there?" He peers at the chart and says, "Ah, yes," as though he has come across Piotr's name. He leans back in the chair, his posture open, and even though I hear voices in the almost full waiting room, the impatient shuffle and cough of the person in the adjacent examination room, his demeanour invites me to take all day to say whatever it is I must tell him. He knows about Piotr, I think. He knows what happened. It was written up in both the local newspapers and in *The Globe and Mail*, *Saturday Night*, *Maclean's*.

"Fairly steady, six years or so." My feet are mottled, have turned blue with the chill of the room. Old feet, I think. "What do you think this thing could be?"

"What do you think it is?" he asks. "What would be your worst fears?"

"I'm not at all worried about tumours. Cancer. Not at all."

"Well, good. We'll do the necessary blood work anyway, if only to reassure you. You're what now?" Again he flips through the chart on his lap. "Ah yes, you're forty-two. Well,

4

you know the body is not perfect. I get people in here who expect that their bodies should be a hundred per cent all the time. Something goes wrong, they expect that I will tinker with it and send them home in perfect shape," he says. "I'm not a mechanic."

The door closes behind him. I dress hurriedly in the cramped cubicle, bending to slip into my shoes, and feel the swollen thing slide back into place beneath my bottom rib and rest there, a slight pressure against the bone. What do I think it is? It's absence, I think. And not the absence of Piotr, either. But the absence of me, Amy Barber. *Oh who can we turn to in this need?* I think of the line from one of Rilke's Elegies. I have turned to the physician. I would like him to operate, carve around it, deftly lift it from my chest.

I had arranged to meet a friend, Daria, at The Forks following my appointment with the doctor, and we rush across the parking lot towards one another, two bright and cheerful birds chirping our greetings; but then, as so often seems to happen, we grow closed and as still as the surface of the river, which reflects back to us the bright June sky and trees on the opposite shore. We spread our sweaters on blocks of tyndall stone still cold from the past winter, the chill a fist curled in the stone's core. We sit side by side for almost an hour, hardly speaking, and except for the dogged drone of a motorboat in the distance, we enjoy the silence.

It's early in the afternoon, mid-week, and the lunch crowd has petered out and drifted back into the office buildings behind us. Although I know it is not possible, still I searched, and had not seen Piotr among them. There is little chance that my eye will find something of him today. Daria has come straight from work and she still wears the heavy make-up she must put on to help her look younger, seamless and smooth for the camera's eye, but in the light of day her face appears soft, swollen. An overripe tomato. I imagine that if I placed a thumb beneath each of her eyes, the slightest pressure . . . I avoid looking at her and stare out across the river, at the great shell face of Saint Boniface Cathedral. The drone of the motorboat grows louder and then becomes a high-pitched whine as a small craft rounds the bend in the Red River and enters the mouth of the Assiniboine; in it, a man and a young boy. The man cuts the power to enter the marina and we watch as the boat glides towards shore. They moor their boat, the man giving instructions, the young boy scrambling about, gathering up life jackets, a pink pail, which he swings up onto the dock. The man glances our way, and then I do see Piotr. I see him in the shape of this man's stocky body, the slope of his shoulders. I lean forward and press my palm hard against my rib to push the swollen thing back into place. I hold it there.

"I wish people wouldn't do that," my friend says and turns her face away.

The young boy has a pair of binoculars around his neck and has raised them in our direction. The man speaks sharply and the binoculars drop to his chest. Daria begins to tell me, then, the reason for wanting to see me. She has broken off with the man she met recently. Not a long-term relationship this time, but still it hurts.

"Well, you know the saying," I tell Daria. "If you love someone, let him go."

"Yes, I know the saying."

"And if he doesn't come back, hunt him down and kill him."

She laughs and then blushes, slightly embarrassed at having laughed. "I must say, I haven't heard that version before." Her on-air voice is carefully modulated and serious.

"I came across it on a tee shirt. It's crude, but to the point. I think I may be that kind of person."

"Maybe you have too much time to think," she says.

I choose not to interpret her comment as concern for my mental well-being, but rather as hidden animosity over the fact that she must deny herself the luxury of self-examination; time will not allow it. She has a job she must go to every morning. She rummages about in the oversize bag on the stone beside her and pulls out a Koala Spring. "I've only got one. But we can share."

"It's okay, I'm not thirsty." I don't want the intimacy a shared bottle of drink implies; my mouth where hers has been.

"On the way over to meet you, I realized," Daria says after a while, softly. "It's June. You must be thinking about Piotr."

It is not as silent as I had thought. Not silent at all as I begin to hear the traffic of the city of Winnipeg behind me, a constant, steady hum. I listen to the wail of a siren, the low growl of another motorboat making its way round a bend in the river, its sound becoming a roaring echo as it passes beneath the Main Street Bridge, a train as it glides across a trestle bridge beyond, a child calling. I begin to hear a hundred different sounds where I once thought there was silence.

1

June 1991

"Look at this one," Amy had said as she held the tee shirt up against her chest, modelling it for Piotr. IF YOU LOVE SOMEONE, LET HIM GO. IF HE DOESN'T COME BACK, HUNT HIM DOWN AND KILL HIM. That was yesterday in a tee-shirt store on Yonge Street. They left Toronto early this morning and are on the highway now heading up towards Owen Sound and the ferry at Tobermory. Hunt him down, Amy thinks as she drives. It seemed hilarious at the time but she wonders now at how the shop is allowed to sell tee shirts like that. More than likely because it says hunt *him* down and not her, she reasons, otherwise there would be a crowd of demonstrators outside the store.

Piotr sits beside her, reading, face hidden behind *The Globe and Mail* he bought outside their hotel earlier. Because she's usually more alert than he is in the morning, she agreed to take on the first shift of driving, but she wishes now that she hadn't. She's still in shock and in the state of heightened awareness that a sleepless night brings. Nerve ends buzz and her mind races ahead, beyond the horizon. The landscape when they'd first entered country was softer, an opaque misty blend of colours, but as the sun rises behind them it becomes too brittle, too bright, and she must squint through watery eyes against the sharpness of it.

9

"Canadian humour is very strange. I don't get it," Piotr had said when she held the shirt up against her chest. He had been tense and wary and I should have known, Amy thinks: doors closing one by one, his flat-surfaced conversations, cheerful voice. I should have guessed.

She'd explained the original saying.

"I still don't get it."

"I think it means, more or less, love me or die."

"Oh, I see." He'd spoken quietly, turned his back to her, faced the window and the street, the shapes of people passing by. "All right." And then he'd told her that the time had come. He was leaving her within a week.

Amy squeezes the brakes to reduce speed. They are approaching another of the small villages and towns that have been strung out all along the way. It seems that she's barely able to gain highway speed before she must slow down again. She's caught by the old-world look of this one. Quaint, she thinks, of the use of stone, the flash of blue lobelia trailing from window boxes, and the gingerbread-house look of the store-fronts. She drops her sunglasses down to cover eyes that brim suddenly with an unreasonable longing, the desire she has to stop and find a house. The two of them, they'll enter it and disappear.

"Nice," she says as they leave the village limits. They could grow to be Mrs. and Mr. Amy Barber, an ordinary, elderly, and tenderly devoted couple who die within months of one another: tree limbs entwined and inseparable. I didn't see it coming, Amy thinks, because I didn't want to. If I had, I would have had to leave him. She watches the needle climb till it reaches a safe ten kilometres above the limit, then she holds it there. This constant stopping and starting, barely gaining highway speed and then having to cut back again, grates on her, and she worries that they'll miss the ferry. She doesn't want to have to wait. She doesn't want to sit beside Piotr on their grassy knoll overlooking the water, or pass the time on the glass-bottom boat peering at rusted hulks of sunken ships, or stand beside him on the deck while he scans the horizon with the binoculars she gave him as a Christmas gift in their third year. No! she says inwardly and slaps the steering wheel with the flat of her hand.

Piotr glances up from the newspaper, his expression quizzical.

"Anything interesting in the paper?" She asks the question he usually asks.

The question posed. Amy: a reasonable facsimile of a civilized person, a mature adult who understands and accepts that when someone says "I no longer love you," there is nothing you can do to change it. You would think she would know that by now. But no, as she sat beside Piotr in the car, driving off into the sunset in her mind, she still believed that as long as she was breathing there was something she could do. Loving and being loved was like swinging on a swing or flying. Both will and action, but will mostly. Her ferocious will would make him continue to love her and never, never leave.

"More on the massacre in the Katyn Forest," he says. He closes the paper and folds it down into a square. He's referring to the killing of fifteen thousand Polish officers and soldiers in 1942. He's told her the story of his father's narrow escape, how he'd stayed home that day, in his study, listening to his short-wave radio while most of his friends and acquaintances were snatched from city streets in broad daylight. "Photographs," Piotr says, "of the burial sight. A witness. They can't deny it much longer." When he asks her the question, "Anything interesting in the paper?" she's always perplexed to find that she can't remember a single item of importance, only incidents, small stories like the one about a woman who loses her wedding ring while out fishing on her honeymoon and then goes back there years later, lands a trophy-size fish, and, when her husband guts it, she discovers the lost ring.

Piotr removes his glasses, lifts the binoculars hanging at his neck, and scans the sky. The landscape has once again opened up to the weathered silver wood of New England-style barns, gently rolling green hills. He's searching for a bird in flight. In

11

their frequent trips across the country, Piotr has followed the gliding flight of many birds and claimed that most of them are hawks. The cords in his neck grow taut as he twists away from Amy. She sees the pebbly flesh-coloured mole at his hairline near the nape of his neck and she wants to put her finger against it and transmit the message: I know you. I know the smell you leave behind in a room, strong, like that of a furry burrowing animal. How you travel constantly to deny that burrowing instinct and a niggling, unsettling suspicion that perhaps you are, after all, a very ordinary person.

He senses her scrutiny and lowers the binoculars. He turns and smiles with a quick little nod and a wink, guessing at what she's thinking. "It will be okay, don't worry," he says, as he had kept trying to reassure her throughout most of the previous night. Where love has ended, friendship will continue on and on. They have become too close, he says, for it not to. Like twins, they read one another's minds. Fuck you, Amy thinks, and returns his wink, daring him to read her mind now. As he turns away his face drops with shock. "Amy! Watch!"

Oh God, she thinks. She has strayed into the path of an oncoming car. Her reaction is immediate and swift as their car swerves sharply to the right and safety. The other driver leans on the horn and its sound is a banner of alarm flapping in passing. Or self-righteous indignation, Amy thinks. Sorry bub.

Piotr breaks the silence that follows. "I think you're tired."

"Probably. I didn't sleep much last night."

"Oh, I see." He turns away, eyes fixed on the passing landscape. "You think this is easy for me?" he asks.

"Oh, yes, I do. I think so." The words are spat and he shrinks from the sound of them. Just once she would like him to experience her savage anger, a seed which had lain dormant during their six years together, grown now, a hard stone.

They don't speak for several moments. Then he straightens in the seat, brushes invisible crumbs or lint from his pants; a signal that he is changing the tone of their conversation. "Would you like me to spell you off for a while?" he asks.

"No, it's okay. I was day-dreaming, that's all." She resolves to be more careful.

"What were you day-dreaming about?" he asks, his voice firm, underlining his determination to set a new, safer course for discussion.

"I was thinking about what I might write next," she lies.

"Well, I thought we'd agreed."

"Maybe we agreed."

Clean, she thinks, of the landscape, restful, pastoral. A bit of mist still clings to low ground in places, and beyond, in a pasture, cows drink from a stream. Green. A Constable landscape. Pasted on for effect. Impenetrable.

She did sign a contract. Last night. She agreed to adapt a novel into a film script. She agreed for her own reasons, that while he goes off to research a project in Belgium, while he pursues his goal to become a Coppola or a Miloš Forman, she'll stay behind and continue to spin his straw, his often convoluted and vague ideas, into words. A friendship of convenience, now that love is gone.

"Are you having second thoughts? Maybe it would be better if you worked with someone else. Perhaps you want to." His voice is hurt, worried-sounding.

"No, no. It's not that. It's just that I think . . . maybe . . . " Amy stalls and her throat constricts. "Well, I think that it's time I write something of my own. For myself." The idea comes as a surprise to her.

"What would you write?" He seems equally surprised.

She doesn't reply. She thinks of the journals lying in a trunk. The pages and pages of years put down, bits of poetry and crude attempts to turn her history into fiction.

He drops the newspaper to the floor, reaches across the space between them, and turns on the radio, scanning through a series of stations until he finds the familiar voice of the CBC. He's concerned about the threat of forest fires on the other side of Thunder Bay and the highway closing down. He has an airline ticket and an appointment with a film producer living in Brussels. He will travel to Belgium to meet her there. A woman he knows from film school in Poland. Elizabeth, an old friend, he explained. Amy feels the warmth of his arm as it brushes against hers. She looks down at the sweep of fine dark hairs on his skin and the sprinkle of moles across it. She wants to touch him. A man's voice breaks the silence, drowning out the hum of tires against blacktop. "Where you white people have gone wrong is that you have forgotten that you are human," his voice says with smooth inflections. "You have forgotten your children. You have forgotten where you have buried your fathers. You have forgotten that the earth is your mother."

You white people, Amy thinks, startled at being addressed in this manner.

"It's true. You white people don't care about your dead," Piotr says. He has often described All Saints' Day, the day set aside to honour the dead with the placing of candles and flowers on graves.

Amy knows and knows. At present all eyes are turned on the Soviet Republic states. But in the past, attention had been focused on Eastern Europe for an entire winter, and hardly a day had gone by when she hadn't been reminded where the countries of Czechoslovakia, Yugoslavia, Hungary, Poland, and Romania were. She has seen countless dreary documentaries on "The Journal" of their religious and folk customs, including All Saints' Day. These people all look the same to Amy, regardless of their nationality. Colourless. Drab. Smiling into the camera and displaying rows of teeth that look spot-welded. Jaws: the character in the James Bond movie with his deadly stainless-steel smile, a parody of the dental work of the people of Eastern Europe. She thinks that All Saints' Day is a good day for those who sell candles.

"I think the man was making a point about the environment. And there's no country more polluted than yours," Amy says. They don't have anything to look forward to, she thinks, that's why they put so much store in looking back, calling it culture or tradition.

"Yes, I know." He lifts the binoculars once again and begins his search for hawks. As he squints, the white scar at the corner of his eye disappears into folds of skin. A duelling scar, he'd said with irony when she first met him. She had perceived his enigmatic response, his self-protective nature, to be arrogance. He had puzzled her. It had never happened before that she disliked a man and at the same time became prickly-skinned with lust by the smell of him, sticky with desire at the sound of his voice on the telephone.

The physical attraction would last about six months, Amy had thought. Six months of eating one another's faces off. Hot, furtive hours snatched from work for rutting. It was laughable in its intensity, the stuff that inspires satirical comedy; they knew that and were secretive, like cats.

But near the end of the first six months he fell asleep one night and stayed. This was a summer night, hot, humid. Amy went outside and sat on the deck in her bathrobe, the smell of him still clinging to her skin. And fingerprints, Amy thought, my entire body covered in fingerprints. She was unsettled by his presence in the room above her, asleep in her bed, as unsettled as he would be, she knew, when he awoke and found himself there in the morning. A light flicked on two yards down and then Daria, Amy's friend, stepped outside. Amy shrank back into the shadows. Daria stood on the steps looking out over her newly landscaped yard. As she turned to go inside, she saw Amy and waved. Wonderful, Amy thought, as Daria tiptoed barefoot down the lane, she'll see Piotr's car and put things together. Daria pushed through the gate, clutching her robe against her narrow body. "God, what a night for sleeping, eh?" she said. Worrying, Amy knew, about her 5:00 a.m. call for work. She entered the yard, seemingly not noticing Piotr's car parked beside the garage.

They sat looking up at the sky, pink with the reflection of city lights. They heard a squeal of tires echo in the street and it was quiet once again. Then Amy began to hear a rumbling sound, the sound of snoring in the room above their heads. Daria glanced up at the window and grinned. "Oh, you have company. I'm sorry," she said. "I didn't know." They were silent for several moments, listening as the snoring grew louder, a ragged guttural sound.

"It doesn't sound like anyone I know," Daria said, and

laughed. She leaned forward and patted Amy on the knee. "Don't worry, I'm not going to ask who. But I am curious."

Amy knew she was expected to say who it was, but she remained silent. She'd aroused Daria's interest with her reticence, she realized, as she sensed the tension in the woman's posture, her surreptitious search of Amy's face, eyes glancing away to sweep across the yard. Light dawned in her face as she noted the presence of his car. "Amy," she exclaimed, "not the L.B.T.! Don't tell me that you and the L.B.T.?" She began to laugh, her laughter saying that she was tickled by the idea. "I'm sorry," she said as she dabbed at her eyes with the belt of her housecoat. "You'll have to excuse me, but I thought you two didn't even *like* one another." She chuckled as she drew a package of cigarettes from her pocket, lit one. "My, my, you are full of surprises," she said. She leaned back into the chair and studied Amy. "But you know," she said carefully, searching for the right tone, "I'm really not. Surprised. I've always thought that there's something quite charming about that man. I'm not sure what it is. Maybe it's that he's so civilized."

"So, what else don't I know about you?" Amy had asked Piotr the following morning. "You snore like a chain-saw." He was standing in the bathroom, a towel wrapped around his waist, holding a basket filled with the usual paraphernalia – various cosmetics, creams, colognes. He picked through the items, his expression one of bewilderment. "Amy, what are all these things for?"

In the months following he began to tell stories about himself. The scar beside his eye wasn't really a duelling scar but the result of a skiing accident, a pole-tip glancing the corner of his eye. He told her about growing up in Kraków. How he'd fantasized about being a North American Indian and that his favourite toy had been a tomahawk, which a friend of his father's had sent as a gift from France. She was intrigued by his stories, especially the legends. The legend of Boruta, for example, the Prince of Polish devils, who had attempted to grab hold of the corner-stone of a church, to shake loose its walls and bring it down. Piotr had been to the Romanesque

16

cathedral at Tum, the church where the devil had been, and had placed his hand into the imprint of Boruta's hand. As she listened to his stories she grew aware of the paucity of her own, that she had nothing better or even of equal value to give him. And so she kept her history where it belonged. In the journals in a trunk upstairs in a closet.

At the end of the first year, he told her that he loved her. He was drunk when he said it. They had just finished shooting a film and it was during the wrap party. She rode the handlebars of a child's bicycle, a prop, and they weaved among the pillars of a cavernous warehouse, away from the echo of rock music, the smell of dope, a wild, fast ride down a tunnel-like corridor into a dark room. There they danced with their foreheads touching, mind mining mind. "I'm so tired of fighting with you," she said. He picked her up and swung her around, his laughter on the edge of hysteria breaking in the back of his throat. When he set her down he licked her cheeks, slathering her face like a dog with his hot saliva. "Yes, Aimless Amy. No more fighting. I love you."

He was sober the following morning when he stood in the doorway watching her bathe. He was fascinated by all things female. "I do love you," he said. Well, she thought, so this is it, then. This will be the end. Now he will lose his shine, his sex appeal. "But there's no future in it," he went on to say. "This doesn't change anything. It's what we agreed. I just wanted you to know that. I do love you." He would tell her that often. It was as though once he learned to say the word "love," he must use it over and over.

"I understand," Amy said. She grew shaky and her scalp tingled. Love, a transient wanting to stay for a time. But she was certain it was love because she hadn't asked him to say it and he hadn't asked for anything in return.

They begin to catch glimpses of the sun on water on both sides of the highway as they head up the strand of the Bruce Peninsula. The air changes. It becomes lighter, moist, and as she relaxes her grip on the steering wheel the knot of tension between her shoulders begins to loosen. Sunlight flashes in the windshields of several vehicles approaching in the distance, and as the cars sweep around a curve towards them the angle of light changes for a moment and the vehicles become scintillating silver balls, shimmering balls of light which seem to bounce down the highway towards them. The angle of light changes once again and the vehicles suddenly become solid. Then the traffic grows heavier, a stream of cars travelling slowly, almost bumper to bumper. "I don't like the looks of this," she says.

As they pull up beside the toll booth at the gates, the sound of the ferry's horn quivers in the air as the vessel moves away from the loading dock. Amy swears silently as the attendant guides her into the outside lane. She's thinking of the room she reserved in Thessalon at the Maranatha Motel and its kitchen closing down at eight o'clock.

"Well, at least we'll be first on the next one," Piotr says. His dark eyes stare at her from behind his glasses, steady and unblinking. He grabs her hand, squeezes. "Thank you. You're a good driver."

His formality is irritating. "Oh, I see. We're practising at being friends."

They walk to loosen stiff muscles and enter almost deserted shops and poke about the displays of souvenirs. Piotr drops a Mountie hat onto her head and places a Maple Leaf flag in each hand and snaps a picture. What will he do with the hundreds of photographs he has taken? Will he find some way to edit her out of them?

When they step out of the store they both notice the iridescent flash of colour, a hummingbird darting among flowers bordering the walk. They pause, Amy silently amazed, feeling that its presence has been arranged for their benefit, as have all the sightings of wildlife they have encountered during their six years of travels, the deer, the turtles, the beaver, the bears, a fox loping alongside a runway as their plane landed; animals stepping out from their natural habitat to view Piotr and Amy passing by. Raising their heads to greet the special children, eyes meeting eyes. They once saw a great egret gliding low above the marshes just outside of Winnipeg. Its presence was a rarity for Manitoba, a wildlife expert assured them. It had

18

appeared, a white ghostly bird, its graceful wings unfolding against the emerald cloth of the marsh, just like that. For them. The egret was herself, Amy had fantasized, hovering above the marsh of Piotr's body, touching, breathing her love into him, sweeping down the breadth of him until he rose up and cried out.

They find their usual grassy knoll facing the water. The ferry's stacks are two sticks disappearing over the horizon. They sit in silence as they eat the bread and cheese they had bought. Later, Piotr succumbs to the warmth of the sun and stretches out on the grass, head cradled in Amy's lap. He dozes while she browses through his newspaper. She reads that a "professional, employed gentleman, early 50s, 6', who enjoys the arts, is seeking a vivacious, slender, attractive, refined lady with integrity." Forget it, Amy thinks. Six feet is too tall. Hank was six feet and all she ever got from him was a stiff neck from looking up. She reads that the Roman Catholic Church in Poland is winning the right to teach its religion to atheists. Power lines must be protected in Manitoba. They don't say against what, but the inference is there. Protection against a group of people who might sabotage power lines in the middle of winter to make a point. The Tories seek billions for farmers, she reads, and thinks of the town where she grew up, how it has become reduced, looks so worn out and abandoned. She reads for almost an hour, all the bits and pieces of information that make up the world today. But not her world. It's as though the events happen on another planet and don't affect her. She reads to keep from thinking about Piotr, who is leaving her. When she closes the newspaper, the events vanish.

Piotr shifts in sleep and settles down once again into her lap, his mouth slack, fists curled. She watches as his chest rises and falls in a deep sigh. "You will always be special to me," he'd said last night. He had been sitting on the bed across from her, leaning forward, hands resting on his knees. He had been silent for almost half an hour, forehead slick and body shivering.

Frightened, Amy thought. Shivering with fear. "This is not easy," he said, he kept saying. "I'm still very fond of you."

"Then why leave?" she asked.

"I don't know." He stared at the floor, silent again for long moments, and Amy couldn't bear the tension. She went to the window, which overlooked an alley below. She'd heard voices out there earlier, the sound of vehicles. When she looked down, she saw what was to be a scene for a film. Two H.M.I. lights at the entrance of the alley beamed eerily through heavy fog steaming from machines. "They're shooting something," she said but Piotr gave no indication that he'd heard. The fog thinned and Amy saw several people emerge at the entrance of the alley and gather around a camera. A pick-up shot, because of the absence of a full crew. "Action!" a voice called and a slight figure darted across the alley and disappeared into the shadows of a darkened doorway. A fugitive, likely, she thought. She watched several takes. She would have liked to drop something down into the middle of their scene, a bottle or the glass of Scotch she held. Just as Piotr had done. He'd dropped a bomb into her scene.

"Why?"

His shoulders sagged beneath his tan shirt. He had a closet full of identical tan and brown shirts and pants. "L.B.T.," "The Little Brown Tub." The tag, a jealousy-induced one, had been pinned on him at the film institute where she met him. "Oh, you mean the little brown tub in baggy pants who pretends he can't speak the language? You mean him?" She'd told Piotr about it and he had laughed wryly, shrugging it off, saying that he was used to being disliked, and immediately he became interesting. She never told him, though, that it was she who had invented the label.

"Why?" she persisted. "If you're still so fond of me, why leave?" She winced inwardly at the word "fond."

"It's too difficult to explain," he said. "Even I'm not sure I understand."

"Try," she said, her voice taut with anger.

"All right," he said. "It's because I think that perhaps I no longer love you."

20

Contrary to Piotr's prediction they're not among the first to board the ferry. The line of cars farthest away is loaded first and then the attendant signals for them to move forward. They drop in behind the traffic streaming on towards the gaping mouth of the vessel. Tires meet the metal ramp at the entrance with a steady rhythmic clank. They'll be on the upper level, Amy realizes. Piotr guides the car up the steep grade, but just as they are about to reach the top of it, the car in front of them stops and they're left hanging at almost a ninety-degree angle. Piotr turns to her in panic. She yanks on the emergency brake. The attendant below is preoccupied with directing the car behind them onto the bottom level. "Hey, you, come on!" Piotr yells from the window and the attendant turns quickly, sees their predicament, grabs a lever, and they feel the car rise and level off. Their ears pop as car doors slam shut and people begin moving towards the stairs. "Hey, it's okay now," Amy says and rubs his knee. He takes these happenstances personally. He is constantly suspicious that the country is one big trap-line set to snare its immigrants and keep them in their place. Amy believes he's right. She takes on his anger directed at the attendant. She had come to believe that she was an immigrant, too, cut off from her country at an early age. It's this ability to identify, she will later come to realize, her ability to take on his skin, to see through his eyes, that caught her.

They find the lounge and a quiet corner and share a beer. Piotr unzips his leather folder and spreads pages across the table. Amy watches a group of teenagers mill about on the deck outside the window. They look out of place, California, in their muted pastel colours. They begin throwing pieces of hot dog to the wind and are rewarded by seagulls treading air, sometimes flying backwards in order to snatch a scrap of bun. A man stands off to one side, watching. He leans against the railing, a sharp visual contrast to the younger people and their exuberant playing at feeding the gulls. A Charles Manson look-alike, Amy thinks. He laughs as a seagull swoops down from nowhere and plucks a piece of bun off a young man's head. He's thin, a bony man, probably undernourished as a child. He digs about in his shirt pocket and then stuffs wads of something in each ear. Licks of dark hair flip in the wind. Most likely doesn't have any money and is reluctant to come in where he can smell the food, she thinks. A rousing cheer rises over a near in-flight collision of several birds snatching at the last bit of food. Then the pastel-coloured young people drift away and the unkempt-looking man watches them.

The squeak of Piotr's fine-tip felt marker sets Amy on edge. He's crossing out line after line of dialogue of a stage play, the work of a Polish playwright, which he hopes to co-produce with his new partner, Elizabeth. Angst-ridden hyperbole. Amy wonders what Eastern European writers will have to write about now. Piotr dislikes what he has read of Canadian literature. Too much kitchen sink, he says. People falling in and out of love with themselves or writers playing around with style and form because they have nothing to say. Huh, Amy thinks, as she searches through her bag for the novel she's been reading at his request. Talk about self-indulgent, getting off on the smell-of-your-own-armpit kind of love. She thumps the book down onto the table. "Huh!" she says aloud. Piotr doesn't look up. The book is *Tristan*. A translation of a novel by Maria Kuncewiczowa. She picks up the book, rests her feet on the chair beside her, and begins to read.

"Look," Piotr interrupts minutes later and points to the window. Amy looks up. The Charles Manson look-alike stands sideways at the railing facing the hull. He shoulders a small rifle. He squints down the sights and they see his mouth go "pow, pow, pow" as he pops off imaginary rounds at the gulls.

"Isn't that illegal?" she says to Piotr. She scans the room for other people's reactions, but they appear not to have noticed. "Shouldn't we tell someone?"

Piotr shrugs. "Tell who?"

In the time it took for Amy to ask the question, the man

22

lowered the rifle. He walks over to the window, bends, and then, several moments later, rises with a knapsack which he hoists onto his back. He's rolled the rifle into his sleeping bag. They see the tip of its barrel protruding out one side of it as he walks away. Piotr returns to his work without commenting. Putting the incident from his mind instantly, she knows. He needs a draft of the script to put into the computer the moment they arrive home. Needs it to take with him when he goes to meet the new person, Elizabeth, his old friend. Amy tries to erase the incident, too, as she returns to *Tristan*. She reads for several minutes and then closes the book. Must be a bad translation, she rationalizes, because she fails to see any of the passion or beauty Piotr speaks of with shining eyes whenever he refers to this work. It fails to engage her. She sets it aside and studies him. His single-mindedness is a discipline he learned during his years as a student. Today it both awes and irritates her. His earlier question, "What would you write?" hurts. It implies that she might not have anything to say. She hasn't, for instance, been caught in the maelstrom of a war. "In Canada, there would never be a war," she remembers a Czech immigrant saying. "It's too cold in Canada for a war," he'd said and laughed. "Canadians wouldn't want to go out and fight. They wouldn't want their toes to get cold."

She hasn't experienced an exotic childhood either, like the one Piotr claims to have had, toddling about in the safety of a beautiful walled garden, playing games on the Planty in the shadow of a castle, beneath his child's feet the remains of ancient moats and fortifications. Cowboy and Indian games in the Old Market in Kraków under a renaissance parapet in a square filled with hundreds of pigeons that were not really pigeons but knights, he said. The knights of dukes, cursed and turned into birds. Unlike his, her dreams have not been thwarted by the invasion of an enemy.

Yes, well, she thinks, even if I did have extraordinary stories to tell, I wouldn't have the patience to put them down. She can remember, though, whatever she wants to. She has a mind for minute detail, shades of a colour, a raised eyebrow. She could, if she wanted to, remember way back to age nine. In a place she will call . . . something unusual, she thinks, exotic. The name jumps forward from the bottle of beer placed between them. Corona. Carrion, Charon. No, something plastic and meaningless. Carona.

If she wanted to she could recall that long, strange summer when she spent almost the entire time outside, on a rope swing.

Sometimes I'd lie on my stomach and wind the swing up and let it fly and then afterwards I'd reel about the backyard, loving that off-spinning feeling of things not being what they were. I'd swing standing up, sitting down, upside down with the rope wound through my legs and chafing the skin behind my knees raw. Once I vomited into my shoes from motion sickness, and near the end of that long, strange summer, I got a sliver in my buttock from the wooden swing seat. Two small sutures closed the wound. I still have the scar. And the doctor's his, too, I imagine, on the wrist where I bit him when he tried to pin me to the table. He joked about it later, saying he'd had to give little Amy Barber as much anaesthetic as he would to put down a horse.

To the left and across the street from my yard stood the red brick face of the school, elm trees, and the jangled shimmer of television antennas. When I think of that horizon of antennas in the Fifties, I think of the word "jangled" because of its connotation of sound, the sound I thought their aluminum arms made as they embraced the invisible signal. It was also the sound of bangles jangling at a wrist: Aunt Rita as she approached the house one morning. I saw her coming. She was up early. Taking her role-playing at nurse seriously. Rita had taken a leave of absence from her job at the Film Exchange where she was in charge of distribution of short subjects and newsreels for Paramount. She had come to relieve Margaret, my mother, in the sick room. I have no idea what, if anything, she may have been doing for my father at that time, but she certainly did something later. As Rita stepped through the gate, I waved and she nodded, concentrating to keep from spilling whatever it was she carried on the covered tray. Food, I suppose. An attempt to seduce Jill's tastebuds and bring some colour back to her waxy, pale cheeks. Rita eased the gate open with her hip and passed by the veranda and down the side of the house along the pathway obstructed by overgrown weedy flower-beds.

The door closed behind her, and her white shoulders disappeared into the gloom of the back porch. She called hello in the kitchen, her heart-shaped face turned up to the ceiling as she passed her greeting through it into the sick room, my parents' room, where they had moved Jill, my sister. Where Jill had spent the past month. I continued to swing, and each time my feet shot forward the swing's metal rings squealed in the wooden crossbar above my head, groaned when I receded into the low branches of the shade tree. Squeal and groan. Squeal and groan. Like someone learning to play the violin. This was the sound of that particular long and strange summer. I remember the look of it, too, almost tropical, pools of water collecting in hub caps beside the road and rusty-looking sprinkles of mosquito larvae floating on top. Maroon and white peonies, blooming fools, the size of dinner plates. And tomatoes. Water-logged and swollen, thin-skinned fruit cracking open and leaking their juices in my Grandmother Johnson's garden.

"Do you want an orange, kid?" Jill had asked me. This was in July when it was still thought that her illness might be rheumatic fever. The middle of July. Possibly only three or four weeks after our trip to City Park on the day of the Lutheran Sunday School picnic. Jill had been kneeling on the bottom bunk bed, the humidity of the day evident in the rim of perspiration popping across her forehead. She cradled a fruit basket that someone had brought to the house. She swung her arm, and fruit bounced off the wall behind me. What I caught I could have, she said, and so, my appetite being what it was, I caught all of it and wolfed it down instantly and hid the fruit rind and seeds inside the doll house. Throughout most of that

July, and all of August, gifts arrived at the house. Paint-by-number sets. Embroidery kits. Sparkle art. Eventually Jill grew weary of these attempts to amuse her and gave the gifts to me.

I hadn't spent almost an entire summer swinging out of resentment over what extra attention Jill may have received. Not at all. I welcomed it because then there wasn't time for their eyes to pinch pieces off of me, to puzzle over, sort through, measure and compare. My parents, Timothy and Margaret Barber, my grandparents the Johnsons, Aunt Rita and my brother, Mel, all the people who entered and left the house that summer more or less ignored me. Occasionally someone would squat and say hello. Or touch my face with a tentative, quick touch, as though afraid I might bite them. They believed that I was being considerate; soft-shoeing my way through Jill's illness.

But I remember something quite different. I was relieved to be left alone because I was teaching myself how to fly.

The house loomed and receded. Moments after Aunt Rita arrived I saw Grandfather Johnson coming down the street. He walked erect that day, shoulders squared, not tight then – or with a snootful, drunk, blasted, the term depending upon whoever witnessed the prematurely retired gentleman walk by on any given day. Grandfather Johnson's pride was as great as his thirst and so he didn't drink in public. My wily and vocal grandmother had lately uncovered his stash of port, and so that day his face possessed a quiet dignity and wasn't flushed or uncertain. He carried a plant. A geranium. A red wound against his black suit. He would set the plant on the bureau at the foot of Timothy and Margaret's wide bed where Jill lay. If she was asleep, he'd stand there, fold his hands as if in prayer, and rest them against the footboard, careful not to press his weight against the bed's frame or jostle the mattress in any way. If Jill was awake, he'd say, "Now, sweetheart. Guess what it was I saw on the way over here?" He believed it was important that Jill never lose sight of the world outside the room.

He walked slower that day, as though being sober made him tired. The rope swing jerked; I felt weightless for a second, then dropped hard to the end of the slack. A wailing sound rose up in the house, high, thin, climbing above the noise of the squealing swing. A dog, I thought at first, but realized that it had come from the bathroom upstairs. Margaret. Margaret had locked herself in, opened the water taps, and was howling. My grandfather turned and looked at me, his eyes jumping with fear. Then Rita appeared at the back door, her white face angry as she looked out across the space between us. "Must you make so much noise? Must you? You're driving your poor mother crazy."

"Here, now," my grandfather said in alarm, "she's just a child amusing herself." He set the geranium down and knelt in front of me. I looked down at his pink scalp shining through thin strands of silver hair. I regretted for an instant my collusion in the past with Grandmother Johnson in ferreting out his latest supply of port. His crooked fingers trembled as he fastened the buckle on my sandal. I was to go down to the locker plant, he said, to ask for more ice. It was the only thing that would satisfy Jill's strange food cravings now. Shards of ice wrapped in a handkerchief which she would suck on. I had listened to the sound of it in the night, my sister's greedy slurping at the cold nipple.

When I returned from the errand, my grandfather waited for me beside the swing. During the walk home I'd hugged the ice-filled enamel bowl against my body and a cold spot radiated from my breastbone as I walked towards him. He held the oil can and pointed up to the metal rings screwed into the crossbar of the swing. He smiled, nudged the swing's wooden seat with his foot, and it swung back and forth, silent now, its only sound a soft whisper of rope rubbing against slippery metal. He set the oil can down on the seat and the swing moved between us, a lazy, hypnotic motion. I remember how he would clear his throat before he spoke. "Here now, Shorty." He had something to tell me, he said, and I wondered how he would say it.

Yes, she can remember. But can she be trusted? Can one trust a person who seizes every occurrence that passes by in the street and changes it instantly the second her eye rests on it?

27

She's the kind of person who believes that when she enters a room, action begins, and that when she leaves it, people freeze in their positions. She thinks, for instance, that Margaret Barber, her mother, is at this moment sitting in her bachelor apartment in Carona, motionless, not at all alive until Amy walks in for one of her monthly hour-long visits. She is a mother, too, of a twenty-year-old son living somewhere in Alberta. She wonders if he, too, is in a state of waiting. She sees him as being five years old, with dark, curly hair, sitting outside on a clothesline stoop, his tongue working across his bottom lip as he concentrates on his task of stripping leaves from a twig. She allows for his father, Hank, to have some kind of life, but she can't imagine what. This is Pergolesi's "Stabat Mater." Amy. Two voices. The learned counterpoint and the new, what she hears floating through the rooms of her mind.

I don't know if you should trust her.

2

The summer Amy Barber remembers is the summer of 1959. The hot season had arrived in May, overnight, with unusually high temperatures that held steady throughout the early weeks of June. The people of Carona could hardly believe their good fortune. And then they worried. "Looks like we're in for a doozer," they warned one another as they ascended the marble stairs of the Bank of Commerce and passed through its Corinthian columns and on into the cool interior. "We've either been living right or awfully wrong, time will tell," is what they said as they waited their turn to see the manager about their seeding loans.

It is now mid-June. Amy was among the students who had polished their penny loafers or saddle oxfords and marched down from the school to the Town Hall where they'd lined up for their injections of polio vaccine, and then, because of the unusual heat and their tender arms, they were sent home early. She's walking home now, alone, as she almost always is. She doesn't realize how ridiculous she looks, comical the way she walks, leading with her chin, her wispy, nondescript-coloured hair held flat against her head with a row of bobby pins on either side. And even though she's nine years old, she still has what looks to be a milk stomach, a doughy protrusion which the waistbands of her shorts, pants, skirts, work down below so that often her stomach sticks out from beneath her shirttail. Her mother, Margaret, has sewn countless tunic-type shifts for Amy, who she worries aloud will turn out fat. But Amy despises those shapeless dresses and paints her fingernails with red polish and pins her hair flat on either side of her head. She dabs Margaret's cologne behind her ears even though it makes her eyes water and mucus run from her nose in two thick rivulets, which she clears from time to time, a reflex action, on the back of her arm. Her knees are bony knobs and often peppered with scabs where the skin has been scraped away. Her feet are large for her body and as she walks home along the sidewalk they flap against the concrete like duck feet.

Her feet stop flapping as she squats and tumbles a large rock away from the base of a tree. Holy, she thinks, as she sees the variety of insects. Holy cow, holy poop. She sees flat grey slugs, rust-coloured centipedes, a pink earthworm already drilling its way back into the dark, damp earth. She sets her pencil box down and picks at the worm, amazed at how it clings tightly to the earth. She yanks and it lets loose and she has it, a ropy pinkish thick worm which curls and lashes about in the air in front of her nose. Musty-smelling. She feels its strong muscles working. Why does it loop and twitch like that? Is it afraid of her? she wonders. She sets it down against the warm pavement. What's inside it? Earth? She knows very well what's inside it. She takes her metal-edged wooden ruler from her pencil box. She hesitates for a moment and then decides. She brings down the ruler swiftly onto the worm and saws it in half. Holy yuck, she thinks, disgusted by the blob of white juice bubbling out. And it's all over her ruler too. Worm juice. Nothing has changed. It's still white worm juice inside. She watches as one half of the earthworm tries to get away. She'll go into the house, upstairs, get Timothy's movie camera, and take a picture of the severed worm. White blood, she chants to herself as she pushes open the front gate. White blood, white blood. White blood is poisonous.

"Hi, Short Stuff," Mel, Amy's brother, calls as she enters the front hallway. "The brat's home," Mel reports to

Margaret, who is in the kitchen, sewing. Oh yes, Amy thinks, and forgets about the severed worm as she remembers what she really had planned to get a picture of today. A surprise for Timothy when he returns from being on the road. She doesn't go into the living room, pass through it to the dining room, and on into the kitchen to say hello to Margaret. Instead, she climbs the stairs to the second floor, to Timothy and Margaret's bedroom, to see if she can find where he has hidden his movie camera.

Margaret leans across the table in the kitchen cutting out a pattern. She'd gotten up with the sun, drawn all the window shades, and tacked a blanket over the window in the back porch to keep down the heat. Shoe polish in tins lining the window sill in the back porch begins to soften, and on the kitchen counter a tall glass pitcher of cherry drink sweats a puddle of moisture. Memory of the recent polio epidemic lingers in everyone's minds. Keep cool. Don't run, you hear? Sit quietly in the shade now. Good advice at any time. Margaret's hair has a life of its own as it switches in the breeze created by the oscillating fan sitting on the countertop. Every morning she jams metal combs into her hair on either side, but by the end of the day the combs spring loose and bounce across the floor or drop down into the dishwater in the sink. Unlike her younger sister, Rita, who is fine-boned and petite, Margaret is lean and sinewy. At certain times of the month her eyes glitter with a look that says, "Ask me no questions and I'll tell you no lies."

Margaret hears a noise overhead. She looks up, takes a deep breath as though she might yell, but gulps back the impulse. Margaret is not a yelling type of person. She knows it's Amy up there, snooping about her bedroom again. The brat is home, she thinks. The voices of Elsa Miller and Jill see-saw back and forth in the dining room, their voices indistinguishable one from the other over the sound of the bent fan blade, which clips rhythmically against the wire cage. Mel's there too. Often Margaret thinks back to Timothy's objection to her wanting another child. Often she thinks that she should have left well enough alone and been content with the two she had.

31

Mel is the oldest. He is fifteen. His full name is Melville, named after Timothy's birthplace in Saskatchewan. And Mel does resemble prairie in a way. He's solid without being fat. A blond, squared-off brush cut. Stubble cut. A fringe of white eyelashes, respectable in length, not too lavish and feminine. His eyes are sometimes blue, sometimes grey. Mel appears to have just the right amount of everything in him, which can be deceiving.

The year when summer arrived so suddenly and early, then lingered long past the time for it, will be recorded as a year of intense sunspot activity, licks of flame spurting from the sun's skin, and remembered for the undulating veils of aurora borealis and frequent thunderstorms. Those storms, and the heavy snowfalls of the previous two winters, ensured the continuing prosperity of the Midwest.

That prosperity is reflected in Timothy's furniture sales. He sells hundreds of three-room groupings through catalogues and sample books to independent stores in the network of towns and small cities in the southern end of the prairie provinces. People line up, he says, to buy the kitchen suite, the five-piece living-room ensemble, and the bookcase bed, bureau, and matching bedside tables, with lamps thrown in. The factory can't ship them fast enough, he complains. The growing abundance of the Midwest is reflected in the Barber house, too, in Margaret's new kitchen, the green-and-white rubber-tile floor polished to a high shine, the Arborite countertop, and in the absence of the cumbersome kitchen table that Timothy had brought to their marriage. "This is an antique," Timothy had explained to Margaret when she objected to inheriting a piece of junk. He told her how the table had crossed the ocean in the cargo hold of a ship. How it had been dismantled and carried off from a thatch-roof house in Northern Ireland to be assembled in a bleak sod hut on the prairie. "Antique" was not then a much appreciated word. Timothy's only fault: being ahead of his time. The table has been banished to the basement behind the furnace and in its place is the new chrome suite, one of Timothy's lines. It consists of a table with bowed chrome legs, grey mottled

Arborite top, and matching chairs with plastic-covered seats, which wheeze when you sit on them. Farting chairs, Amy calls them. Margaret's brother, Reginald, runs the family hardware store and so Margaret has been fortunate. She's been among the first in town to own a steam iron, the Mixmaster, the not so very portable sewing machine, the television console. Bill North from Bill's Electrical Service has recently rewired the Barber house and connected Margaret's new stove and the clothes dryer sitting out in the back porch. The next thing on Margaret's list is a floor polisher.

When Margaret finishes cutting out the blouse pattern, she sits for a moment behind the sewing machine, head bowed as she studies the sewing instructions. "The breast darts," she reads and feels her nipples tighten pleasantly, pulling taut the string of desire between her legs. Margaret has "artsy tits." The expression coined by Timothy. It describes the breasts of the fashion models in *Vogue*, the magazine her sister, Rita, buys at a drugstore near the Film Exchange where she works. What Margaret is thinking about as she reads the instructions is how she is going to look tomorrow when she wears the new blouse to work, her one day a week at Reginald's store. She imagines Bill North entering the store. Sees his eyes veer to one side. Not shifty, just a swift blink of recognition of Margaret's "artsy tits" moving beneath the soft ecru fabric. She sees Bill all at once, solid and hard, the thick mat of chest hair creeping up to the base of his throat. Even though the humidity weighs heavily in Margaret's limbs, she's acutely aware of her desire to make love with Bill.

Jill's voice pushes through the clicking of the bent fan blade from the other room. "Ring, rang, rung," Jill says, instructing Elsa Miller.

"As in ding, dang, dong," Margaret hears Mel intone in a church-bell voice, and his attempt at humour surprises her. Mel has joined Elsa and Jill at the dining-room table because, for the very same reason Margaret is suspicious of Elsa Miller, Mel is attracted to her. He's drawn by the exotic sound of her German tongue. George, Mel's cat, lies curled in his lap as Mel stacks coins into piles so that he can roll them and deposit them into his savings account. Through the fringe of his lowered white eyelashes he studies the curve of Elsa Miller's mouth as she reads aloud from a grammar book, Jill looking on. Will she or won't she? Mel wonders. He's thinking about the dance at the end of the month. Elsa senses his scrutiny and picks up the book and tips it on its end. She raises it then, obscuring all but her and Jill's eyes and foreheads. Silently the girls agree to gaze out over the top of the book at Mel. Elsa's eyes are pale blue, Jill's green with flecks of brown like chips of varnish floating in them. They're sticking their tongues out at him behind the book. He watches his too-large squarish hands stack the coins. The hands of a banker, Timothy once said, thinking to please Mel but making him squirm. The remark hit too close to home. Mel had always wanted to have the hands of a piano player or a card shark, nimble fingers, the casual flair of dismissal over a fortune lost. A disguise to cover his desire to one day be rich. But the desire could be thought of as piggish, he would have said, greedy. Well-off would be okay. Carona was filled with well-off people. Several were on their way to making their first million. The farm-implement dealer, for instance, and a man who was experimenting with raising germ-free hogs. The word "rich" was a crude one for Carona. It carried the connotation of ill-gotten gains, indolence, a bloated mind. There were, after all, seven churches in the town of Carona. There still are.

Elsa and Jill turn and face one another behind the book. Jill's child features are becoming sharp, giving way to the high noon of adolescence. Two profiles, a soft and a sharp one. Mel's fingers freeze as the crack of light between their foreheads closes and their mouths meet in a soft, quiet kiss. He skirts around these displays of affection. It unsettles him when Jill and Elsa dance together, their breasts touching. Elsa's are small swellings flattened by tight undergarments. Jill's, two proud chocolate rosebuds. Mel has seen them when she's come from the bath, those two hard buds nudging against her pyjamas.

Amy hears the three of them talking as she comes down from upstairs, carrying Timothy's camera rolled inside a towel. She hears Jill say, "Elsa really likes you," as she stands in the dim hallway where their sweaters and jackets hang on either side of the front door. She waits to hear more. "Ha, ha, ha, very funny." Phoney, Amy thinks. Doesn't Mel realize how his voice changes when Elsa is around? They begin to whisper and chair legs scrape against the hardwood floor. Scheming, Amy realizes.

She steps onto the veranda and into the immediate contrast in temperature. The heat is a sudden blast beating through the window screens. She steps outside into the bright sunlight and her eyes tear. She hears the sound of the sewing machine in the kitchen and then a beeping on the radio that signals the two o'clock news. At two o'clock Amy's grandparents will arise from their afternoon nap, irritated and quibbling over who has been awakened how many times by the other. Her grandmother will freshen up, dab hard at her temples with astringent to swab the prickle of whatever accusations are left unaccounted for in the bedroom. Then she will put on her garden hat and go out to straighten things up and Amy will be there with Timothy's movie camera.

Heat ripples above the baseball diamond in the school yard across the street. Amy feels the pressure of the sun, a white hot thumb pressing its mark into the top of her head. She sees the flash of a curled tail in the air above the smouldering road. She raises the camera and frames the circus performer in the viewfinder: the squirrel which now dashes across the high wire of electricity leading into the school. It's Amy, she thinks. She chooses to believe that every squirrel she sees is the one she once found lying stunned on the ground beside the school. She'd brought it home in Mel's paper-route bag. Timothy had named the squirrel Amy because of its impulse to be on the move. Incessantly it climbed the rungs of the bird cage, its temporary home, or up their legs to their heads. Up the walls to the rafters of the garage. Amy felt the urgency in its oversized feet and understood its need to move was serious and so she agreed with Timothy that they would take it back to the school. She'd stood beside him and crossed her fingers and watched as the animal climbed up the sheer brick face of the building, up three floors to the hole just beneath the eaves troughing.

The muscles in Amy's arms ache with the weight of the camera as she follows the movement of the squirrel. She's disappointed with what she sees. It would be a fine waste of Timothy's film, she thinks, and so she lowers the camera. She can picture Timothy stroking his long chin when the image of the squirrel flickers on the dining-room wall, wondering where in hell it came from. A fine waste of film, he'd say. She hears the now steady *chugga chug* of the sewing machine and the grumble of a man's voice on the radio. It's too hot, she realizes. Fear of polio or sunstroke will keep her grandmother inside until later. She hides Timothy's camera among the chunks of broken concrete beneath the veranda and follows the grumbly voice, Diefenbaker's voice, to the back of the house. She steps into the porch and is enveloped instantly by the sharp chemical odour of melting shoe polish.

"There's nothing to do," Amy says as she enters the kitchen.

Margaret starts, her concentration broken. She spits out a row of pins into a china dish beside the sewing machine and peers at Amy through heavy locks of auburn curls. "It's too darn hot to do anything anyway. And tell me, what were you doing up in my bedroom?"

Just then the spring on the screen door twangs as the door opens. Bunny North enters the porch, calling "Howdy," and Amy is spared the necessity of inventing a reason or denying having been in Margaret's room again.

"Hi ya, Short Stuff, what're you up to today?" Bill's wife, Bonny North, or Bunny, as she has been called since she and Margaret attended grade school, puckers her pink little mouth and kisses Amy on the end of the nose in passing. Bunny's top lip has not grown since she was ten years old. A bicycle accident, Margaret had explained to them as a warning. A fall, and Bunny lost three permanent teeth. The original bridge with its porcelain buck-teeth was never replaced, and as she grew into adulthood her top lip shrank to compensate for the child-size teeth. Bunny is short and on the chubby side and seems to

36

bounce rather than walk as she crosses the kitchen. She carries a paper bag, which crackles noisily as she sets it down on the floor. "We definitely haven't been living right," she says, flapping the top of her blouse to fan her chest. She pulls out a chair, sits down. *Woosh*, it says. "Bet you could cook an egg on the sidewalk." A newspaper reporter had done just that the day before and the kids in Carona are stealing eggs now from their mothers' refrigerators and scrambling them on the hoods of cars parked downtown. As Bunny leans forward Amy sees that freckled hump at the base of her neck. A dowager's hump, Margaret calls it, a warning against incorrect posture. The fleshy hump, the atrophied top lip, the ever-present dark shadows beneath her eyes make Bunny appear perpetually wounded.

Margaret's eyes flicker across Bunny's body. She wonders if she and Bill had made love the previous night. "Heading up to the lake this weekend?" she asks.

"Will Tim ever finish work on the jalopy?" Bunny snaps back. They laugh. "Lucky to go before summer's over." Bunny has recently inherited a cottage at the lake but they seldom go there because Bill's electrical business has become a thriving enterprise. He works long hours, weekends, installing new appliances, pushing and pulling wires through walls of wooden slats, plaster, and horsehair insulation, crawling across roofs to adjust television antennas towards the signal, electrifying the barns outside of town for milking machines and automatic feeders. Bill's reluctance to take time off work is a source of irritation for Bunny; the amount of time Timothy spends working on his Whisky Six '29 Studebaker when he's not on the road is Margaret's sore spot.

Amy likes to study the contrasts between these two women. Bunny North wears her sleeveless blouse hanging free over her red pedal-pushers, safety pin at the side closing, and a bra strap slides halfway down her arm. Her voice is like her mouth, child-size. Sometimes whiny or sing-song, inflected with exaggerated emotions. Any sternness she has is fake and gives way in moments to a soft recanting of whatever empty threats she's uttered. Her children are scamps, Margaret says, unruly scamps.

Margaret is more complicated. She's like her bedroom upstairs. Its papered walls, dull-green with delicate apple blossoms unfolding from floor to ceiling, the white wicker furniture say to the observer "cool," "calm." But there's an edginess in the careful arrangement of the room, in the studied placement of her engraved silver vanity set, its brush and comb and jars reflected in the three-sided mirror of her bureau. Amy can't look at the wide bed without thinking of a line she read in Margaret's "Blue Book." "My bed is winter," Margaret had written.

Amy listens as the women's talk leaps from the progress of Bunny's garden, which she complains is too wet to weed and growing fast, and the bed-wetting problem of Mindy, Bunny's thumb-sucking oldest child, to Margaret's complaints about mosquitoes and the price of blade roast at the butcher shop. Throughout this their voices mix with John Diefenbaker's monotonous intonation of promise for social justice. Amy has seen this man on television amid all the remedies advertised for the relief of indigestion, bloating, irregular bowels. She's seen him in the newspaper. In posters in windows his eyes follow her wherever she goes in Carona. He wags his finger at her and his hound-dog jowls quiver as he winds up to make a speech.

The women's conversation takes on a new tone. Their voices drop and the talk becomes coded, punctuated by a raised eyebrow and the occasional shift of a shoulder in the direction of the dining room where the voice of the girl Elsa Miller, clipped and precise in her determination to rid it of its German accent, rises above the radio and the rhythmic pinging of the fan blade.

"Why would she do such a thing?" Bunny repeats the question Margaret has asked. "Well, because she doesn't want anyone to know that she's used goods, I suppose. It's convenient. She passes Elsa off as being her mother's child and she becomes the big sister."

Margaret appears to savour this idea as though it's a piece of chocolate but she waves her hand to dismiss it. "Go on, Bun, that's just gossip."

38

"Wait," Bunny says, clearly offended, but Jill enters the room then and their talk breaks off. Margaret's eyes follow Jill as she crosses the room. She enjoys the image of Jill reaching for a glass in the cupboard, her thick dark braids shifting against her back with the movement. The sight of Jill's long, tanned legs and bony child-haunches beneath the pink-striped shorts pleases Margaret. When she looks at Jill she imagines herself at the same age. She doesn't see the presence of illness in the bruises on Jill's shin and thigh or notice her paleness, a shadow lying beneath her strong, tanned face.

Elsa enters the kitchen and Margaret's pleasure vanishes. She tries to conceal her dislike for Elsa as the girl swoops down on the blouse pattern lying on the table, gushing over it. Yes, Margaret replies drily, she *is* making a blouse. Yes, it should be quite nice when finished. The tendons in her neck grow taut with the effort to be civil. Elsa senses Margaret's hostility and retreats. She fiddles with her earring, turning the gold hoop around and around, and wonders why the woman doesn't like her. She dresses old, Margaret thinks, a miniature of the two women who had accompanied her to the skating rink last winter. They'd made a noisy entrance, stamping snow from their boots and speaking to one another in German. They'd headed straight for the bench nearest the oil burner; brassy, Margaret thought. When they shrugged free from their heavy fur coats, they revealed clunky and overdone-looking amber and coral beads. Their leather gloves concealed rings, too, with large and well-cut stones. *Meine Mutter*, Elsa had said, as she introduced the older grey-haired woman to them, and the young woman, whose harsh-red hair and preference for orange lipstick made her appear sullen and hard, was her sister, she'd said. But Bunny could be right, Margaret thinks now. The woman is too old. She would have been well past child-bearing age when Elsa was born. The rumour that the younger woman, Adele, is really Elsa's mother, makes sense. But while the illegitimacy of the girl is a delicious melt-in-the-mouth thought for Margaret, it's their jewellery she wonders about; she has come to think that there's something sinister about the time-worn look of it.

Mel appears in the doorway and leans into its frame. George, a ginger tabby, winds around and through his legs and then settles down in its favourite spot directly in front of the refrigerator door. "Anyone seen my bank passbook?" Mel asks.

Jill sloshes cherry drink into two tall glasses. "Amy had it, yesterday."

Until then they had all ignored Amy, but as they turn and stare at her, their eyes accusing as usual, she feels cornered. She feels the ridiculous sadness in Mel's eyes. His meek disappointment. "I haven't seen your shitty little passbook," she says.

"I won't stand for that!" Margaret's voice is cutting.

"She's lying," Jill says.

Amy lunges for her and Jill laughs as she gracefully twirls away swinging the glass of cherry drink, not spilling a drop.

"Stop it, you two." Margaret grabs a fist of her own hair and twists it as if she wants to yank their voices from her head. Amy lunges again and Jill darts behind Elsa.

"If you don't stop fighting this minute, you'll make it storm," Margaret warns.

Amy wants to pinch Jill's arm but Jill raises them above her head. The movement causes her halter top to ride up, exposing a slash of tanned midriff. Amy pinches her there instead. Hard. Jill shrieks and glass shatters against the floor. Cherry drink spatters on their legs and spreads out in a crimson pool around their feet.

Bunny leaps up and rushes to the sink for the dishrag. Elsa stoops and begins to gather bits of broken glass. "It's the heat," Bunny says. "It's getting to all of us."

"Oh, I know. You're right." Margaret's arm drops to her side. "But it's no excuse for bad behaviour. You need a paddling." She shakes her finger at Amy. Mel snorts. As if Margaret has ever paddled any of them.

As Amy retreats through the back porch she hears Mel speaking to Margaret. "What do you think?" he says. "Elsa has invited Jill and me to go to the Lutheran Sunday School picnic tomorrow. In the city. Think it would be okay?"

Amy stops in the doorway to listen. "I don't know," Margaret says after a slight pause. "I suppose so. Well, all right, but only if you take Amy too." Amy smiles, sensing their immediate disappointment. She opens the screen door as wide as the spring will allow and lets it fly.

"Amy!" Margaret howls. "When will you learn how to close a door!"

I remember that I ran across the school yard, carrying my father's camera against my chest. The day seemed to be bleached by the sun, the colours faded. The baseball diamond, the school building radiated heat. I cut through the RCMP compound and its squat two-storey red brick building. Behind it, and seemingly ironed flat against the sky, was the silver bullet-shaped water tower, CARONA painted in shiny black enamel. Once I was out of view of the veranda, I slowed to a walk. I cut through the front and back yards of houses, heading towards the cemetery at the edge of the town and, beside it, my grandparents' house. I walked head down, watching my feet. I imagined that I floated across a body of water. I became the girl on the inside cover of *The Book of Knowledge*, floating on top of a book towards a strange new horizon. I passed by a Chinese junk with red and gold sails, going on towards a city where a rocket thrust up through a yellow and turquoise sky. I floated towards faces carved in the side of a mountain, cannons aimed at belts of snow hanging above valleys, a fountain spewing, water arching over menacing-looking totem poles. There was just one thing about the picture on the book that puzzled me, though. It was the presence of tiny yellow moths fluttering alongside the book the girl and boy stood on as they held hands and floated towards their future. Why moths? I wondered, as I turned and entered the broad alley-way behind the town's oldest hotel.

On one side of the alley, the white stucco wall of the hotel's

41

back side reflected the sun. On the other stood the sagging livery stable, doors removed, dark insides gaping open like an old man's mouth and emanating the odour of another era. It was a thick, comforting odour and I became Amy the squirrel, age two and heading out for the first time, way the hell and gone down the street before Margaret snagged me by the hem of my dress and reeled me in. Where was I going? "She was going to buy an ice cream," Timothy had said, and would repeat the story at my every birthday and at the same time plunk down a brick of ice cream for me to eat. Spoonful by spoonful, the whole quart of Neapolitan ice cream disappeared inside my round little body. But Timothy had been curious. "Don't chase her," he instructed. "Let's just see what happens." They sent Mel to follow me and I took him places he'd never been. Somehow, through a wandering, circuitous route, we wound up on the back steps of Andy's Cafe behind which, beyond a row of rusting oil barrels, flowed the swollen Lucy May Creek. Afterwards Timothy built the fence and screwed a hook closure on the outside of the gate. He watched with a mixture of pride and despair when, later, I wheeled the baby stroller over to the gate, climbed into it, and then went up and over the fence.

As I passed by the hotel I heard the rumble of voices inside it. Then the back door opened and a grey-looking man reeled unsteadily into the bright sunlight. "Holy cow," he muttered. He couldn't see me. He turned his back, bent to fumble with his pants. I heard the splash of his stream hitting the wall. I wanted to raise Timothy's camera and record this but decided not to. Margaret had warned me often to steer clear of the men who went in and out of the old hotel, those who would wave me over and call me "lass" or "darling" or "princess." "Go on, help yourself," they'd say, urging me not to be shy but to come on over and take a coin from among the change held out in their soil-stained hands. I would be invited to choose a nickel and buy a treat. An ice cream. I had been warned often about the promises of ice cream. But there was nothing sinister about these men, so often I did pluck a nickel from their palms, or a quarter. They didn't seem to care or know the difference. The grey-looking man was lean and stoop-shouldered. He turned and saw me as I passed by. "Hey now, get on out of here. No place for a girl," he said.

I crossed the road that bordered the cemetery; beyond it was the golf course and clubhouse. I set the camera down on top of the stone wall enclosing the cemetery and searched for Alf, the groundskeeper, but the grass appeared to be freshly clipped so I knew Alf had already been and gone. I hiked up the wall and dropped down inside the cemetery and the air felt immediately cooler. I walked among the hard stones and smooth columns of marble and granite headstones. In the golf course beyond a red kite climbed unsteadily into the cloudless sky. Two boys. Cam and Gord, I recognized, a year older than I was. Their backs were brown, impervious to the sun. They looked up at the kite, pulling on its string as they walked backwards, coaxing it to fly higher. Behind me at the front gate of the cemetery stretched the highway and I heard the sound of vehicles gearing down as they approached the town's speed limit. There was a lot of traffic around Carona then. Transport trucks moving in and out of town, bringing dry goods, groceries, television sets, washers and dryers. The merchandise was transported from the city to the town where it would be uncrated in the stores, the shelves stocked, banners painted to proclaim coming sales. The merchants were anticipating another record harvest, the mounds of silver coins in the callused palms of the men who stepped from the beer parlour – while inside it was the click of billiard balls amid the raucous roar of male voices, all saying the same thing in different ways, congratulating themselves and sometimes God for the absence of hail among the pillars of clouds at night, for the heavy rainfall at the right time, grain prices, the record-breaking yields per acre, and all of them loving to love the prime minister, "Dief the Chief."

The hinges on my grandparents' fence squealed. I stood still for a moment, watching for movement behind the curtain at the window. Grandfather Johnson would be sitting at the table spooning sugar into strong coffee. I dropped down behind a row of dogwood shrubs, unrolled the camera from the towel, and waited. All at once the back door opened and the elderly woman stepped outside. Her loosely woven garden hat, tilted at an angle, cast a latticework of shadows against her face and I worried that her features would be hidden. She stopped at the bottom of the stairs to pull on a pair of gardening gloves, jerking each finger down into place with the same determination that shaped all the movements of her life. I picked up the camera, held my breath, and waited. She slid rather than bent to her knees in front of the flower-bed. I framed her in the viewfinder. She wobbled forward and her straw hat became a flat beige circle as she leaned over the flowers. Then what I waited for happened all at once. She started, and leapt to her feet out of view, darting towards the house, holding up a green bottle. She held it away from herself as though it stank, not stopping to realize that it didn't make sense for my grandfather to hide it where she was bound to find it, or that the fluid inside the bottle was not port but clear water.

I thought of how Timothy complained that it was strange the way you couldn't get people to stand still for an ordinary camera but with a movie camera you couldn't get them to move. My grandmother's voice inside the house was sharp and accusing, my grandfather's injured-sounding. I felt discouraged and disappointed. I had anticipated Timothy's laughter at the sight of the usually staid and prim woman running across our dining-room wall waving a port bottle.

I left their yard and cut back through the cemetery, feeling the mystery of the place in Alf's carefully tended graves, rectangles of bright flowers or crushed stone marking out where people lay, waiting. Their silence brushed against my legs as I skittered along narrow pathways between headstones. On the golf course, Cam and Gord were still staring heavenward at the red kite. Its ribbon snapped as it found a stream of air and began climbing higher. I stood behind a tall column of marble, leaned into it to steady myself, and raised the camera. I felt the vibration of the film unwinding against my cheek as the cogs began to feed it across the camera's eye. When I couldn't see the kite, just the boys walking backwards with their arms stretched to the heavens, it looked as though they were engaged in some kind of ecstatic worship. And then I remember clearly how the air in front of me suddenly quivered. It was as though the air in front of my face became water, two thin streams rippling, their currents going opposite ways. I felt a sudden harsh sting in my nostrils and gasped, rearing away from it. In the moment it takes to blink, in the instant I staggered back from the odour, the water parted and a thin white line zig-zagged down in front of me. Light swirled, became a ball turning, and then a concussion of air whomped me hard, dead centre in my chest. I felt myself fall backwards, and in the final dim split-second of consciousness, I remember hearing voices.

I opened my eyes. Overhead, a green canopy of branches swayed, and beyond it I caught glimpses of the sky, high and clear, and of the red kite, a tiny triangle now, gliding gracefully across the face of it. Sunlight exploded in brilliant pockets of light among the trees, and I realized that the air moved now. I could see, in the swaying branches of birch, that the air had begun to move.

I became aware of the ground beneath me, as though it had just materialized, damp from the previous night's rainfall. There was a bitter metallic taste in my mouth. I pushed up onto my elbows and felt an ache in my breastbone. As I sat up the movement rocked inside my head, making the world tilt and then gradually steady. My knees shook when I stood and so I reached for the headstone for support. I touched it, and felt its cool surface beneath my hand. I knew I wasn't dead, then. The stone was real. The boys' voices from the golf course were real too. I looked down at my feet where the camera lay. Its metal casing was completely ruined, battered, a deep dent in its side as though it had been smashed with a hammer. Then I saw my feet. The buckle on one of my sandals was black and bent, like it had been crimped with a pair of pliers.

The boys' voices, the cool dampness in my tee shirt, the sound of the wind swaying in the branches above me, were confirmation that the world was still there. But I felt that I stood somewhere outside of it, looking in. I left the camera and towel lying in the grass and walked towards the front gate and the wrought-iron angels flying across it, the trumpets at their mouths heralding my passing. I still tasted metal on my tongue, and felt that my limbs were somehow lighter. I began to walk towards Main Street where there would be people and traffic. The sky seemed to be much higher and brighter and the store-fronts vivid, sharp outlines against the day. My feet barely touched the ground as I ran across the school grounds towards home. I remember how I pushed off and sailed, my stride yards long and high, the pull of gravity much less than it had been before. I thought it might be possible to challenge gravity, to stretch my arms and will myself to leap and rise above the houses and follow the path of the telephone wires, thread my way through the forest of television antennas, become a ghost in the screens of all the television sets in the living rooms of Carona. I had been struck by lightning and survived.

"Well, it's possible. I might find the time to do it tomorrow after work," Margaret says to Bunny. She stands in the centre of the kitchen with her fingers against her throat as though she's tracking her pulse. She has pushed her hair back from her forehead with one of the silver combs and it stands straight up now, a curly auburn tiara.

Bunny and Margaret watched in mock horror as Jill made two mustard sandwiches, which she said she must eat instantly or die. A stage, Margaret said, and shivered as she watched Jill suck the remaining smears of mustard from her fingers. Mel roamed about the house in search of his bank passbook and the women resumed their visit. Bunny slid a pair of men's dress slacks from the paper bag she'd brought with her. The woman who usually does alterations for Bunny is away and Bill needs the pants for Sunday, she explains. It's his turn to usher at church, Bunny says, otherwise they wouldn't bother going.

"All right." Margaret feels the heat of her answer rise in a blush beneath her fingers at her throat. She sees Bill North, hard and hairy, lean, and feels her body pushing up against his. "Tell Bill he can come over tomorrow, then. After work." If she'd known the purpose behind Bunny's visit, she wouldn't have said yes, the children could go to the city to the picnic tomorrow.

"Around four would be good," Amy hears Margaret say as the screen door closes behind her. The muted light of the sun permeating the pink blanket on the window and the women's voices are like an arm around her shoulder as she passes through the porch. They turn and look at her as she comes into the kitchen and it occurs to Amy that she might be marked in some way. Like the story she'd heard. Cain, going around with a big X on his forehead. But Margaret is frazzled and preoccupied and looks straight through her.

Bunny puckers her tiny pink mouth and blows a kiss off the palm of her hand. "The coast is clear," she says and winks, meaning that she's run interference again, smoothed Margaret's ruffled feathers. A faint crackle of static cuts through the music playing on the radio. Margaret's eyes dart nervously towards it. Damn, damn, damn, Amy sees in her mother's eyes. She's worrying, Amy realizes, that the static signals the possibility of a storm. She knows then that there isn't anything noticeably different about her appearance. For a second she thinks she might tell them: I have been struck by lightning. But she decides not to, believing that she would lose the experience if she told them. *Woosh*, the chair farts as she sits down at the table behind the sewing machine. She notices the crooked lines of Margaret's sewing. How she's repeated herself in a seam, over and over. The skin next to the ruined buckle has begun to sting. She swings her foot up and down, wanting them to notice the strange look of her buckle, but they don't.

Later that night Amy lies naked beneath cotton sheets, body still cool from the tepid bath Margaret had run for them before bed, a dash of Mr. Bubbles for good measure, and they'd

47

soaked up to their necks for a full fifteen minutes each. Then, sensing a storm brewing, Margaret swished through the rooms banging windows down into place. It's necessary to close the windows because lightning could follow the flow of air into the house and become a current of electricity that could very well turn them all into glowing lamps for Jesus if they stepped down into it, Mel has joked to frighten Amy – which, over the years, has been Mel's and Jill's main occupation. They have jumped from closets in dark rooms, hidden around corners and leapt out at her. Sometimes they have dropped down from a tree like ugly spiders, swinging upside down in front of her face. They make pig faces at her. Mel plays at Wolf Man, and his face changes, fangs sprout to suck her blood dry when she's asleep. She has looked in the mirror in the morning and seen red dots, the puncture marks drawn on her neck with a pen. They have put a field mouse, frogs, in her bed. Two against one is never fair, Margaret chastises until blue in the face, but Margaret can't be everywhere. Lately, though, Jill and Mel seem to have lost their interest in teasing Amy. More often their heads are together as they whisper, and it's become difficult to uncover their secrets.

The smell of cigarette smoke spirals up from the living room where Margaret sits in the dark, smoking and waiting for the storm. "Stop fighting," Margaret had said earlier in the day, "or you're going to make it storm." When their moods changed suddenly and they became irritable, or their play turned into punches and slaps, Margaret didn't think to attribute it to a coming change in the weather; rather, it was their behaviour itself which would bring on the storm.

In the bed below Amy, Jill's quiet and steady breathing says that she's already sleeping. Across the hall in Mel's room a beam of light swings against the wall as he plays with his flashlight. Mel has $120 in his savings account. Amy saw the figures melting away, streams of blue ink trailing across the water in the toilet where she'd dropped his passbook. She admitted this finally and apologized because she wants to go with them to the Lutheran Sunday School picnic tomorrow.

She wants to find out why Mel has packed a mickey of whisky in his school bag.

Margaret stiffens at another crackle of static in the radio. The wind rises and begins to sweep down into the streets of Carona. The red brick face of the school flickers with the first round of lightning. Amy hears her mother's swift stride up the stairs. She turns away from it and faces the wall. She can hear the shade tree swaying, its branches scraping against the side of the house. The television antenna begins to hum and then emits a high-pitched whine. Amy hears the squeak of Mel's bed springs as he gets up and waits for Margaret outside his doorway. His flashlight casts a circular pool of yellow light against the wall. Once Amy awakened to see Mel standing in the doorway of their bedroom with the flashlight stuck down the front of his pyjama bottoms. "Chicken," Jill said and so Mel dropped them, shone the light onto his rubbery-looking penis, and then turned around, bent over, and showed her his brown anus and wrinkled testicles. "You have hair there," Jill whispered. "That's disgusting." Amy couldn't see any hair at all.

Margaret enters the hallway now and pushes past Mel and on into their room. Amy keeps her breathing flat and even. The bed shakes as Margaret jostles Jill awake. "Your pillow. Bring your pillow," Jill moans in protest. Amy feels Margaret's hands against her ribs. "Wake up." The antenna continues to whine, steady and high, and the roof begins to vibrate with the sound. Thunder cracks and Margaret gasps. "Amy, wake up." Her touch is more insistent. "It's only thunder," Jill mutters, but she pulls on a tee shirt and clutches her pillow against her chest and joins Mel out in the hallway. The sky opens suddenly and rain falls in a great gush against the roof.

Amy curls up tightly, facing the wall. She opens her eyes. The wall leaps with white light and she sees once again the air splitting open in a zig-zag pattern in front of her face. No beginning to it, no end, it is that fast. Branches tear free and tumble across the slope of the roof. Amy uncurls suddenly, her legs shooting straight out then swinging up and over the

49

side of the bed to dangle in front of Margaret's astonished face. "I'm not going downstairs."

"It's going to be a bad one." Margaret's face leaps forward in a flash of lightning, flat, white, eyes wide with fear.

"I'm staying up here," Amy says. But after the next crack of thunder and another long sheet of light that follows, illuminating the room, the crayon drawings on the walls, Jill's doll collection on the shelf, Amy sees that Margaret has already fled, leaving her there. She flops back onto the bed, surprised but satisfied that Margaret has given up so easily. She listens to the whisper of their feet scurrying down the hallway, against the stairs, drowned out then by a clap of thunder and the rising wind. "Be good or you'll make it storm," Margaret has pleaded often. But Amy doesn't think about this now, the idea of possessing the power to unleash a storm. She thinks only about what happened in the cemetery. That she had been inoculated by a streak of lightning and become immune to gravity and to the violence of any kind of storm. Immune to what normally struck other people down.

Margaret's inference that their behaviour can somehow influence the weather doesn't occur to Mel or Jill either as they lie beside their mother on the floor in the living room, damp with heat and the weight of her arms, heavy protective wings stretched across their sweating bodies. But, as they listen to the growing force of the storm beating against the walls of the house, they become infused with her fear and vow silently to try and be better children.

"Requests?" Mel asks, and wonders if he'll find enough spit to play the mouth organ he's brought with him.

Amy listens to the music as she drifts into sleep, the song Jill's request, she realizes vaguely by the wavering Hallowe'en tune about witches and goblins. The eerie melody doesn't keep her awake to worry about who or what might creep up on her just as she is about to fall asleep. She sleeps and dreams of rising up from the bed, up through the roof of the house, floating in the clear night sky, while below her lies the town of Carona, still, dark, asleep.

Hours later when she awakens, the storm has passed, but she can still hear something outside in the yard. The swing. She recognizes the squealing and groaning sound. Someone must be out there, she thinks. She climbs down from the bunk bed and crosses the hallway into her parents' empty bedroom. The clouds have thinned and the moon casts its light into the room. Through the wet glass Amy watches the stirring of the shade tree's branches, uncertain arms flinging about this way and that. An erratic dance, an attempt to ward off the wind and the sound of the rope swing as it moves back and forth with its invisible rider.

3

The following day Margaret stands in front of her brother Reginald's hardware store and watches as her children prepare to leave for the Lutheran Sunday School picnic in the city. Her children, Elsa Miller, and the oldest Miller woman, Esther, cluster about waiting for old Josh to finish packing the trunk of his car. Josh Miller agreed to drive them the forty-five miles to the city and then to return later on in the day to pick them up. He gestures to Mel to hand him the school bag but Mel declines, indicating that he wants to keep the bag with him. A sign above their heads reads MILLER'S TELEVISION AND RADIO. The sign is hand-painted with blue and white letters and streaming across it is a trail of egg yolk, hardened now to a glossy shine.

Josh had inspected the vandalized sign earlier and then shrugged in resignation. "Will have to chisel the darn stuff off," Josh told the older woman. He's related to the two women and Elsa. A cousin or second cousin, it was rumoured, and that he was responsible for their immigration to Canada. Recently he'd purchased the property across from the hardware store. An investment, he said, for the future of his new family. Carona was a better place to raise a family than most, he said, and so he bought the boarded-up wood-frame building which had once been a cafe. The remains of the previous

52

business can still be seen in the counter and stools, which Josh prefers to leave intact because he says he wants people to take their time when they shop at his place, take a load off, and have a cup of something and a chat before they shop. He opened up the front of the building, installed two display windows, and lined up in front of them are television consoles, picture-tubes flickering night and day. The children of Carona whose parents are less fortunate, whose rooftops don't sprout the required spire, park their bicycles in front of Miller's Television and Radio and watch. Taped to Josh's window is a faded newspaper article alerting the public to an advancement in the technology of television. A British invention. A television set that emits odours to match the image.

The shop door opens and Adele Miller, hair bound up in a green scarf, skips down the stairs and walks over to the car. She sees egg splattered across the sign and shakes her fist at it. A gypsy, Margaret thinks of the woman with her green turban and large hoop earrings. Adele shoos the children towards the car and climbs into the front seat beside Mel, and the older woman goes back up the stairs. Margaret feels betrayed. Mel neglected to tell her that Adele would be going with them. She feels a surge of irritation and is about to cut her farewell short when Bill North's half-ton pulls into the curb beside her. The door slams shut and he walks towards her. "Reg in?" She nods. His presence, in the worn jeans and the wide leather belt which clanks with his tools as he walks by, passes through her.

Sunlight flashes in the car windows as Josh Miller's green Oldsmobile backs away from the curb. Margaret waves goodbye. Jill raises her hand, fingers fluttering, and then points at her head. See this, her exaggerated gesture says, I am wearing my hat. Just as you told me. As the car sweeps by Jill smiles at Margaret and it isn't the same toothy bright smile Margaret is accustomed to seeing, but something else. A trick of light, or one of those rare occasions when the idea is a breath of panic inside Margaret's chest: Do I really know these people, my children?

She hears Bill talking to Reginald inside the store. His voice, which is strangely flat and neutral-sounding, neither friendly nor brusque, has become coded with messages, she believes. Messages meant for her. She ponders at length the messages she hears in a single line of greeting. Margaret knows exactly when it was that Bill, who had always been Bunny's boyfriend and was now her husband, suddenly became Bill. It was last winter when they'd come over to play cards that she'd noticed Bill, the man. He'd complained about having a stiff shoulder and Margaret led him upstairs to the bathroom as though he were one of the children. The lamp beside her bed had been left burning. Bill paused in the doorway of Margaret's bedroom and looked inside it. "Just as I pictured," he said.

What has he pictured? she'd wondered as she searched through the medicine cabinet for the liniment. Her mind sorted through the casual disorder of Bunny's rooms and she thought that his comment had to be a favourable comparison. Later, she would take what he'd said a step further. At a certain moment, Margaret thought, perhaps as he crawled across a rooftop or drove past the house, or lay beside Bunny in bed, a damp Mindy wedged between them, Bill had imagined not just her bedroom but her inside the room. He sat on the toilet seat, with his back to her, and dropped his shirt off his shoulders. "It's the witch's kiss," he said, and indicated the aching spot in his shoulder. Margaret turned from the medicine cabinet to face him and her heart lurched. She stood paralyzed, bottle of liniment in hand, thinking, So much hair, broad back. Not a boy but a strong-looking muscular man whose physical presence filled the entire room. He grew wary, waiting for her to smooth liniment across his shoulder. Waiting for her touch, she thought. She felt his careful attentiveness and her skin prickled with desire. She concentrated on her outstretched hands, the slight tremble as they moved down against his skin, and she tried not to think of the texture of it or the roughness of his hair against her warm palms.

"I think Jill is having a bad dream," she said when she rejoined Bunny and Timothy downstairs around the new chrome suite. She could still feel the warm imprint of Bill's hand on her breast. She was flushed with excitement over

54

having dared to step over the line. The lie, she hoped, covered the change in her. They would read the bright spots in her cheeks, her unusual silence when Bill came into the kitchen and they continued the card game, as concern for Jill.

"Strange crew, those." Reginald turns away from the window as Margaret steps inside the store.

"Eggs, Josh's sign?" Margaret asks.

Reginald shrugs his lack of concern. "You heard from that man of yours?"

"Due home tomorrow, why?"

They're interrupted by Garth, Reg's middle son, as he bounds up from the basement, singing. Margaret smiles as she notices his shoes. "They're blue all right, but not suede," she says, "so they don't count." She tilts her cheek up for him to kiss.

"My favourite aunt."

"Where in hell does that guy get his money, that's what I'd like to know," Reginald says, asking the question he has asked constantly since the opening of Josh's shop across the street. Reg has stopped stocking televisions and radios because he can't compete. Loyalty to a three-generation family business wears thin in the face of a bargain. He's at the window constantly, shaking his head in disgust when he sees one of his old customers enter Josh's store.

"Have you heard the latest about the 'strange crew'?" Margaret says casually and notes Reginald's quick attention. Garth squats in front of a carton and begins unpacking it, listening, she knows. "The latest is that Adele is really Elsa's mother. Not the older woman."

Reginald snorts. "You just figured that one out?" He goes behind the counter to a shelf and takes down a box of account books. He begins to lay out the individual books, each lettered with a customer's name. "Think Tim will come in when he's home and put something down?" Margaret is stung with embarrassment. "You want the real latest on that bunch?"

"Sure." She's thankful for the distraction.

"Adele goes into the city at least three times a week."

Garth abandons his pretence of work and adds, "She gets on the bus at night and comes back the next morning."

"So?" Margaret asks.

"Dolled up, fit to kill," Garth says.

"So maybe that babe is bringing home a bit of bacon," Reginald says. He winks at his son. "Plying the trade in the city."

"What trade?" Margaret asks.

Reg laughs. "Guess."

Margaret's stomach tightens with a picture of Mel in the front seat and the woman's thigh rubbing against his leg. She senses Reg's and Garth's keen attention as they wait for her reaction. She reaches for the wall switch and flicks it on. The fan above their heads whirs, stirring the air. "You're full of prunes," she says. "When it comes to gossip you're an old woman, Reggie."

She goes down into the basement to the coffee room to set water to boil. As she passes through the dimly lit interior she immediately senses the presence of Bill. Then she sees him through a row of shelving as he stands against the far wall. She sees just his head, framed in a rectangle of fluorescent light. He looks down, absorbed in a task. She has watched him secretly as he rewired their house, up on a ladder, arms and face caked with plaster powder, whistling softly as he worked. She invented reasons to enter rooms where she knew he was and realized by the stiffening of his spine that his tension matched hers. She painted the veranda's wicker chairs white and carried them upstairs and set them on either side of a table in front of the bedroom window. From there she can see the light in his bedroom at night or his truck backing down the driveway in the morning. She began to drape her nightgown over the back of a chair instead of folding it and setting it back into her nightie drawer. She arranged perfume bottles on the table and set in its centre a tin of Chantilly dusting powder, the lid opened, the powder puff flecked with scented beige granules, as soft as skin. *Just as I pictured.* She'd thought that on closer inspection Bill would have seen more than he had first imagined.

She thinks of Bill as being a young Ernest Hemingway and of herself as Catherine and that she will make him love her. He senses her watching now and raises his head. She has known since that night last winter that something would eventually happen between them, that the lines would one day converge: Timothy's absence, her being mid-cycle, when her desire for sex was at its peak, the children away. Her throat clicks with dryness. Be quiet, she thinks. Stop this. But she's certain that when she rises up to meet him, skin against skin, she will meet the substance of her intemperate dreams.

Bill North feels compelled to look up from the spool of electrical wire he's been unwinding and looping around his elbow. He sees Margaret's face and the self-satisfied look of her mouth. He's become impatient with her game, the signals she telegraphs with her eyes and then takes back moments later, retreating behind a mask of pleasantries. She needles Bill into remembering the act. The night she'd picked up his hand and pressed it against her breast and then walked away as though nothing had happened. He feels uncertain and off balance in the presence of that self-knowing look. She's too old to play at cock-teasing. "Howdy," he says. "Bun says after work. Still okay by you?"

"Yes, sure." Her voice is brisk and businesslike. "Around four."

I watched through the back window of Josh's car as Margaret receded from view that morning. Goodbye forever, I thought, without knowing why I had thought of the word "forever," except that seeing her standing there in the street, wearing the new blouse with its crooked collar, growing smaller and smaller, made me think of the song "Clementine." "You are lost and gone forever, oh my darling Clementine." I prefer to remember Margaret looking like that, uncertain, vulnerable. Elsa and Jill had rolled the windows halfway down and I leaned into the upholstery enjoying the pressure of the windstream against my face. I took short gasps of breath through it and felt beads of cold water form inside my nostrils, and I thought, Maybe I can breathe under water now.

Josh patted the dashboard. "Rocket '88," he said to Mel. "Hydra Matic. But it won't get you to the moon. Maybe those old Americans can make better cars but they'd better get the lead out if they want the moon." He turned on the radio. "It's a push button," he explained. "Go on, have a go at it." Bits of music and voices popped from the speakers as Mel began pushing buttons at random.

"Hey, that's not a toy, boy," Josh warned. I laughed inside, thinking that Mel was just that. Not real. A toy.

The seat bounced as Jill fidgeted, moving her knees in and out as though she needed the bathroom and signalling her impatience with the long ride to the city. It seemed to take longer to get there than to return. We called it "the city" because Winnipeg was and still is the only real city in the province of Manitoba, a sprawling island with half the population of the province living on it. We had all been to the city before, of course. Timothy made a point of taking us in for the Santa Claus Parade each year. Occasionally we accompanied Margaret when she took the bus in for her appointment with the doctor. Mel, Jill, and I had the distinction of having been born in the city because Margaret wouldn't go to the clinic in Carona where the receptionist snooped and your health became everyone's business. Or else we would go with her for a short day's shopping excursion which always ended on the mezzanine floor at the Hudson's Bay store. She would collapse into an overstuffed sofa, bags strewn about the carpet at her feet, while we waited for Rita to get off work at the Film Exchange and join us for a Denver sandwich and ice-cream floats. "She puts all her money on her back," Margaret said often about Rita, and when she appeared, causing all heads to turn, my mother's expression was clearly envious, sometimes genuinely admiring. But the trips in to the city were few and far between and our travels were always confined to an area of three city blocks, which encompassed Rita's office, the Winnipeg clinic, and several department stores in the vicinity of the bus depot. Now we would see new sights, new streets, the park.

We passed through Carona and gained speed. We approached the golf course and then sped past the cemetery and its wrought-iron gates. Behind them, dark spruce, white birch, and the slender willow trees screened from view the place where the dead people were lined up, waiting. I wondered about the camera. If it was still there, whether Alf had found it. Alf was always riding the mower. He wore coveralls that were too large and which sagged beneath his armpits and his behind. Alf had a freckle-faced mentally retarded son, Harry, who was Mel's age but really only about three years old.

"So, how's your daddy's old jalopy coming along?" Josh inquired. Mel squirmed and muttered his reply, but I knew Mel was petrified that Timothy might finish restoring it one day and actually drive it down the street or, worse still, insist that Mel join him. The tires thumped rhythmically over the cracks in the concrete, the highway cutting straight and clean through the prairie where the sky reached down to touch the rim of green fields. The stream of air had grown stronger and I gasped to breathe through it, feeling that my skin might pull away from my bones and slide off and then Josh turned and told Jill and Elsa that it was time to roll the windows up. The sound of the car's radio leapt forward in the silence. "It is with deep personal satisfaction, my fellow Canadians, that I am able. . . . The clouds are beginning to disappear . . . that we are on the verge of a turn in the tide of gloom and fear which was the legacy we inherited. . . ." The voice of John Diefenbaker droned on and on, following me into the city.

"What is 'legacy'?" Adele Miller asked Josh and listened carefully to his explanation. "What does he mean, legacy of fear and gloom?" she said with scorn and laughed sharply. "This must be a joke." Then she swivelled her green-turbaned head towards Elsa and spoke rapidly in German. Elsa tensed as though she'd just swallowed an ice cube. Adele turned back and fumbled in her beaded drawstring bag and came up with a cigarette. The match flared and I smelled the same acrid odour that had stung my nostrils in the cemetery. Jill leaned across me and whispered to Elsa. "What did she say?"

"Nothing." Elsa's mouth went crooked as she spoke from

one side of it. "The usual thing. Stay in the shade. It's easy for me to sunburn."

I studied the translucent flecks of dried skin where Elsa's gold hoop pierced her lobe. Did it hurt to have a hole in your ear? Elsa must have sensed my scrutiny because she turned to me then. Her pouty mouth stretched in a wide smile across wet teeth. She was cute in the soft, puffy way often preferred by adolescent boys. Even though she was a full year older than Jill, she'd chosen my sister for her closest friend, and Jill took on the responsibility of guiding her through her first year in a strange country with some pride. "You will have a good time at the picnic, yes?" Elsa said to me, her voice going several pitches higher than normal. For a moment I thought she might tweak my nose or chuck me beneath the chin.

"Adele is really your mother, isn't she? And not your sister?" I said, and felt Jill's elbow jab into my side. The corner of Elsa's eye crinkled into a white line and I saw the sudden squirt of moisture there. She turned her moon face to the window and didn't speak for the remainder of the drive to the city.

Mel's school bag thumped heavily against his leg as he walked on ahead of us in the park. Jill, solicitous of the withdrawn and weepy-eyed Elsa, stayed close to her side, as she had ever since we'd arrived at the picnic grounds, and held her hand now as we struggled to keep pace with Mel's single-minded march. Josh had dropped Adele off downtown at a hairdressing shop and us at the park with instructions as to where and when we should meet him later. It was easy to slip away in the confusion of activity: the bustle of families gathering at the picnic site, the setting of tables, and fires spitting to life in the brick pits in the cookhouse. We hadn't been noticed as one by one we bundled our sweaters and hats into our picnic blanket and stashed it among the bushes beside an overgrown path that led through trees and then out into a clearing and the remainder of the park.

We followed Mel as he passed by a sun-dappled pond where self-possessed swans ignored the offerings of bread in people's hands. Then we dutifully walked through the zoo, pausing only once to look at the cages where raw-bottomed baboons shrieked their discontent. "From the family of Cercopithecidae," Mel read from a plaque. "So you can tell Margaret what you learned today. But don't tell her that," he said when the animal squatted in front of us and pulled its penis, stretching it like a rubber band until it looked like it might tear loose.

In deference to Elsa's pale skin, we waited in the deep shade of a vine arbour while Mel went inside the pavilion to the concession and bought a bottle of cola. The haunting melody of piano music floated out from the top floor of the recital hall in the pavilion, seducing us into silence and turning our thoughts inward. Elsa's eyes grew redder and the tears that had threatened to erupt during the ride into the city spilled over and ran down her cheeks. "What?" Mel's face dropped in dismay as he walked towards us. I saw the wet stain in his school bag where he'd jammed the bottle of cola down inside. I heard the hard clink of glass against glass.

"Amy's got a big mouth, as usual," Jill said.

"What now?"

Elsa dabbed at her face with the back of her hand and laughed, a breathy bit of laughter that was meant to convey to us that it was over now, she was sorry for having been such a cry-baby. "Is that what you think?" she asked them. "That Adele is my mother?"

"Does it matter?" Mel frowned to cover his uneasiness with this delicate topic.

"Yes, it does." Elsa's temper flared suddenly. "It does!" Her shoulders dropped then and her arms fell to her side as the anger subsided as quickly as it had risen. She slung her shoulder bag around against her stomach and unzipped it. She took out a bottle of white pills. We watched as she unscrewed the top. "It matters to me because I don't know who my mother was. I was born in a bomb shelter and left there. They never

61

found her. I'm adopted and so is Adele, and so you see she really is my sister." The tiny pills spilled into the palm of her hand. She ducked her head, and one of the pills disappeared into her mouth on the tip of her tongue. "Esther Miller adopted both of us." She dropped the remaining pills into the bottle and screwed the top on tightly and put the bottle back into her purse.

Jill wound her arm around Elsa's waist and glared at me. "You always try and spoil things, don't you? Jerk."

The three of them turned then and began heading out across an open field in the park. The piano music grew softer and then ended. Scattered applause rose up in the recital hall. I watched as Mel's blue shirt, Jill's pink shorts and top, and Elsa's yellow sundress became spots of colour moving across a green carpet. When they reached the centre of the broad field, I followed. Head down, I watched my feet glide swiftly across the damp grass. The crimped buckle looked like an oddly shaped black bug on the side of my foot. The rhythm of my feet pulled me forward while I floated across the harbour on top of the book, heading towards my future. I looked into a yellow and turquoise sky and saw against it a pagoda, a Gothic cathedral, a rocket. I noted something different in the future then: a volcanic mountain, its cone trailing smoke and at its base a city whose buildings were pink and pyramid-shaped. The flutter of yellow moths billowed up around my ankles.

When I looked up, searching for Mel, Jill, and Elsa, I realized that they were gone. Vanished. In their place, riding against the dark backdrop of trees, were three boys on bicycles. They rode in a circle, swerving now and then to cut across one another's path. Their raw-sounding voices were like the screeching baboons', as they exclaimed loudly over near collisions, daring them to happen. I slowed down instantly and searched beyond them for a path, one Mel and Jill and Elsa may have taken to enter the belt of trees. One of the cyclists – dark-haired and I thought him to be the oldest and the leader – looked up and saw me. Immediately he veered from the circle and headed towards me across the grass. I stood still as he wheeled about me slowly in a wide circle. I turned with him, wanting him to speak. I couldn't guess at his intention if he didn't speak. A thick hank of hair lay across his forehead almost obsuring his eyes. The other two followed and joined the first boy, circling around me again and again. Then, as if on signal, they stood up, straddling the crossbars of their bicycles and, legs pumping in short spurts, they tightened the circle and began making clucking noises like chickens. I looked for an opening to dash through and escape. "Chick, chick, chick," they called without humour, taunting. Their faces became a blur and their bodies exuded something I had not met before. Not anger or revenge, but an intense maliciousness. I became rigid inside with panic. Where was Mel? Stay together, Margaret had instructed.

"Here chick, chick, chick," they called. "Pock, pock, pock." I cautioned myself not to cry. They passed so close now that I could feel the heat radiating from their bodies and smell their unwashed hair. An arm flashed in the air and I felt my head snap back as one of them yanked at my hair. Another arm flashed and my rump stung with the blow. Their mouths, mean thin slits, sneered as I yelped. And then the circle loosened, widened, and I thought that they had grown tired and were deciding to leave me alone. Beyond them I saw the arch of a footbridge and beyond that cars moving steadily on a street just outside the gates of the park. I held my breath and waited for the opportunity. I leaned towards a space between their bicycles, but it was what they'd been counting on, I realized, as they whooped loudly and circled in more closely. *Mel, Mel*, I cried silently. I sensed that something was about to happen. Something dangerous. Mel, I thought, and heard myself say, "You assholes!" And then I began yelling in desperation all the swear words I knew. "You bitches!" I yelled and stamped my feet, making them thunder against the ground. "Pigs! Fart-faces!"

The leader's mouth flew open in astonishment and he slammed on his brakes. The others, caught off guard, crashed into him, and instantly all three toppled to the ground. I began to run. I headed towards the footbridge and the street on the other side of it. "Shit-faces! Hoors! Flake-heads!" As I ran across the bridge I heard the sound of water rushing beneath it. The sound matched the rush of exhilaration in my chest. Their raw voices rose up in shouted oaths and then an explosion of laughter. "Hey! Hey you kid! We're not bitches. We're sons of bitches!"

I looked back and saw them rising slowly and untangling the mess of bicycles. They had no intention of following me and so I slowed down to a fast walk, swinging my arms, trying to appear as though I had a definite destination. I was furious, filled with righteous indignation. Margaret had said we were supposed to stay together, and Mel had deserted me. He was going to pay for it. I wanted to plot my revenge but the boys' taunts echoed inside my head and I saw myself in their circle, heard myself speak, and saw again their bicycles fall to the ground. I made thunder with my feet. They fell. I said "Pigs" and they fell. I became infused with energy and confidence, and as I felt my new weightlessness return, the colours, sound, and movement in the busy street began to emerge. I hadn't needed Mel after all.

I watched cars idling at an intersection, waiting for the traffic light to give them permission to go. Music rose up from a white convertible. A Cadillac. A woman with platinum hair and red sunglasses that matched the convertible's leather interior smiled and nodded at me. Jayne Mansfield, I thought. The light changed and the car sped away. I was standing in front of a cafe. Through its windows I saw people sitting in bright vinyl booths, and the sound of rock and roll music vibrated against the windowpanes. Across the street a bearded hobo painted on the side of a building pointed out the way to the next town. A man and a woman approached me, parted, and passed by on either side. I watched as they joined hands and crossed the intersection. I decided to follow them. I walked by a row of new cars, the sun reflecting in spotless chrome bumpers. Overhead, red and blue plastic banners swayed limply in the heat. The couple swung their arms as they walked. Ahead of them an amplified voice rose up and echoed between the buildings. A man's voice, twangy, nasal, and then I heard the thrum of a guitar. I looked back. I could still see the entrance to the park and down from it the tall hobo. It would be easy to find my way back. Walk in a straight line and don't go down any side streets no matter how interesting they might look, I told myself. I would find my way back easily. In the meantime I thought it only fair that Mel chew his fingernails over where I had got to, so I continued to follow the couple who headed towards the sound of applause and then laughter crackling in a PA system. "You all get in a little closer now, you hear?" cajoled a man whom I would come to know as Stu Farmer. "You all gotta get in close if you want to hear this musical genius." I followed the voice and hurried towards meeting a player in his country and western band: Hank. The man I would some day marry.

Mel whistles softly as he stands, hands on hips, looking up at a maple tree. "Holy Toledo," he says, and then, "Wow!" because Elsa and Jill are ignoring him. The rye whisky he's drunk buzzes in his limbs and he feels inches taller, that his movements are athletic and fluid. "You girls should come and see this."

Elsa's pale moon face seems to glow out at him from the deep shadows where she sits halfway up a gentle embankment. She leans against a tree and Jill sprawls on her back beside her. It has only taken several timid sips of Mel's spiked cola and they've become stupid, bird-brainy, Mel thinks. *"Du bist ein kleines Schwein."* Jill has been chanting the sentence Elsa taught her, over and over.

The maple tree has been blasted open by lightning. Its trunk looks as though giant hands have grabbed hold, wrung it dry until the trunk split open with the force. Reduced to a pile of toothpicks, Mel thinks. Its wood is streaked the colour red, veins that glisten with wet sap. Mel's imagination fails him when he examines the destroyed tree. He can't imagine the power, can only be awed by it and admit silently that he lies when he tells himself that he accompanies Margaret downstairs during thunderstorms because he has promised Timothy to be the man of the house when he is away.

They had waited several minutes for Amy to follow them into the trees, and when she didn't, they reasoned that she knew she wasn't wanted and her nose was out of joint as usual, the spoiled brat that she was. They reasoned that Amy went back to the picnic. So they skirted the border of the park, walking through a narrow band of trees growing beside the Assiniboine River, picking their way among the sinewy tree roots, dragon tails writhing up through thin soil, until the sound of the Lutheran Sunday School picnic, the cheering on of participants in the sack races, three-legged races, grew fainter. They agreed to rest where the trees grew wilder and thicker and the earth smelled musty, of mushroom spores and wild fern. They smeared their bodies with insect repellent and Mel revealed the contents of his school bag. Then they sat beneath the umbrella of shade, felt insects light against their arms and legs or attempting to crawl inside their noses and ears and then bounce off at the scent of repellent. They watched a fat beaver waddle along the river bank on the opposite shore, sipped at the spiked cola, and felt themselves take on the veneer of sophistication.

But while the girls are now languid and content to loll in the shade, Mel becomes energetic. Behind him the land drops away sharply to the rain-swollen river that flows swiftly on through the city. Its water, coloured by the yellow clay of the region, grows muddy-looking where sewer conduits empty out storm water and the refuse of the city. Mel finds a path and climbs down its bank to scout for wildlife. Otters, he explains later to Elsa, hoping to impress upon her the other side of him, his outdoorsy spirit of adventure. But Mel is always just a step behind. He hears the slap of a tail or the soft *plop!* of an animal's body meeting water, turns quickly, only to see the ripple of its wake. He sees the river's course, how it passes beneath the arch of a stone bridge at the park's entrance and on into the centre of the city. At the horizon, a crane's boom swings in an arc and hovers above the skeleton of a building. Mel imagines that he enjoys the shushing of traffic, its steady sound muffled slightly by the row of newly constructed apartment blocks. In his altered state he believes that he would like to sit out on a balcony and smoke a cigarette and watch traffic stream by below. The rye whisky causes him to forget how city people make him feel so out of place in his own skin. They seem noisier, almost hostile in their indifference to his presence. Margaret often embarrasses him when she goes shopping in the way she engages clerks in long conversations, not noticing how the clerks' faces look pained with the expression of boredom or disinterest or, worse, how their faces turn smug and seem to say "hicks." He climbs back up along the path until he gets to the shattered maple tree.

Elsa rests her elbows against her knees, cups her chin, and smiles down at him. "Don't you want to see this?" Mel is desperate to gain her attention. She smiles again, shakes her head no.

"See what?" Jill sounds half asleep.

"This tree. It's been hit by lightning."

"If scientists could discover a way to harness a bolt of lightning," Jill recites, "they'd be able to light up a billion light bulbs."

"New York."

"Whatever."

"Or the City of Lights." Elsa laughs.

"She's been to Paris," Jill says. "She's seen the Eiffel Tower." Her legs flash as she rocks herself up into a sitting position.

"Was that before or after Germany?" Mel hopes he sounds sarcastic.

Jill pulls at the ribbon around one of her braids. She unties it and lets it drop. Then her nimble fingers tug at her dark hair as she unravels the plait.

"I was born in Germany," Elsa says.

"Dresden. She showed me on a map," Jill adds.

They have become like Siamese twins, Mel thinks, with a surge of envy.

"Then I went to Poland. Was taken to Poland, I don't remember. That's where Esther found me and adopted me. And Adele."

"In Warsaw," Jill says.

"Zelazowa-Wola. Not far from Warsaw."

Mel likes the strangeness of Elsa's voice, her style. The way she wears her woollen tam in winter, for instance, not tilted to one side but pulled down over her ears and forehead, a frame for her round face. Her leather shoulder bag seems to be a part of her and not just something she wears when she wants to dress up like the other girls, who carry their bags stiffly on special occasions or with a hint of self-consciousness when they bring them to school. Then, the bag betrays that it's that time of the month and they keep their little secrets in it for when they go to the bathroom and come back with lumps at the back of their skirts. Mel runs his hand over the tree's shattered bark and then reaches inside its core where splinters bristle like a porcupine. He wants to pull a sliver loose and present it to Elsa, and say, Here, a toothpick carved by nature. He winces as a splinter pierces the back of his hand. He sucks at the wound and tastes salt.

"Then Esther took us to France," Elsa continues, "England, and now here."

Jill has unravelled her other braid and shakes the thick hair free. "Turn around. I think you'd look good like this," Elsa says and begins to gather Jill's hair up on top of her head. Mel glances at them and then turns away with a blink of shock. Elsa isn't wearing underpants. Earlier she'd made a tent of her dress, made a careful point of tucking it in beneath her thighs. But as she reached for Jill's hair her dress slid up and in his quick glance he believes that he saw bare skin. Well, all right, Mel thinks as he drinks the last bit of spiked cola. He tells himself that maybe it's a custom or something, not to wear underpants. Elsa fusses over Jill, declaring her envy, her desire to possess such thick shiny hair. She twists it into a knot, drawing the skin on Jill's face taut.

"Hey, Mel, look," Jill says. She pulls the skin beside one eye up until the eye almost closes in a slanted slit. "Mother Chinese," she says in a sing-song voice. Then she pulls the skin beneath the other eye and the lid droops. "Father Japanese." She finishes the joke by pulling one eye up and the other down at the same time. "Me." She laughs. Elsa laughs too. A bit uncomfortable, Mel thinks, probably embarrassed because she doesn't get the joke. It doesn't occur to Mel that perhaps Elsa thinks it's in bad taste. His eyes are drawn to her bent knees. The dress has hitched up higher, and he sees the pout of flesh between her legs. His scalp goes tight with the realization that he's right. She isn't wearing underpants. It looks like a mouth, he thinks. What Elsa has down there is a sideways plump mouth. Not the slender, elongated shape of Jill's.

"I want your hair," Elsa says to Jill. "I wish we could trade heads." She turns to face Mel as she speaks. Her blue eyes shine out from the shadows. She smiles and then very slowly draws her dress back down into place.

She wanted me to see it, Mel thinks. But even as he thinks this it seems to be a preposterous idea or the result of an over-active imagination. It must be that she's foreign, he thinks. He goes over to where the school bag rests beneath a clump of bushes. He searches through it while his mind races around a maze of possibilities and comes to a thudding stop at the word "fuck." While the word is used frequently by others around him, he doesn't use it. Even when he looks at the magazines or the hand-drawn cartoons that circulate at school, he thinks "screwing" or "banging." "Fuck" is something dogs or trashy poor people do. Elsa's blue eyes meet his and there is a knowing there, an understanding between them. "I'm thirsty," she says.

Mel holds up the mickey of rye and shakes it. It's still about three-quarters full. "We need more mix."

Elsa lets go of Jill's hair and it ripples around her shoulders. "Why don't you go, Jill? When you get back I'll do your hair up and you'll see what it looks like. I've got pins in my bag."

The protest in Jill's mouth dies as she looks first at Elsa and then at Mel. She grins. "Sure." She slides down the incline and slaps dirt from the seat of her shorts as she walks towards Mel. Her eyes flash with amusement. She stands in front of him almost nose to nose while he flips through his wallet. "Just one cola?" Her hair, a frizzy loose cloud, obscures Mel's view of Elsa. He hands her a dollar. Her fingers close around it as she leans forward and says the words softly: "Elsa says she's not a virgin."

Mel's throat goes dry as he watches Jill climb up the slope again and wind her way among the trees. She's like pieces of a jigsaw puzzle, he thinks, as he watches bits of Jill, the glimmer of a tanned calf, forearm, a swatch of pink cotton, flit away among the black tree trunks and into the deep shadows. He's aware of Elsa in the foreground holding up a little mirror, the aura of gold around her head as branches sway in a light breeze and a beam of sunlight shines through her wispy curls. His body pulses with heat.

"Melville," Elsa says. She uses his full name and Mel wishes Jill hadn't told her. "Why don't you come and sit down."

"Sure." To his surprise he feels his legs propel him forward. He still believes that's all he will do, sit beside her and wait for Jill to return. That this may be the time he needs to ask her to go to the dance with him. She'll say yes and he'll enter the gym with her beside him and see all eyes turn, evaluating, second-guessing Mel Barber. Mel studies his father when he returns from the road, how his bloodshot eyes still peer over the rim of the steering wheel, steady on some fixed and predictable destination, the slump of his narrow shoulders beneath his white shirt, its starch gone soft, saying "ordinary" to Mel. He feels pity and something else that he will come to identify later as being contempt. Elsa is different. He, Mel, will be different. "Sit," Elsa says. She reaches out and pulls him down beside her on the cool, damp ground.

Mel has studied the bawdy cartoons that from time to time exchange hands. The most lewd of all is one titled "What Happened When They Put Spanish Fly in the Office Cooler." Couples in an office are depicted in various positions of copulation. To Mel, every position seems equally erotic. Sometimes Mel studies the cartoon characters' faces. The women all wear ecstatic smiles, signifying bliss, and the men leer. Only the women have drunk from the tainted cooler, Mel supposes, because the men's crooked smiles indicate that they think they have just pulled one off. But mostly Mel studies the act itself, engorged penises entering female bodies, and he thinks that he doesn't care what position, he just wants to do it. And Elsa had assisted him. When he fumbled, searching for the way inside her, she held him and shifted her pelvis and guided him. The moment he felt her heat, he groaned, realizing that he couldn't hold back, he was going over the top.

Elsa lies beneath him. Her rib cage rises and falls against him and her breath is warm against his chest. When he opens his eyes he sees his curled fist against the brown earth, the skin scraped away by the tree. It's as though the hand belongs to someone else. "Heavy," Elsa murmurs.

Mel pushes himself up and off her body in one swift movement. He feels himself slide back inside his own body. He averts his eyes from the sight of Elsa's milky-white torso as he stands up and steps around her. He walks down to the damaged tree and stands there, plunging his hands deep into his pockets and whistling softly through his teeth to deny the creeping sense of disappointment. What he does with himself in secret is a desperate act inspired by images of Spanish fly in the office cooler. He thought that the real thing would be more intense than a small shudder of pleasure. He thought there would be arms holding, mouths kissing. But Jill had barely disappeared among the trees when Elsa lay down. She'd flung her arms above her head, a bent knee swaying lazily. When he tried to touch her breast, she shook her head no. Instead, she reached down, pulled her skirt up around her waist, and closed her eyes. Nothing left for Mel to do but climb on. And then it was over.

Mel hears Elsa step up behind him. Her fingers pluck something from his hair. Then she walks around to face him. She closes her eyes offering her mouth for him to kiss. Her pouty lips move towards his and his stomach heaves. He thinks wildly, I can't do it. I can't kiss her. Suddenly her eyes fly open, pale agates stare into his with a question. "Did you hear that?" she asks.

Then Mel hears a voice too, calling out. His name.

"It's Jill." Elsa turns and scrambles up the embankment.

Mel runs after Elsa as she sprints among the trees. The soles of his shoes are too smooth, and he keeps losing his footing on the damp ground, stumbling and crashing into trees.

"Mel!" Jill's voice has become sharp with fear. Mel feels as though he's knee-deep in water, trying to run, impeded by his awkwardness, and he wants to weep in frustration. When he reaches the edge of the park and climbs up onto the grassy hill, he's red-faced and panting. Elsa is far ahead. He tucks his chin into his chest and runs, aware through the hammering of his heart that there are voices other than Jill's. When he looks up he can't see her, only boys on bicycles, riding in a circle. Elsa stops running and waits for him to catch up. Her eyes bulge with anger. "Tell them to stop." Mel sees Jill in the centre of their circle, cowering, her head tilted at a crazy angle while the boys ride around her making clucking noises. They have her by the hair. Mel feels the pain of it in his own scalp. He steps towards them, angry, his eyes fixed on the crouching form of Jill. They see him coming and brake to a stop. "Hey look! It's Howdy Doody." Jill tries to move towards him. She whimpers as they yank her back into place. They're older, taller than he is, Mel realizes with a sinking heart. "Let her go. That's my sister." He spoke quietly. He almost said, Let her go, please.

"Well, way to go! Howdy Doody has a sister." The leader laughs, pushes out of the circle, and heads over to Mel. He rides at top speed, brakes at the final moment, and the bicycle slides sideways in front of Mel. "Make us stop." Mel smells stale cigarette smoke. He can see the hairs in the boy's nostrils, he's that close. Mel swings, wanting to knock him off balance, but the boy is quick and has Mel by the wrist with one hand and slams him hard in the stomach with the other. Mel hears himself grunt as he falls backwards onto the grass. The bicycle thuds to the ground beside him and he sees a running shoe swing forward and he thinks, Oh God, I'm dead. The shoe stops inches from his chin and then comes down slowly. Mel feels the pressure of it against his chest. He's pinned. Elsa's legs flash by his head. Mel hears her scream at them, high-pitched, in German. "Hey you guys," the voice above Mel says, "check it out, eh? It's the Tasmanian Devil."

As Elsa runs towards the other two, their faces betray their uncertainty as they see the rage in her twisted features. Jill is freed suddenly as they back away from Elsa's onslaught of words and her fingernails clawing at their faces. Mel lies still, not daring to lift his head but wanting desperately to know what's happening. The pressure against his chest lifts suddenly as the leader swears and bolts away. Mel sits up. One of the boys is cupping his nose and blood runs between his fingers. Elsa grabs Jill and pulls her to her feet. The leader strides towards them, his fists curled at his sides. "I'll show you what fighting dirty means." Beyond them Mel sees an adult running in their direction. He jumps to his feet, waves, and calls out. The man waves back. "Here now! What's going on over there?"

The leader swipes at a dark hank of hair trailing across his forehead. He squints over Jill's shoulder at the approaching man. He raises his hands, backing away in submission, and the other boys follow. They pick up their bicycles and walk away. The man stops and watches until they mount their bikes and begin to ride. Then all at once the boys turn and ride back, heading directly towards Jill and Elsa. They gain speed and as they go by, the leader veers inwards, kicks, attempting to get Elsa and missing, hitting Jill instead. She moans and doubles over clutching at her groin. "Now see here!" The man yells and chases after them. Jill's face grows pale as she gathers her shorts in a fist and presses against the pain. Mel stifles an incongruous impulse to whistle a nonchalant tune as he watches the cyclists round the corner of the pavilion and disappear. The man stops running and then shakes his fist in their direction. "Hoodlums! Punks!" He turns. "Everything okay?"

Mel carries the imprint of the boy's shoe in the middle of his shirt. He brushes at it and hunches his shoulders, crinkling the fabric to obliterate its shape. His shame makes him want to vomit. He follows Jill and Elsa as they head back along the path among the trees. Jill sucks air through her teeth to keep

73

from crying. Mel doesn't think of the word "shame." He feels it, thick, hot, rising in waves as he fixes his eyes on the centre of Elsa's back. It's her fault, he thinks. If she hadn't sent Jill for the cola this wouldn't have happened. He feels some of his shame give way to anger.

When they reach the clearing where moments before Mel had lain on top of Elsa, he steps onto the spot purposely, grinding his anger and their act into the ground and burying it. Elsa's murmured concern rises up among the trees as she kneels in front of Jill and examines the blue mass spreading beneath the pale skin of her groin. "I forgot the cola. It's back there where I dropped it," Jill says.

Mel squints against the rush of tears. He picks up the school bag and unbuckles its straps and carries it down the path that leads to the steep river bank and the rush of yellow water below. The rye whisky bottle is cool in the palm of his hand. He promises himself to throw it into the river and to never take another drink of booze again.

She heard their voices and crept softly through the trees towards the sound. She saw Mel first. He stood with his back to her, facing the river, the school bag dangling at his side. She saw the back of Jill's head and Elsa kneeling in front of her. A complete picture, the three of them, and she stood as usual on the outside looking in. But what became apparent to her, what she had in the past only suspected, was their complete lack of concern for her well-being. This revelation shouldn't have caught her by surprise but it did, and her chest ached. She wanted to limp into their picture, bruised, cut, and bleeding. It would have served them right, she thought, if she'd been struck by a car or offered too many ice-cream cones by strangers.

If she had died and not Jill, she would have had them all in the palm of her hand forever.

"Shorty!"

Elsa and Jill crane their necks to get a look at her.

"Well, so how was the picnic?"

Mel sounds so phoney, Amy thinks.

"How was the whisky?" It's their loss now because she won't tell them what she just saw in the other park down the street.

"What are you talking about?" Mel frowns.

She points to his hand.

Jill titters and covers her mouth.

"I found it," Mel says.

"So who's the liar? Drop dead, Mel." Amy is amazed to see Mel's legs fly out from beneath him as though someone had just given him a quick shove.

The bottle flies from his hand and he whoops in panic. He's lost his footing on the slippery path and his feet take off. Still clutching the school bag, Mel feels himself being propelled forward and unable to stop. His body can barely keep up with his churning legs as the uneven ground, knotted tree roots, pass beneath his feet. Fall down, he tells himself as he sees the path in front of him end in the steep drop of the river bank and the swift current of flowing water below. He can't swim. He sees his death happening before their astonished eyes and yet he thinks that he can't bear the indignity of falling down. He doesn't want to die this way, either. But, still, he can't risk making a fool of himself. "Drop the bag," Jill screams. Before Mel can comprehend what she's said, it's the bag that saves him. The bag flailing at the end of his arm snags a tree branch and Mel's feet leave the ground as he falls backwards, landing on the path with a thud. Wind slams from his chest and for a moment his lungs refuse to open as he gulps air. He raises his head and looks down the length of his body. His feet jut out over the bank. He hears the rush of water below and then Jill and Elsa running down the path towards him.

Amy watches the scene from above. She watches as Jill sits down beside Mel, lifts his head, and cradles it in the crook of her bare legs. Her hair falls forward, a dark curtain rippling around his face as she rocks him, laughing and crooning. Elsa stands to one side watching for a moment and then she squats beside them. She pulls loose a frond of wild fern growing among the trees and begins to fan Mel's chest with it. Mel's hand shoots forward and knocks the fern aside. "Take off!" His shoulders twist and he hides his face in Jill.

Interesting, Amy thinks, how she said to Mel, "Drop dead," and it almost happened.

4

We rode home in silence, drowsy with heat and our eyes half-closed against the press of sun on our faces. Our mouths were rimmed with the black licorice Mel had brought along to overpower any lingering odour of whisky on his breath. Jill had pulled her hat down low onto her forehead, hiding her eyes and feigning sleep, but now and then she would massage her groin. Adele, whom Josh had picked up at the hairdresser's, chain-smoked and hummed, studying her reflection imposed upon the landscape gliding past the car window. She no longer wore the green turban. Her hairstyle was smooth, too perfect, I thought, like a store mannequin's hair. Occasionally her humming broke off as she flicked bits of tobacco from her tongue or exclaimed in a scoffing or resigned way over some private thought. Mel stared straight ahead, as though hypnotized by the broken white lines of the highway. A wall of cumulus clouds banked high in the north as concrete as a range of mountains. The clouds, coloured by the sun, had their own purple valleys and snow caps streaked with pink and gold. A screen for me on which to replay the adventure I had after Mel and Jill abandoned me.

I had followed the couple walking in front of me as they headed towards the sound of music echoing in the buildings along the street.

"What we have here is a musical wonder," the man called Stu Farmer said as I hurried towards his husky amplified voice to join the crowd standing around an elevated platform in the small park beside Portage Avenue. "My little partner has been playing the guitar ever since he was knee-high to a grasshopper and he ain't much bigger now. Sat on the floor beside my guitar when he was only two years old and started strumming the heck outa it just as easy as eating apple pie. I thought old Chet himself had dropped by for a visit. When the boy comes out here to play, I want you to pay attention. You're gonna hear something downright amazing. So get ready! Ladies and gents, let's give this cowpoke the welcome he deserves! Welcome Stu Farmer Junior!" He flung his fringed arm in the direction of the blue curtain strung up behind him on the stage.

"Well, well, well," I heard someone say and then I felt a man step up to my side. From the corner of my eye I saw grey flannel. A grey suit. The man stood beside me and made a church steeple of his hands, tapping his index fingers together. The curtain on the stage billowed suddenly and a woman's voice rose up from behind it, pleading. Stu Farmer chuckled. "Come on out here, son. Ain't a thing in the world that'll bite you." He leaned across his guitar and winked. "Unlike his pappy, he's a bit on the shy side, folks." The crowd tittered in appreciation and watched the curtain. Traffic in the street slowed down as people leaned from windows to catch a glimpse of what was happening on the stage, which had been set up in the centre of the park among rectangles of flower-beds.

A woman who was later introduced as Loretta, Stu Farmer's wife, pushed through the opening in the curtain with her back to us and dragged Stu Farmer Junior onto the stage. A tall, sandy-haired man stepped out behind him and sauntered off to one side of it. He grinned at us and tipped his Stetson to the back of his head. This was Hank, the man I would meet again not too many years later. Junior, a shy teenage boy, wore a gold satin shirt identical to his father's, and a white Stetson. He flinched when he saw the crowd and his chin dropped to his chest. Loretta nudged him and he bowed. When he straightened, his Stetson dropped low over his forehead. He looked off to one side, as though concentrating on something happening in the wings.

"I've been telling the folks here about how you can play two songs at once on your guitar. That true, son? You haven't been putting us on, have yuh?" The Stetson said no. "Well, let's do it then. Let's play for the good folks out there."

"That's right, son," murmured the tall man in the grey suit who stood beside me. "You can do it, son. The people of the plains who till the soil, they plant, they hope, and they do not surrender. Whether the forces of nature destroy their years' work, their life work, or when world events . . ." I glanced up. His Adam's apple bobbed as he paused to swallow saliva. Grey whiskers glinted among the soft folds of his jowls. I stepped away and threaded in deeper among the crowd, working my way closer to the front. When I turned and looked back it was to confirm what I already knew. It was John Diefenbaker. He stood among the crowd, smiling strangely, his head wobbling from side to side as though he was agreeing with everything and everyone around him.

"You ready now, son?" Stu Farmer asked. "Well come on, let's do it then." A-one, two. Their feet stomped, hands flashed against strings, and music flowed from their instruments. "Yankee doodle went to town," they played for several moments, and then they keyed up and began playing another song, which the couple began to sing, "Home on the Range." They harmonized in a fake mournful tone over their son's head. Then their instruments fell silent and Junior continued to play. He lifted his head and his gaze grew fixed on the air above us as he concentrated, as though reading from an invisible score. "Yankee doodle went to town, riding on a pony." I heard the words in his strings. As I listened, I heard another melody emerge at the same time. "Where nary was heard a discouraging word and the skies are not cloudy all day." The people grew still. I glanced back and saw John D's head wobbling and his mouth moving as he recited the words to the song.

The boy played for several minutes and then, as he neared the end of the performance, he became impatient to be finished and the melodies blended together. He bowed and stepped to the back of the stage.

People clapped and several turned from the stage, about to leave, while others shifted sideways to the edge in order to politely slip away. Stu Farmer grabbed the microphone. "Say folks," he said. "If you have to go, I understand. But if you can stick around you'll see that we've been saving the best for the last. What you're about to see and hear would make my grandpappy roll over in his grave. Heh, heh, heh. Rock and roll, that is." He nodded at the other musicians. A-one, two, one, two, three, four. Their feet began to stomp again, and then their instruments jumped with the rock and roll beat. Junior played with them, a little smirk pulling at one corner of his mouth. The curtain parted and a skinny, young, pimply-faced man leapt to centre stage. The sequins on his bolero jacket sparkled in the sun as he swung his arms, and his legs scissored back and forth in time to the beat. His black hair shone as though it was wet and his squared-off sideburns appeared to be painted on halfway down the sides of his narrow face. The musical introduction ended and he froze in position, legs splayed, pelvis thrust forward. In the slight pause that followed I heard a snuffling sound as Stu Farmer Junior ducked his head. Laughing, I realized.

"Ladies and gents, boys and girls. I kid you not, straight from Nashville, I give you Elvis the Pelvis Presley!"

I was startled when the women around me shrieked. Several men shoved their hands into their pockets or stared at their shoes, refusing to look at the gyrating performer. "Elvis Pretzel, you mean," someone said sardonically. "A friggin' impersonator. No way they'd get that guy to come up here." I watched as Junior began to edge to the back of the stage. He grinned and winked at Hank. Then he glanced up and our eyes met. He smiled, shy, and put a finger against his mouth, the gesture saying, "Don't tell anyone." Then he backed through the curtain and disappeared.

As I left the crowd, people streamed past me towards the

stage, coming out from the houses bordering the park, some running, others doing a little jive in time to the music. I saw Junior sitting on a picnic table at the back of the park, which, I noticed, was in a square bordered by houses and apartment blocks on three sides. Spirals of water twisted outwards above freshly mowed lawns. As I approached Junior I heard reedy music. I dropped to my haunches beside a tree. He was bent over a mouth organ and a bluesy bit of jazz echoed in his cupped palm. Then the music broke off as he lifted his head, swung his legs up and over the table, and swivelled around to face me.

"Hi." He whacked spit from his instrument. "You all enjoyed the show?" His eyebrows were like black wings flaring up with his question.

"It was okay."

He laughed. "It was a piece of dogey doo doo, you mean." He began to play a jazzed up version of "Heartbreak Hotel." His voice had been soft, low, as though he was weary and didn't like to expend the energy required to talk. I noticed a bottle jutting up between his legs. "You ever hear me play on the radio, kid?"

"No."

"You ain't missed a thing. Care for a little swig of porch-climber?" He held up the bottle.

I shook my head no.

He tipped the bottle, drank, and then set it down on the picnic table with a bang. "Come here, little kid. Come on. Ain't nothing here's going to bite you."

When I refused he slid down from the table and waved me over. "Come on! I just want you to stand beside me. I want to measure."

I got up and stood beside him. "Look. Top of your head is level with my ear, right?" The brim of his Stetson brushed against the side of my head. "I'm five foot two, but my eyes aren't blue." He laughed at his own joke.

"Well, so how old are you? Let me guess. Nine? Ten?"

"Almost eleven," I lied.

He sighed. "Know how old I am, kid? Sixteen. But they

81

don't mind if people think I'm about twelve." He plucked a cigarette from his shirt pocket, lit one, exhaled smoke while studying me. I noticed the shadow of whiskers beneath his stage make-up. "You come here alone? Think that's a good idea?"

"Ain't nothing here's going to bite me."

He laughed and reached for his guitar resting against the table. "Stick around." His voice had lost its thin twangy sound and fake accent. "I'm going to play something. Just for you. This is the real show. Why don't you hop up?" He patted the table.

"It's okay." I went back and sat down beneath the tree, leaning against its trunk.

He bent over his instrument as he played and I liked how his hair had been flattened by his Stetson, a band of dark hair shining with perspiration. "You live around here?" he asked.

I told him the name of my town.

"*Really*?" Again his black wing-like eyebrows shot up. "We're going out that way. Near the end of summer. Me and my parents and Hank, if he can ever get it together. And Old Elvis there." He laughed. "Doing a string of towns."

The singer's voice echoed in the apartment blocks behind me, but as Junior stopped his wandering through the strings and began to play, his music dominated.

He closed his eyes and his head dropped lower and lower until his pale cheek rested against his guitar. I stretched out on the grass and cradled my head, immersed in the exotic spiciness of music that seemed to flaunt its colours, boasting of a place where there was more than what I had. More than a two-tone flat landscape where people sang about cheating hearts or blue suede shoes. I closed my eyes, yearning to see it. Gradually the steady wind-sound of traffic streaming by on Portage Avenue, the voice of the man called Elvis, receded completely and Junior's music remained at the centre.

I was nine years old and my mind not yet cluttered with what might or might not be possible. I lay there, eyes closed, face turned into the damp grass, and, as in my dream of the previous night, saw myself floating in the air. I could do it, I knew. I could rise up, it was simply a matter of possessing the fierce desire. I tried. I imagined sparks shooting from my head in my intense concentration to move. Move, I urged my body. I clenched my teeth and my head buzzed with the pressure of it. Move, *move*. I had been struck by lightning, been subtracted, and I was light now, feet swift. And then it happened. I felt my body inch across the grass. I held my breath. *I was moving!* Slowly, but I felt the grass brush against my face as I moved forward, an inch, two, perhaps three, inches. *I was moving without doing anything but willing it to happen!* And then it stopped. I heard footsteps pounding in the ground beneath me, opened my eyes, and looked up the tall length of Hank.

"Who's the dopey kid?" he asked Stu Farmer Junior. Junior stopped playing. I sat up and the world rushed forward to meet me. "I want you to hear this. I've been working on it," Hank said. Junior nodded. "Tell me what you think." He began to play.

"Ah, Hank Snow," Junior said. Hank nodded and cleared his throat, opened his mouth, and then closed it again.

"Come on, we're waiting."

"Well, there's –" Hank began to sing and then stopped to clear his throat again.

"Ain't nothing here's gonna bite you," Junior said.

Hank grinned and began to sing a song about driving an eighteen-wheeler away from a woman who has broken his heart.

When they return from the picnic, Margaret is upstairs in bed. They hear the soft scuff of her slippers as she hurries down to greet them. "I wasn't sleeping, just having a wee lie-down," she calls out to them, sounding like her mother, Grandmother Johnson. She steps out onto the veranda and they don't recognize their mother at first. She's pulled her wet hair straight back into a ponytail and her clean face looks younger, almost boyish. She wears Timothy's blue-plaid housecoat.

She smiles and crosses her arms against her chest and taps her foot. "What if I don't let you in?" She laughs. Then she bounds towards them and unhooks the screen door. "I hope you're as tired as I am." She yawns. "And I hope you're hungry too because I made sandwiches."

Amy notices how her voice doesn't match her eyes, which veer towards the sky in search of a storm, the look of apprehension dawning. Humid air holds the smell of Carona on a Saturday evening: potatoes frying in butter, apple pies cooling on countertops for the Sunday after-church meal, nips and chips cooking in Sullie's Drive In and Take Out outside of town.

One by one they pass Margaret on the veranda. She smiles over their heads, not at them, and doesn't wonder over the dirty footprint in the centre of Mel's chest. Jill stops to wind her tanned arms around Margaret's long white neck and kisses her ear. "I wore my hat all day." She winces against the pain in her groin but she is careful not to limp.

"Go on up and wash." Margaret slaps each one playfully on the rump as they ascend the stairs. Her eyes embrace the image of her children in the dim light of the upstairs hallway, the square man-look of Mel's maturing frame, the glint of gold in Jill's dark rippling hair. Sparks of the sun clinging to it, she thinks. And then there's the short-legged, stubby-bodied youngest child. Amy. The child she had ached for. And so unbearable had her longing been that she'd made the decision to stop using her diaphragm without Timothy knowing. An accident. It happens. The result: Amy. Obstinate, moody, too silent, always wanting to run before she walks. She has confessed to Timothy that she doesn't understand this one. From the very beginning Amy struggled to be free of her embrace, preferring Timothy's arms instead. She's not like my other babies, Margaret had complained to Bunny. Not round, plump, and gurgling, eager to please with a smile. Amy had been born covered in downy black fur from the back of her neck to her buttocks, breasts enlarged and nipples oozing. She was not the Amelia Margaret had envisioned, a porcelain doll whom she would put in smocked dresses with lace collars.

84

She was muscular, hard, and resisted Margaret at every turn. The daily bath routine became a tussle. But it wasn't this or the fight to dress Amy that had filled Margaret with resentment. It was the way her second daughter had eyes only for Timothy. Let's face it, Margaret had said to Bunny, I was an incubator and that's about all.

Mel ducks into his bedroom to change his shirt. He stands in front of the mirror stripped to the waist. He turns sideways, examining his profile, flexes his muscles, and checks to see if his pectorals are larger. He looks to see if something has changed because he has "banged" a girl. Then he feels a pressure in his chest, the imprint of a foot. Hangers clank in the closet as he pulls free a clean shirt. He tucks it down around his waist and turns to the mirror. He imagines he can see the treads of a sneaker.

Jill sits on her bed holding a mirror to her groin. Blood pools beneath her skin, becoming an angry-looking bruise. She runs her finger across it lightly, back and forth, and feels something else. A lump. It will disappear when the bruise fades, she thinks. Jill believes that the lump is from the boy's kick but the node has been swollen for a month or so and is rapidly growing larger.

Amy washes her hands in the bathroom. The air is moist and smells of Chantilly, and bubbles from Margaret's bath still cling to the side of the tub. When she steps from the bathroom she looks inside Margaret's bedroom. The new blouse her mother made lies crumpled on the floor. The Blue Book, Margaret's journal, lies open on the white bedspread. Amy's stomach sings with hunger and so she decides that she'll wait for another opportunity to discover what her mother has written in it today.

They sit waiting around the table as Margaret unwraps a damp tea towel from a plate of sandwiches and sets the plate down. She hovers over her children, pouring ice tea into their glasses, and then sits down to watch them eat. Amy's hands shake as she tears apart her sandwich and stuffs chunks of cheddar cheese, ham, and bread into her mouth.

"So, what did you do today?" Margaret chooses to ignore how Amy's cheeks bulge with food, that she barely chews it before she swallows and reaches for another sandwich. Often, they lose their appetites when they watch Amy eat, and so they have learned not to watch when she sometimes stirs everything together into a soupy mush so she can eat it more quickly with a spoon. They can always tell where she has sat by the sticky globs of food left behind, the dribbles of milk, the litter of crusts or bits of fat or rind picked off and discarded.

"We went to the zoo. We saw monkeys," Jill says.

"Baboons. They belong to the family of Cercopithecidae." Mel's voice is deep today. Baritone.

"Oh really?" Margaret replies as though this information is surprising.

"The usual picnic stuff." He raises his arms, stretches.

"And swans. We saw swans. They were in the duck pond."

"I have always loved the swans," Margaret says to Jill. She leans into the chair hugging herself as though suddenly chilled. "And what did you see, Amy?"

She will tell them absolutely nothing about the country and western band because they ran off on her. "Three boys on bicycles," she says through a chunk of bread and notices how Jill's and Mel's faces grow sharp. "In the duck pond. Quack, quack." She draws her lips back to reveal a wad of half-chewed bread stuck against her teeth.

Mel shoves his sandwich aside, his appetite gone. "I think I'll go out for a while. That okay?"

Margaret appears not to have heard. "I think your father should be home quite early in the morning."

"I'll go with you," Jill says.

Margaret becomes suddenly alert and Amy, anticipating her next move, plucks up another sandwich before she can clear them away. "Haven't you all had enough of the outdoors today?" Margaret asks.

"Just for a while. It's so cool now. I thought I'd look up

Garth," Mel says casually, although he knows that his cousin is probably waiting for him.

"Well, all right. But don't be long," Margaret says as she goes to put the sandwiches away. Her foot meets George napping in front of the refrigerator door. Her face turns red and all three look up in astonishment as Margaret heaves the plate of sandwiches at the cat. "Melville Barber! I have had it up to kingdom come with that cat of yours! You're going to have to do something about it!" She turns and flees the kitchen.

"What now?" Mel stares at the shattered plate, the sandwiches fallen open, meat and cheese and egg salad scattered across the shiny new floor.

Jill shrugs. "I'm not a walking encyclopaedia."

They leave together and Amy sits at the table alone. She sets her hands onto her lap, palms up, lying there limply. Her head drops forward until her chin almost rests on the table. She hears Margaret's heels thumping on the ceiling overhead and then the squeak of bedsprings. She stares at the wall as she chews and wonders, Why did Margaret throw the plate of sandwiches at the cat? She eats methodically, steadily, to still a gnawing at her centre. Why does Timothy have to go away? Why can't he stay home and work in town like other fathers do? She remembers Timothy out back, chopping wood, heat radiating from the woodstove, the happy smell and crackle of it. She remembers it being more orange when Timothy stayed home. A glowing orange fire, friendlier than the house is now, warmer. There is something about the house that is too hard and shiny with Timothy away. She gulps back tea to wash down the sandwich, and reaches for Mel's half-eaten one. "Born July 4th, 1946. Jill Anne. A beautiful, bouncing baby girl. Eight pounds, four ounces." Amy has read this in Margaret's Blue Book. Sometimes the entries are cryptic: "I don't know." Or, "Over my head." Sometimes they're clearer: "Tim goes away." "Tim returns Thursday." Margaret records her cycle, the onset of menstruation, with single words: "bloated," "cramps," "depressed." Amy has read pages of tiny script that summed up a day or a conversation, or their own antics recorded in a tone of high exuberance, her love for them declared in a flourish of curlicues, sometimes followed on the next page by an abrupt printed sentence such as: "I can't stand this any more."

"Amelia Jane, born April 29th, 1950, seven pounds, twelve ounces." Amelia's a name for an old woman, Timothy had protested, and so, although the birth certificate said otherwise, she became Amy. Amy has read puzzling descriptions of herself in Margaret's Blue Book which, if it weren't for her name written there, she would not have recognized as being herself.

Usually when Margaret throws herself onto the bed it's over a slight disagreement with Timothy or after a visit from her mother. And usually the springs squeak again only moments later when she gets off the bed and comes back down to them, subdued and shamefaced with apologies. Amy listens now. The silence in the house draws back and up, at its centre a hole, the pause before the wind rushes in and fills it. She scoops globs of creamy mayonnaise from bread and sucks it from her fingers. When she finishes the insides of Mel's sandwich, she pushes away from the table, her stomach distended.

She leaves the house, going out the back way to avoid a chance meeting with Mel or Jill. As she crosses the yard towards the garage, the rope swing is a dark silhouette, a skinny U suspended under the branches of the shade tree. Gravel crunches under her feet as she follows the driveway to the back of the yard. The air inside the garage rushes forward to meet her as she opens the door, hot, heavy with a sweet smell of paint. Timothy's jalopy is covered with a tarpaulin. When he works on it, she sits behind the wheel practising for the time she will drive it. She feels through the dark until her hands rest against the rungs of a ladder. She lifts it down from the wall. A can of paint topples from a work-bench as she swings the ladder around and out the door. It scrapes against the roof of the garage as she sets it in place, teetering beneath her feet as she climbs upwards.

"Where are we going?" Jill hears a noise in the backyard but she doesn't mention it. She's afraid Mel will leave without her. They lean against the side of the veranda. Across the street the cries of several children playing in the school yard float up to meet the coming night, and, set against it, is their light-coloured clothing, phantoms dancing, gliding in a strange waltz.

"You mean, where am *I* going." Mel leaves the yard and walks down the street, quickly passing from view into the shadows cast by the trees.

"Mel!"

He turns and his heart becomes sick with the sight of Jill's limping, gimpy walk as she tries to catch up to him. He drops to the grass beneath a tree and waits. "So Howdy Doody has a sister."

Jill sits down beside him. "Jerks. They were just jerks."

Mel yanks at a blade of grass. He cups it and blows. He's been trying for years but he never succeeds in making it shriek. "Howdy Doody. They meant my ears, of course." He feels the flutter of her cool mouth against his cheek. "I should have gone for the cola. Not you."

"I don't think it would have been the same." She laughs and he feels himself blush. She hugs her knees and presses her face into them, running her tongue across the taut, smooth skin, tasting salt, and feeling the slippery smoothness of her kneecap against her lips. Is that what it's like, she wonders, a wet kiss? A wet mouth sliding across another wet mouth? "So?" she asks.

"So, what?"

"So did you and Elsa do it?" She grins at him and her white teeth shine out from her wet lips.

"Yes." And he would like to do it again. Soon. He feels the rush of desire.

"I thought so." She leans back onto the grass and shivers as dew soaks through her thin cotton top. She looks up at the dim pinpricks of new stars. The children in the playground still seem to be dancing, their muted voices saying, We have secrets. Adults will call from doorways. Come on in, now, they will say. You'll catch your death. Time to pack it in. Time for sleep. Children having fun seems to make adults nervous, Jill thinks, as she hears the first call and listens to the anguished pleading. Adults want to stop their children's playing quickly with a warning that is really a veiled threat. The children continue their play, choosing for several moments at least to close their ears to the beckoning cries of their anxious parents, who offer safety in the rooms of houses, as they wait in doorways for their children to return and for their own lives to continue.

"Well, so? What was it like?"

"I don't want to talk about it."

Jill springs on him, beats him down onto the grass with her fists. "You have to. You have to." She straddles him with her thin bruised legs and wraps her hands around his throat. "You have to." She threatens murder. Mel's eyes bulge, his tongue lolls grotesquely, and then his head drops to one side as he feigns death. She flicks the end of his nose and rolls away. It's not fair, Jill thinks. She picks at a small scab on her knee. It stings as she pulls it away. And then her tongue stings too with the sudden craving for something salty. "Pickled herring," she says. She would die to sink her teeth into a piece of pickled herring. Her tongue shivers as she imagines the salty taste of it, her teeth slicing clean through its blue skin, feeling the texture of its flesh, salty, tangy. She feels the heat of Mel's fingers against her cool ones. "God, I'd kill for some pickled herring." He lifts her hand and sets it against his groin. She feels the bump that is his penis. "It's hard!"

"That's what it was like."

She withdraws her hand. The children playing in the school yard have all gone home. She misses their voices. "What's it look like? Hard."

He groans. "Aw, come on."

"I'm serious."

"For the love of Mike," Mel complains but he unzips his fly and shows her.

His knob is bluish, cold-looking, she thinks, as though it must hurt. "It's – "

"It's what?"

90

"Kind of . . . " Ugly, she thinks. "Show-offy."

Mel leaps to his feet and walks away.

"Hey, wait up! I meant big. It's big." She grabs his arm and slows him down. Her mouth fills with saliva as she thinks of brine and sucking at a chunk of pickled herring. "So are you and Elsa going steady now?"

"No. I don't think so."

"But you are going to ask her to the dance, aren't you?"

"Maybe." He wouldn't be caught dead going anywhere with Elsa.

They walk down towards Main Street, their destination the hardware store where their cousin Garth Johnson waits for them. Beyond, cars pass beneath the yellow bug-repellent lights at the filling station.

"I don't think you have Howdy Doody ears. I really don't." Laughter bubbles in her throat. "Actually, your ears are more like Prince Charles's ears."

"Thanks a lot."

The air has grown cool and goose bumps rise on Jill's arms as she and Mel walk downtown. The sudden chill is a reminder that spring had been swallowed up overnight in May, causing those who had murmured against the unusual almost-tropical weather and its offspring (salamanders spawning in sump holes in basements, clumps of moist penis-shaped mushrooms erupting in lawns during the night, their pale new skin turning leathery-brown beneath the sun of the day) to wonder aloud now whether it has been just too darn good to be true, this marvellous weather. "Don't you forget, it's only June," they remind themselves as they step out onto back stoops, hands on hips, confronting their wet gardens. "At least there's no sign of rain tonight. Good thing, that. Enough is enough, eh? About all we're gonna wind up growing this year is slugs and mosquitoes and little boys." They bite back the dreaded thought of punishment, an unseasonable frost.

As Mel and Jill walk beneath the street lamps, past houses and then the shops of Main Street, the streets they pass through feel as familiar as the lines running across the palms of their hands. Unlike Amy, who treats her travels through Carona's streets as something she has to do in order to arrive at her destination, Mel and Jill have the ambling gait of landowners. They pause in front of Hardy's Gem Store. While all the other stores are closed, windows dark, there's a light in the Hardys' window. The abalone shell lamp has been left burning. Jill has always been drawn to the shell, by how its colours appear to vibrate, iridescent waves curling over a landscape of spiky coral. Usually when Jill looks at it, she thinks that it's what an ocean would look like on the moon. But tonight as she looks at it, she thinks of pickled herring. The craving is for more than its tangy brine, it's the texture of its flesh she desires as well. The sensation of shredding thin skin between her teeth.

A display of jewelled ties and key chains hang from a wire in the window, their semi-precious stones gleaming in the shell lamp's light. Mel sees Mr. Hardy sitting on a stool at the counter, his visor pulled low on his forehead as he hunches over a pool of light. He must have just emptied a tumbler, Mel thinks. He taps on the window. Jill protests and then groans as the man beckons for them to come inside.

The bell above their heads tinkles softly as they open the door. The shop smells arid, of sand and of the elderly couple Mel and Jill know from the United Church. Mr. Hardy used to usher. The Hardys are rock hounds and have turned their hobby into a business. They travel to New Mexico or Arizona every winter in search of precious and semi-precious stones. Jill follows Mel through the narrow aisle in the centre of the cluttered shop. Dusty showcases display oddly shaped rocks, rocks split open to reveal bristly purple quartz crystals, and some shells too, a polished moon shell, its centre resembling an intense blue eye. It's the sound of Mr. Hardy's shop that Mel likes. He likes the grinding sound of the drums on shelves all about the room, rocks tumbling and sliding through sand and water, each canister seeming to revolve at a different speed. Mr. Hardy holds a stone out for them to admire. "Moss agate. I sent for it down in Iowa." His hand shakes with excitement. The cream-coloured stone feels cool and heavy in Mel's

92

hand. Green trees of moss sprawl across its convex surface. "Look at that, son. There's a world inside that stone."

Japan, Jill thinks. A volcanic mountain range framed on both sides by bonsai trees. "Nice."

"Oh my, yes, I should say so." He chuckles softly. The man has always been rather solemn; taciturn, people say. But he's become a new person now, he tries to explain to anyone who cares to listen. He met Jesus Christ in the desert of Arizona and gave his life over to him. In the past his faith had no substance, he says, like the faith of most of the people who worship in the seven churches of Carona. So he crossed the road to the new church, the Alliance Gospel, and was pleasantly surprised. However, the congregation of worshippers, who came from all over, weren't surprised to see the Hardy couple; they'd been expecting them because they had been praying for them. The people of Carona have noticed the change, how the reclusive couple has become more outgoing, friendlier, though most aren't comfortable with the weekly meetings the Hardys have begun to hold in their living room. A prayer cell, they call it. An exclusive holy few who are tight-lipped about what it is they pray for.

Jill goes over to the pan sitting on the counter and stirs through wet silica sand and polished stones. The man's hand drops down on top of her head. "Choose something you like."

"It's okay," she says, wondering what makes adults think that children like to be touched by them. She almost prefers the crabby, aloof Mr. Hardy to this new model.

"Go on." His long fingers reach down and pluck up an almost clear purple stone. "Amethyst. It's an ancient gem. Even mentioned in the Bible. In the new Holy City. I could set it into a nice little pin if you like."

"I like it like this." She hears car doors slam and then people's voices as they pass by the window. Her tongue quivers for the salty fish. Mr. Hardy reaches around her, picks up the pan filled with polished stones, sand, and water, and holds it beneath the lamp. He swills them around. "I was a proud man, once." His voice becomes scratchy and unnatural. "See this?" He tilts the pan so they can see. "This is what God's doing to me now. Smoothing the edges off the old curmudgeon."

Jill drops the stone into her pocket. "We promised our mother we wouldn't be late," she says, nudging Mel in the side.

Mr. Hardy smiles down at her and nods his approval. He puts the pan aside and plucks a tract from a stack beside the cash register. "Here." He hands it to Mel. "You might like to read a bit of this before you go to bed tonight."

"Amen," Jill says as they step from the store.

"Where does he get off? He gives you a stone and me a lousy religious tract." He crumples it and tosses it into the street. "What am I, second class?"

"A sinner." Her laughter echoes in the buildings across the street. "Here." She presses the piece of quartz into his palm.

They pass by Ken's Chinese Food. The ivy-covered windows glow with light and activity as Ken, a tiny man, and his two equally diminutive sons dart from table to table in the almost-full cafe. A fan above the door turns out warm air and the smell of ginger into the street. Beyond they see the flare of a match: Garth standing on the steps of the hardware store, lighting a cigarette.

"So, what's up?" He sounds annoyed, as though he had better things to do than meet Mel.

"You're going to have to get me some pickled herring." Jill's craving throbs like a toothache. She sits down on the bottom step and hugs her knees.

Mel slides the mickey of whisky from his back pocket and holds it up to the light. "We didn't drink much. Must be two bucks' worth here."

Garth snatches the bottle from Mel, and, as the headlights of a car sweep across them, he slips it inside his shirt. "I don't give refunds," he says. He smiles with one corner of his mouth. He spends hours in front of the mirror practising that smile.

Mel feels a surge of envy as the grey Impala sweeps by and he recognizes several grade-twelve students who will soon graduate. Probably going to the city to take in a movie. He imagines them entering a nightclub using false identification.

"Come here." Jill reaches out and pulls Garth down beside her. She winds an arm around his neck. "Come on, Cuz, you can do it. Go over to Waller's and get me a jar of herring."

"You serious?"

"Serious."

"What, is she really serious?" Garth asks Mel.

Mel shrugs. Television screens in Josh's store window flicker with bright images, and, above, in the suite of rooms where he lives with the two women and Elsa, the windows glow with the light pressing softly against orange curtains. One of the windows darkens with the shape of a person passing back and forth behind the curtain. Mel wonders if it's Elsa.

Garth yanks at Jill's hair. "It has to be herring, eh? Nothing else will do? What brand do you want?" he asks as he gets up and shakes the creases from his drape pants. "Not bad, eh? Thirty-six inches at the knee."

"And twelve at the ankle. We know, we know," Mel says drily. Garth has been the first in Carona to wear the baggy draped pants which, he boasts, he wheedled his mother into bringing back from Grand Forks, U.S. of A.

"I'll see what I can do," Garth says and saunters off into the shadows. But he knows he can get what Jill wants because he is a thief. He was born a thief. He possesses a cunning intuition about people and their movements. He knows which of the young women in town "has the mitt on," which women "have a bun in the oven." What kind of underwear they have on beneath their clothing. He admits to having snuck into houses and stuck pins into packets of condoms lying inside drawers of bedside tables. But few people in Carona know this side of Garth Johnson. They know him as a congenial, if not a bit smart alecky, boy. He is, after all, the son of Reginald, who is the son of Thomas, and so on. Those who know him well keep silent and Garth delivers whatever it is they want.

He emerges minutes later from an alley halfway down the street. His white shirt shifts from side to side as he passes beneath the streetlights. Cocky, Mel thinks as Garth flips something in the air and catches it with one hand. Pickled herring, Jill realizes. Saliva swells in her mouth.

"Waller's working overtime," Garth says. He grins. "Had a hell of a time getting past him to get these." He sets a carton of eggs down on the steps beside the jar of herring and Jill plucks up the glass jar and twists open its lid. "Oh, I love you, I love you, I love you."

Big deal, Mel thinks and glances up at Josh's window again. There are two shapes in front of the window now. Two women; he can tell by the outline of breasts.

Jill reaches through sliced onions at the top of the jar and the smell of fish and brine rises. Blue skin slides up through the opaque slivers of onion. She opens her mouth, bites, and feels immediate gratification. Yes, this is it, her tastebuds say.

Garth and Mel watch in silence as Jill sucks brine from her fingers and then eats another large chunk of fish. Her mouth glistens as it moves up and down, sideways, grinding flesh between sharp teeth, gulping back the salty liquid. She is oblivious to all as she eats and eats. When she has devoured half the jar of herring they can no longer bear to watch the brine dribbling down her chin and her tongue darting forward to clear it away. Garth opens the carton of eggs and gathers up a few. Several people leave Ken's Chinese Food and so he waits for the noise of their car engine to cover the sound of eggs breaking against Josh's sign. He drops back into the shadows. He glances at Mel who is still standing there, hands in pockets, looking up at Josh's window. The two women have moved together in an embrace. Their heads come together. Dancing, or kissing, Mel thinks.

Garth laughs, a brittle fox bark. "Didn't think old Josh could still get it up." The two figures part and it becomes clear to him then in the silhouettes of their bodies that it is two women. Garth's jaw drops and then his lips curl in a half smile. "Dykes. Bloody dykes, I'll bet." He laughs and throws an egg and Mel sees it break against Josh's sign. "Here, your turn." He offers Mel an egg.

"No way. Forget it."

The egg arcs through the air and they hear the soft crack of it as it hits a window. White eggshell slides down the glass pane. The curtains part suddenly and a face appears and hands cup eyes against the light in the room. "You're a little chicken shit," Garth says with a touch of bitterness.

Mel is stung by the inference that he's a coward. He wonders if Garth can see the imprint of a foot on his shirt. "Elsa fucks like a mink," he hears himself say and instantly wishes he could take it back.

Garth, who is about to throw another egg, stops, arm still held above his head. He brings it down slowly as the news sinks in. It's seldom that he is not the first to know something. "You're kidding. Interesting . . . "

The light in the room blinks out and Mel can see the sharp features of Adele as she peers out at them. "We'd better get going." Mel looks down at Jill who is hunched low between her knees. Her body convulses as she begins to retch, and then she vomits and half-chewed herring splashes down onto the sidewalk.

Jill and Mel cut through the alley behind the hardware store, walking towards home in silence along a tree-lined street that runs parallel to Main Street. They pass by the Hardys' small cottage where in the living room a handful of people kneel in front of couches, chairs, the piano bench, unmindful of creaking joints or sore knees as they pray for individual people in the town of Carona, including Margaret and Timothy Barber. They pray that the breath of the spirit will quicken the steps of the unredeemed towards their Redeemer. As Jill and Mel walk down the street, the sky above Carona begins to grow lighter. Slowly the eerie light rises, imperceptibly at first so that they aren't aware that the faces of the houses have become brighter. Mel notices as the light beams stronger and he thinks that there must be a fire outside of town. But there's no smoke, no smell of anything unusual, and the light doesn't flicker or jump, rather it grows brighter, as though someone's in control,

97

turning a knob and bringing the colour up stronger and stronger until the television antennas pushing up among the trees shine with light, taking it on full strength so that their arms appear to be neon tubes, vibrating hot-pink. Mel and Jill walk past the Alliance Gospel Church, the United Church, the row of houses on either side of them bathed in pink light, and then they see flower-beds emerge from front lawns, a tricycle sitting on a sidewalk. People inside the houses abandon the images shifting erratically across television screens, turn off their sets, and come to the window or step outside to look heavenward, at first mildly puzzled, and then, as the sky turns red, they reach for their telephone or books of prayer.

The brick face of the school radiates as though lit from within with burning embers, while its tracery windows above the entrance appear to be solid, a sheet of glowing metal. Margaret watches for Jill and Mel from the veranda and beckons for them to hurry.

"Come inside," she urges. "This is just too strange."

"I think it's aurora borealis," Mel says as he closes the gate behind them.

"All right, yes." But Margaret doesn't like them having been touched by it.

It is not yet daylight when Margaret opens her eyes and hears the rhythmic squeal and groan of the swing. She feels Timothy's presence in the room and there's the clink of coins and keys on the bureau as he empties his pockets. When Timothy returns from his travels they seem almost reluctant to cross the space that has opened up between them while he was away. They find that they walk around one another for a time before they can slip back into each other. They have discovered the giving up of that space is accomplished quicker and more gracefully in bed. Margaret listens to the sound of his clothing dropping to the floor. The mattress dips beneath his weight.

"Tim?"

"Amy," he half whispers. "The little beggar was sitting on the stairs when I came up. Waiting. Now she's out there in her nightgown."

"Oh great! She'll wake the entire neighbourhood."

Timothy slides in beside her and moves up against her and his cool limbs draw her from her state of half-sleep. She shivers as he curls about her and cups her breast. "Drove all night," he whispers and then sighs with weariness. Gradually his body grows limp and his breathing slower and Margaret wants to try to sleep again, to drift inside his encircling arms. His limbs begin to warm from the heat of her body. His fingers twitch in muscle spasms against her breast. She closes her eyes and falls into the rhythm of his breathing pattern so as not to disturb his drift into sleep, but her heart thuds too loudly against the mattress and she grows tense with the sound of it. She opens her eyes and sees the arrangement of wicker furniture, a vague grey outline in the first light of sun, and she thinks: Fool. Cosy, she'd thought when she'd put the furniture there. The chair backs face one another across the low table, an almost grim arrangement, she thinks now. Her heartbeat quickens and she winces against an image of Bill North that keeps rising unbidden behind her eyes. Fool! She wants to pound the word flat against the bed. Timothy's hand clutches at her breast.

"You want to sleep?" he murmurs.

"Yes." That is her wish, to stay curled into him while he sleeps for several hours. But he begins tracing her nipple and then his hand drops from her breast down across her hip and he begins to draw her nightgown up over her legs, her hips. "All right. Sleep then." She feels his palm in the small of her back urging her to curl forward so that he can enter her from behind and watch himself make love to her, whispering that she should continue to sleep until their lovemaking becomes so unbearably pleasurable that she cannot lie still any longer but will moan, or thrust up against him hard, wanting him to go deeper, or turn and straddle him, her lean body becoming a hard straight plane set against his, moving on him until he comes. She believes that Timothy, caught up in his own desire, never suspects that she feels little. She is certain of this; otherwise she would have to think that he didn't care.

"No. I can't. I'm not fixed." Margaret draws away from his probing.

"Well, go and get fixed," he whispers into her neck.

"No." She turns to face him, weeping softly.

"What is it?" he asks, mildly alarmed. He touches her cheek. "Tell me." Their eyes meet. What does he see when he looks at her without his glasses, she wonders. A featureless blob of jelly wobbling on a pillow?

"I missed you," she says, though she knows that because of the house renovations, the new appliances, the third child, she doesn't have the right to say this.

He sighs. They agreed not to speak about their loneliness when they were apart. "When you say that," Timothy explained once, "it makes me feel guilty. It's not my fault that I have to be away." There wasn't enough business in the hardware store any longer to support two families.

"Hey." His mouth is warm against hers. "I'm here now."

"Yes." She smiles. The wee cry is over. The sound of the rope swing beats against the house, a squealing, groaning metronome, steady, monotonous. "I caught that kid up on the garage roof last night. My heart was in my mouth." She sees the soft pouches of flesh beneath his eyes that come from squinting against the sun and at the flash of white lines passing through the beam of the car's headlights.

"Hello." She laughs lightly and he releases her. She's grateful for his poor eyesight, that he can't see her features clearly. He moves away from her, rolls over onto his side of the bed, and falls asleep instantly.

Margaret looks up at a dust mote dangling in a corner and wonders how she will arrange her face while he is home. What will she think about to keep the image of Bill North firmly beneath the surface? The light in the room has grown stronger and the pale apple blossoms on the wallpaper begin to bloom their dusty pink colour. She hears footsteps in the hall. Jill, she realizes as the bathroom door closes softly. She lies still, barely breathing, forcing herself to stay at Timothy's side

100

while he sleeps but wanting desperately to be downstairs, her mind engaged with familiar chores. She hears the scrape of the bedroom door against the carpet. George. Amy must have let the cat into the house. She listens to the soft pad of its paws against the carpet and then George springs up onto the bed and creeps across the foot of it, settling on top of Margaret's feet. She looks down at the animal as it crouches and blinks at her with amber eyes. It's only an animal, Margaret tells herself. It knows nothing.

Several hours later, Jill, Mel, and Amy cluster around Timothy at the kitchen table. Amy sits on his lap and listens to his voice push through the top of her head and feels his breath stir in her hair. She hears the strange, almost water-like sound of air moving in his chest as he inhales smoke. She has shown him the mark on her foot and he has slathered it with ointment and put on a Band-Aid. "How did you manage that?" he'd asked. "That's a nifty little surface burn you've got there." She said she didn't know; she had just wanted him to see it and to dress it because it seems to her that Timothy's hands possess something Margaret's don't and that the burn will heal better and faster if Timothy cares for it. Jill stands behind his chair leaning into it, arms wound about his neck. She rests her pointed chin into his shoulder and begs him to make smoke rings for her finger. Mel sits across from Timothy listening intently as he describes the display of northern lights he saw outside of Regina last night, like the underside of an umbrella, he says, red, green, violet, the colours absolutely streaming down from the centre of the sky. They are drawn to him, all of them, like metal filings to a magnet.

Margaret prepares breakfast and listens to their voices. She moves between the stove and counter, stirring scrambled eggs, buttering toast, catching glimpses of herself in the mirror. She is not satisfied with the look of the green grosgrain ribbon against her auburn hair, and does not recognize the expression on her own face, the eyes are too wide, there is a strange

101

half-smile. She stacks toast onto a plate and is about to put it into the oven to keep warm when she looks out of the window and sees Bunny and Bill's Fairlane pull into their driveway behind Bill's truck. Home from church, she thinks bitterly, and notices that Bill is wearing his new dress slacks. "I'm going to be out. The pants will be on the dryer in the back porch," Margaret had said to Bunny on the telephone and had lain still on her bed hardly breathing as she heard the door open and then close. The telephone rings in the hallway, startling her so that she almost drops the plate of toast.

"I'll get it," Mel and Jill both say at once.

"No, I'll get it." Margaret wipes her hands on her apron and goes into the hallway and picks up the receiver. She hears the bright voice of her sister, Rita. "Say, kiddo, okay if Louie and I drive out for supper tonight?" Margaret holds the sound of her sister's voice tightly against her ear to stop her hand from trembling.

"Amy?" Rita says when she doesn't answer. "Go and get your mother for me. *Tout de suite.* This is long distance, you know."

Margaret laughs. "It's me. Sure, come out for supper. I have to talk to you."

"Oh." Rita is quiet for a moment. "I guess you don't want me to bring Louie, then?"

Why is it that you always take it for granted that I want to talk to you about you? Margaret thinks. She has already said everything there is to say to her sister about the folly of being in love with a married man. She and Bunny have talked to Rita until blue in the face. Let her learn the hard way, I guess, Bunny had said. It was the way Rita had learned almost everything, which was why discussion in their family always centred around her. "No, that's fine. Tim plans on working on the jalopy today. Louie can keep him company."

"Well, that should be fun for Louie."

As Margaret goes back into the kitchen she hears the porch screen door open. They all turn at once and see Alf, the groundskeeper, step into the doorway. He wears his coveralls and stands blinking for several moments, looking embar-

102

rassed and out of place. He clears his throat and then abruptly thrusts an object in Timothy's direction. The camera, Amy realizes. "My boy came across it yesterday when he was helping me with the mowing," Alf says. "I knew it was yours."

"Holy Toledo," Mel says and whistles at the sight of the ruined camera.

Amy is jammed between her father's legs and can't escape. She watches as Timothy examines the camera. She stands deathly still as everyone's eyes swoop down on top of her head.

"Ain't none of my business how she got there. My boy just come across her. A shame."

As Amy tries to squeeze out from between Timothy's knees, he holds her fast by the neck of her tee shirt. "Look." She's forced to confront the shattered camera which is already pitted with rust. Ashes to ashes, she thinks.

"Thanks for coming by." Margaret hopes to dismiss Alf, disliking the smell of manure that emanates from his straw-encrusted boots.

Alf nods. "You been talking to Reginald this morning?"

"No, why?"

"He was putting cardboard over the store window when I came by. Seems someone chucked a good-size piece of cinder block through her. Smashed pretty good and then some."

"Seems like it got broke," Mel says with a slight scoffing tone in his voice.

"You betcha." Alf nods, oblivious to the mockery.

"Was anything stolen?" Margaret is thinking about the display she'd arranged in the window the day before, remembering what tools, toys, and kitchenware.

"Reg didn't seem to think so. So it don't make a heck of a lot of sense to me." He turns, about to leave.

"Wait up." Timothy hands him the camera. "Think your boy would like to tinker with this?"

"Think so." Alf's smile reveals teeth stained from chewing-tobacco.

"Perhaps he can fix it," Mel says. He seldom uses the word "perhaps" and Amy thinks he sounds mealy-mouthed.

"Well, if he does manage to fix it, then bravo," Timothy says. "I don't want it back."

"What on earth is happening to this town?" Margaret wonders aloud as the door closes behind Alf. Mel and Jill exchange a glance and slip from the room. Amy moves to follow them but Timothy holds her fast. He slides a chair out from the table and indicates that she's to sit down and face the music.

Margaret does not say a word. Although she doesn't agree with Timothy that they should overlook Amy's covert behaviour, she goes along with him because she knows the girl too well. The moment Margaret makes an effort to pick up on something Amy's interested in, Amy discards that interest. Film is cheap, Timothy had once said to Margaret. "She just likes to think she's pulling one over on us but in the meantime she's learning something, don't you see?"

Amy slouches down into the chair, head lowered, and Margaret sees the veins in her stem-like neck which make her appear small, vulnerable. Amy, the shadow between them; the child whose presence while in her belly Timothy ignored, refusing, too, any physical contact throughout the entire pregnancy. The child he never wanted became a delight instantly, the moment he saw her elf-like face. Margaret's secret joy, her relief, gave way to puzzlement in the following months. "She sure is the apple of her daddy's eye," Bunny once remarked. "I told you he'd come around in the end." "Yes," Margaret said, "I'm glad." But she felt that she was being punished. Amy's pug nose, the constant trail of mucus beneath it, the fingernails embedded with dirt, her perpetual determined frown, do not say vulnerable. "Sit up straight, you'll get a dowager's hump sitting like that," Margaret says. But even though Amy listens and pulls herself into the proper sitting position Margaret can still see the veins behind the strands of the child's wispy hair, and she feels anger. Perhaps, Margaret thinks, it is Timothy's unreasonable patience with the girl that is the cause of her anger.

"Well, so what happened to the camera?" Timothy asks.

The plastic chair-seat sticks to the backs of Amy's thighs and so she begins to lift her legs, one and then the other, again and again, and they make a satisfying sucking noise. Timothy must have been in a hurry this morning, she thinks, as she notices that he's forgotten to do up the middle button on his shirt. She watches his white shirt move in and out as he breathes. She would like to put her hand against it and feel the rhythmic moving, the warmth of his breath.

"I think you should go up to your room for a while. I'll come up in a few minutes," Timothy says.

As Amy climbs the stairs she listens to the soft murmur of their voices. She goes over to the shelf of dolls and spies the trap Jill has set for her, the tiny sliver of paper cunningly placed among the folds of the green velvet dress of Melissa, Jill's favourite doll. Its dislocation will be the proof Jill needs that Amy tampers with her dolls. All right, Amy thinks, as she goes over to the window, I won't touch your shitty little dolls and I won't tell you either about the man who can play two songs at once on his guitar. She sees Amy the squirrel dashing across a telephone wire across the street and then her heart lurches as the squirrel stumbles suddenly, almost falling. Then she sees Elsa Miller standing beneath a tree under the telephone wires, hidden. Elsa wears the same yellow sundress she'd worn the day before. Sunlight reflects off her sunglasses as she looks at the house. Amy sees Mel's sandy-coloured square head move out from beneath the slope of the veranda roof. Jill limps after him, following him to the gate. They sling their arms across it and turn their faces to the ground as though their main concern is to count ants marching across a crack in the sidewalk. They ignore Elsa.

"I bet she does it with everyone," Mel says.

Amy hears the telephone ring in the hall downstairs and Mel and Jill turn, hearing it too, and then look down again, two people, one motion. Margaret's voice rises up from the hall. The telephone call is from her brother, Reginald, who relays the latest news about "that weird bunch" and repeats the gossip concerning the Miller women's sexual proclivity.

"Elsa does what with everyone?" Jill asks, goading Mel into saying the word.

"Screws."

"I don't know about you." Jill's voice rises in a haughty tone. "I thought that's what you wanted." She flicks the gate's latch, pushes off, and rides it open, then strides across the street towards Elsa, her arms swinging. Just then Margaret steps out onto the veranda.

"Breakfast," she calls sharply. "Right now."

"I'll just be a second," Jill says over her shoulder.

"Now."

"I'll wait here for you," Elsa says.

Then Amy sees Timothy's head appear from beneath the veranda roof. He goes over to Mel and winds an arm about his shoulders. "Hello, Elsa," he calls. As Jill reaches his side, he puts his other arm around her and draws her away. "This gal's gotta get some food into her," he calls. "You know, Mel," he says, his voice dropping, "I think that girl has a serious crush on you." Their heads disappear beneath the roof of the veranda. "Ha, ha, ha, very funny," Amy hears Mel say as the door closes behind them.

There is a strangeness in the house, a tension, and even though Timothy is home, Amy feels that she must be very careful. She must remember to look inside the closet before she goes to bed. She imagines that the scatter rugs in the hallway conceal gaping holes which she could fall through. She'd read her mother's journal entry before going to bed last night. "I am a fool," she had written. That was all, and so there was no way she could determine why Margaret threw the plate of sandwiches at the cat. Or why she was wearing Timothy's bathrobe when usually she wore it only if the house was chilly or if she wasn't feeling well. Amy believes that she is somehow responsible for this new strangeness in the house. That it may have entered the house with her the day she was struck by lightning.

She hears Timothy's step on the stairs and so climbs up onto her bed and waits for him. She could tell him about the dirty pictures Mel has stashed in the left-hand pocket of his winter coat in the back of his closet. She could tell him that the reason why Jill got 95 per cent on her arithmetic final was because Mel paid Garth to smuggle a copy of the test from the principal's office. But she can't tell him that she was struck by lightning. The knowledge is hers and never to be given away. When she turns her head she looks straight into his face. He smiles and she feels secure in her nest of pillows. She likes how the gold fillings in his teeth shine with saliva when he smiles, how his voice always sounds as if he's on the verge of a cold. She likes his round wire-framed glasses and how their lenses magnify his blue eyes. She loves the feeling of his lean and prickly jaw, the smell of tobacco that clings to his skin.

"Will you let me help you work on the car today?" Amy asks.

"Maybe."

"Who was that on the telephone?"

"Your uncle."

"Does he know who broke his window yet?" She could tell him that Mel had been drinking whisky. She knows most of Mel's and Jill's secrets but has learned the hard way not to tell. She has learned through the pranks they've played on her, the stealthy little hard pinches against her arms that leave her with bruises. "Amy certainly bruises easily," Margaret says in a tone that implies that it is somehow Amy's fault.

"Amy . . . "

"When Elvis comes to town, can we go?"

"Amy . . . so, what happened?"

"I saw him, in the city, in a park."

"What happened to the camera?"

"The camera." Amy realizes for the first time that she doesn't have to say what happened to *her*. He only wants to know what happened to the camera.

"It was struck by lightning."

Timothy's cheeks puff with air. Then he expels it in a pop which she feels against her face. "In other words, an elephant sat on it. Okay, Sugar. I give up. It doesn't matter."

His hands cup her armpits as he swings her down from the bunk bed. She winds her legs around his narrow frame as he carries her down the stairs. She buries her nose in his warm neck. "Hey. No wiping boogers on my shirt, you hear?" She laughs and her heart burns with the desire to tell him that she may be able to fly. Although she didn't wear one in her dream when she floated in the sky, she believes that she may need a cape, and so, to deflect her desire to tell him that she has been struck by lightning, she asks instead if next time when he comes home will he bring her a cape.

"What, as in a Red Riding Hood kind of cape?" *Huh, huh, huh*, his breath spurts from his chest as they descend the stairs.

"A magician's cape. But it doesn't need to be black."

"You want the rabbits too?"

Amy thinks sometimes that the ache of her swelling heart will hurt her too much.

Mel and Jill sit at the table waiting for Margaret to serve their breakfast. "You will not be seeing Elsa today." Her voice is strained and curt.

"How so?" Timothy asks and then grows silent under Margaret's warning glance that says I'll tell you later.

"So, what happened to the camera, then?" She asks the question to divert attention from a much more dangerous topic.

"It doesn't matter what happened. That matter has been cleared up." He drops Amy into her place and the farting chair says *Woosh*. He bows his head and they follow his example while Margaret hurries through a learned prayer. "And thus to thy service" signals the end of it. "Amen."

As Margaret spoons scrambled eggs onto her plate Amy thinks about the mysterious entry in the Blue Book. When Margaret is finished serving and comes to sit down, Amy waits several moments and then she asks, "What does it mean, to be a fool?" and feels Margaret start forward in her chair.

5

It was mid-July and a day of rain; a fine mist which seemed to fill the air like a cloud rather than fall from the sky. As I stepped out the back door of the Alliance Gospel Church, I breathed the mist deep into my lungs. The hall inside the church echoed with the sound of children's voices singing the closing hymn for the day. I imagined Jill among them, leaning forward to look down the length of the pew, surprised to see that I had already left. Then I imagined Jill staring straight ahead, engrossed in the words of what had become her favourite song. There would be a pucker of flesh between her eyebrows as she sang the words, the expression that said she was thinking deeply.

> When He cometh, when He cometh
>   To make up His jewels,
> All His jewels, precious jewels,
>   His loved and His own,
>
>> *Like the stars of the morning,*
>> *His bright crown adorning,*
>> *They shall shine in their beauty,*
>>   *Bright gems for His crown.*

Jill said she liked the song because it was strange. She sang it and crept around on tiptoe, curling her fingers and making I'm-coming-to-get-you shadows crawl up the bedroom wall at night. She wanted to frighten me with the notion of an invisible being reaching down in the dead of night to kidnap me and keep me hostage in heaven. "Why are you always in such a rotten mood these days?" Margaret had asked Jill constantly during the past several weeks, believing that it had to do with her not being allowed to chum about with Elsa any more. "It's for me to know and you to find out," Jill answered one day, and that time it was Jill who was sent to her room to think things over.

Bunny's right, it must be the heat, Margaret had said to herself, after sending Jill to her room. I think it's gone to all of our heads. She went to answer the knock at the front door. It was the elderly Mrs. Hardy. She barely recognized the woman, whose normal attire had been baggy twill trousers and moth-eaten sweaters. "The old dame was wearing a floral two-piece," Margaret would tell Bunny later, "a picture hat and nylon stockings with hiking boots!"

"Well hello," Margaret said politely, but beneath I heard her impulse to laugh. "What a nice surprise."

Mrs. Hardy nodded her greeting, some of her former curt self returning momentarily. She held out a mimeographed invitation for the three of us to attend the Alliance Gospel Summer School of the Bible. "We'd surely welcome their presence."

Margaret had rolled her eyes dramatically as the door closed. "Not in a month of Sundays," she said, but changed her mind when Grandmother Johnson arrived to worry at the prospect of the three of us going off to that "club thing" at the "Alliance place." She wouldn't say "church," because the building didn't resemble one. The square plain building looked more like a bingo hall, she said. "I know, dear," she said to Margaret, "that it is important for the children to be occupied in the summer, but don't you think those people are a bit too emotional in their approach to religion?" After she'd left, Margaret smiled and said, "Yes, I think you girls should go." Mel couldn't, of course, because Mel had a part-time summer job delivering groceries for Waller's. Then Margaret wound woollen sweaters around her feet and skated up and down the kitchen floor singing, "May I go a-swimming mother? Yes, my darling daughter. Hang your clothes on yonder tree, but don't go near the water!"

And so we had gone to Bible school, Jill and I. We listened to the lessons, coloured in our lesson books, stitched pictures in embroidery cotton, glued macaroni onto jars, sang songs, learned the steps we had to take in order to obtain eternity and how to say prayers that did not rhyme. I didn't mind going because the basement where the classes were conducted was cool. It was new and smelled of raw wood and concrete, and behind the girl's washroom there was a hole in the floor. Sometimes I slipped away from the lesson and squatted beside that water-filled hole and stirred its surface with a Popsicle stick and watched the slick-bodied salamanders slide away through the water.

As I walked away from the Alliance Gospel Church through the fine rain, the voices of the children grew fainter. More and more I had been thinking about the film inside Timothy's camera, remembering the whirr of cogs feeding the film across the eye. I wondered if it was possible that I had captured the image of water parting and lightning streaking down in front of my face. I walked on a street that ran parallel to the one we lived on so that Margaret would not see me and wonder why I had left Bible school early. I could see our shade tree towering above all the others on the street. Green, I thought. There was one word that the people of Carona kept repeating that summer when they stopped to chat beneath the white columns of the bank or on the granite steps of the post office. It was the word "green." "Isn't it green?" they'd say as they looked out across the town, the lush trees swaying with leaves the size of saucers. "Sure is green." Or, "This is the greenest summer ever." I felt the lump of quartz as I pressed my hand against my pocket and the film box already addressed and ready for mailing off to the Kodak Company, protecting it against the drizzle of rain, not wanting it to soften.

I watched my sandalled feet move against the sidewalk. I passed by the legion hall, by a row of cars shiny with rain in front of the medical clinic, and by several people walking across its parking lot. I saw a grey-haired man in a dark suit get out of a car. "If the free world sacrifices its idealism to godless materialism there will be nothing to choose between communism and democracy," he said to me. I crossed the street before he could say more. "It sure is green," he called after me. The houses on either side of me began to disappear and I floated on top of the book, heading across the harbour and towards the city of my future.

I was almost clear of the town, having crossed two sets of railway tracks and passed the grain elevators. The sidewalk ended in tall grass and so I took to the gravelled road, until that gave way to black soil, as powdery and soft as the cornstarch Margaret used to thicken pudding, and the toes of my socks turned black. The misty rain was now so fine that I could barely feel the tingle of it against my skin. I heard the clatter of mower blades and then Alf's voice geeing and clucking to the team of horses in the agricultural grounds, but I couldn't see him. He was hidden from view by the covered grandstand that almost completely surrounded the racetrack. Alf would be in the centre of the track, cutting the grass to keep down the mosquitoes for the harness races.

And then I saw Mel, clearly not on his delivery route for Waller's. Just his head and shoulders at first, as he ducked out from under the grandstand. He went over to his bicycle propped against a tree, turned, and headed off along the road that wound through Carona's Family Park, passed by picnic benches that gave you splinters when you sat on them, the playground where children swung on rows of swings or made pretend cakes in the tractor tire sandpits where stray cats did their toilet. Margaret hadn't allowed us to play in the sand when she used to take us there on hot summer days, Mel and Jill splashing in the cement dish of the wading pool, practising swearing, saying "cat shit," while Margaret spread her blanket off from the other mothers so she could be in the shade, she said. She'd lie on a blanket reading Ernest Hemingway and

112

wishing, I suppose, that she was in a tent in Africa with hyenas prowling about the edge of a camp. She could make him love her, Margaret probably thought while she read his book. I once took pictures of the Ernest Hemingway house in Key West and showed them to her. I told her about the cats, the urinal in the garden he'd carried home on his shoulder from Sloppy Joe's bar, but at that time she showed only polite interest.

But when I was growing up I had the impression that the writer was somehow related and sent his books to Margaret, books that she read over and over while I wandered off by myself in the park, searching for acorns which I'd split open and eat. I paid for my grubbing about in the dirt with frequent invasions of pin worms that nearly caused me to dance with the itch of their movement in my anus, and Margaret to dance with fury while she boiled our bed sheets and towels and dispensed to the entire family regular doses of bitter-tasting pills. The reason why I preferred to wander by myself and not play in the wading pool with Mel and Jill was because of their constant whispered threats to hold me under and drown me when Margaret wasn't looking.

"I could make him love me," Margaret had written in her Blue Book. Even before I had learned to read, she had written those words. Maybe she had written them when Timothy was off in Peterborough, Ontario. Margaret's brother, Reginald, and my father had been fortunate during the war. They'd spent the war years in Ontario and Quebec in Supplies and Services. Reginald had been spared overseas duty on compassionate grounds, his age and large family. Timothy, because of his severe myopia. Bill North, the youngest of the three, wound up in the infantry and was sent to England to train on the moors and beaches in the First Canadian Army Tank Brigade and then sailed for Sicily. They had all returned and, unlike others in Carona – the Smythe brothers, for instance, who had been rewarded with jobs at the post office because one had a steel plate in his head and the other had returned uncommunicative and given to fits of ranting – the men in Margaret's and Bunny's lives returned unscathed.

Except for Decoration Day fifteen years after the war when we, the children of ex-service men, lined up on Main Street to march to the cenotaph and lay a wreath in memory of the dead, the war was a reality only in the minds of the fathers who had returned and refused to speak of it. The memory faded quickly and, in 1959, it wasn't bomber planes people craned their necks to watch passing far above, but rather jet airplanes, which had begun to ply the highways of the sky. On clear nights I had watched for that dot of light, Sputnik, to sweep across the dark hemisphere. For us, the war was Audie Murphy crawling across no man's land on a big screen, and when we'd return from the movie and go to bed we'd pray for God to send us portable radios and dream of becoming stewardesses and airline pilots.

"I could make him love me," Margaret had written beneath a newspaper clipping of the author Ernest Hemingway. What did you do the three years Timothy was away? I once asked her. She seemed surprised by my question. "We waited," she said. "And wrote letters to each other."

I had almost passed Carona's Family Park when I saw Garth Johnson. I saw the flap of his wide drape pants as he approached Mel beneath the trees by the swings. Mel straddled his bike, stopping to talk. Garth slapped Mel on the back as they parted. Garth continued on, walking in my direction for several moments, and then he noticed me and stood still. He looked off into the trees as though something had happened in the branches that had caught his attention. I turned away from him and kept on walking and when I looked behind me moments later I saw him, where I had seen Mel emerge, stoop down and disappear under the grandstand beside the racetrack.

The town of Carona seemed to end at Alf's place. Or else it opened up to something else and Alf's place was the door through to it. At that time I had never been further from town than his tiny two-acre farm. There were spaces between the boards of the rickety fence that enclosed the yard and I could see bales of straw, some broken open and strewn about the barnyard, washed by the rain and bright yellow. The barn door was open and I could hear the buzz of bluebottles inside it. If the horses had been out in the yard I wouldn't have entered. While I liked the smell of the animals, I didn't like them. I didn't like the way they seemed to look at me sideways, snorting suddenly and stomping their hairy hooves against the ground. Their twitching, rippling muscles said you couldn't trust them. But I knew where the horses were that day and so I unwound the strand of wire on the gate and went inside. I passed by the house. My interest was in the shed behind the house. It was a strange-looking building; it seemed to wear a hat. Alf had built a platform on the roof for his mentally retarded son, Harry, with a solid, waist-high wooden fence to enclose it. A ladder resting against the shed led up to the entrance to the platform. It was not a playhouse, but a kind of look-out for Harry. I didn't see Harry at first, just his telescope. I'd been up there once, had bribed Harry with Mel's alarm clock to let me come up. Harry could see almost the whole town from his perch and with the telescope he had a close-up view of people approaching in the distance. The telescope rotated in a half circle and rested on me. I waved and it dipped down. Harry's soft pumpkin face rose up from behind the fence. He rested his chin against it and stared down at me, his little pink eyes unblinking. He grinned and saliva dribbled down his chin.

"I've got something for you." I put my hand in my pocket. He made a gurgling sound in the back of his throat and bobbed his head; his way of laughing. "Come down and I'll give it to you." I spoke louder than I cared to. I didn't want the woman inside the house to come scurrying out in her bedroom slippers to see if bad children had come to play a joke on her poor old Harry, or to teach him swear words or naughty tricks.

"Yup, yup," Harry said, but remained there, his head a round jack-o'-lantern set down on top of a fence.

I went inside the shed. It had an earth floor and smelled musty. I ducked through harnesses hanging from the rafters. All about the room on old doors set up on trestles was an assortment of objects, old clocks, radios, dishpans spilling with nuts and bolts. Harry moved across the platform and dust rained down from the rafters. As my eyes grew more accustomed to the dark interior, I looked among the objects for the camera and saw several items that I recognized: a battered metal dump truck, which had once belonged to Mel, a wooden duck on wheels that may have once been mine. I heard a monotone humming sound behind me, and I turned and saw Harry, a silhouette crouching in the doorway. He pointed the movie camera at me and hummed, thinking, I supposed, that that was the noise the camera made when it was operating. He lowered it and stared at me, his pale freckled face expressionless. He was almost as tall as Mel and certainly towered over his diminutive elderly mother who would take him by the hand on Hallowe'en night and try desperately to keep up with him as he galloped through the streets wearing a bandanna and hooting like an owl, believing he was repeating our echoing cries of "Hallowe'en apples, trick or treat!"

I took out of my pocket the stone that I'd found in a tobacco can in Mel's room, a piece of purple quartz crystal, and held it out to Harry. "You want this?"

He nodded. He set the camera down on the table and then snatched the quartz from my palm and popped it into his mouth. He rolled it about on his tongue, tasting it, feeling its texture. Then he spat the stone into his hand and ran with his strange gallop out of the shed and into the daylight where he stood, shoulders hunched, and examined the chunk of crystal. I picked up the camera. The side of it had been pried off and the inner workings exposed. The film was gone and in its place was a narrow strip of paper fed through the cogs. I set the camera down and just then caught sight of the reel of film. It rested on a shelf above the table, bound tightly with an elastic band. As I put it into the canister that was inside the box I carried in my pocket, I heard the stone bounce off the side of the shed and Harry began to wail his disappointment. Must have thought it was candy, I supposed.

Harry spidered in sideways through the door and lunged for the camera on the table. He followed me outside and down along the house, all the while humming as he filmed the back of my head. When I stepped outside the gate he was right behind me. Because Harry wasn't allowed to wander unattended, I knew I should go and get his mother, but she would interrogate me about my trespassing, and so I didn't. Harry followed me for several minutes, a long-legged scarecrow with a pumpkin for a head. As I grew closer to town I worried about being seen with this weird, humming person, and so I yelled, "Go home!" as though he were a dog. And like a dog, he retreated, but only several feet, and when I turned away he continued to tail me. I was reluctant to walk all the way back to his house and so when I saw a stick lying by the side of the road, I picked it up and threw it at him. He didn't react. His reflexes were not quick enough to shield himself or make him step out of its way. He watched the stick coming, and when it smacked against his chest he appeared not to feel the blow. He stopped humming and lowered the camera, hugging it to his chest. Then he veered off the road, away from me, wading through the tall grass in the ditch. I walked quickly in the event that he might try to follow again, but when I looked back, he was travelling far out across a field.

The drizzle of rain had almost stopped and now and then the sun seeped through the thinning clouds, warm against my arms. I looked up as I approached the agricultural grounds and this time I saw Elsa. She was hurrying away beneath the trees on the road leading through the park.

Later when I reached the post office where I would mail off the film, Mel walked towards me wheeling his bicycle along the sidewalk, its basket loaded with an order of groceries for delivery. "Hey, Short Stuff," he said. "So where's the darn fire, eh?"

I sprinted up the post office steps and yanked at the heavy door. Like Jill, I could have replied, It's my snot and I can eat it if I want to. Or like Margaret, Ask me no questions and I'll tell you no lies. They were connected in some way, the three of them, Garth, Elsa, and Mel, but I didn't know how and so I said, "Why don't you ask Elsa," to try and find out.

"It's just like the rain we got in B.C.," Bunny North is saying to Margaret in the kitchen. Out of the blue, Bill had suggested they take off for two weeks and so they'd packed up the kids and car and driven through Banff and Jasper and then onto the ferry boat to Vancouver Island. "It rained, the entire time, almost every single day, just like today. Not enough to keep you indoors, but enough that you felt damp all the time."

"It's nice. Good for the old complexion," Margaret replies. "And it's turning everything so green."

"I don't know," Bunny says, "the holiday was nice, you know. But hectic? Maybe we just tried to see too much in two weeks. I'd just as soon have spent the whole time up at the lake relaxing." The table in front of her is littered with snapshots. Earlier, Bunny went through the pictures with Amy and Jill, describing their trip. Look how Takakkaw Falls seems to tumble right out of the sky! See those goats leaping across the face of a mountain! Bunny picks up a photograph. She goes over to the counter where Margaret ladles stewed tomatoes into jars. The timbers beneath the floor creak with her movement and Margaret wonders with a lurching stomach how to arrange her face. Bunny leans against the counter, resting her elbows against it. Margaret feels heat radiate from her body and smells the sweet scent of baby powder that always irritates her. "Have a look at this one." Bunny slides a photograph across the counter. "This is where we stayed the night Mindy thought she heard a moose outside snorting." A tiny smirk forms in her baby Cupid's bow. Bill and their four children stand posed in front of a log cabin. A pair of deer antlers mounted beside the door appears to grow out of Bill's head. "It's pretty hard to manage sex when you're surrounded by four kids for two weeks," she says. "Bill got pretty desperate. The moose Mindy heard was actually Bill."

Margaret laughs. She has become a straight line inside now and she wants to stay that way. She doesn't want to think about that day. The moment she'd seen Rita step from Louie's car on her last visit, wearing that white linen suit, carrying the box-shaped red leather bag, and sporting new red shoes, Margaret knew she wasn't going to say anything to her sister about Bill. She'd cooked for them and tolerated the smell of Louie's cigar and Rita's lively chatter, how she seemed able to talk to all of them at the same time, the hint of the flirt she had become evident in the way she answered Tim's question about what she had been doing for fun lately, the following quick wink she cast in Louie's direction to appease him. Rita told them about being among the first in the city to see *The Naked and the Dead* at a private showing at the Film Exchange for the bosses in from Minneapolis. Even the children seemed mesmerized by their Aunt Rita and loved it when she clipped her earrings onto Mel's lobes or imitated Louis Satchmo Armstrong's deep, scratchy laughter. Margaret was relieved that she hadn't talked to Rita about the day Bill came over to have his dress pants hemmed up. She had simply grown to believe that nothing significant had happened to her. She had made a fool of herself, but it was over now. The inner wincing, the cringing, was gone. She watches tomatoes drop into the jar with a soft plop, their yellow seeds trailing down its sides. "What do you think lesbians do with each other?"

Bunny blinks with the shock of Margaret's unexpected question. Then she nods. "Oh yes. I heard. Do you think it's true?" Then they're silent as they ponder over the Miller women whose lives have suddenly taken on a whole new dimension. Margaret no longer thinks about their jewellery and her speculation that it has been gained at the expense of unfortunate, desperate people. Jews, perhaps.

"They say the women share the same bed."

"I couldn't tell you what they might do," Bunny says. "Even thinking about it gives me the willies."

Kiss, lick, hold, what? Margaret finds that she's slightly aroused by the notion of it.

Bunny plays with a silver chain at her neck, sliding it back and forth across her bottom lip. She sighs. "I haven't been able to bring myself to face it. Mindy failed her grade."

"Oh, Bun, I'm so sorry." Margaret sets the ladle down and hugs the woman. Deceit, she thinks as she embraces her friend, isn't at all like a home permanent that has gone too curly. It won't eventually straighten itself out. The feeling of having been deceitful always rises to the surface in Bunny's presence. She pats Bunny on the back for several moments and then holds her at arm's length.

"I was afraid this was going to happen. You wouldn't believe what the teacher let that girl get away with during the year."

Margaret nods in sympathy. She knows she's supposed to agree and quote a statistic she's read about poor reading skills and give Bunny something to alarm the other parents with at the next Home and School meeting. But she can't. Something has shifted inside Margaret. With the straight line comes a flatness too, the inability to feel anything strongly.

"Cam and Gord are real snot buckets," Jill says as she enters the kitchen and slams the Bible school lesson-book onto the table. "I caught them throwing stones at George."

"Now, now," Margaret says, indicating her displeasure with Jill's choice of language.

"Well, they are. They're retards," Jill says as she leaves the kitchen.

Holding her side again, Margaret thinks. She's noticed how the girl seems to favour one side. What side is the appendix on, she is about to ask when Bunny stops her with a question.

"Would you like to come up to the lake with us for a couple of days? Bill says it's okay by him," Bunny says and blushes. "Well, actually it was his idea. He says he plans on spending the time working on the outboard. You'd be company for me." Bill's suggestion puzzles Bunny though. She knows of his dislike for her friend. She's so tight her ass squeaks when she walks is Bill's observation of Margaret, or, She's stuck on herself. Often Bunny is compelled to try and explain or defend Margaret.

Margaret searches for the message lying behind Bunny's statement that it was Bill's idea. "I'll see," she says, compelled and repulsed at the same time by the idea of going to the lake with them. "When?"

"Tomorrow, if you can get things together that fast. He's still got Frank in looking after things at the shop until the end of the week, so we may as well take advantage of it."

"I'll have to talk to Tim." Margaret hears Jill's footsteps in the upstairs hall. Her mind picks apart the words "it was his idea." When Bunny leaves, she returns to her chore of filling jars with stewed tomatoes and forgets completely that she promised herself to wipe her hands, go upstairs, and find out what's bothering Jill. It will be up to Timothy to decide, she thinks. If he thinks it would be good for them to go, then she will go. Then she does wipe her hands and goes out into the hall and asks for the long distance operator. She gives her the number of the motel where Timothy always stays in Brandon. She leaves a message for him to call her when he gets in that evening. It will be up to Tim to decide whether or not Mel is old enough to be left behind for a couple of days while she and the girls go up to the lake with Bunny and Bill. She looks down at her hands, which have begun to shake. Why am I doing this? Why can't I stop myself?

That night Amy lies in bed and listens to the sounds in the house. The sky outside the window flickers with light. For an hour there had been faint flashes of lightning which grew in intensity, but the thunder never amounted to more than a rumble in the far distance. And then, gradually, the lightning grew less frequent as the storm skirted the town, though the tension of its threat remains. She feels it around her, thick and humid. Downstairs Margaret stubs out her cigarette and gets up from the couch. Her waiting for the storm that never comes is over. "I think it would be great for you guys to get away," Timothy had said. She thinks about going to the lake in the morning. About her folly.

Amy hears the toilet flush and then Margaret brushing her teeth at full speed. An up and down furious sound of brush against her teeth, a single spurt of water rinsing the brush clean, and then a sharp *ping!* as the brush hits the bottom of the glass, saying, Finished! That's done for the day. Amy feels her bed rock as Jill changes position. "Oh hurry up," Jill says, wanting to creep out of bed, needing to talk to Mel. For the

121

past hour she has thrashed from side to side, had been still only for moments, sometimes muttering under her breath or growling with impatience like an angry dog. Now she begins to hum softly as Amy hears the bathroom door open and close and then Margaret's door scraping against the carpet as she shuts it. They listen as she moves about the room. "When He cometh, when He cometh," Jill begins to sing softly, "like the stars of the morning, His bright crown adorning." She stops and Amy feels the jab of her foot against the mattress. "Hey, you sleeping?" she whispers. "Guess what? You're not really a jewel, you know that? You're a pearl. An affliction, that's what you are."

"I don't care." Good, Amy thinks, then God won't want me. There's no way I'm going to go to heaven, not now or at any time in the future. No one's going to reach down and grab me off for His crown.

"You better care or you might wind up in Hell and turn into a lump of coal."

"Shut up."

"You will, you know. You'll burn and turn into coal dust."

"I'm not going anywhere."

"Everyone does. When they die."

"Not me."

"Idiot. As usual."

Amy feels another sharp jab of Jill's foot against her back.

They hear Margaret opening and closing drawers, putting away, straightening up before sleeping so that her dreams may be as tidy as her room. She neatly sets out what she will take with her to the lake tomorrow. Amy watches the light of a passing car sweep across the ceiling and she thinks, Maybe I'm already dead. I was killed by lightning and everything that's happened since then has just been a dream. Maybe I'll wake up and find myself on the ground in the cemetery and all this will happen again in the same order.

Jill sighs. "I sure don't want to go to the lake tomorrow."

Maybe I can breathe under water, Amy thinks. Then all thoughts scatter with the sound of the telephone ringing in

122

the hall below. Light beams across the floor as Margaret's door opens. They listen to her feet moving against the stairs. Whenever the telephone rings unexpectedly in the night they think *Timothy*, and their hearts go stone-cold with fear. Margaret picks up the receiver. They hear her soft, anxious murmur. She talks for a short time and then comes back upstairs, pausing outside Mel's door with a question. Then she stands in their doorway. "That was Bunny." Amy feels her heart begin to beat again. "Harry has wandered away and Alf hasn't been able to find him. Have either of you seen him today?"

"No."

"No."

"Well, all right. Didn't hurt to ask. Try and get to sleep now."

Amy sees the stick smack against Harry's chest, watches him walk down into the ditch and travel far across the field. Harry has wandered away before. They always find him. They hear the creak of springs as Margaret drops down onto her bed. She writes in the Blue Book, "Going to the lake tomorrow." The lake, like the city, needs no name. It's huge, an ocean set down in the centre of the prairie, not one of the smaller lakes in the chain of lakes in the Whiteshell where Margaret once sent Jill to CGIT camp. Perhaps Margaret is writing "Bloated," or, "Sore breasts," or, "I can't stand this constant shifting of emotions up and down." The bed sways as Jill gets up. She stands in the dark, the top of her head just level with Amy's bed. Her head moves away as her feet pad softly against the floor. Then she stops.

"Hey, Peewee. You didn't touch the dolls today," she whispers. "What's the matter, are you sick?"

"Sick of you."

"Thanks."

Mel hears Jill enter his room. He feels her presence beside his bed and smells the faint coconut scent of her limbs. "Move over." She slides into his warm spot. "I can't get to sleep." She draws the covers up beneath her chin. "Talk to me."

"What about?" Mel cradles his head in his arms and looks up at the ceiling.

"Anything. You're a naturally boring person. Anything will do to put me to sleep."

"Speak for yourself."

"Elsa."

"What about her?"

"How's Elsa?"

"How would I know?"

Jill feels a squirmy little shift in his body. "Liar." She nudges his ticklish spot and he twists away from her, gasping to contain his laughter. "Get out of my bed." He kicks at her leg. "Right now."

Then they lie still, side by side, lost in their own thoughts. Mel slides an arm under her neck. She watches the curtain on his window swell with a light breeze and then recede, sucked flat against the screen. Out and in. Each puff of wind brings the smell of rain. The mirror on his bureau at the side of the bed, which had reflected faint light passing through the breathing curtain, dims now as clouds sift across the face of the moon and the room darkens. Mel feels her growing heat and thinks of how they used to sleep in the same room, he in the top bunk and Jill in the lower. About reading comic books together on Saturday morning and eating food smuggled from the kitchen. Sometimes a bad dream or a cold room or a shared secret brought them together to curl around one another's bodies in the night while Amy slept in this room, in a crib and then in the bed that became his when Amy took his place in the room across the hall with Jill. Mel flexes his bicep, making Jill's head jump up and down. "So, what's up?"

"Nothing. Just talk to me."

He pulls his arm away and reaches under his pillow. His hand cups the end of a small flashlight in order to focus on a cartoon drawing. He has done almost every position with Elsa now, except for the chair one, of course. There are no chairs

124

under the bleachers at the agricultural grounds. "You wanted to know how Elsa was. Look." It's been so easy. He simply tells Elsa what he wants to do and she does it with the same strange detachment as the first time. Jill's hand closes around the cartoon, crumples it. "I don't want to see that thing." She throws it across the room and they hear it hit the wall.

Mel is stung. He turns away. "I want to sleep." But Jill doesn't leave. She lies there and listens to the soft swish of the curtain as it swells and subsides. She hears Amy moving about in the room across the hall, rearranging the dolls to make her angry in the morning when she'll discover number-one doll at the wrong end of the shelf and the last doll she's been given in the centre. Thirteen years of dolls out of their chronological order in the morning. I don't care, Jill thinks, and is surprised to realize that she really means it.

Mel feels Jill's touch at his back as she begins to walk her fingers down his spine. "Hey, you mad?" When he doesn't answer she begins to draw. "I'm tracing a snake upon your back. Guess which finger did it." She plays their child game, which was at first just a game, but then their drawing snakes began to move further afield from their backs, exploring almost all creases and folds of skin, except for one. Jill won't let Mel feel her between the legs. Mel pulls away. "Come on, Mel, please. I didn't want to look at the picture because I want to show you something else."

Mel allows himself to be drawn to face her. Their noses almost touch on the pillow as they breathe in each other's breath. "Give me your hand." Her hand is cool and firm as she guides his beneath the elastic waistband of her pyjamas. His hand passes across her flat belly. The skin is moist and clammy. Mel tries to still his breathing which has grown uneven. She holds his hand still against her abdomen and Mel thinks that maybe she's changed her mind now and has decided not to let him touch her. "Feel this." She shifts his hand to the side. "There. Just run your hand up and down. There." Mel presses lightly and feels the large swelling beneath her skin. "What's that?" He pulls his hand away quickly, but she catches it and makes him feel the swelling

125

once again. It's egg-shaped and hard. "It's where that guy kicked me. You know."

Oh shit, Mel thinks. "But what is it?"

"I don't know. It keeps getting bigger. I can hardly walk straight." Her stomach jerks with the attempt to hold back tears. He feels the movement and is stricken. "You should show it to Margaret."

"No. She'll take me to the doctor."

"You don't have to tell her how it happened."

"It's not that." She moves into his side and rests her head on his shoulder. He winds his arm around her, holding her against him. "It's just that I think . . . that if I don't tell anyone, it'll go away." She begins to cry.

It's all my fault, he thinks. "I'll tell Margaret, if you won't."

"I shouldn't have told you." She cries silently for several minutes and then grows quiet. As children they had always been sick together, measles, mumps, and even later on they seemed to catch one another's colds and flu. A sadness settles in Mel's chest. The presence of the lump in her body is like when he first noticed the swelling of her breasts. It is something he cannot share, and he knows she has stepped further away.

"I'll wake up one morning and it will be gone. I know it," she whispers. "So there's no need to tell anyone." He feels her hard chocolate rosebud nipple nudge his arm as she reaches across him for his hand. "Do you want to draw a snake?" She takes his hand and guides it down between her legs.

When Jill left the room, Amy got out of bed, and she lies on the floor now beside the bed, the navy-blue cape Timothy bought for her spread out around her. She lies with her arms straight out, toes pointed, and nose flat against the floor. The muscles in her neck and back have begun to ache from her intense concentration. She closes her eyes and sees herself rising up above the road outside the house. She is wafted gently upwards until she's level with the telephone poles, and the ground begins to glide swiftly beneath her outstretched body. She imagines herself flying for seconds, minutes, an hour, she can't tell how long, but is jarred suddenly by the sound of breaking glass. It has come from the kitchen. And then she hears Jill wailing. Lights flick on in both Mel's and Margaret's rooms almost at the same time. Amy leaps up and follows Margaret and Mel down the stairs.

They enter the kitchen to the sight of Jill sprawled on the floor in a pool of brine and broken glass. "Oh, leave me alone," Jill cries. "Just leave me alone. All I wanted was a damn pickle, for God's sake!"

6

Margaret Barber lies between Jill and Amy in a mouldy-smelling bed, which is not even a full-size bed and which, once their bodies heat the mattress, exudes the odour of urine. Her head pulsates with what has been a two-day headache caused by the heat, the glare of sun on water, the airless hours spent playing lifeguard to Bunny's children, watching them sculpt the shapes of turtles, Popeye, and an airplane in the sand while Bunny stayed back at the cabin reading from a stack of magazines. All day Margaret listened to the children's cries and their heat-induced whining, their skirmishes over ownership of territories and sand toys.

Jill moans and turns suddenly, her arm thrashing Margaret in the chest. How can I sleep through this, Margaret wonders, through this damned headache, the awful-smelling room? Jill curls against her, hands tucked between her knees, and sleeps a dreamless sleep. Margaret must lie flat on her back because if she tries to sleep on her side she smells the perspiration of another person in the pillow. Bill? she wonders, and her stomach twists. Jill murmurs in sleep. Moody and silent by day, Jill only begrudgingly agreed to play with the younger children. But she wouldn't go swimming; she had resisted Margaret's pleas to put on her bathing suit. Margaret sighs when she thinks of this now, and attributes it to shyness over her developing breasts. Jill had been content to wade, as deep as her shorts would allow, through the sunlit water, beads of it spraying up around her body like multi-faceted crystals, diamonds, white fire.

Oh, Margaret thinks as she stares up at the ceiling through the throbbing of her headache, she'd been such an idiot to agree to come. "I think that's a terrific idea," Timothy had said when he returned her call. "There's no reason at all why you shouldn't go. Mel will manage perfectly fine on his own."

And Mel is managing perfectly fine, too. At that moment in Carona, Mel is upstairs in his room about to have a go at the last position depicted in the cartoon. Garth lies naked on Jill's bed across the hall, waiting his turn.

So, although a little drunk, Mel is managing fine. Do this, he says, and is delighted when Elsa flips up her skirt and turns her little white bum up to greet him. But then suddenly Elsa does something quite different. She stiffens and both legs shoot straight out. She's as rigid as a board as she topples sideways from the chair onto the floor and lands on her back. Garth hears a thud, and then a steady thumping sound, and comes to investigate. Mel stands over Elsa, his eyes wide with shock. Her heels bump against the floor, up and down in a steady rhythm, like a wound-up toy soldier knocked onto its back, and her head thrashes back and forth in time to it. "Christ," Garth says as foam begins to bubble at the corners of her mouth and her eyes roll up inside her head. He gathers up his clothing, dresses swiftly, and leaves a terrified Mel to manage alone.

Margaret and Timothy will be proud of Mel in the end, of how he had been man enough to go downstairs to the telephone, to pick it up and call Josh Miller.

Josh doesn't talk much as he mounts the stairs to the bedroom. "Epilepsy, a seizure," he says, and, "blanket." He kneels beside Elsa and wipes her mouth with his handkerchief while Mel strips the blanket from his bed. Josh rolls Elsa into it and cradles her in his arms as though she were a baby, or a limp doll, Mel thinks, as Josh pushes past him and out of the room. Mel sees Elsa's round white face, the flutter of her eyelashes closed in deep sleep, and the soft pout of her mouth; the corners turned down in a look of extreme disappointment. His heart constricts. She has consented to bare her breasts for him, and still he has refused to kiss her. He would like to now. He doesn't understand this desire or the feeling of guilt that he interprets as pity or sorrow.

The car door slams shut and Josh drives away leaving Mel with an incredible regret: to not be able to erase the past few weeks and unlearn what he knows. He imagines that Elsa loved him and that he betrayed that love. He wanders about the empty house and stops to turn on the radio. He listens to Buddy Knox singing that all he wants is a party doll, which only increases his sense of remorse, and so he goes out to face the still and dark town.

He takes the back way, choosing the street that runs parallel to Main Street. He walks through the shadows cast by the United Church, past houses, then the Alliance Gospel Church. A soft light burns in the window of the Hardys' cottage. Behind the curtain people kneel in a circle. They're praying for a spiritual revival to occur in the town of Carona. They continue to pray for individuals who have been brought to their minds in dreams or while they were out weeding the garden, for those whose names they've heard in soft but distinct whispers across their shoulders. They continue to pray for Margaret and Timothy Barber.

Mel steps out from the alley beside Johnson's Hardware and into the street. Garth is nowhere to be seen. Hiding under a bed, Mel thinks, and suddenly feels self-righteous as he looks up at the window above Josh's shop. He wants to gaze up at that lit window and wallow in his regret, but a figure darts across the street towards him, and before Mel realizes that it's the woman Adele, she leaps on him, striking his face with the palm of her hand, and then her fingers become claws raking the skin beneath his eyes. Mel ducks, backing away from her, arms raised to ward off the blows. He gasps as she punches him in the stomach. "You swine! You dirty little coward! You have to use little girls!" she shouts. Her fists pound against his shoulders. Mel wants to say, Wait a minute. Not once had Elsa indicated that she didn't want to do it. She was the one who offered it to him in the first place. Mel doesn't know that Elsa's behaviour is, sadly, a learned one. Adele brings her knee up between Mel's legs, going for his balls, and so he swings, blindly but hard, connecting with the woman's head, and is astonished and sick suddenly to see her hair go flying away into the street. Adele crouches, glaring, her orange mouth contorted in anger, and her bald head, with a scar running in a crooked line from one side of it to the other, shines silver in the light of the street lamp. Mel has never seen such rage, or a bald-headed woman. Such ugliness. "Jesus!" he says, turns, and flees from it. As he runs, he hears the sound of the hardware store's windows shattering, one and then the other.

Margaret hears a mewing sound coming from the adjoining room in the cabin. One of Bunny's children, wanting to be led through the bushes to the back of the property and the privy. Well, she will ignore it tonight, in the same way Bunny and Bill seem able to ignore all their children's requests during the night. A terrific idea, Timothy had said. Bill's idea, Bunny had confessed. So far Bill had only joined them for the evening meal, eating quickly and almost silently, speaking only to bring order to the children's unruly behaviour or to ask Bunny to pass him something. Bunny's basset-hound eyes appeared hurt and uneasy the whole time. Bill would already be gone in the morning when they gathered in the large room that served as both kitchen and living room to feed the brood, as Bunny put it. Feed the sharks, you mean, Margaret had thought as she worked at preparing sandwiches and filling jars with lemonade for their day beside the water. At night they all went to bed at the same time, Margaret with her two girls in the evil-smelling and cobweb-draped room, Bunny's four children crammed into an equally small room, and Bill and Bunny out

131

on the veranda on a fold-down couch. Then the cabin grew still and silent as everyone but Margaret, with her grinding headache, fell asleep. Absolutely useless, Margaret thinks. She gets up, dressing quickly, and goes out through the back door so she won't have to pass by Bill and Bunny.

Whenever Bunny had spoken about the cabin she'd inherited at the lake, Margaret imagined something more than the little wooden unpainted box with its tilting veranda and the cluster of equally decrepit, festering cabins around it, dark and empty. She had imagined the sound of water breaking in waves against the shore just outside the door and the light of the moon dropping down against the lake, illuminating the room, and Bill standing there in the doorway, pausing in that light before moving towards her. Not his absence, not the almost fifteen-minute walk to reach the water.

The road is a dark corridor but at the end of it she sees light moving against the face of the lake. She steps out onto the beach, hears the soft wash of waves against the sand, and her headache begins to diminish. She walks by the children's toppled sculptures, by shovels and pails strewn here and there. On she goes, beyond the dock and away from the main beach to a rising in the land and a sand bank that forms a gentle cove. She burrows down into the sand, its warmth an embrace, the cool breeze off the water a caress against her hot skin. She tries not to think of Timothy asleep in his motel room some-where in Saskatchewan and focuses instead on a white shape that appears to hover above the surface of the black water. A sail. A sailboat. She watches it for several moments and it doesn't seem to move. A pelican? she wonders, and finds its silent white presence comforting. Margaret thinks of Timo-thy returning home and reaching for her beneath the blankets. And how she once confessed to Rita that she was frightened about turning thirty-five and facing the possibility of never having sex with a man other than Timothy. "Why on earth would you want to?" Rita asked and Margaret was surprised to see the blush rising beneath the heavy beige pancake make-up Rita wore. "Just to know what it would be like," Margaret said. "Let me tell you then," Rita stated rather strongly, "once you've had one, you've had them all."

But Margaret doesn't think so. Margaret knows there's something she's missing. She knows this from her strange and sometimes bizarre early-morning dreams of making love with strangers, or with Timothy, her children, Bunny, Bill. Margaret has even had several dreams of being made love to by a large black dog. Dreams of wet and slippery sex that bring excruciating pleasure and leave her aching for more. Then Margaret lies awake and listens to the sounds of the house to determine if the children are still asleep and will not hear the squeak of bedsprings as she replays the dream beneath her eyelids and seeks relief. Margaret has even dressed up and gone to see a doctor in the city and sat out in the waiting room with all the other patients, those whose broken parts – in their wrappings of bandages or plaster, in their fevers manifested by blotchy rashes – were more evident. And after the doctor had poked about her insides, Margaret had got dressed again and sat across from him on a Naugahyde chair and said, "What am I supposed to feel when I have intercourse?"

"There's no indication of fibroids," he said. "Are you experiencing discomfort?"

"No," Margaret said, determined to be clear. "It's just that I don't feel anything."

He laughed. "Well, what do you expect? That you'll feel the earth moving? Hear bells?"

Yes, Margaret thought. Yes, yes, yes.

Margaret's eyes remain fixed on the white triangular shape that hovers above the lake, only several yards away or perhaps a mile. It could be three feet tall or thirty, solid or the substance of the evening air, a reflection cast down from the other side of things, it's difficult to tell. Fool, Margaret thinks, and winces against the image that leaps unbidden behind her eyes. She sees herself kneeling on the floor of the kitchen, looking down at Bill's feet, at a contrast of colours, his brown socks set against the green-and-white tile floor, which she had polished earlier that day, before everything else, before the heat, before

133

the children had come down from their beds, still warm, wanting cold cereal and milk and listening to her instructions on how to behave at the Lutheran Sunday School picnic. Before she had put on the new blouse she made. Two coats of paste wax polished to a high shine with woollen sweaters wrapped around her feet. The new liquid waxes don't give as high a shine: her mother's voice, speaking to her as she worked. "Your account at the store is too high, I can't let you add to it for a floor polisher at this time," Reginald had said, sounding like Mr. Block, a high-school teacher they had once played Hallowe'en pranks on. Bunny and herself and others she had forgotten who had left Carona. At night, first snow-fall, hiding and waiting for the man to make his regular journey to the back of the yard and the privy, she remembered as she polished the kitchen floor and tried not to think that Bill North would be coming over later on in the day. The floor shone like a mirror all around Margaret as she knelt in front of Bill, the tape measure, clammy against her neck, swinging back and forth. The cat was at her side, batting now and then at the tape as it moved.

Or, the floor shone like fresh ice, its surface having just been flooded with water and hardened. But already there were scuff marks on it. She could see them from the angle at which she knelt, the little hook-shaped marks her children's shoes had made on its surface, and when Bill spread his feet apart, she saw the outline of his socked feet in perspiration on the shiny floor. Heat radiated off his leg as she held up the tape to take his inseam measurement. He had touched the back of her neck and her skin tingled.

"Margaret," he'd said as he ran his fingers across her hot skin, and she heard in his voice what she believed to be amazement that he was finally, at last, able to touch her. "Margaret," she whispers to herself as she leans back into the warm sand, saying her name the way she thinks he'd said it, examining its tone. I wonder whatever happened to Mr. Block? Bunny had asked recently, and she'd told Bunny what she'd heard, that their bachelor teacher had found happiness in the arms of a widow in another town. You have to let the first coat of wax harden thoroughly before you apply the second, she hears her mother instruct. "Margaret," she repeats to herself, but she cannot put away or change or deny the sound of Bill's zipper sliding open or the memory of the yeasty smell of him as he drew her head towards him. Oh my God, she'd thought. Oh God. The light finally dawning. What am I going to do? How can I get out of this gracefully? He doesn't smell clean, she thought, as he thrust his hips towards her. She hadn't been able to think of a single graceful thing to do and so she gave in to the pressure of his hand at her neck and became a reluctant child, eyes closed, mouth opening to receive him.

She had wondered how to do it. How to arrange her mouth, what to do with her tongue and teeth. She'd thought suddenly that Bunny's small mouth was probably not large enough to hold him. "Good," Bill said. "Good, good," he repeated with each thrust and Margaret wondered how not to gag. "Good," he said as he came. His stream bubbled in the back of her mouth, filling it, and she wanted to pull away from it but he held her head in place. She waited for it to end, and at last he grew limp and slid from her mouth. There was more liquid than she'd expected and so she kept her mouth large inside, holding it, not wanting to swallow, and waited until he turned away to fix himself. She looked around quickly to see what she might do with it and saw the tray of pins resting on the freshly polished floor. She bent over it, opened her mouth, and the semen dropped in a gush down onto the pins. The cat crouched beside Margaret, watching, and then rose to his haunches, padded over to the small plastic tray, and sniffed at it.

Idiot, Margaret thinks as she burrows more deeply into the warm sand. Twice a fool to have agreed to come here. She scoops up handfuls of sand, imagines time trickling away, minutes, hours, years. "So what if you're turning thirty-five?" Rita had said. "I'd give my eye-teeth for someone like Timothy."

The sound of male voices begins to push through Margaret's thoughts. Sometimes she wakes up in the middle of the night to a similar sound of voices and thinks she's left the radio playing downstairs. It goes on all night, the voices, and

Margaret accepts it, thinking that it could be the residue of a conversation that occurred during the day, the outward ripple of soundwaves reversed by the barrier of a weather front. Or it could be a conversation that took place in another time, blown back now by stellar winds, and perhaps the television antenna fed the sound into the room. She realizes then that the white shape on the water has disappeared and wonders if it was a sail after all and if the boat has come ashore. The voices rise and she hears soft laughter. Sound travels far in moisture-laden air, they could be miles away, but she decides to investigate. She walks until she comes to a wall of dark rocks, a solid arm laid down against the water. She kicks her sandals free and wades along the length of the rocky peninsula, thinking to walk around it, but the sand bottom drops away too steeply and too soon she's thigh-deep in water. She returns to shore, puts on her sandals, and decides to attempt to climb over it.

As she reaches the top of the rocky arm, she sees the light of a bonfire in the distance where the shoreline appears to draw back into a seemingly endless curve of white sand. The breeze off the lake feels cool against her legs and thighs and she begins to shiver as she approaches the fire and two men; young men, she realizes, as she draws closer. One leans forward and pokes the fire with a stick, causing the flames to flare brighter, sparks to snap and shoot off in all directions. How would it look to turn away now that they've seen her coming? Unfriendly, she thinks, and so she will stand beside their fire for a moment.

"Hello," one of the men calls. "Nice night for walking."

The man who has stirred the fire smiles widely and waves.

"Yes," Margaret says. She's close enough now to see the beer bottles shoved down into the sand between the two men and then she sees the carton of beer half-submerged in the water. There's no evidence of a sailboat. Their faces flicker with the light of the flames. Early twenties, she thinks. She begins to shiver violently.

"You're welcome to join us," the young man who greeted her says. "Why don't you come and get warm?" He's spoken quietly, with the proper degree of respect. Well brought up,

Margaret surmises as she drops to the sand and tucks her long legs up beneath her.

He senses her uneasiness; she realizes this in the way he smiles, clear, open, and friendly. Only he speaks, while the other man nods occasionally in agreement or draws stick-figures in the sand. They wear white tee shirts and boxer trunks and Margaret notes a well-muscled calf and hopes for Mel to be as healthy and strong-looking one day. He explains that they're graduates of architecture on an extended gradua-tion celebration before they part and go their separate ways to work. One to Toronto, the other to Montreal. They have been friends since grade school, he explains, and names an area in the city, Silver Heights, which Margaret doesn't recognize. She can't fathom anyone having been born in the city, much less growing up in its streets. When she says this they laugh and he tells her that they have backyards and neighbourhoods, too.

There's a lull in the conversation. She realizes that they haven't once sipped at their beer and thinks that it's out of deference to her presence, or perhaps they believe they ought to offer her one and don't want to. She thinks it's time to leave and is about to get up when the silent man speaks. "The water's as warm as a bathtub," he says. Then he peels his tee shirt up over his head, rises, and strides down towards the lake. His white legs reflect the dancing light of the fire. She sees him sprint through the shallows and then hears the sound of his body meeting water as he plunges in. The other man looks Margaret full in the face for the first time. He smiles. His features are even, a perfect drawing, no blemishes, not even the hint of whiskers. His eyes are the darkest she's ever seen. She hears the smooth rhythm of the swimmer's stroke.

"Why not go in for a swim?"

"Oh, no." Margaret laughs. "I'm afraid I'd sink like a stone."

He stands up and takes off his tee shirt and then holds out his hand. "Come on. It's true, at night the water is as warm as water in a bathtub."

Margaret allows herself to be pulled up, thinking that she'll dust sand from her shorts and say, Well, it's been nice meeting the both of you, but instead she lets him lead her down towards the lake. It *is* warm, Margaret thinks, as it rises up about her knees, thighs, and then her waist. She gasps as the water rises beneath her armpits.

"Put your arms around my neck," he instructs.

She does and he walks out further and Margaret feels her body rise in a float. The rhythmic sound of the swimmer has become fainter and then fades completely under the sound of their own breathing. It's just the two of them now, faces only inches apart, breathing each other's breath. "There," he says. "I'm treading water now. Isn't it warm?"

"Yes," Margaret agrees. "Like water in a bathtub." It's beautiful, she thinks. It seems they are dead centre in the path of moonlight that leads to a vanishing point in the dark horizon.

"And you are not sinking like a stone."

"No," Margaret says and laughs. His eyes are clear and steady.

"That's because I'm holding you." His hands grasp her arms and gently he pries her hands loose from his neck. Margaret floats away from him, secured only by the lightest touch of his fingertips. "You trust me," he says.

She can no longer see his face. "Yes."

"I could let go," he says, "and no one would ever know."

Yes, he has that power, she thinks. She's given it to him by agreeing to come. She sinks then and sputters as water fills her mouth. His strong hands circle her wrists and draw her towards him. She rises in front of him gulping for air and then he turns her away from himself. She feels his hands under her armpits as he lifts her and throws her out across the water.

Margaret breaks through the dark surface of it and it closes over her head. She sinks further and then feels the sandy bottom rise to meet her. When she stands up she discovers she's only in waist-deep. She turns to speak to him but the words are forgotten as he raises a hand in farewell. "You'll be okay now," he says and rolls over and swims down the broad path of moonlight.

As Margaret waits beside the dying embers of the fire for them to return she becomes aware for the first time of the roar of night sounds all around her, a constant chattering and sawing of crickets, the hum of mosquitoes, the rustle of poplar leaves flipping in the breeze.

When the sky begins to lighten and still there's no sign of the two swimmers, Margaret decides to head back to the cabin. She thinks that she'll listen to the radio, search the newspaper for mention of bodies washing up on the opposite shore. She will find nothing, though. Later, when Margaret embraces the ecstasy of her new religious faith, she will remember the man's parting words: "You'll be okay now." After Jill is gone, Margaret will come to believe that the young men were sent to deliver her a message.

Her clothing is still wet as she walks back towards the cabin. Suddenly she sees the thick dark hair on Bill's chest as he advances along the path through the trees. She imagines lifting her head and looking him square in the eye and that if he should happen to make the slightest move to touch her, she would say, "Not on your life, buster." But at the same time her eyes veer from the path and search among the trees for a suitable hollow where they could make love.

Bill hears her coming and looks up. "Oh good," he says, "I found you. Bunny says she thinks you ought to come and have a look at Jill."

7

At first it was thought that Jill had rheumatic fever but when Timothy returned home he said he wanted another opinion, and he and Jill disappeared into the city and returned several weeks later, Jill thinner, her limbs sensitive even to the slightest press of cool breeze against them. Then even the weight of a single bed-sheet would cause her to cry out. Timothy grew morose and silent and took an extended time off from work, spending the majority of it out back in the garage, and hardly a day passed when I didn't hear the whine of his electric sander. I spent most of my time on the swing, and as the summer drew to an end, a huge splinter from the swing seat pierced my buttock and began to fester into a boil. I began to limp but no one noticed.

"You know what happens to a caterpillar," Grandfather Johnson said to me one day near the end. He was trying to explain to me that my sister was dying. I had just returned from the locker plant where I had been sent to get a bowl of ice. Mr. Beever, the owner, said that I should help myself. I suspected that he wished to avoid the eye contact that would have been necessary through the giving and receiving of the bowl. I entered the cloud of frost that billowed out from the door of the walk-in cooler and passed among the hanging carcasses of pigs, sides of beef, to the end of it and the bin of ice. Above it, hanging upside down, was a row of eviscerated turkeys. Their stiff limbs seemed stretched and thin as though in shock and their skin had turned pebbly yellow with fleshy blue bumps.

When Jill finally did die early in the month of September, Margaret ran from the house with her hands covering her mouth. She ran out of the yard and across the street and stopped just inside the school grounds as though she'd run into a wall. She turned and retched into the grass. I went inside the house in time to see Timothy carrying Jill down the stairs to lay her out on the couch. Aunt Rita walked behind him, carrying a blanket, and when she saw me she tried to shoo me away, but I was mesmerized by the sight of Jill's stiff, yellowish limbs, which bobbed as Timothy descended the stairs. I thought, Jill looks like a frozen turkey.

The day following the funeral, silence in the house radiated outward, pushing against the walls, so that it seemed to me that the sides of the house bulged into the yard. I felt tension in the house's groaning timbers as I walked out onto the veranda. There were hands out there, I thought, palms raised against the windows to contain our bulging silence. A silence faintly permeated by an odour that to me would forever be connected to the smell of a sick child. The odour came from cankerworm droppings, a dry, dark stain on the sidewalk and in the street beyond; the smell almost gone now. But throughout the previous month the stink of worm droppings rose from sticky patches, overpowering all other smells. Timothy had raged against the fetid sweet odour, and each evening attempted to get rid of the droppings by taking the hose to them and washing them away into the sewer. By morning, the smell and wet stain would have returned. "It's like the abattoir in Saint Boniface," Aunt Rita had commented. But it wasn't that, nor was it the wind blowing in from the direction of the sugar beet factory, nor leaves erupting with sap, as we'd first thought, but the effluence of millions of chewing worms. It was September now, cooler. The worms were gone and in their place were sluggish wasps, crawling across spattered veranda windows, feeding.

Mel was upstairs in his bedroom. I stood out on the veranda with my navy-blue cape, which I wore constantly now, wrapped tightly around me. Margaret was closeted in her room with Mrs. Hardy, who had been sent, she said, to give meaning to Jill's death. Mrs. Hardy was attempting to teach Margaret to raise her hands in prayer and say, "Thank you, Jesus, for taking Jill away from me." Timothy was out driving the countryside. He was out in the rolling Pembina Hills watching through blurred eyes how the road climbed to meet the late summer sky. Beside him in the car, with a solicitous hand placed against his thigh, was my Aunt Rita.

I noticed the absence of birds on the television antennas, and even Amy the squirrel could not be seen. Out of respect for our loss, the school had been closed for several days to spare us the pain of the sight and sounds of happy children playing in the school grounds. No one walked or drove past the house. It was as though Jill had taken everyone with her.

Ashes to ashes, I had heard someone say as I watched the clumps of black earth drop from Timothy's hand. Because I had been struck by lightning, I should have been the one reduced to a pile of ashes, I thought. Elsa Miller stood behind me. I heard her weeping. Josh had driven her out from the city, where they now lived, closer to the medical care Elsa required for her epilepsy, Josh explained. And much to my Uncle Reginald's relief, Josh had closed up his shop. The cape Timothy had bought me absorbed the heat of the sun, which beat down against my shoulders and back. I was hot. I hoped we wouldn't have to be there much longer. I recall seeing the groundskeeper, Alf, standing on the periphery of the group of mourners, Jill's classmates, the teachers, distant relatives, the whole town of Carona. Alf looked out of place, as usual, in his manure-stained coveralls. He bowed his head and clutched his cap against his chest, thinking no doubt about his own boy, Harry, who had narrowly escaped death from a vicious bout of pneumonia after wandering soaked to the skin for several days. A shame, that, the people of Carona said. A shame that Jill had died and the mentally retarded Harry hadn't.

I'd seen Harry later on in the day, after the mourners had left our house and the United Church women's auxiliary had cleared away the mess in the kitchen, wiped it down, and restored its counters and floor to Margaret's usual high shine. Timothy sat at the end of the living room in the easy chair, smoking. The ashtray in the smoking-stand beside him was filled with cigarette butts. Margaret sat on the couch, legs crossed primly, the same pose she'd maintained during the time visitors streamed steadily into the house. Earlier, Bunny had sat beside Margaret, almost ignored, until Margaret turned to say that she would be fine, she didn't want Bunny to stay the night, continuing to punish her friend for being the one to discover the swollen lymph node in Jill's groin. Aunt Rita posed on the edge of the piano bench, elegant in a narrow black sheath dress, her white face framed by a careless-looking but careful arrangement of hennaed curls. The silent trio barely moved as I passed through the room, into the hallway, and out the front door.

What did I hear as I stepped out from the veranda that evening? The chirp of crickets, perhaps the sawing of cicadas, whose sound has been recorded in almost every new novel and story I have read recently. Cicadas in Mexico, for instance, Brazil, Greece, Minneapolis, the insect leaps off the page before I can squash it, its purpose meaningless; only to be there? What's with the plague of cicadas in contemporary literature, I asked Piotr once, and vowed that I would never put the sound of a single cicada in any of my scripts.

That evening after the funeral I wanted to go and ride the swing as high as I could, but as I walked towards it I felt the boil on my buttock rubbing against my underwear. It had been painful to sit up straight on the hard pew during the service. I stood in the centre of the yard looking up at the gold filigree, the paper-clip shapes of the television antennas set against the purple rim of the twilit sky. A cat crooned in a neighbouring yard and then another cat joined in and then both of them began to scream. I couldn't move without feeling the bulge of the boil and the sharp prick of the sliver swimming in its centre, so I lay down on the grass and spread the cape over my shoulders. I smelled the damp earth and the spores of

143

toadstools exploding beneath it. I spread my arms out beneath the cape and closed my eyes.

It's now or never, I thought. I had practised long enough. I said the word, "Fly." And, as in all my dreams and imaginings, it was just that easy. I felt myself rise and the wind blowing against my face and scalp. I opened my eyes and saw the fence pass beneath me. As I had suspected, flying was similar to swinging, both will and action, I noticed, as I brought my arms forward and swept them back again and felt myself climb higher. When I tilted my right arm, I moved in that direction and down the street I flew, passing directly over the red roof of Bunny's house, across the wrought-iron steeple of the Presbyterian church, the silver shell of the grandstand at the agricultural grounds. I had risen so high that the houses were like pieces in a Monopoly game. Too high, I thought, and clapped my arms against my sides and felt myself plummet. Quickly, I spread my arms and felt the air cushion my body. Below me lay the clutter of Alf's yard. I wanted to see Harry. I wanted to say that I was glad he was alive and that I was sorry for having chased him away that day. Light flashed in my eyes, the setting sun reflected in glass. I realized that it had come from Harry's look-out tower on top of the shed. I circled for several moments, knowing that he was watching. "Sorry," I called down to Harry. "You hear that, you little pumpkin head? I'm sorry."

Then I tilted my left arm and veered off across the top of the grain elevator, away from Carona where farmhouses lined a gravel road every mile or so, and then I saw the top of Uncle Reginald's Ranch Wagon parked beside the road. Both front doors were wide open and the radio was turned on full volume. Garth sat on the car's hood, tapping out the beat of the song with a pair of chopsticks. Mel was inside the car in the driver's seat, crying. I am not a coward, Mel cried. I am not a chicken shit. Am I? Am I? he asked, still blaming himself and not cancer for the lump in Jill's groin. The melancholy sound of a train's whistle rose and Mel lifted his head. A beam of light shone steadily on down the track. The passenger door slammed shut and then the driver's door too. Mel reached for the keys in the ignition and turned on the engine. A startled Garth leapt from the hood as the tires spat gravel and Mel drove away. I watched yellow dust roiling up behind the car as Mel made a bee-line for the rail crossing. He would meet the train at a ninety-degree angle. The train's whistle shrieked several times and I wanted to close my eyes to the explosion of metal and glass. I blinked and Mel was gone and the train streaked across the road, its cars swaying wildly. Then I saw the glow of the station wagon's tail-lights appear intermittently in the space between the swaying boxcars. Garth saw it too. "You idiot!" Garth screamed and then ripped off a rebel yell and flung the chopsticks into the air. As the train's caboose clattered across the road, Garth ran towards the car. Mel got out from it slowly and walked towards him, wearing an uncertain grin. "How was that for a chicken shit, eh?" "Not bad," Garth said, "except that you've gone and pissed yourself." He pointed to the stain in the leg of Mel's new suit pants, and it was true, Mel had.

The day following the funeral I had expected that Margaret would have somehow tidied up the world while I had slept and that the house would be back to normal once again. I stood on the veranda feeling slightly nauseated by the sight of the feeding wasps. I heard the soft voice of Mrs. Hardy upstairs in Margaret's bedroom. Steady, monotonously solicitous, and holy. At some point during Jill's illness Margaret had moved the wicker furniture back down to the veranda and if it hadn't been for the wasps I would have sat down. I opened the door to the house thinking that I would go back inside and wait for Timothy and Aunt Rita to return. I opened it as wide as its spring would allow, changed my mind and let go and the door slammed shut. I liked the sound of its spring being stretched to the limit and so I opened it again and once again let go. The door slammed. I liked this sound too. So I opened the door again and let it fly. Then I did it again. Open and slam. Open and slam. I continued to do this until I heard feet pounding on the stairs, and then I saw Mel, his face a mask of fury as he ran down the stairs towards me. He'd wound his belt around his fist and he grabbed me and swung the belt, hitting me on the backs of my legs, my buttocks, hitting the boil there, and it burst wide open.

"Now, now, dearie." Mrs. Hardy came down the stairs and clasped me to her bony chest. I strained against her because I had only yelled once and wasn't crying and didn't need her ministrations. "You kiddies have had a difficult time," she said. She took my face in her hands and peered into my eyes and said slowly and distinctly, "You must realize this: Jill is safe in the arms of Jesus now." I laughed because I saw Jesus cradling a frozen turkey against his chest. Then Margaret entered the hallway still wearing her funeral dress. She'd slept in it and she looked old, used, defeated; a crumpled paper sack. I try to remember Margaret this way. It is the last picture I have of her where she looked natural.

I untangled myself from the woman's embrace, needing, longing for Margaret's touch at last. I wanted to confess that it was my fault. I wanted to tell her that I had been struck by lightning. That I felt I had enough power in me to light up a city the size of New York and that perhaps, at one time, I might have secretly wished Jill dead. As I walked towards my mother, my arms coming forward to embrace her, she noticed my limp and her eyes filled with horror. She shrank from my touch and backed away, her fingers gouging deep into her eye sockets. "Oh God, not another one," she moaned and then her voice rose in a high, keening sound. "Please, God, oh no, God, you can't do this to me."

Mrs. Hardy stopped Margaret as she attempted to flee. "My poor, poor child," she said, and Margaret lurched into her arms. "Jesus, God," Margaret howled, "I don't deserve this."

"But, my dear," Mrs. Hardy said, "won't you see that the Lord is calling out to you? He has taken Jilly to be with Him for a reason. Can't you see?" She stepped back and raised her face and hands and began to chant a prayer. At least I believe it was a prayer but I couldn't be certain because the words, though they sounded like words, didn't make any sense at all. When I left the house, Margaret's voice joined with hers and I heard my mother say, "Thank you, Jesus, for taking Jill away from me."

146

When I woke up in the hospital, the sliver removed and my buttock throbbing with the pain of sutures, I became aware of a figure in black at the end of my bed. It was Grandfather Johnson, come to visit, standing there just as he had when he visited Jill, holding a geranium plant, a red wound against his black suit. "Now guess what I saw on my way over here?" he said. I heard myself yelling at him to go away, to get out of my room.

Once Piotr asked Amy if she would like to go and visit Jill's grave. They were leaving the Grandview Apartments following a visit with Margaret. She linked her fingers through his, knowing that Margaret watched from the window. "Heavens no," Amy said, it wasn't All Saints' Day, after all, and she didn't have a candle. The girl who had sat in her sickbed throwing fruit at Amy no longer existed. Visiting Jill's grave would be like visiting the scene of an accident. In dying, Jill had taken both Margaret and Timothy away.

Amy made a point that day of driving past the family house, without telling Piotr she had grown up there. She took him to see Carona's "historical point of interest," Sullie's Drive In and Take Out. Over forty years old, known throughout the land for its hot dogs, she told him. And then she drove down Main Street for no reason at all except that the dissolution of it, the boarded-up store-fronts, the spent greyness of Carona were reminders of the danger of false expectations. Do this and you're sure to get that. The promise of the faith of the Fifties, the structure of fictions past: conflict and resolution, when constant change was what was real.

She took him to see all the seven churches of Carona and he was puzzled. Six of them were Protestant but so different that each required a separate place of worship? The Prince of the Polish devils would have his work cut out for him here, she told him. In all his twenty-plus years living in Poland he'd never once met a Protestant. They stood side by side in front of the United Church. She didn't mention that her wedding had occurred there. A cold wind stung her face. She reached for Piotr's hand, the one he'd set into the hand of Boruta, wanting to wind her fingers through his and warm them. But he drew his hand away to point out something he wanted her to see. She should have noticed how often it was that he would do that.

8

Amy and Piotr have left the ferry, *The Chi-Cheemaun*, and are travelling across Manitoulin Island heading towards the town of Little Current. He drives and she's relieved that he doesn't appear to be in a hurry but seems to have sunk into a reflective mood, content to wander along in the stream of slow-moving traffic. Pensive, Amy thinks. Perhaps doubting his decision to leave her? "I wouldn't mind living here," she says, and envisions at once blue gingham at a window, a plant on a sill, a pottery bowl cupping wild rice and sweetgrass drying in a sun porch. Being still and not moving. The two of them, in a village on one of the outermost points of the shore, just the sky and water. They would build something. Yes, she thinks, stay and build.

"I don't think it would be a good place for a person living alone. You'd go crazy here in the winter. It's pretty isolated, I think. Little Current, six kilometres." He reads the sign at the side of the road.

Alone. "Will we stop?" She reminds them of their ritual of stopping at a particular store to pass the time browsing while they wait for the traffic from the ferry to move through the bottleneck of the single lane on the narrow bridge just outside the town.

"Sure." His hand drops away from the gear shift and crosses

the space between them. She feels its warmth against her thigh and the gentle reassuring pat. She covers it with her own. He brought very few things with him when he entered her life. A single suitcase of clothes and several canisters, the films he'd made in Poland – no excess baggage from a previous marriage or even a short time lived with another woman. He came almost penniless, with only a halting grasp of the language. But his eagerness to learn, his child-like inquisitiveness she found seductive and took on, her world-weariness fading as she acquired his capacity to celebrate simple things such as a dish of blueberries, a cloud formation. Look! he exclaimed constantly, pointing, and she was seeing a sunset as though for the first time. But although he came to her with very little, when he leaves, the rooms of her life will have a hollow echo, she knows.

"Look," he says now, and draws his hand from beneath hers to point out a man crouching beside the road. The man from the ferry, Amy realizes. He's wearing a jacket, now, red plaid, but nevertheless she recognizes the backpack and green sleeping bag rolled up on top of it.

"Should we?" Piotr touches the brakes and the car slows down. The man rises in anticipation.

"No. It's him, the guy we saw on the ferry."

"That's not the same person," he says, but jabs at the accelerator and they shoot away. He watches in the rear-view mirror. "The other man was much smaller."

"It was him," Amy says. He knows well enough not to argue against her memory.

They drive in silence for the next several minutes and Amy remembers the last time they picked up a hitchhiker. They had been on another island. The Sanibel Island in Florida and heading up towards a reef of smaller islands. The man had appeared so suddenly, emerging from a dark screen of mangrove, that they stopped more for fear of hitting him. They couldn't have known that the round, soft-faced middle-aged man was mentally handicapped. Once they did realize, they had travelled too far to take him back. His shirt was neatly ironed, his cotton pants had a sharp crease, and his shoes shone. He has a mother, Amy remembers thinking, reminded of Harry in the town of Carona and his tiny, caring mother. As she travels across Manitoulin Island sitting beside Piotr in the car while outside a saw-toothed, pine-tree landscape divides land from sky, she thinks of a pink and turquoise horizon, of the round man they picked up in Florida, and wonders how long it took his mother to track him down. BEWARE OF CROCODILES CROSSING, the road signs had said. She imagines that he might still be out there, heading across those shell-strewn beaches, on and on he goes, right into the Gulf of Mexico. Then she sees herself cradling a huge conch shell against her chest. Piotr stands so close to her that his wet bathing suit touches the side of her leg. They are waiting for the orange ball of sun to drop into the ocean. They long to see the phenomenon of the green flash occurring just as the sun sets.

"We should go back to Florida, it was so beautiful there," she says. He doesn't answer.

Yes, it was beautiful, but it was rotten too. After they spent the entire day shelling they sat out in someone's backyard looking out over the Gulf. It was dark and lanterns bobbed on skiffs, nodding across the violet water. From a patio behind her, there was music, a jumpy Ry Cooder song, "Get Rhythm," and voices; the voices of people reclining beneath pastel umbrellas, the soft murmur threading through the music. She and Piotr sat side by side on the beach that night but rather far apart for a couple in love, she sifting white sand through her fingers and Piotr wondering aloud for the third or fourth time what it was that these people did that allowed them the waterfront property, the cars, the boats. She didn't sense the growing frustration that lay behind his question, his disappointment over what he perceived to be a lack of opportunity for himself, the small gains he had made. She didn't think of the Russian proverb he often quoted: "Not married by thirty, not rich by forty, always an idiot." Rather she thought that he wanted to be far away from her, out on one of those lamp-lit boats, scuba-diving or snorkelling and not beside her, a comparatively mature woman who must

*constantly diet and exercise and suck in her stomach and try
to ignore the quizzical glances they received from strangers
on the beach, in restaurants. The odd couple.*

*When they did go snorkelling she encountered a manta ray
that had lain hidden in the sand. It rose up in front of her
suddenly and she'd darted to the surface, terrified. Piotr left
her side to pursue it and, abandoned, she felt claustrophobic
in the underwater world and swam back to the boat alone.
She watched the yellow tip of his snorkel move further and
further away. That was when Piotr began to leave her, but she
chose not to notice.*

They enter the store in Little Current and Amy enjoys all at
once the smell of deer hide and the dry, pleasant odour of
sweetgrass. She follows the scent to a display rack and takes
down a braid of grass. She will buy it and hang it in the car.
Good luck and all that; a blessing of some kind. She searches
for a clerk. A radio plays in a room behind the counter but
there's no sign of anyone. They wander for several moments
among the shelves of moccasins and hand-knit bulky sweaters, both of them feeling as though they're being watched.
Piotr grows impatient. He fills his cheeks with air and expels
it slowly. "Come on," he urges the invisible clerk. Moments
later a woman appears from the room behind the counter.
She's heavy-set, a plump native woman with clear, silky-
looking skin. Amy sets the sweetgrass down onto the counter.
"You people just off the ferry?" the woman asks.

"Yes."

"Aren't you the lucky ones," she says with a slight smile.
"The ferry's going to be shut down for a while now."

"What's up?"

The woman explains that she's just heard it on the radio, a
barricade has gone across the highway just south of Tobermory, blocking off traffic. A slender teenage boy enters the
store. He wears his baseball cap low on his forehead and leans
into the counter, studying them.

"I guess we are lucky," Amy says as they get into the car, but she doesn't feel lucky. She thinks of the extra days they might have had together if they had encountered the barricade and not been able to board the ferry. They would have had to backtrack, take a land route up around Georgian Bay. For the past two summers there have been similar occurrences of short-term blockades by native people in all three of the Prairie provinces. The incidents that have sparked them are sometimes sketchy and forgotten almost as quickly as the barricades come down. Piotr turns on the radio, still concerned about the possibility of heavy smoke from forest fires reducing visibility and causing the highway to be closed. The news report says the fires burning north of Thunder Bay are still under control. They learn, too, of other blockades by the Ojibway Indians at the Saugeen and Cape Croker reserves.

The sun has begun to drop low on the horizon as they drive through Espanola. YOU ARE ENTERING INDIAN COUNTRY, a yellow spray-painted message on a train trestle bridge announces. "Where isn't it Indian country?" Piotr comments, and, as if to confirm the message, two dark-skinned children appear beside the highway, carrying fishing rods. There are probably six more where those two came from, Amy thinks, and sure enough three more dark-haired children rise up from reeds beside the road. "Watch." But Piotr has already touched the brakes. Beyond the children a woman stands in front of a sagging, unpainted house, an axe in hand. The children turn and look at her; she has obviously shouted a warning. Then she returns to her task of chopping kindling. Amy imagines a warm setting, fried potatoes browning in a pan on the stove inside the house, fingers dunking pickerel fillets into a bowl of flour.

While Piotr is forever raising the binoculars in search of distant shores, Amy sees bits and pieces of the whole. It doesn't occur to her, for instance, that there is dioxin in the fish the children aspire to catch. As the car passes by the house she turns and notices the satellite dish set up on a rock behind it. "You okay?" she asks Piotr. She noticed that his skin has become slick with perspiration as his body works to slough off the poison of the Scotch he drank last night.

"Amy, I am okay." He's peeved because it's the second time she's asked him this in the last half hour. She supposes that he objects to her asking because it draws attention to the fact that even though she had drunk more Scotch than he had, been awake the entire night while he had slept soundly, she has driven the larger portion of the distance so far. That even though she is nine years older, she seems to have much more stamina. But she discovers her error as he begins to tell her he's worrying about how to adapt the stage play *The Emigrant* for film. He has already discussed the problems at length with the woman he will meet in Belgium; how he will take the two men in the play out of the basement room where the entire action is supposed to occur without sacrificing the tone of the play or the sense of the immigrants' isolation in a foreign society. If he takes them from their basement room and puts them out on the street, he will lose, he worries, the important factor of their self-imposed imprisonment in a new country, how they choose to cling in desperation to old ideas, ideals, philosophical stances. As Amy listens to his monologue, she hears this Elizabeth person speaking through him and bitterness rises in her throat. She, Amy, is his translator. It's up to her to pick apart the tricky analogies he draws in awkward and convoluted sentences. Only she can paraphrase them and repeat them back to him or write them down. The reward, his relief and astonishment that she appears to have read his mind, belongs to her alone.

"Well, what do you think?" he asks as he finishes describing how he will go about dramatizing what is already dramatic.

Corny, melodramatic, hyperbole, Amy thinks. If she said this his face would darken and twist with anguish and he would lash out at her, say that she doesn't understand the nature of real drama. Later, after he had looked up her words in a dictionary, he would circle her with cautious, tentative questions. An endless screen of dark trees flies past the window, a seemingly impenetrable wall. But suddenly there's an opening, a logging path cutting through that wall. "Stop the car," Amy says.

The car idles beside the highway. A man's voice on the radio predicts rainfall during the night. "I see that you are angry," Piotr says.

Amy picks up the binoculars from the dash and raises them. A speck on the highway leaps forward, a truck, slightly distorted by the lenses. "I'm not angry."

"Tell me what you're thinking, then."

My chest will explode, Amy thinks. She has come to imagine that in breathing one another's breath across the pillow, cells have fused and they have given birth to a third entity, which is both of them, yet exists apart from them, and whose singular and omnipresent shadow somehow confirms their own existence. She knows that if he leaves, this third person will be murdered. She shoves the binoculars back onto the dash with more force than is necessary. He calls after her as she leaps from the car and jogs down the gravel shoulder. She cuts down through a spongy ditch and up the other side of it and enters the logging path. Hard, mean, confining, she thinks, and musty, like the inside of her head right now. Mean country. A relentless gloominess. She squints up at the corridor of sky at the top of the path and watches as a hawk wheels, riding the air's currents, its keen eye noting minute movement, discerning what is prey, what is not. There's a sudden scrambling sound in the underbrush off to one side and she stops dead, the hair on the back of her neck prickling. A bear. She fears the lumbering but swift and deadly violence of a bear, but then she sees the sweep of antlers as a deer rises up among the trees.

Piotr steps up close behind her, watching as the deer ambles off into the dense forest. "Oh, nice." She feels the push of his words against her cheek. His arms circle her waist.

"Tell me what you're thinking."

She leans against him for a moment. "What I am thinking."

"Yes."

Amy turns into him and they stand face to face, noses touching. "What I am thinking," she says, "is that I'd better take off about ten pounds if I'm going to find another lover."

She's gratified by the mixture of fear and grief in his eyes.

"Oh, I see." He releases her. "You are being perverse." As he turns away she sees that pebbly pink mole sticking up through the bristles of his fresh haircut. You have a thick neck, she thinks. Believe it or not, your head is perfectly square. I don't know how your mother ever managed to give birth to you. You are ridiculously pigeon-toed. You have the legs of a woman. The reason I love your penis is because it looks so funny when it's stiff, the way it sways and dips, the flagpole of your body so large yet friendly-looking and eager to the point of being almost obsequious and not at all as menacing as you may hope. Shut up, shut up, she tells herself. I love you. She steps forward and holds him and presses her face into the back of his head. "Everyone always leaves me." She tastes the saltiness of his perspiration. This isn't entirely true, she knows it. She was the one who left Hank and their child, Richard.

"You knew it would come to this. I never said anything different. This has always been the understanding."

Because you have your goal, Amy thinks, which probably includes a younger woman with wide enough hips to allow for the passage of another square-headed person just like you.

"Amy, please, don't cry, you'll just make it more difficult." But it's he who is crying. She feels it in the trembling of his stomach muscles and in his words.

"I can't help it."

He turns to face her again and they stand joined from knee to face, crying. Amy is feeling rather than actually thinking about Timothy becoming withdrawn after Jill died, turning into a collector and hoarder of the past. How the family, after the initial surge of sympathy it received over Jill's death, became the source of ridicule and gossip as a result of the junk Timothy began carting home in the trunk of his car. They were small things at first, licence plates, bits of pottery, and then almost anything he could fit into the trunk – hub caps, wagon wheels, washstands, scrap metal. And then he began to tow home whole vehicles. In the same way Margaret's new ecstasy spilled into the town of Carona – as she seized every opportunity to proselytize in the street or in the hardware store, telling people the good news, that Jill's death had been for Margaret's salvation, and theirs too, if only they had hearts willing to listen – Timothy's junk filled the basement, the garage, and spilled out into the yard.

"Oh, I don't know," Piotr says as they walk hand in hand back towards the car.

While last night in the hotel room in Toronto he was quietly determined and concise, speaking as though he had memorized what he wanted to say, his steely but quiet resolution to leave her is now giving way to sadness – doubt? She squeezes his hand and he returns the squeeze and she feels hope rising.

They wheel in off the highway outside of Thessalon and pull up at the office of the Maranatha Motel and to the sight of adolescent children, exuberant and daring as they skateboard up and down a set of shallow steps in front of the service building. Parents push toddlers on swings in the playground while a black Lab dodges in and out among their legs and then lopes off to fetch a stick someone has thrown into the lake.

Mr. Kruik, the efficient, brisk-mannered motel owner, is behind the counter in the office and hands them the key to the room Amy always requests, the one at the very end of the units, facing the water and a large outcrop of rock. He tells them that the kitchen is still open if they hurry and so they go straight to the dining room without bothering to park and unpack.

They're the only people sitting in the cool, dimly lit interior. Feeling sticky and weary, they're content to lean back into their chairs and passively watch the panorama of the end-of-the-day activities through the wall of tinted windows. Several bare-backed children skip stones, and the black Lab prances and dives where the stones dimple the water's surface. Clouds begin to change from pink to deep oranges and reds, their bottoms heavy and ballooning down to meet the horizon of the North Channel. Amy and Piotr watch as the waitress fills their wine glasses. They lift them in a toast to the end of the day.

Later, their stomachs full, and slightly light-headed from the wine, they decide to walk and regain their equilibrium, hoping to banish the humming sound of tires and the drone of the engine from their ears. They follow a path they know well. It cuts through bush at the side of their motel unit down to the water's edge. They skirt the shoreline, climbing up and over granite slabs jutting out into the water. They emerge at the highway, cross it, and head down towards a modern two-storey building. CRAFTS OF THE NATIONS, its sign proclaims. Passengers begin to stream from a Greyhound charter tour bus in the parking lot. As they enter the store, Piotr goes off to look at the tooled leather belts but stops instead to try on an expensive anorak, which he won't buy, Amy knows, though he insists, nonetheless, that she watch as he tugs it down around his hips and turns slowly in the full-length mirror. The bus passengers begin to enter the store and mill around. Amy overhears the driver talking with one of the store clerks about the barricade at Tobermory, how it has thrown a monkey wrench into the tour. He hasn't told the passengers yet. As people crowd about Amy she hears foreign languages, smells garlic and fish. Hands reach for and examine billfolds covered in various tartans. Sun-catchers – bevelled-glass trinkets in geometric shapes – clank together as people turn them and exclaim over the wildflowers pressed inside.

The tourists haven't yet discovered the second floor where there are more crafts and a gallery of lithographs, and so Amy escapes up there and wanders about the almost empty loft among shelves filled with raw lye soap, beeswax candles, dried weed arrangements. She picks up a round ivory-coloured box from a shelf and admires the look of the quills decorating it in a precise arrangement, a star inside a circle. Interwoven among the quills are strands of sweetgrass. She opens the box and inhales. The whispering sound of denim thighs moving startles her as she realizes that she's not alone. Her eyes meet the eyes of a person standing on the other side of the shelf. She sees long, black, slightly matted hair and recognizes the red plaid jacket of the hitchhiker, the man they had seen on the ferry. He smiles but not at her. It appears to be his natural expression. Bad teeth, she notes, as he laughs aloud and jiggles something in his hand. Then his head dips forward as he tosses whatever it is he has in his hand into his mouth.

"I see you managed to get a ride," Amy says.

He blinked at her. She had startled him. Daydreaming, she supposed, of sitting at the window at the Husky station just outside of Ignace, looking out over the iron-coloured hills and yellow tamarack; such a stark contrast to what he'd seen from the ferry that day, the band of clear water and sky. He blinked and saw her in front of him, realized that she had spoken to him.

"What?" he asked, pulling a wad of cotton from his ear.

"I saw you earlier today. Beside the highway. Been on the road for long?" She speaks to him through a display of English bone-china ballroom dancers.

"A day and a half. Outa Owen Sound. Took a whole day and a half to get this far."

"You from Owen Sound?" More Prairie or Maritime than central Canada, she thinks. He has the look.

He shook his head at her indicating no, and poked the cotton wad back inside his ear. Perhaps, when he was in the iron-coloured hills in Ignace, he craved the sight of water and how the sun changed the light against its surface, breaking it into particles as bright as fire, white fire that he could barely look into, and, perhaps, once he'd seen it, he craved equally to be in Ignace and feel the trees and hills surround him.

Amy waits for him to say more and is disappointed when he doesn't. She wants a clue to this person so that she can begin to rearrange and shape him, mimic his manner of speech – a story for Piotr later on, one of the stories that he loves for her to tell and listens to carefully, laughing at the right places.

"I guess it's not as easy to get rides as it used to be in the Sixties." She realizes with chagrin that he probably wasn't around during that decade.

"What?" Once again he blinks as though startled. She notices how his jaw moves sideways as he chews, rather than up and down.

"People aren't as willing to pick up hitchhikers now."

"I have to get to Ignace by tomorrow." He speaks louder than necessary. His eyes shift suddenly and fix steadily on her face.

"You live there?"

There's movement behind his face, it's as though he's having an argument with himself over what to say next. "Yes," he says finally and then runs his fingers through his matted hair, shaking it into place. His face becomes still and unreadable.

Strange person, Amy thinks, as she backs away from the shelf of figurines. "Well," she says brightly as she turns to leave. "I guess we're lucky we got this far, eh? Seems we got the last ferry going for a while."

"Don't leave your headlights on," he calls down to her as she descends the stairs.

Weird person up there, Amy will tell Piotr.

She imagines him, the hitchhiker: sitting in the Husky restaurant outside of Ignace in his booth across from the cash-register counter, close to the doorway. Perhaps every single day he recognizes someone, but they rarely recognize him. When he hitched up and down the strip of highway that was his, moving once every month between Ignace and Owen Sound, he recognized the licence-plate numbers of the four-by-fours, the pick-ups, the swaying rust buckets of the locals, but mostly the compact Japanese imports like the one she drives, a silver Nissan SX.

It is likely that he had seen her before that day on the road with Piotr. He could have seen her at the Husky station where she and Piotr may have stopped for gas on one of their several trips between Winnipeg and Toronto. Where the hitchhiker waited for his shift to begin and drank coffee and watched travellers pull in off the highway and cross the apron of cement surrounding the restaurant. "Don't forget to turn off your headlights," he'd said as she went down the stairs in the giftshop. And it could have happened. She could have forgotten to turn off the headlights of the silver Nissan and he'd noticed. "You've gone and left your headlights on," he'd said and watched her eyes widen with gratitude.

Amy looks for Piotr and then hears his voice rising above the murmur of many voices. He speaks rapidly, unusually loud and animated, in Polish. She's irritated by this. She hears the same animation, vitality, when he speaks long distance to the woman in Brussels. The story of the weird man upstairs disappears from her mind as she wanders among the giftware, listening for familiar-sounding Polish words that will give her a clue to what they're talking about with so much energy. Walesa, she hears the name. *Tak, tak, tak*, she thinks. Damn. When this happens there is nothing she can do but wait.

Still damp from the shower, Amy wraps a towel around herself and joins Piotr on the couch. He flicks through the television channels in search of news. The faces of native people appear behind a tangle of barbed wire at a barricade, then the knowing smile of Sam the bartender on "Cheers," three seconds of an old movie. He flicks through channels until he finds news of Poland. Then he hunkers down, legs crossed, hand cupping his mouth and chin. Like the day she first met him six years ago at an orientation meeting. They had both been selected for training at the film institute. He was sitting like that, his posture saying he was being defensive. Amy was late, there was only one empty chair, the one beside him, and when she sat down she smelled his strong odour. His eyes were almond-shaped, tiny and dark. Seed-shaped, she thought, Mongolian-looking. When she stood to shake hands, his palm was too moist, his smile enigmatic, and she noticed that they were almost the same height. "I don't want to work with this person," she later told the powers that be. "He can barely speak English, for God's sake. We're supposed to be able to communicate." But she could understand everything he said perfectly. She couldn't explain that his odour and intensity frightened her. The first thing Piotr said to Amy was, "I am very sorry, but I don't like your script." And she replied, "Well, I'm very sorry too, but I can't take very seriously the opinion of someone who can't read the language." Six months later, they were living together.

At the end of the first year, she finally took Piotr to meet Margaret in Carona. Amy walked behind them in the garden at the back of the Grandview Apartments and watched how Piotr thought to offer Margaret his arm as they walked along the path between the strawberries. Amy thought it was strange how Margaret, who had never in her entire life grown a garden, demanded one then. She requested that the developer, who owned a vacant lot behind the apartment, have it ploughed up for the tenants who wanted to grow gardens. Piotr, attentive and soft-spoken, leaned forward to catch Margaret's every word as she poured tea and served sponge cake and strawberries in her tiny apartment.

He was thinking about his own mother, Amy realized, by the way he scanned the room, his expression extraordinarily tender as he took in the stiff crocheted doilies spread across shiny surfaces, the bric-a-brac carefully set down in their centres. He had just learned that his passport would not be renewed and had received an official letter requesting that he return to Poland. He had decided to ignore it. He didn't believe in Gorbachev's new word "perestroika" and he thought then that he'd never be able to return to his country. He rose to examine the photographs on the buffet. "My children's school pictures," Margaret explained as though Amy wasn't one of them. Margaret joined him to point out a young and well-scrubbed Mel; Amy, pug-nosed and buck-toothed. Her voice dropped when she said "Jill," and Amy felt the air in the room quiver.

When Piotr first heard the word "glasnost" he said he didn't trust it. But Amy thought that he both wanted and didn't want to believe in the immunity of the demonstrators they had watched, thousands of people teeming through the streets of Warsaw. Part of him wanted it to be true because he remembered too well the tanks rolling in and martial law thwarting his desire to study filmmaking in the United States. But he also didn't want to believe in the word "glasnost" because it changed things. It interfered, she suspected, with the vision that had driven him: of earning the stature of a major filmmaker and of fame affording him special status, the privilege of being able to move freely between his home country and the free world. Now, supposedly, the whole world is free.

He's lost in the flickering images of people milling about in the market place, complaining that prices are climbing too fast, beyond their means, and so Amy gets up and goes over to the bed that is heaped with their belongings. She clears it off in the event that this is one of those nights when he'll sleep alone with a pillow over his head, body tucked into the fetal position and twitching with nightmares.

"Want a beer?" He nods quickly, indicating his desire for silence so that he won't miss any of the news. She goes into the bathroom and puts on her robe. She fluffs her wet hair. She believes that she looks younger than she is. In any case, she often tells herself, her body is young. The absence of cellulite, stretch marks, is reassuring. She didn't breast-feed Richard and so the skin of her breasts is still fairly elastic and smooth. She dabs gloss on her mouth, plucks two beers cooling on ice in the sink, and steps back into the room. Piotr is gone. She sees him then, through the window, his silhouette against the sky as he stands out on the rock. He's walked out as far as he can to the edge of the outcrop with its sheer fifteen-foot drop into the water. It's dark, she thinks. He might trip over a fissure or a lichen-encrusted node. Don't fall. Don't jump.

Piotr turns, places his hands on his hips, and looks back into the room. The bathroom light shines behind her; he can see her, she knows. His citizenship card, the airline ticket he purchased in Toronto lie on the foot of the bed. Maybe, she thinks, he's brave. The brave arrow in Rilke's *Elegies*, collecting his energy to free himself from this, his first love. Shooting away, not remaining, being brave enough to have "no place to stay." All right then, Go, she thinks, and nudges him with her eyes over the side of the rock.

June 23, 1991, Amy writes the date in her notebook. Piotr is in the shower, face turned up to its tepid stream, eyes closed. She must be careful how to write about this day. She wants to get it straight, to be a knife paring down to the bone of this day so that when she rereads the entry she can trust it to be an accurate recording. They are both marginal people, she has come to realize. He, living in a culture he was not born into, she in one of her own making; Piotr has become her country. She smells him in the mound of clothing on the chair beside the desk. The room is dark except for the light of the lamp spilling across the clean page. She turns the lamp off for a moment, listening to the stream of water in the shower, the sound of a television in the unit next door. As her eyes grow accustomed to the darkness, the outside landscape emerges. A faint wash of light bands the horizon above the water; to the right, headlights press through the darkness on the highway. A car approaches and for several seconds she sees captured in the headlights a person standing beside the road. The hitchhiker? she wonders, and tries not to feel smug about being where she is, in the clean, friendly room, while he, the matted-haired slightly weird person, must face the night in the open, alone. God, she thinks, and turns the light back on, don't do that. She must not forget what it was like to be him, on the road and alone.

Piotr comes out of the bathroom and stands naked beside the bed. "Aren't you tired?"

She looks down at the pen between her fingers and at the blank page. Maybe that's it, she thinks, the attraction of Piotr is like the attraction of a clean page. I thought I could write myself on him.

"Amy."

"I'm coming." Sometimes she imagines a "Made in Canada" stamp on his buttock and, beneath it, a tiny red maple leaf. She wishes she could tattoo her name onto his rear, a message to the women who might come after her that they have Amy to thank for whatever sexual prowess he now possesses. She slides in beside him. His body is cool from the shower, while hers, she knows, is hot. His cock is already stiff and so she grasps it and then rises to her knees beside him and kisses its shaft and then spreads his legs and kisses his moist, mushroomy-smelling testicles. He sucks air between his teeth. "Don't please. I want it to last all night."

She rolls away from him, laughing. He moans and then turns to her, climbs on, and enters. She winds her legs around his waist. "You're up to here," she says. "I can feel you in the back of my throat." He swells inside her, comes quickly, and collapses against her.

"I'm sorry." He kisses her again and again.

She strokes the mole at the nape of his neck. When this happens, when he comes too quickly, she knows that he'll rest. Have what he calls his love nap and then he'll make love to her. He rolls off onto his back and she moves away to a cooler spot in the bed. "No, stay." He draws her into his side. She listens to the thud of his heart in his narrow chest as he falls asleep almost instantly. So much for the love nap. She moves away from him and lies still, hearing the sound of water running in pipes, the murmur of a television from another room, feeling not the least bit sleepy.

She gets up and goes out into the bathroom. Nytol or Scotch? Or will she stay up and write in her notebook? She sees the high rosy flush of desire in her cheeks and when she passes her hand across her pubic mound her swollen nub rises to the touch. As if her need for him was only that. She needs him for all of herself, all her bones and muscles and her heart. She hears the rumble of air in his chest and the small puff of the explosion as it passes through his lips. Wake up, Amy thinks. I have lived longer than you and so I know. This is about as good as you're ever going to get. She widens her eyes, leans towards the mirror, and makes her face go flat, clear, willing the lines to disappear and wanting to see herself as twenty-five, not forty-one, but it's no use. Tonight she is what she is.

They slept together for the last time with their limbs entwined and curled towards each other, foreheads almost touching. While they slept, the hitchhiker walked beneath the northern sky, which blazed with lights that appeared to have been flung randomly across it; the systems of stars and planets of unfathomable numbers and age, their presence a taunt, a reminder of our inconstancy.

But the man didn't look up at the sky as he walked or see the meteor streak across the northern sky. He looked straight down the highway, hands shoved into his jeans pockets to warm them. His ears are sensitive to loud voices, the pitch of the "s" sounds when the radio is set just slightly off the station, to the wind. He may have, as a child, had severe ear infections that went unattended, and there's been some scarring in the tissue. He left Lethbridge, Alberta, where he grew up, because of the wind. But the wind that night was light – intermittent cycles of warm air becoming cool, moist, and the traffic was sporadic at that late hour, mostly tractor rigs. The force they created when they passed by threatened to push him off the shoulder. He wasn't hoping for a ride, though. He preferred to walk at night. Sometimes he'd walk as much as forty miles at a good steady pace.

The hitchhiker is no one, really. He's like many who go unnoticed, who appear to be steady, fixed on a goal, whether that be simply to move between two cities every month or so in a straight line as she thought she had been doing, beginning with the birth of her child and continuing until he was launched into adulthood. Yes, she too was supposedly fixed and steady, like many who don't recognize their own inner aimlessness and are as surprised as the people around them when they explode suddenly one day in a seemingly senseless act. Violence. A random shot by a random man.

This is as much as she cares to surmise about this man's life. Except that she supposes he has spent some of the time on the road thinking about his parents. Perhaps on birthdays or Christmas he had mailed them a card that said "Good luck. Robbie" and a Lotto 649 ticket. But if he'd sent them a picture of himself they wouldn't have recognized the inward-turned person who had gradually quit hiking into town to shoot pool on a Friday night and then eat Chinese food before hitching a ride back out there to his cinder-block room beside the dark highway. Perhaps it didn't make him feel good when he sat at his table in the restaurant watching families and listening to their conversation. It didn't make him feel normal.

A beam of light appeared in the distance and then that single beam of light split into two, headlights of an approaching vehicle. He veered off down into the side of the ditch because it happened at night mostly, when at the last moment the vehicle would swerve in his direction as though the driver deliberately aimed for him. It was an older model car. A GM product. A Pontiac. Green. Alp 985. Friendly Manitoba licence plate. "Pardon me, ma'am," he could have asked her once. "Do you drive a silver Nissan?" Again he was enveloped by the darkness, and while she and Piotr slept, the lights of the sky fell down around him.

Part Two

9

It is almost impossible to erase the memory of a child's face when from the very beginning you are drawn to study it, compelled to memorize the pucker of its milk-flecked mouth, the sweep of delicate eyelashes, the slightly squat nose. As you turn away from it, the face remains in your mind's eye. Even as the child leaves for adulthood, you retain the image of a younger face.

She can recall her son, Richard, perfectly. She can conjure him up as a five-year-old sitting out on a back stoop beneath a clothesline. Dark, thick curls tumble across his forehead. His tongue slides across his bottom lip as he concentrates on his task of stripping leaves from a twig because he wants to turn it into an airplane like the one he stops to watch as it passes low over their house. Look, Richard says, as he pushes the twig across the sky. I made an airplane and it's flying, he says, and, because he thinks so, it is.

Where was she then? Oh, reclining on the chaise lounge probably, wearing her new zebra-striped two-piece bathing suit, watching the garden Hank had planted, grow. Or else she was lying on the lounger on the tiny patch of grass between the house and the garage, swaddled in a blanket, gulping shallow little breaths of air and waiting for the pain that attacked her body from time to time to subside.

Whenever she stops moving long enough to look into her mind for her son, she sees him out there on the stoop behind the house. She can imagine him at age ten, with large square teeth and a longer neck, glancing off to one side, looking puzzled. Or at twenty in a denim jacket and blue jeans, tall like his father. She can see the intelligence in his eyes, the questions he will never ask.

For Margaret, it is different. It is two years since the death of her child, and as she leans into Timothy's side while they drive across open country, she envisions Jill in the cumulus clouds banking above the gravel road, their flat slate-blue bottoms threatening freezing rain or an early snowfall. She sees Jill in the billowing white tops of the clouds, transfigured, the substance of butterfly wings now, or angels, she thinks, silvery, almost translucent. Margaret doesn't wish to recall Jill as flesh and blood, as she was when she danced in the kitchen, her slender, tanned arms swinging wildly at her sides, her wide grin. If she did, she would be engulfed in raging grief. Unlike Timothy, who makes a point of stopping at the cemetery on his trips in and out of Carona, Margaret has only visited Jill's grave once, and that was to inspect the headstone her mother had purchased, a white marble lamb with the inscription "Safe in the arms of Jesus" that Margaret had insisted upon. She finds peace in her image of Jill, a larger-than-life face smiling down at her as they drive along the road.

Timothy and Margaret have been driving for almost an hour in the countryside. The intervals between their safe, flat murmurs grow longer as the minutes pass, and eventually they are lulled into silence by the drift of warm air from the car's heater. Outside, the trees, their limbs stripped clean of their foliage during the night, stand naked in the chilly wind. It happens that quickly, Margaret thinks, a big wind and overnight the landscape changes. The road they travel cuts up through tarnished-looking fields of stubble, past brightly painted red and green barns.

The drone of the car's engine and the unchanging panorama

of the beige late-autumn landscape have a hypnotic effect and Margaret feels as though she is going nowhere, that she has not set out from anywhere and is not about to arrive. She's in between. It's a comfortable state, not having a beginning or an end – like not possessing a body. Let's keep on going, she wants to say to Timothy. She imagines dust collecting on furniture and her two remaining children, Mel and Amy, wandering through rooms and wondering where their parents have gone.

"We're almost there," Timothy says, as though he were soothing an impatient child.

No, please, let's not arrive, Margaret thinks. Let's just aim the car and keep moving. They could sleep in it and quiet their hunger pangs with nips and fries, live like gypsies. She's not certain if it's right for her to want this. Whether the desire is a spiritual or carnal one. Anyway, it's impossible. Tomorrow is Sunday. On Sundays she must get up early and meditate and bathe and dress with exquisite care and hurry off for her tryst with the Lord, her new lover. She will rise up among all the others around her in the Alliance Gospel Church and receive with open arms His sustaining manna and drink from the fountain of His love until her thirst is quenched and her heart swells with joy.

The car skids as Timothy touches the brakes suddenly, jerking Margaret out of the circle of his arm. "Almost missed it." He points to a plastic ribbon tied to a stick. Beyond it, the faint hint of a path curves through tall grass, ending, it appears, in a thicket of trees. The car sways as Timothy eases it down into the shallow gully beside the road and up the other side of it. He grabs his gloves from the dash and pulls them on.

"You want to come?"

She shakes her head no.

"Well, I won't be long. Keep the car running so you don't get cold."

She watches him wade through the grass and then stop to examine a sun-bleached log lying directly across the path into the clump of trees. He rocks it and then stoops to try to lift it, but it appears to be too heavy. He waves, turns, and enters the grove, and his yellow jacket becomes a splash of colour moving among the trees. And then she can no longer see him at all.

"I suppose you're busy," he'd said, referring to the Bible lesson she was studying at the dining-room table. It was her turn to lead the discussion at the weekly prayer cell she attended at the Hardy house. She'd seen the wish in his eyes, the heavy drooping lines at the corners of his mouth, the defeated look of his thin shoulders, his hands, scoured from his scavenging among cast-off rubble, flesh gouged at the knuckles in various stages of healing. "Of course I'll go with you," Margaret had said, closing the lesson book, and immediately Timothy had regretted asking. She doesn't realize that he has grown to despise her constant cheerful acquiescence, how her expression has become self-satisfied, almost smug. Her belief that there's a larger reason for every incident in their lives makes him seethe with a feeling of impotence.

Beads of moisture cloud the car window, but through it, in a field beyond, Margaret sees the sudden flare of a fire in a distant field, a farmer burning off stubble, she realizes. She reaches for the keys in the ignition and the engine shudders and dies. The outside world rushes forward in the sound of wind moving in waves across the couch grass. A barren and miserable sound, Margaret thinks, and feels her eyelids grow heavy. She wraps the car blanket around her shoulders and closes her eyes.

When she awakens a few minutes later, it's to the sound of honking. A flock of Canada geese passing overhead. Only a thin band of daylight encircles the horizon. She gets out of the car, hugging herself against the chill of the wind. Although she can still hear the geese, they're no more than black specks in the distant sky. She calls for Timothy and hears a sharp crack of a branch underfoot as he emerges from the trees instantly, as though he has been standing hidden the whole time, watching and waiting for her to call.

"I want you to back up the car!" he shouts. "Try and get in as close as you can."

The engine sputters once and then catches hold and Margaret shifts into reverse. Grass sweeps against the underside of the car as Margaret backs it carefully in his direction. She hears a clunk and then a grinding sound. A rock, she thinks, and so she decides not to venture any closer. She watches in the mirror as Timothy hurdles the log and sprints towards her with an agility she hadn't thought possible. She rolls down the window as he approaches.

"Good stuff." He presses his chilled mouth against her cheek.

"What's up?"

"Come and have a look."

Margaret walks through the bush behind him, twigs scraping against her body. She dislikes the mouldy smell of rotting bark and dry leaves underfoot. Finally he stops, pushes aside a large branch, and gestures for her to step in front of him into a fairly large clearing. She enters it and immediately sees the car, an old one, similar to the one he's been working on for years.

"Some luck, eh? It was covered with branches and I almost missed it. It's got just about everything I need to finish mine."

"Whose car is it?" She sees a stack of branches lying off to one side of it.

He shrugs and turns away from her. "I heard about it from one of my customers." His voice has become less animated, disappointed, she knows, by her lack of enthusiasm. He walks around the car, re-examining it. "It's even got the name plate."

"But, Tim, it must belong to someone."

Hinges squeal as Timothy pries open a door. The interior is littered with broken beer bottles, dried leaves, and rain-soaked newspapers. "It shouldn't be too hard to tow it out of here. We'll just have to move that log first."

Oh God, no. This is what was behind his unusual request for her to accompany him, she realizes. She leans into a tree and crosses her arms over her chest. She knows what's going to happen. He'll tow it home and push it into place at the back of the yard, where it will collect snow and leaves as it rusts away, and neighbourhood dogs will come and squat and strain beside it, squirrels will prance across its hood to store acorns behind the seats.

Timothy lights a cigarette and sits down on the running board. He exhales, and Margaret's tongue quivers. Unlike others in the church she hasn't been freed of her craving. "The car's been here for ages," he says quietly, head lowered, rubbing a finger against a sore knuckle.

"Come on, Tim. Someone went to the trouble to try and hide it. The car belongs to someone."

The slouch of his shoulders becomes more pronounced. "It's really only good for parts. It's worthless as it is."

"I don't want a stolen car in my yard, Tim."

He sighs, pushes himself up off the car's running board, and flicks his half-smoked cigarette into the bush. He sweeps aside the branch at the entrance to the clearing and as Margaret falls in behind him it springs back and whacks her hard against her thigh. She winces and cries out but Timothy, who is far ahead of her, has begun to whistle and doesn't hear. She catches up to him at the car. The tow chain falls to the ground between them in a heap. "I'll tell you what to do." Her protest dies as he continues to whistle.

Sick at heart and feeling sluggish, Margaret reluctantly starts the engine. Pray, she instructs herself, as Timothy winds the chain through the rear bumper. She sees him in the mirror as he walks back to the log and winds the chain around it. Then he returns. "Okay," he says through the window, "now as soon as you feel the chain pulling, you give it the gas. But take it easy. We'll have to move that log out slowly. Okay?" he says, cheerfully.

She watches as he runs back to the log and yanks at the chain, testing it. Then he whistles, the signal that all is ready. Margaret presses down on the accelerator and feels the car move forward inch by inch as the chain unwinds slowly through the grass. Her foot begins to shake. Jesus, please get me out of this one, Margaret prays. As she reaches the end of the chain's slack the car jerks slightly and holds steady.

"Okay. Remember what I said, slow is the ticket!" Timothy shouts. "Slow and easy!" He bends over the log, ready to swing it off to one side once it begins moving. Slowly, she

176

instructs her shaking foot. A steady, even pressure. She feels the back tires grab and begin to hunker down into the soft earth. The muscles in her calf tighten in a sudden spasm and her foot hits the accelerator sharply. The car leaps forward and then stops dead as though she's run into a cement wall. Her body flies forward with the impact. She feels a stab of pain in her chin as it hits the steering wheel, and then behind her, dully, as though it's happening far away, she hears the sound of glass shattering as the severed chain whiplashes through the back window.

She cups her chin and rocks back and forth. She drops her hand to look at it and is relieved by the absence of blood. She runs her fingers across the tender spot. A bruise, nothing more. She turns, and through the spikes of glass hanging in the back window she sees Timothy down on one knee beside the log. He rises slowly, then walks towards the car, stopping at the shattered rear window, and stoops and peers in at her.

"Maggie? Are you okay?"

"My chin. But I think it's just a bruise."

"What happened? I said to go slow."

Though his face is a blur through the throb of pain in her chin she notices that he's not wearing his glasses. "I'm sorry," she says, "but I thought the car was going to get bogged down." Then it becomes clear to her what has happened. God has answered her prayer.

"The chain snapped." His voice sounds as though he has a full-blown cold.

"I know." The approaching darkness is punctuated by many fires now, flickering in the distant field. "Tim," she says. "Do you think that it's God's way of showing us that we're not supposed to take that car?" Thank you, Jesus, Margaret breathes. She feels the tickle of her new language on the tip of her tongue. *Alla, alla, lingal, mia, mia, alla, alla*. In the name of the Lord I command you to stop hurting, she prays, and the pain in her chin subsides. Then Timothy's face comes into focus. Blood. A trail of blood runs from his nose. She notes, too, that the skin beneath his eyes has turned purple and swollen, and then she sees the strange new angle of his nose. *Alla, alla, mungle, teckle, mia, mia,* her tongue desires to speak. The wind sweeps down the shallow ditch, its movement swimming in the top of the yellow grass. We'll have to put cardboard in the window until we get it fixed, she thinks.

Timothy bangs his fists against the roof of the car. "You stupid bitch!" Timothy shouts. "Margaret, you're an ignorant, sanctimonious bitch!"

That is how Margaret came to be a divorcée. Though not the cause, this was the event that propelled Timothy out of the marriage and into the city and the scandal of Rita's apartment. Then the two of them drove west until they could go no further, to where they still live, on a small hobby farm just outside of Victoria in a stone house filled with washstands, robin's-eye oak bureaus, and bookshelves, which they bought at flea markets and refinished, mantel clocks that chime the hours of their lives, and glass cases, which are mounted on walls, displaying Timothy's pocket watches and Rita's plate and rhinestone jewellery collection. Years later, Timothy mourned the loss of the farm kitchen table, which, when Margaret moved to the Grandview Apartments, fell to Amy and Mel to lug out from behind the furnace in the basement.

Amy sold the table to one of the many "collectibles" stores in her neighbourhood and was amazed to find that the chrome suite, which Mel took, had also become a sought-after item. When she and Mel had flipped the chrome table over to unscrew the legs, she'd seen the wads of dried chewing gum where she used to sit, at her place between Timothy and Margaret. Timothy at one end of the table, Mel at the other, Jill across from Amy, and Margaret beside Amy and close to the stove and counter so that she could jump up quickly to bring more hot food or wipe a spill from the table. "Whatever you think you can make use of just take," Margaret had said to Amy and Mel, because she didn't know how she would fit everything into her scaled-down life. Amy prowled through the house and searched through closets, which still held remnants of Jill in a single bouquet of dried flowers, a chocolate box filled with Get Well and Sympathy cards, one remaining doll. But she was unable to find anything of herself, not even a scrap of paper with her large uneven scrawl, for her to puzzle over and ask, Is this me? She had been there, though, it was apparent in the greyish hard spots of chewing gum stuck beneath the chrome table and in the films Timothy had made with his camera. "Just these," she'd said. "I want these." She'd left the broken projector behind on a shelf and filled its box with the reels of eight-millimetre films. She took the box of films home and put it in a trunk in an upstairs closet along with all her journals.

Mel and Amy became "products of a broken home," which, though growing more common in the 1960s, was still an anomaly in a town as small as Carona. They were objects of pity and scorn as though, like Alf's son, Harry, they were defective and deserved bad luck. Mel excelled at capitalizing on the pity end of the spectrum, and because the size of Timothy's monthly cheque to Margaret did not take into account Mel's ambition for further education, Mr. Waller, the grocer, was moved to take "the lad" under his wing. He offered Mel steady employment in his final year of school and later through his four years of university, lending him money to buy a car so that he could drive back and forth to the University of Manitoba, from which he would graduate with a degree in economics. Mel was a well-liked student, though he was not ever at the centre of things. He had to rush back to Carona at the end of each day, to put in two hours at Waller's and then four more at his desk studying. Mel proved to be even, predictable. He would achieve notoriety in his final year with the surprise win of the silver medal and by his equally surprising boast, made once when he was inebriated, that he was an expert on female genitalia and could determine the ethnic origin of a woman by the shape and colour of her labia.

Amy drew the short straw when it came to being pitied, because after Timothy left, she took to cussing in earnest. "That little Barber kid went and caught a bug of some sort," people remarked. "What a shame. She's come down with diarrhoea of the mouth." And she became bossy, too, to the point of being belligerent in the playground, feverishly writing down playscripts and handing them out at recess to make her classmates say and do exactly what she wanted them to say and do. And if they tried to be original and change their lines (as Mindy North once did, and instead of being the queen decreeing, as the script indicated, that the prisoner standing before her be sent to the dungeon to be tortured, decreed instead, "Off with his head!"), they were excluded from the next play, and found their bicycle tires flattened. She didn't want to hear their taunts of her "old man" having "buggered off," "flown the coop," gossip the children had overheard around their dinner tables. "My dad's on a buying trip," Amy had told them to explain his absence. "He's taking on a new line," she'd said without recognizing the irony in the explanation. She threatened her schoolmates into silence with her swearing and directed them through her playscripts away from the topic. "Manipulative," the teacher complained to Margaret on Parents' Day. Margaret was worried, and so she began to take the problem of Amy to her weekly prayer cell.

For some reason Mel was exempt from Margaret's attempts at proselytizing; all her efforts were forcused on Amy. But Amy realized fairly quickly that even if she were to take on Margaret's faith, become born again and baptized in the spirit, even if she prayed with the tongues of angels, possessed the miraculous gifts of healing, prophesied and dreamed visions, it would not be enough. She would still be found wanting in some way. She was flawed simply because she was alive.

When Amy was thirteen she put a black rinse in her hair and twisted strands of it into spit curls and pasted them into place with Dippety-do gel on her forehead and either side of her face because she thought it made her look Spanish. At night she lay in the top bunk bed aware of the silence in the bed beneath her, sometimes imagining she could feel the nudge of a foot against the mattress. The unchanging porcelain and plastic faces of Jill's dolls on the shelf across the room seemed deliberately cool and impassive as they watched with sightless glass eyes Amy propping a notebook against her knees and writing long letters to Timothy, telling him that she felt anxious, as though the heart in her chest had grown faster than her body and she had too much power. She told him that Margaret was still a "holy roller" – his expression for the people at the "Alliance Gospel Circus."

Margaret still thanked Jesus for taking Jill away from her and was willing to embrace any catastrophe that might serve to bring the rest of her family into the Kingdom of God. Margaret wrote in her Blue Book that she would give up anything, even her own life, for that to happen. Amy might have been frightened when she read those words, wondering what terrible lesson Margaret or Timothy had yet to learn that might tempt God to reach down and pluck her up next to become a gem in his kingly crown. But she wasn't. Amy reasoned that because she'd been struck by lightning and survived, she was immune to killer diseases, accidents, the force of gravity. She suspected that she might be immortal.

Timothy had been gone for over two years and still she wrote to him, letters that she sometimes mailed, but usually not. She had grown disappointed in his replies. She had looked in them for the father who had bought her the cape, but his letters were too carefully written, as though writing her was an assignment that he strove to do well. "You must come and visit us sometime," he once wrote. She hadn't the courage to ask, Sure, when? Then his unsatisfying letters dwindled to greeting cards sent on the occasion of holidays and special days such as Valentine's or St. Patrick's, and which, Amy suspected, had been chosen by Aunt Rita.

Margaret allowed Amy to make one telephone call a month and it was the same thing, the same stiffness in his voice as in his letters. There were long silences between their sentences when Amy wanted to but could not ask, "When can I come and live with you?" And so she stopped calling him as well. She began to write Timothy's replies to her letters. "I want you to come and live with us soon," Amy wrote Timothy saying. "You should be with your mother right now. But once you're older, then I want you to come." She invented his life with Aunt Rita, and an Irish setter named Pal. On Saturday afternoons they'd play bingo at the legion hall while Pal waited for them outside. But they didn't play for money. They played for things, and Timothy had won an ironing board and a kitchen clock that was shaped like a Dutch windmill and which he was going to send to Amy because it wasn't an antique. She looked up Victoria, British Columbia, on the map at school and took them out of the legion hall and put them instead on a sandy beach with the sound of surf crashing as they looked out over the Strait of Juan de Fuca, Aunt Rita throwing a piece of driftwood into the water and Pal bounding after it, eager to please. She had Timothy explain how, from the beginning, he really had been attracted to Rita more than to Margaret but didn't want to hurt Margaret's feelings.

Amy tried to write a story about the time when Timothy had taken her to visit Santa Claus at Eaton's and the line-up of children and parents to Santa's throne was too long. She had grown impatient and so, rather than wait to see him, she'd pulled Timothy over to see the electric trains. She wrote about what she saw: trains winding through tunnels past gumdrop signal lights, train-station roofs encrusted with frosting and embedded with jewel-like candy, candy cane lampposts, trains crossing bridges over orange soda-pop rivers. She stopped writing when she remembered that Timothy had let go of her hand and she'd been frightened that he'd abandoned her. Dad! she'd cried out, then saw how the faces of several people around her had gone soft with pity, and so she'd swallowed her panic and set off angrily to find her father, who was only an aisle away, his back to her, engaged in conversation with a store clerk. *Dad!* she had yelled, and when he turned she punched him in the stomach.

Dad! Amy sometimes cried silently and punched her pillow, but it wasn't the same thing. One Saturday before Father's Day, resentful over the absence of mail at the post office, Amy went into Black's Dry Goods and marched to the men's section at the back of the store. On a table was a display of gift suggestions, ties encased behind plastic in narrow boxes, plaid shirts, handkerchiefs, fishing lures. Her compulsion to pick up the items and one by one throw them across the room began to recede. A fishing lure, she thought. Yes. Perfect. She chose the largest one, a silver spoon with red glass beads for eyes. She bought it and mailed it away to Timothy in Victoria.

At age fourteen, Amy refused to get out of bed one Sunday morning and told Margaret that she no longer wanted to go to the "Alliance Gospel Circus." Mel didn't have to go, she reasoned, and, besides, it had become a boring affair; they repeated the same stories over and over, did the same tricks. Margaret, who had become somewhat of a spiritual force in the congregation, perceived Amy's rebellion to be an attack by the evil one and she rose to the challenge.

When Amy is sixteen, and Shirley Cutting walks into her life, Margaret puts in a request to her prayer cell for "prayer warriors" to come to her aid, those who will fight on their knees daily for Amy. And Amy becomes a redhead like Shirley and Shirley becomes her best friend.

Amy meets Shirley for the first time in Ken's Chinese Food when Shirley walks in one day with a self-possessed air, as though she'd been coming to Ken's all her life. Her thick red hair is pulled back into a ponytail, drawing her features taut, accentuating their sharpness. A fox, Amy thinks, when she first sees Shirley. "Foxy" is what Cam and Gord will nickname Shirley later on, the name muttered under their breath, for their ears only. Shirley sits on a stool at the counter, looking unconcerned as she puffs furiously at a rollie and blows the smoke towards the ceiling. She turns and looks at Amy, Cam, and Gord where they sit in the back booth, and her eyes become slits as she studies them coolly and with a great deal of contempt. When Amy goes over to the jukebox, Shirley speaks. "Play fifty-six." Curious, Amy punches the number and the song turns out to be an old one, Sarah Vaughan singing in a clear, bittersweet voice, "I'll Be Seeing You." Shirley hums along like a slightly drunk, love-lost woman in an old black-and-white movie, sitting at a bar nursing a drink. Fade to black.

That was Shirley. She was seventeen.

Amy sits down beside the young woman and begins talking past her to the waitress, well aware that Shirley is listening in, and Amy is not surprised as Shirley's mask of contempt begins to slip and that she almost smiles. As the song ends and the waitress is called away to another customer, Shirley turns to Amy. "You come across as being a snob, but you aren't. What a relief. This is such a tight-assed town." Amy had won Shirley over, she knew, because she had peppered her conversation with swear words. She invites Shirley to join them in the back booth, the one they have come to think of as being exclusively theirs. Cam, Gord, Amy. Over the years they've been hanging out at Ken's there have been others invited to join them in the back booth, those who were in the transient stages of rebellion. But it's Amy, Gord, and Cam who have proven to be the hard-core oddballs. When they were younger they were explosive and loud, sometimes laughing for no reason other than that someone had belched. Ken, the good-natured proprietor, doesn't object to their presence as long as they buy a reasonable amount of food. Each year he paints over the graffiti and names they have carved into the plywood booth. Now that they're older they've grown quieter, tense, a rather pitiful-looking group sitting there wearing silly little masks of bravado. At sixteen and seventeen, they are edgy about where they might be heading. Shirley is a welcome diversion.

"You guys want to help me do the shopping?" Shirley asks.

Shirley's question is a challenge, and because her green eyes promise an adventure, Amy, who has become a lazy, mediocre student, is all too willing to skip school and accompany Shirley on her hitchhiking jogs into the city, and to try her hand at shoplifting. She reasons that she's simply helping Shirley out with "her problem" – the problem being Shirley's father dying too young of a heart attack and her mother remarrying. Her new husband is foreman of the Hydro crew, recently arrived to rewire the town of Carona, and there is another child. Shirley's presence is barely tolerated by the new husband. When he comes home from work Shirley leaves the house. She calls from the cafe before returning, to check if the coast is clear. Her stepfather does an inventory of the refrigerator before he leaves for work in the morning and again when he returns, to determine if she's eaten anything that belongs to him. Amy figures she is helping out, because at first all they steal is food and cigarettes.

It takes them only two rides to reach the city. Then they get on a transit bus and head towards Shirley's old neighbourhood in the north end. Amy sits next to the window, watching people strolling along Memorial Boulevard. Several young men and women, hippies, she believes, are long-haired and wild-looking in their frayed jeans and floppy hats. She imagines herself walking among them, wearing white cotton, sandals, wooden beads maybe, her hair long and straight to her tail bone. As Amy watches the "flower children," she thinks that while she's the one on the bus and moving, it seems as though she's the one standing still.

When they get off the bus, the long face of Stanley Knowles stares out at them from an election poster taped to the window of Pete's Grocery and Meats, the store Shirley remembers going to with her real father on Friday nights, treat night, to spend her allowance. The politician's face is a solemn one, Amy thinks, as she enters the store behind Shirley. The man, she will learn, though unpopular and feared in the municipality of Carona, is this neighbourhood's totem.

"Pete!" Shirley shrieks as she enters the store. She opens her arms to receive an embrace. A tall, muscular man grabs her in a hug.

"Doll! How you been?"

"I told you, this guy is a mark," Shirley says later, and winks. "While we talk you get me tuna, solid white. It's the only kind I can hack."

The houses in the neighbourhood where Shirley lived in happier days with her mother and real father are identical wartime prefab single-storey houses built on cement slabs and constructed on lots so narrow that their eaves troughs meet over the strip of walkway running between them.

185

There's a stingy look about the neighbourhood in the way most of the yards are enclosed behind chainlink fences. Amy feels she is intruding as she stands with Shirley in front of the house where Shirley used to live. Amy doesn't know that in not much more than a year she'll leave Carona and wind up in this neighbourhood, in one of these very houses. That several years later she will bring home a bundled up spring baby, and in summer watch, amazed, as he zooms around the front yard on all fours, stopping now and then to taste a bug. That in autumn the child will pull himself up at the chainlink fence, suck at the wires, and screech with delight at the sight of a garbage truck lumbering by. Or that in her memory she will always frame her child, Richard, as being five years old and out behind the house sitting on the clothesline stoop, making an airplane, the summer she almost killed him.

Amy comes home late one night in December, and Mel, diligent in his final year at university, is still up, at the kitchen table studying, as usual. But he is also waiting for her, she realizes, as he stretches and pushes his books aside.

"Look," he says and begins to scratch at his chin exactly as Timothy would do when he was forming what to say. "You're going to make a mess of your life. Why not play it smart for a change? Why not put the necessary time into the books and then you can get out of here. Because the time's going to pass by anyway, and you do have the brains to accomplish something if you want to, you know."

For a moment Amy is struck dumb by this rare display of brotherly concern. Mel goes on to tell her what their cousin Garth discovered while riffling through the secretary's files at school: the results of a recent test which show that Amy's intelligence quotient is among the highest of all the students. As Mel talks, it dawns on Amy why the teachers have suddenly begun to take an interest in her. It explains the reason for their requests that she remain after class so they can have a friendly but concerned chat. They use hackneyed phrases

186

such as: Nose to the grindstone, Apply yourself, Pull up your socks.

"Were you ever tested?" she asks.

"Yes."

"Know your score?" She notices the blood rush to the tips of his ears.

"Average." His candid expression disappears as he reaches for a textbook and begins flipping through it. "But I'll get there."

The old tortoise-and-hare crap, she thinks. She laughs and tosses a package of Black Cats across the table. "They're on me."

"Hey, thanks," he says, genuinely pleased.

Steady, plodding, dull, Amy thinks. And poor. Mel only smokes when he can get o.p.'s. "Shirl and I are going Christmas shopping tomorrow. You got a wish list?"

He grins and then attempts to look serious. "That's another thing," he says. "You're going to wind up in reform school if you're not careful."

She laughs to cover what she's feeling as she leaves the room: dread. Not of being caught and being shipped off to a reform school, forever wearing the badge "juvenile delinquent," but because it's true that Mel is going to get where he wants to go, while she doesn't even know what she wants. When she looks around at the people of Carona, there isn't a single one among them that she'd like to be, and this confirms her growing suspicion that being struck by lightning may have made her unsuitable for a life of normalcy.

She undresses in the dark and boosts herself up onto her bed. She falls asleep instantly and dreams of flying. She dreams she is borne upwards, up above the street and far away she flies, now, outside of town, above other towns, and above the giant sleeping city to the east.

The following morning she dresses for her date with Shirley in baggy too-large pants, an oversized shirt. She puts several bangles on her wrist and at least two rings on each hand. She will not wind up in a reform school. She will not get caught. No sweat, she tells herself, as she stands in front of the mirror

187

brushing her henna-red hair until it crackles with static and puffs out around her tiny white face. Witchy, she thinks, and likes it. She ties her hair back with a black velvet ribbon, like an r.b. She studies her profile. Snobbish-looking, perfect, she thinks. I look like a rich bitch from Balmoral Hall.

Frost crystals hang in the air, and the snow-packed road crunches loudly beneath her feet as she walks to the other side of town to meet Shirley. It's a hollow sound, as though during the cold night the earth's core has shrunk, and walking now across its fragile mantle, a thin crust of frozen earth, makes Amy feel a bit off balance, wondering if she's wrong to think it will support her weight.

Shirley has taken Amy from piking cans of tuna and cigarettes from Pete's to the Metropolitan Store downtown where she has learned to tie several scarves onto her head, slip rings onto her fingers, bracelets onto her arms, and stroll away, selling them later to the kids in Carona. Recently, they have graduated and begun to "shop" at Simpsons. For Amy, these trips into the city to shoplift are like touching an electrically charged wire on a dare and then spitting on her finger and touching the wire again for an even stronger jolt. She likes to see how long she can stand the buzzing of electricity in her body. That day, as they enter Simpsons, Amy imagines that she has become a well-oiled machine, precise and with no nerves at all.

They join the flow of people moving down the centre aisle of the store, beneath the sparkling revolving snowflakes suspended from the ceiling. They walk among the sounds of paper rustling, the whirr of cash registers, and the murmur of many voices. Gold and silver garlands wound around pillars glitter harshly, and poinsettias appear like red clots on the wall in front of her. She sees the whole floor at once and yet every detail of it too. She misses nothing. She sees her mind as a camera clicking and storing information. They're on the first floor, near the south exit, she notes, and near the car park. Sporting Goods is to the left, Toys to the right, where a baby howls in disappointment as its mother pries a package from its fingers. Paint and Wallpaper directly across from Toys.

They step out of the traffic moving down the centre aisle and stop to look at a display of skis. Amy notes three clerks, two at the sports counter and one speaking to a customer. She's searching for security personnel. She and Shirley cross the aisle and stand in front of a counter of model airplane kits. Shirley takes one from the shelf while Amy scans the toy section for security personnel, and spots one, a middle-aged woman in Paint and Wallpaper. What she is doing, Amy sees, is pretending to tidy up shelves, while really watching two kids huddled together on the other side of the model airplanes. Amy knows where that security person will be for the next little while. Shirley sets the model kit back onto the shelf and they move into the main artery once again. Amy follows her as they pass by Optical and the row of green vinyl chairs where people wait to have their eyes tested.

They enter the jewellery department. Shirley stops at a carousel of gold chains and begins to rotate it slowly, as though deep in thought, and then appears crestfallen, as if she can't find what she wants. There are only two clerks in Jewellery. One leans against the counter with her back to them, chatting, while the other tidies up around the cash register. That means two counters of jewellery unattended, Amy realizes. Another display rotates slowly, Shirley searching for what she wants, but Amy knows that she already has several gold chains hidden inside her coat sleeve.

Just then a woman steps up beside Shirley. At her side is a little girl, mitts dangling from both sleeves on idiot strings. The girl twitches with impatience as her mother stops to browse. "Gosh, they cost the earth, don't they?" the woman exclaims, and Amy detects a British accent. It's not Security, but Shirley moves away, not taking any chances. Chicken, Amy thinks, and steps into her place.

"I'd like to have a look at the rings, please," she says loudly, impatiently, as though she's been standing and waiting for some time now for the clerks to be finished with their little visit. They both turn, surprised and then a bit annoyed. The woman with the child moves up beside Amy to look, too, as she examines the tray of rings the clerk has set down. She hovers at Amy's shoulder as Amy slips onto her finger a pearl ring surrounded by a cluster of emerald chips. "It's for my mother," Amy says. "For Christmas."

"Quite nice," the woman comments as Amy holds up her hand to better admire the ring. The child at her side sighs deeply and begins yanking at her mother's coat.

"Not bad. But she has a large hand. I don't think this will suit her." Without removing the pearl ring, she selects another, a plain band with a single clear stone. Too much like a wedding ring, she thinks, and puts it back into the velvet tray.

"I beg your pardon?" Shirley calls for attention from the other jewellery counter and draws the remaining clerk away. Amy picks out a third ring, a large moonstone surrounded by tiny red stones. She slips it onto her middle finger and spreads her fingers, on each one a ring, two that are her own. "I just don't know," she says. "What do you think?" she asks the woman.

"Your mother must have a November birthday, then," she says. Their attention is arrested suddenly by the sound of a carousel display crashing down against the glass counter. The clerk turns from the tray of rings, watching as Shirley, profusely apologetic, assists the other clerk in righting it. Too much make-up, Amy thinks suddenly. Exaggerated. Shirley has plastered on too much eye-shadow and mascara. But this works to Amy's advantage, because the clerk handling the tray of rings becomes suspicious and her attention is diverted.

With the moonstone ring still on, its stone now twisted to the palm side of her finger, Amy removes the pearl ring and wedges it carefully back into the velvet display case. "It's okay, thanks a lot," she says to the distracted clerk. The bulge of the stone is cool against her skin. A seventy-five-dollar ring. A gift for Margaret for Christmas, if she can think of a way to explain how she came to afford it. The clerk smiles in answer, still preoccupied by the fuss at the counter where Shirley and the other clerk gather up the spilled cards of earrings and pins. Amy wants to grin and hold the ring up for Shirley to see. Check this out, eh? Got you beat this time. But her exhilaration vanishes with a sudden chill of fear. She's being watched, she senses it. She looks down and into the face of the young girl at the woman's side. The girl stares at the moonstone's silver band. Amy's stomach lurches. Even while she knows it's not possible, it is the face of Jill she's looking into. The child's mother crosses the aisle, calling for the child to follow, and the girl walks backwards, mitts dangling like another pair of hands at her side. She grins up at Amy, her expression knowing, and at the same time her dark eyes are filled with scorn. Then she turns away and, with a little skip, catches up to her mother. Amy watches brown braids shift against the child's red coat until the girl and her mother are swallowed up in the jittery kaleidoscope of Christmas.

"Have you decided if you want the moonstone?" The clerk's voice intrudes bluntly.

Amy swears under her breath. She twists it from her finger and drops it onto the counter. "I don't want it. It's overpriced garbage."

The clerk's mouth drops open. "Well, I am sorry," she snaps. "I don't price it. I just sell it."

Amy hears Shirley call her name, looks up, and sees that she's on the escalator, going to the second floor. Behind her, and staring straight at the back of her head, is Security, a man wearing glasses and brown cords. Come on, Shirley beckons, and then looks puzzled as Amy turns away and walks towards the north exit of the store.

It had begun to snow while they were in the store, light dry crystals, but now as Amy walks along Portage Avenue, heading downtown to the bus depot where she'll wait for Shirley, the snow grows heavier, like huge wet pieces of tissue, and melts in her hair, making it stringy and limp. Her white bucks grow sodden from the stinging cold and her toes stiff, as though welded together. The sky turns mauve and begins to brighten the closer she gets to downtown, the avenue becoming festive then with the coloured lights of Christmas entwined in wreaths of spruce boughs mounted along the centre boulevard. When she reaches the Hudson's Bay store, she stops for a moment. Recorded carol music floats out across a manger scene above the main entrance. The window display is a living room on Christmas morning. A tall blond man is standing in a plaid bathrobe off to one side, one hand in his pocket, the other casually holding a pipe. Two mannequin children crouch at the Christmas tree looking at the gifts. Their beautiful, well-groomed mother smiles and watches from where she sits in a Queen Anne chair, an unopened gift on her lap. Wet snowflakes tumble down from the top of the department store, down through the music, children's voices singing "White Christmas."

The warm and happy family Christmas display fades and in its place Amy sees her reflection in the plate glass, hands plunged into jacket pockets, thin shoulders hunched up to her ears. Reflected above her head in the window is the sign on a building directly across the street: ROYAL BANK. She walks to the intersection and waits for the light to change. Tinny-sounding, she thinks of the carol music pushing through the traffic sounds.

When Amy returns moments later and enters the Hudson's Bay store, her pocket heavy with five dollars' worth of quarters, she thinks, What do I want for Christmas? Anticipating Timothy's question. Her fingers begin to thaw and tingle in the warm air as she feeds quarters into the pay phone. I want to get on a bus. Visit you for Christmas. She frames what she will say. Her breathing becomes fast, suddenly, with the quickening of her heartbeat. She listens as the first ring cuts through the crackling of static. I want to live with you. He has been waiting for her to make the first move. Perhaps he's been hurt or puzzled over why she stopped writing and calling, thinking that she doesn't care or is too happily occupied in her own life. On the third ring he answers and her mouth freezes. She thinks her heart will stop.

"Hello?" He asks once again when she doesn't speak. "Margaret? Margaret, is that you?" He pauses and Amy hears what might be a heavy sigh. "You know you really should give it up, Margaret. This must be costing you a fortune," Timothy says, his voice suddenly hard. He hangs up.

When she steps outside the air seems colder, and once again

she feels the bite of dampness. She stamps her feet, waiting for the green light. She's stunned by the revelation that Margaret calls Timothy. That her mother stands in the hall at the telephone listening to his voice and not speaking.

She waits on a bench in the bus depot, watching the clock and the patrons in the Salisbury Coffee Shop as they come and go. Pain shoots through her toes as they begin to warm up. The skinny ticket agent behind the Grey Goose wicket has been glancing at her off and on and she knows she looks bad, like a runaway, a drowned and decrepit rat. She smiles at him from time to time to try to convince him otherwise. For half an hour a young man in a U.S. Air Force uniform recounts the story of his life and what it's like to live in the city of New York. When his bus leaves, an old man takes his place on the bench beside her. He sets several bulging bags onto the floor at his feet and begins telling Amy how lucky she is to be living in this time and country. His tongue is thick and slow with an accent. He's fifteen minutes into his speech when Shirley, flushed with excitement, enters through the arrivals and departures gate. They go up to the washroom so she can show Amy the sweater, cosmetics, and jewellery she has stolen. "So, what's with you?" she stops to ask. Amy shrugs and says nothing. Shoplifting has become boring, that's all. Not her scene any more.

Margaret Barber looks at the clock and wonders why Amy isn't home from school yet and whether she has gone downtown again. Whether she will even show up for supper. She dusts flour across the kitchen-table top and begins rolling flat a chunk of cookie dough. She works from the inside out, applying an even pressure to the rolling pin so that the dough doesn't crinkle or crack. When she's satisfied with the result, an almost perfectly shaped circle, she begins to hum to the music playing on the radio as she dips a Christmas tree cookie-cutter into flour and presses it into the circle of dough. "For unto us a child is born," the choir sings on the radio. It's the Mormon Tabernacle Choir, but still it's quite beautiful, Margaret thinks. "And the government shall be upon His shoulder," the choir sings. It doesn't matter to Margaret that she's not going to eat the cookies. Or that, because Mel and Amy are going to parties, she will pass Christmas Eve taking communion at the Alliance Gospel Church, and then the remainder of the evening alone, and that the following day, while Mel and Amy sleep off their party hangovers, she will walk down to her parents' for a pinched, silent Christmas meal. The cookies are for others. For the Christmas boxes she and the other women at the Alliance Gospel Church will pack and deliver to the less fortunate. Secretly, when it's dark outside, she'll set the boxes down on the back steps or just inside a porch door; the recipient need never know the hand of the giver. " 'For unto us a child is born, unto us, a son is given. . . . And his name shall be called. . . .' " Margaret sings along with the choir. " 'Councillor! . . . The Everlasting Father! Prince of Peace!' " She sings loudly, feeling joyous, trembling with the beauty of the music and with the vision she has of the Prince of Peace standing white-robed and barefoot on a rim of clouds, eyes filled with the terrible white fire of his love, and at his side is Jill. Then suddenly she thinks of Amy and the picture falls apart, her joy vanishing. There's a reason why she has just thought of Amy. She wipes her hands on her apron and goes out into the hallway and calls Mrs. Hardy.

"Edith? I'm worried about Amy. I'm not certain why, I just am." She listens to Mrs. Hardy's response with a slight bit of annoyance and she has an unloving thought. It is easy to say to trust in the Lord with all your heart and not to worry when you haven't had a child of your own to worry over, when you have your man at your side. "Do you think we could take a minute and pray for Amy?" she asks.

The woman agrees and begins to pray, and Margaret closes her eyes and presses her forehead against the wall beside the telephone. "Oh yes, Jesus," Margaret sighs. "Oh yes, oh yes, oh yes," she breathes while the woman prays, believing, trusting with every single cell of her body that there is still time and God will yet save Amy.

10

And then, when I was seventeen, I made a date with a rapist. His name was Dave. He was a six-feet-six, size-fifteen-boots man endowed, I discovered, with an enormous mouth and a rather small prick.

Dave was part of a rotating Hydro crew, a group of thirty or so men who lived in a trailer camp just beyond the agricultural grounds. They had arrived all at once to rewire the town of Carona and they made every night jump like a Saturday night. The rumour was the men from Hydro had been given strict instructions not to form relationships with the local girls, in other words not to risk dipping their wicks, but they did so anyway, and this was why the crew was changed every few months for the year and a half it took to get the job done. I met Dave when he stopped by Sullie's Drive In and Take Out where I worked for part of that 1967 spring and summer.

Sullivan, a stocky, balding man, a World War Two vet, and the proprietor of Sullie's, wanted to take his family on a vacation for the summer, he'd explained, and I was surprised and secretly pleased that he had sought me out. I was to have complete charge of his food establishment, located just outside of town, working full time for the whole summer and supervising a part-time evening staff, which was made up of students, some of whom were older than I was.

195

Shirley hinted that she'd be more than willing to hang out at Sullie's and give me a hand. But I didn't want Shirley Cutting around for many reasons, one of which was that I had begun to notice that she had an off-putting body odour, like mouldy apples, and that the little black flats she wore were always scuffed and chewed down at the heels and that the patches of skin at the back of her ankles were mottled with dirt. I was also concerned that the hand she'd offered to give me would likely end up in the cash box, and I couldn't watch her and everything else at the same time. But Shirley did come by anyway, off and on, walking the mile and a half and pushing the stroller with Cheryl, her anaemic-looking stepsister, inside it. The first time, she came around through the back door carrying Cheryl in her arms, and I said I was sorry but the work space was too cramped and dangerous for a young child, what with the hot fat and grill. After that, Shirley would only stay long enough for Cheryl to eat an ice-cream cone while she leaned against the outside counter, smoking a cigarette and speaking to me through the order window. But in June, once summer really set in and we became busy, I couldn't do any more than wave and say hi in passing, and Shirley got the message. She stopped coming all together and would wait down at Ken's Chinese Food for my shift to end.

I had surprised myself, and no doubt Margaret too, with my enthusiasm and energy as I set off after school on the bicycle Mel had long ago abandoned, down the highway each afternoon to get to Sullie's place around four o'clock to prepare to be open by six. I liked anticipating the evening's trade and estimating what we would require to see us through the night without being caught short or left with too much thawed and seasoned meat.

I liked the people who came, too, especially the little kids. I got a kick out of how they had to stretch up onto their toes to reach the order window, and the way they lisped their requests. I adored these children, their shyness, and how they stared at me with obvious admiration. It was my new look, I reasoned. I was different. I hadn't opted for the current fad and become the Big Bopper's girl in "Chantilly Lace." I didn't wear my hair in a ponytail like most. The novelty of my friend Shirley had worn off, and I was no longer a redhead but a blonde, my hair cropped short, hugging my skull. I tugged feathery tufts of the stiff bleached hair down onto my forehead. I wore matte, almost-white pancake make-up, which covered any identifying moles or marks so that my face was blank and I could draw onto it the features I wanted. I pencilled around my eyes in a way to make them appear larger, and I drew a small bright orange-red mouth. While their parents probably regarded me with a raised eyebrow behind my back, these kids, I could tell, thought I was terrific.

Dave had dropped by Sullie's early in the season shortly after his arrival in town and had become a regular, always ordering a double cheeseburger, loaded, and a chocolate milkshake. Because his purple Ford had Hollywood mufflers I could hear it a mile away as it headed towards Sullie's at least three or four times a week, and I'd have the patties on the grill before he pulled into the parking lot: two acres of gravel surrounding the drive-in booth. I'd begun to add an extra scoop of ice cream to Dave's milkshake because the man was a giant, and because even though he was stunningly good-looking he didn't appear to know it, which is more or less why I let my guard down one night and agreed to get into his car. Of all the men in the Hydro crew, Dave seemed to have some class. I never saw him with an open beer between his legs or laying on the horn at a girl and leering, or shoving his head through the order window and saying, "I've got the wiener and you've got the bun, honey, let's hot dog."

One night near the middle of June, the heat made everything sticky, and even though the exhaust fan above the grill roared at top speed my shirt was pasted to my back. Outside, the sky ballooned ominously, heavy purple clouds threatening a downpour, and so I let Patsy, one of the part-timers, take off early. Except for Dave's car the parking lot was empty, and with only half an hour to closing I shut the deep-fryer down and began cleaning up. Patsy hadn't been gone more than ten minutes when raindrops like heavy stones began pelting against the side of the booth. I peered out through the window

197

at the solid sheet of rain slashing across the parking lot and decided I would have to wait this one out. The headlights of Dave's car pressed through the rain towards the booth, to circle around the back of it and head out the other way to the highway, I thought, but the car stopped behind the booth. I rolled the day's cash receipts into cheesecloth and then into a paper bag as I heard the car door slam, footsteps, and then Dave's fist banging against the booth. I put the paper bag into the freezer and went to the door. Dave was so tall I had to step back in order to see all of him at once.

"You can't bicycle home in this. Want a lift?" he asked. Rain streamed down his hair and across his face.

"Okay, thanks." But not home, I said. He could drop me off at Ken's where Shirley waited.

I sat inside Dave's car listening to Marty Robbins singing about a white sports coat while Dave crammed Mel's bicycle into the trunk. Then he slid in beside me, the shoulders of his denim shirt soaked, and rain dripped off the end of his perfectly shaped nose. The cleft in his chin deepened as he grinned. He was what was known as "rugged," I guess, but twinkly-eyed too, like a young Robert Taylor. He hugged the steering wheel for a moment, staring through the sheet of rain, which, on the car's roof, sounded like applause as Marty Robbins finished his song. Then he turned and looked at me, pulling a face, his mouth twisted and one eyebrow shooting up, a wicked cartoon villain. "Nee-ah, ha, ha. Nice night for a murder!" he said.

"Yeah, sure," I said as we drove away, and I was relieved, then felt a bit stupid for having felt worried, when he pulled up at the curb on Main Street outside Ken's.

I felt awkward having this giant dogging my heels as we entered the cafe. Several other men from the Hydro crew sat together in a centre booth and I felt their eyes follow us as we went to the back of the cafe where Cam, Gord, and Shirley waited. "Meet Dave," I said.

"Yeah, we know Dave," Cam said, without looking up. Gord, too, was acting a bit strange in the way he seemed to be preoccupied, fiddling with a pack of cigarettes. Just then, the waitress, an older married woman from another town, came over to the booth and began clearing away their dishes, and I felt the air between her and Dave become charged with tension. "Howdy," Dave said, but the woman turned her back on him and loaded her tray swiftly. Then she hesitated, took a swipe at the table with a damp cloth, and looked me straight in the eye. "You're not going out with him, are you?"

Later I realized how she had emphasized the word "him" and had attempted to telegraph a message with her eyes, but all I noticed then was the flush of blood in her cheeks, and I thought, Well, imagine that. She's jealous. Dave wrapped his arm around my neck, pinning me in a fake headlock, and rubbed my bristly hair. I saw Shirley's face flare with undisguised envy. What a pain in the ass Shirley has become since I got the job, I thought.

"It's your funeral," the waitress sang under her breath as she walked away.

"Brenda's working the night shift," Cam said. "She said it's okay to go up."

Brenda was an affable, chunky farm girl who worked as a telephone operator and rented the suite above the old Miller's Television and Radio shop. She invited people up to her apartment to see the life-size poster of Elvis Presley pinned to her bedroom door. When Brenda worked the night shift, we often went up there to play records and drink beer and watch Shirley's nose turn red and her green eyes glitter with tears as she retold the story of how she'd found her father pitched forward at the breakfast table, face resting in a plate of toast she had just buttered for him moments earlier. When Shirley's nose grew red, she'd slip off into Brenda's bedroom with Cam or Gord, or sometimes with both of them.

When this happened, I told myself that it was none of my business. I'd watch midget wrestling to drown out the rustling and the muffled sounds coming from the bedroom and think about the foolish girl who went to bed with Elvis hoping that he'd give her a Cadillac when it was over and all she got from him was a watermelon. I knew how it worked in Carona. That there were only two kinds of girls, and even though I was a

199

virgin, I was guilty by association. But I didn't care. Even if Shirley was the town bicycle, as Mel so succinctly put it, there was a whole lot we had between us that never needed to be said. But that night, as I looked at the three of them sitting in the back booth of Ken's Chinese Food, I thought, Misery loves company. They were a miserable lot with nothing better to do than use Brenda's place for their group grope, and so I asked Dave if he would take me home.

Once we got back into the car, Dave changed. His face became serious and unreadable and he didn't talk. He backed away from the curb too quickly and the tires squealed against the wet pavement as we took off. The rain was coming down so hard the wipers barely cleared the windshield. "Here." I indicated the intersection and my street. He turned into the street, but as we approached the school, the car sped up, and through the rain I saw my house flash by, the light in the front hall shining through the screens of the veranda. "You passed it."

He didn't answer, just continued staring into the sheet of rain, clutching the steering wheel in his huge hands. I grew intensely alert, mind tumbling with scenarios and ways I might extract myself from each of them. I don't remember what music played on the radio or what, if anything, I may have said between the time we passed my house and when the car stopped in front of the gates of the cemetery. But I do remember seeing framed for an instant in the beams of the headlights the wrought-iron angels on the gates, horns lifted to their mouths, angels forever frozen, forever calling forth the sleeping people lying in orderly rows beneath weeping birches and spruce beyond. Dave doused the lights, and the angels, the buff-coloured stone wall, vanished.

Up until this point no one had ever touched my body. Cam and Gord had learned early from my kicks and hard slaps not to even try. I liked my body. I liked its extreme slenderness. Margaret worried over this. "She eats like a horse," she complained to the doctor, "so I don't see what's happening." The doctor, to satisfy her, ordered me to go down to the lab in the basement of the clinic to have blood samples drawn off and sent to the city to confirm that my cell growth and formation were normal and that there was nothing poisonous robbing my body of nutrition.

I liked the way my body was made. Every aspect of it, from my small breasts to the deep, pink folds which turned inwards, into me. Myself. I had sat on a mirror in the bathroom once and examined every crack and crevice of myself, probing with my finger and declaring myself sound and pretty amazing actually, the way my muscles sucked my finger up high inside me as I brought myself to orgasm. I had begun to enjoy my body's cycle, the rising and falling rhythm of menstruation, and took some satisfaction in squatting over the toilet and feeling huge clots slide out of me and land with a soft thick plopping sound in the water. And then in the ensuing decline of my slightly swollen breasts as my body, like a waning moon, became sliver thin, sharp once again. For this reason I was particular about who might touch it and, so far, I had not allowed anyone but myself.

Dave moved forward as he groped at the floor and then, slowly, the car seat slid backwards. I stared into total darkness. Think, I instructed myself through the sound of rain drumming on the roof. Once, when in the city waiting for Shirley, who had gone into the Salisbury on Main Street to use the washroom, I had been surrounded by several young boys who became cocky and then menacing and I disarmed them by swearing more than they did. In the end they showed me their sharpened jackknife blades and the knuckle-dusters they'd made at school in shop, and invited me to attend their little gang-war skirmish, which was supposed to happen later that night in Vimy Ridge Park. But Dave wasn't a scrawny street punk. I couldn't read Dave.

"So, where you from?" I asked. I knew I sounded stupid.

"A small town in the northwest of the province near the Saskatchewan border."

"And what do your parents do?"

"Farmers," he answered in a monotone.

Several quiet moments passed. I waited, hoping he'd say more. "What do you think of Carona?"

201

Dave turned to me. "Cut the cute crap. You know why we're here." Then he lunged at me, obliterating the world outside the car window. In one second I was pinned flat under his body, feeling his weight and then his belt buckle cutting into my thigh. He began grinding his hips and I felt his hard penis pressing against my leg. This isn't the prick of a giant, this is about the size of a pencil, I thought, as Dave snorted and chewed at my hair, and then his fist balled around my breast. He scrunched it and I yelped in pain. He squeezed harder and again I cried out. "You like that," he said into the top of my head and I realized that he wanted me to cry out. His breathing became raspy and he began to yank at his jeans and then at me, at my shirt, the zipper of my jeans, all the while whacking and thumping away at my leg with his pencil-thin penis.

Later I described it to Shirley as being about the size of my finger and she said that was Gord, too, and although Cam was a much smaller person, his was the size of a Polish sausage. "Thick, like that," she said, making a circle with her thumb and index finger. And then she said, as though reciting a rule of grammar, "It's not the thick of the prick, but the throb of the knob that does the job." She asked was I absolutely certain he hadn't gone off inside me. "Certain," I said.

My jeans and underpants were down around my knees, pinning my legs together, but Dave kept jabbing at the crack between my legs with his pencil until I thought it might snap. We were half on the car seat, half on the floor. "Wait, wait, wait," I said over and over through his frantic probing to get inside. I felt his body become rigid as he began to hear me and to realize that I was stroking the small of his back. His thick dark hair had fallen across his forehead, almost obscuring his eyes. Greasy, I thought, and my stomach heaved. "Dave, I can't." I forced myself to touch his mouth. "I'm wearing a tampon."

He reared back with laughter. "Shit," he said. "Tell me something new, why don't you?" But his hand snaked down between my legs just the same, and he began fishing about, searching for a string.

I crossed my legs, trapping his hand. "It's my first day. It'll

202

be one bloody mess on your car seat. We can do it on Friday," I said. "I'll be finished on Friday."

His head came up over mine and he opened his enormous mouth and covered my nose and mouth with it, his fat, slippery tongue licking, thrusting down the back of my throat. I had to swallow his saliva to keep from choking, and then he slathered my entire face, my eyes, licking my ears, his tongue going up inside my nostrils, and at that point I became more frightened of being suffocated than penetrated. My face was sopping wet with his saliva as I fought to breathe through his tongue, now pressed flat against my nose. I began thrashing my head back and forth. He groaned, and I felt the gush of hot wetness between my thighs as he came. He swore and collapsed against me.

I listened to the sound of rain washing against the car's roof. Our breath had misted the windows and we were encased in a moist, musky-smelling cocoon. Not a single car had passed by in the short time we'd parked there. His breathing grew quiet then, and he slowly untangled his limbs from mine, slid back behind the steering wheel, and began tucking himself in. He plucked a tissue from the box on the dash and threw it at me. Nausea rose in my throat as I dabbed his sticky semen from the insides of my legs. He checked his reflection in the mirror and smoothed his hair into place. "How old are you?" he asked, looking in the mirror; checking for scratches, probably, Shirley said afterwards. I told him.

He grinned, resembling a combination of Rock Hudson and Robert Taylor, but I saw the maniac lurking behind his smile. "I guess that makes you old enough to know better."

My hands shook as I pulled my jeans up around my hips and my breath was still quick and high in my chest. Okay, I said to myself, you made a stupid mistake. Don't waste time slitting your throat over it. But no bloody way will I ever get inside a car with this man again.

We didn't speak during the drive home. When we arrived at my house, he pulled over and reached across me to open the door, but I had already opened it and had one foot on the ground.

"What's the rush?" He brought his arm up against my chest, pinning me against the seat.

"It's late."

"We have a date. Friday, remember?"

When I didn't answer he tweaked my nipple and then he pinched it hard. I grabbed at his hand and curled forward, gasping with the pain, but I couldn't pry his hand loose. He released me when he was ready to release me. I got out of the car and stood waiting for him to get my bike. When he didn't make a move, I said, "Hey, my bike."

He winked. "On Friday." He tooted the horn lightly, and then the car's muffler coughed and rumbled as he sped away. I looked up at the house, hugging myself to keep from shaking. My nipple throbbed. Great, I thought, as I saw a light go on upstairs. Wonderful.

Margaret stood at the top of the stairs. "Oh, thank God, you're home. I couldn't sleep. I've been awake half the night thinking about you."

I walked towards my mother who waited for me, clutching her pink flannel nightgown closed at her throat. Her hair, tousled from sleep, puffed out around her head in an unruly, wild-looking auburn mass. I wanted to push my face against the soft swelling of her belly and climb back inside.

"What is it?" she asked. I saw fear rise in her eyes and her body grow stiff as I approached.

"Nothing. Just waited out the rain before heading home."

"But I heard a car."

"Chuck and Brenda."

"Oh. You're sure? Nothing's the matter?" she asked as I climbed to the top of the stairs and walked past her.

"Just tired."

"Well, I'll say a prayer for you anyway."

Anger would always replace my desire for a caress from Margaret.

I went up to the bathroom to wash the smell of this man from my body and then to search for bruises.

I lay awake most of the night repeating over and over in my mind his words, my own, inventing new scenes for what had actually happened, things that I had not said and done but wished I had. By morning I had almost convinced myself that my reconstruction was the truth. I rehearsed what I would say and then called Shirley. "You'll never guess what happened last night," I said softly, hearing Margaret puttering about in the kitchen.

"Why don't you come over. His royal highness, the pain in the butt, had to make a trip into the city today, so the coast is clear."

Shirley was upstairs in the bathroom when I arrived, and her mother, a small sinewy woman, sat at the table in the kitchen rolling her day's supply of cigarettes amidst the cluttered remains of breakfast. She worked with quick, furious motions, as though she was frightened that her husband might walk in at any moment. "You can go up," she said, barely glancing at me.

I heard Cheryl squealing, and when I walked into the bathroom Shirley was kneeling beside the tub squeezing water from a sponge, letting it trickle down Cheryl's stomach. "Hi!" she said. "Cute, eh?" Cheryl's eyes were always red and her nose dripped. Allergies, Shirley explained. I didn't think she was cute at all. I sat on the toilet and watched while Shirley bathed her stepsister, her hands moving across the child's pale body. Shirley's flaming red hair, freed from its usual ponytail, fell forward as she bent over the child, and Cheryl reached up, her baby hands pushing through that red curtain of hair, and pulled Shirley towards her until their foreheads touched. I watched as they giggled and rubbed noses, Shirley completely oblivious to my presence, cooing in a small voice, "You little monkey, you little monkey."

I felt tough and strong as I told her about Dave while she chased Cheryl across the bed and wrestled her into her clothing. "The guy's a sex maniac," I said. "All hands and mouth. A fucking-machine. Sweat city." Shirley gave up on chasing Cheryl and I had her full attention. "Watch out for that one," I

205

said, and didn't notice how her eyes narrowed as she listened. She began chewing at the cuticle on her thumb, deep in thought. I didn't tell her that I was certain the only reason why he'd let me go was because I'd made a date with him for Friday. Or about the bruises on my breasts. Instead, I told her the story as a kind of boastful joke about the funny thing that happened to me while on the way home the other night. But she grew tense as she listened and her features hardened with her silent calculations.

"That's it," she said and immediately took charge of my life, insisting that she meet me at the end of my shift at Sullie's and walk back to town with me.

Which she did, beginning that night, and arriving almost an hour before closing. She would keep out of the way, she said, as she hiked herself up onto the counter, swinging her legs, the heels of her flats making black marks against the cupboard door. "Here comes a great pair of falsies," she'd say, or, "Check out lard arse, there," offering a running commentary on the customers who had left their vehicles and were lined up outside at the order window. But she never stole so much as a nickel and I was thankful for that.

In the days leading up to Friday I began to feel cornered by Shirley's concern and regretted having told her anything about Dave. She watched for his purple Ford and made me duck into alleyways or zip into the post office when it approached in the street. On Thursday night, as I lay in bed exhausted and gratefully moving towards sleep, the throaty purr of a car's muffler startled me fully awake. Dave, passing by the house. Twice. My scalp tingled as I lay there drenched in a cold sweat, making plans to cover myself for Friday night. On Friday, Patsy would close up and Chuck, Brenda's boyfriend, could be persuaded to take all of us to the town down the road to catch the current movie.

But Shirley didn't show up at Ken's on Friday night as we had agreed. Cam, Gord, and I waited an extra half hour, and then Cam phoned her and her mother said Shirley had left well over an hour ago. Gord had arrived at the cafe still angry from an argument he'd had with his parents before leaving the house. They'd begun to nag him to do something useful with his life, threatening to make him enlist in the army. Gord swore over Shirley being late, refusing to wait any longer. We left Ken's and headed off to meet Brenda and Chuck. I didn't know it then, but this was to be my last night in Carona. The night before I left the town for good.

As I walked down the street between Cam and Gord, I suppose I looked as though I could have been their kid sister tagging along. Still short, at four feet eleven inches, I nevertheless *felt* I was their equal in height and superior in all other ways, although I was careful not to show this. When we reached the intersection we didn't bother to wait for the traffic light to change. This was one of several lights installed recently. These lights, and the cavernous hall of the beer parlour, transformed now into a lounge with recessed lighting, and "mixed" drinking, and the beginning construction of a new school to accommodate the influx of students who were being bused in from outlying areas, were just a few of the many changes in Carona, but they didn't affect me. Nor did the displays in store windows that were designed to catch our eye – the new consumers. I had watched the events of the Cuban Missile Crisis on television, Martin Luther King telling a crowd of thousands they were "free at last," the killing of President Kennedy, the young man who attended classes wearing a black bag to test the conformity of the university students around him, and none of this touched or affected me, except to confirm what I already knew about impermanence and change.

As we walked down the street the warm night was soft and the texture and colour of navy suede. Underlying that softness, however, was the hard edge of tension. I could feel anger in Gord's body as I walked beside him, impatience in Cam's. From time to time a car passed by and I would call out and ask if any one had seen Shirl. No one had.

Brenda and Chuck, whose face flamed with fresh eruptions of acne, waited for us outside the telephone company building where Brenda worked. Gord said he wasn't interested in going to a movie to see "the fag" Elvis, and when Chuck protested,

Gord surprised us by grabbing him around the neck and threatening to kill him. "Easy," Cam cautioned, pulling Gord off an astonished Chuck. Cam explained the fight Gord had had with his parents and suggested that we cool off, pick up some beer, and drive out to the pits for a swim. The suggestion didn't please Brenda, but Chuck agreed to drive the eleven miles to the gravel pits if we paid for the gas. Cam and Gord looked at me, and I said okay, and so we stopped off at Sullie's and I paid myself for the last two weeks' work. Patsy said that Dave had been around, asking for me.

The further we drove from Carona, the better I began to feel. I was giddy with relief that I had escaped Dave, and as we scrambled down the face of a gravel cliff towards the turquoise pools of clear water, ankle-deep in an avalanche of crushed rock and sand, it seemed to me the night itself was like the water in the pits, deep and soothing. I laughed as a naked Gord, a white fish shining in the light of the moon, posed on a ridge of gravel, showing off, calling out to us, "From deep in the heart of Africa comes the cry of the Fug Owee tribe. Where the fuck are we?" Then he yodelled a Tarzan cry and leapt feet-first into the water.

I stripped down to my underwear and went over to where Cam sat naked on a sandstone slab of rock, watching Gord swim laps. Gord had the tough, jerky swimming stroke that most self-taught country boys had. They'd thrash, hold their heads too high, and punch the water with their hands as though fighting their way through it. Cam appeared comfortable in his nakedness and sat with one knee raised, his flaccid penis lying against his other leg. The summer had bleached his hair to such an extent that it had turned silver, complementing his narrow face and high cheekbones. He was a good-looking person, though I never regarded Cam as being anyone other than a boy I had known since grade school, not seeing past that constant cigarette clenched between his teeth, the raw-boned look of a not yet mature body. When I did meet him again some twenty-five years later in Red Deer, Alberta, he said I'd been responsible for ninety-five per cent of his wet dreams. I liked his sharp wit and how he clearly enjoyed the company of women, and I would have given anything to have been his lover, but, having been happily married for almost twenty years, he was impervious to my flirtations. He told me I'd be the first to know if it ever turned sour.

As I sat down on the rock beside Cam, he grinned and tugged at my bra strap. "Hi, No Tits," he said. "Hey, Chuck, Barber here doesn't want us to see her no tits." Chuck, who was now treading water in the centre of the pool, laughed and dove under. I laughed, too, and slid off the warm rock down into the tepid water. I wasn't ashamed of my small breasts. It wasn't that. I didn't want them to see the bruises, the thumb-prints the colour of tobacco stains. Music floated down from the car window and Brenda appeared at the top of the gravel ridge carrying a blanket. She scooped out a hollow for herself and sat up there, watching while we swam.

Then Cam built a fire and we dried ourselves beside its heat and sipped at beer for an hour while the sky swept its arm of stars over us and Gord roamed the gravel hills. I recognize that night now as having been one of those few moments in life when I didn't want to be moving towards another place. But when Gord reappeared, and I heard the sound of a beer bottle shatter against rock, I knew that my state of contentment was bound to end soon.

Instead of returning to Carona, we drove on further west, towards a larger community where Gord directed Chuck through the streets, making him stop behind a hardware store. Brenda, Chuck, and I waited as Cam and Gord disappeared into the shadows and returned moments later, jubilant with success, carrying a length of chain and a carpet knife. Then we drove to the outskirts of the town where there were several car dealership lots and, once again, without saying why, Gord instructed Chuck to pull over.

Chuck groaned and began to bang his head against the steering wheel, saying that his father would kill him if he ever found out, and Brenda made frightened noises behind her hand as we watched Gord darting through the car lot, hooking the curved knife into tires and slashing them open. Cam stood beneath a streetlight, hands plunged deep into his jeans pockets, on guard. I sat in the back seat waiting for Gord to be finished, watching impassively while in the final venting of his anger he swung the heavy chain and shattered a windshield. They ran back to the car and slid in beside me. Gord hugged himself and shivered and his laughter was tight and barky. Idiot, I thought. I could tell by the silence in the front seat, by the rigid fix of Chuck's and Brenda's heads, that they agreed. Cam moved away from me, pressing up against the door, staring into the night. I knew that something had ended.

When we got back to Carona I asked Chuck to let me out at the top of the street and I walked the remainder of the way home. There were no lights burning, which meant both Mel and Margaret were asleep. I didn't want to risk waking her, and so I felt my way through the closet in the front hall and pulled free a blanket, and, without undressing, curled down under it on the couch in the living room and instantly fell asleep.

When I opened my eyes the following morning the sun streamed in through the front window and I saw Margaret sitting across the room in the easy chair. She played with the asparagus fern, which trailed like dangling fingers, stroking the plant, sometimes twisting its fronds and letting them spring back. This chair and the couch I had slept on were from one of Timothy's lines, and now the worse for wear. Silver threads had pulled loose from the fabric and were prickly against the arms and legs. On one side of the chair stood Timothy's smoking-stand, which I could never look at without my stomach doing a strange turn. From time to time, Margaret collected bits of things when she went walking, pine cones or small pebbles, and she'd place them in the ashtray to remind herself that her lungs were now clean and taking in nature's pure air. The way she sat there, fondling the plant, deep in thought, unsettled me and I wanted to make my escape upstairs. "What time is it, anyway?" I asked, startling her.

"Oh! You're awake," she said. She got up from the chair and

210

walked towards me. I looked down at her bare feet, the long, narrow boniness of them, her large, square toenails. Ugly feet, I thought. I felt the warmth of her body as she sat down beside me and I inched away from it, slightly repelled by the uncommon nearness of her. She began rubbing the small of my back, small circular motions, which filled me with apprehension. I knew there was a hidden reason behind everything she did.

"Honey."

I groaned inwardly. Spare me, I thought.

"Honey." She took a deep breath. "I'm sorry to have to tell you this, but Shirley is dead."

The words jolted me awake. I freed myself from the blanket and Margaret's touch and sat up. She was silent for several long moments, eyes cast down, studying her hands lying open in her lap. Then our eyes met, hers searching deeply into mine, body alert, waiting for my reaction. "She was killed last night. In a car accident."

I wanted to know all, immediately, the how, when, and where. But even while my skin crawled with shock and my mind did not yet firmly hold the tragic news, I sensed the shadow of something other than sympathy pass across her face and I became wary.

"It happened about six miles from town. On the highway." She reached and clasped my hand, which had grown icy. I couldn't comprehend that Shirley was really gone. Then Margaret said, "With a man. She was with a man. He was killed too."

I knew then why Shirley hadn't shown up at Ken's last night. "Dave."

She nodded. "A David Warren. Only twenty-one years old."

I wonder what happened to Mel's bike? I thought, and at the same time I was appalled by my stupidity, callousness even, for having thought that. Shirley was dead, after all.

"Did you know him?"

I sensed her careful scrutiny and became frightened, wondering when the hole would open up for me to fall through. "I know who he is. But I don't know him very well." The truth.

"Well, that's strange," Margaret said, "because he called

211

here for you last night. Not too long after you left the house. He was very polite, gave his name," she said, "and explained why he was calling. He said you and he had a date."

I withdrew my icy hand from her hot, dry palm. I wanted to flee because I suspected where the conversation was heading. Then I heard Mel's footsteps on the stairs. He entered the room wearing his plaid bathrobe, exuding the sour smell of someone who has slept too long. He passed by without even glancing in our direction and went on into the kitchen to make a pot of coffee.

I got up from the couch, left the room to escape to my bedroom, and Margaret was behind me. "They said on the news this morning that two people were killed," she said. "And when I heard that man's name, I was almost certain the other name would be yours."

She followed me up the stairs and so I headed for the bathroom instead with the intention of running the water taps and flushing the toilet for as many times as necessary to drown out the sound of her voice on the other side of the door. When I reached it, I turned, and we faced one another. She stepped back and clasped her hands across her stomach. Her cheeks burned with a ruddy, dark flush, and her eyes beamed with unconcealed joy. "Amy! Don't you see? It could have been you in that car! Not Shirley. It was the Lord's hand – "

I wouldn't let her finish. I swung my arm and my clenched fist connected with the side of her face. Her head snapped back and her eyes grew wide with shock. In the seconds of silence that followed, we stood and stared at each other. She pressed her palm against the spot where I had struck her. "You hit me," she said quietly.

I waited for something to happen. For the walls of the house to topple inward or the roof to fly off. For a giant hand to reach down, pick me up, and throw me away.

"Your mother. You hit your mother."

"Yes."

She turned then and went down the stairs.

I found Cam and Gord waiting for me in the back booth at Ken's. I slid in beside them. We did not speak for several moments, the three of us in shock and avoiding one another's eyes because we didn't know yet what we wanted our faces to say. I wondered if they were remembering being inside Shirley's body and, if so, did it cause them to grieve more deeply. Ken hovered behind the counter, glancing our way off and on, and then he came over to the booth with mugs and the coffee pot. "Very sad," he said quietly. "You stay. You be sad." I accepted the coffee but I couldn't be sad. I didn't feel anything.

"Dave was a pig, a maniac," I said once Ken had left, breaking the silence and not wanting to ask myself why Shirley, who had been warned about Dave, would agree to get into his car.

"We know all about Dave," Cam said. Then he went on to tell me that, unlike Shirley, Dave didn't die instantly. Cam had learned this from an RCMP officer who had come into the cafe earlier. Dave had pulled a U-turn on the highway and the car was hit broadside on the passenger door by an oncoming vehicle, crushing Shirley's chest and rupturing her heart. Dave was still alive when the ambulance arrived, screaming his lungs out and banging his feet up and down against the pavement until he, too, died. Good, I thought. It was a waste of time, and dishonest as well, for me to attempt to dredge up sad feelings over Dave. I was glad he was dead.

"It's not fair," I said to no one as the three of us walked down to the police compound where Dave's car had been towed.

Crushed chest, she remembers, ruptured heart. Perhaps Shirley's heart had already been ruptured years before.

Whenever she remembers the friend from her youth, she sees Shirley with her stepsister, Cheryl, and is amazed by what she didn't see before, the tenderness of Shirley's hands on the child's body. She sees Shirley leaning over the bathtub, cascading red hair, a satiny curtain, and the baby girl's chubby fists grabbing handfuls of it. She hears a mushy, soft, cooing voice saying, "You little monkey." Only several years

213

later she herself would be as blind as Shirley was to the rivulets of yellow or greenish mucus trailing from a tiny nose and experience and understand what passed between Shirley's hands and the child's body.

When she remembers Shirley she sees, too, her scuffed black flats and the flaky skin at the backs of her ankles, and then she turns her chair to the centre window in her work-room and gazes into the bright new leaves of an elm tree in early summer, or into bare branches beautifully encased in glassy ice taking on the sunlight and appearing as though lit from within, dripping beads of light onto the dirty patches of snow on the walk below.

She sees Shirley walking towards her in the street, her fierce macho stance, ponytail and arms swinging, head and breasts held high, betrayed by weak ankles that turn her feet inward. A van pulls up alongside Shirley, she imagines, and the man inside it winds down the window. "Hey you!" he calls. "You wanna fuck?" Without condescending to glance his way, Shirley gives him the finger and says, "No, but I've got a dog at home who will." As Shirley strolls nonchalantly out of this scene, she walks on the insides of her shoes, making her seem child-like, vulnerable, but grimly deter-mined not to be.

As I looked at the wreckage of Dave's car I wondered at what moment of our evening Shirley had seen the oncoming head-lights and what her final thoughts were in that split second when she realized that the accident was inevitable. The pas-senger side of the car had been crumpled so badly that its door was now in the centre of the car. I walked around the destroyed vehicle and noticed that the trunk lid was twisted and gaped open at one corner. I squatted to look inside. Mel's bicycle wasn't there. I would never learn what became of it. Perhaps it wound up at the trailer camp beside the agricultural grounds and when the men from the Hydro crew were slightly drunk they rode it crookedly and wildly. They rode that bike until its wheels fell off and then they threw it away into the ditch. Perhaps.

Cam stood back from the car, a silvery wedge of hair hanging across his tanned forehead. He squinted against the morning sun and his blue eyes grew watery-looking. Gord appeared to be puzzled as he walked around the car, as though he was only just realizing that the accident hadn't been staged for our benefit after all but was real. He kicked at the hanging bumper, dropped to his knees to peer beneath the car, and got to his feet, his puzzlement replaced with relief. He declared that the undercarriage had snapped in two places. "Ford products," he scoffed, blaming the car for the death of its occupants. "Never would have happened if this was a Studebaker." Then he stuck his head inside the broken side window and leapt back saying, "Jesus!"

I went over. I saw the blood, too, on the nylon green-plaid seat cover, a dark, sticky-looking puddle crawling with flies. Crushed chest, ruptured heart, I thought, and saw in my mind the patch of mottled dirt behind Shirley's knobby ankle bones. The flies were feeding on a part of Shirley. I thought, Go forth and multiply, flies, then forced myself to study the mess on the seat and saw the flecks of yellow tissue, pieces of fat or lungs. That's life, I told myself. Just so you know.

After that, everything seemed pointless. There didn't seem to be anything worthwhile to do, so I didn't go back with Cam and Gord to Ken's where several other teenagers, having heard the news, had gathered like the flies on the car seat. Those who ordinarily would not have given Shirley the time of day if she'd stooped to ask, wanted their fill now of the gruesome details, and would retell the story among themselves and grow fat with smugness.

So I went instead to the Carona Family Park and sat on the rim of a tractor-tire sand pit and watched an ant struggle to carry the wing of a moth many times its size. I listened for the sounds of children's voices. I listened for our voices, Mel's, Jill's, and Timothy's, too, shouting encouragement as he thumped his catcher's mitt, saying, Put her there, Mel! I tried to imagine Margaret spreading a plastic cloth across the splintered surface of a picnic table and laying blankets down on the seats to protect us from the rough wood. I wanted to picture

215

her setting down lime-green and purple melamine plates, a quart sealer of lemonade, waxed paper crackling as she unwrapped egg salad sandwiches. "Me, me, me!" Jill cries, small hands demanding a turn at the catcher's mitt and Timothy's attention. I sat still for a long time and my imagination failed me. This is a dream, after all, I told myself, and you will wake up and find yourself looking out through the bars of a crib. Or else you will find yourself lying on the ground in the cemetery.

Because of Margaret's habit of drawing all the blinds first thing in the morning to keep down the heat of summer, the house was cool and dark, and, as I stepped inside, I sensed her absence in the settled quietness and was relieved. I went up to her bedroom. The room had remained unchanged throughout the years. Her Blue Book lay open in the centre of the bed, as always, and I was curious. "Amy struck me." Or, "Today I have been slapped in the face by my own child." Or had she written, "Oh, most High and Holy Father, who has spared my child Amy this day, has for reasons I don't yet understand desired to take Amy's friend instead. Oh, Lord of all, comfort the girl's mother at this time. . ."? But Margaret had written nothing.

I went to her closet and reached for the movie projector on the top shelf, smelling a faint odour of mustiness which I now know to have been a dried funeral bouquet, out of place among the careful arrangement of her shoes and clothing. I carried the projector downstairs and to the dining-room table. Tucked in all around the projector were boxes containing reels of film with Timothy's concise square printing of the dates and subjects. "The Robin. Amy," Timothy had written, and I knew what that reel contained. The whole film was images of leaves, a tree bobbing in the wind, and, occasionally, if you looked closely, you could see the flutter of the red breast of a robin among the branches. "Now where in hell did that come from?" Timothy had asked once, scratching his chin.

I lifted the projector from the box and set it up on the table. The metal pulleys had long ago broken and the bottom of the box was littered with elastic bands and sealer rings which

Timothy had used as a replacement for them. I picked up another box of film which said, "At Grand Beach." I couldn't remember having been at Grand Beach and so I decided to look at that one.

The film was underexposed and grainy, the colours off, the sky, sand, grey-looking, and the picture, fed unevenly by the elastic band, jumped erratically. I saw a stretch of sand, water, and then the back of a head come out from under the camera, shoulders in a green sweater. Mine. The sweater had been knit by Grandmother Johnson. I watched myself appear whole in the frame, watched my round body being propelled on stubby legs down the side of a sand cliff, falling, getting up, my legs churning awkwardly. Then I stopped at the edge of the water and looked back at Timothy, who held the camera, as though I didn't know what to do next. And perhaps he told me what to do, because I bent over suddenly, kicked my fat legs up in an attempt at a head stand, and tumbled over.

The light in the picture changed suddenly and became brighter, another time and day and the sun had come out. Margaret walked towards the camera wearing a head scarf and black shorts, her legs looking pasty-white. She carried a plastic pail and in the background was a screened dining tent. She waved the camera away as she passed by but at the last moment stopped, dipped her head sideways, and stuck out her tongue. I would later remember Margaret that way, a bit of the child still there.

Once again the picture changed and, amazingly, there was a baseball game. For some reason Timothy had filmed it at high speed and the players darted about with jerky movements. The camera panned past Mel, standing on a base, looking knock-kneed and skinny in baggy shorts. Suddenly, Jill rounded the base, and as she ran by, Mel stuck out his foot, tripping her. She tackled him, faking a huge rage, and Timothy moved in to record Jill pretending to bite his leg. Did she already possess the seed of destruction? I wondered. Had it lain in her body from birth, dormant, or festering, and poisoning the air around her and Mel, turning them against me?

217

The remainder of the film was of me. Me, standing waist-deep in water, clasping myself, shivering. Me, squatting and patting sand cakes and decorating them with shells. Me, attempting to stuff a huge piece of chocolate cake into my mouth and wearing most of it on my face. Timothy loved me, I thought. He must have.

When I entered the kitchen, later, I was struck by the sameness of things. The same pearly-grey chrome suite. Mel's battle-scarred, now elderly cat, George, parked directly in front of the refrigerator door, paws tucked up beneath him as he crouched and blinked up at me, daring me to just try and get past him. But in spite of the intense familiarity of the room and the things in it, I felt as though I had become a stranger to the house.

Margaret had left the fluorescent light on above the sink. The radio sat on the counter wedged between the toaster and the red and white canister set whose labels read FLOUR, SUGAR, COFFEE, and TEA. Radio, I thought, and my eyes veered back to it. "When I heard that man's name, I was almost certain the other name would be yours." It came to me then that when Margaret listened to news of the accident that morning, she had to have known it wasn't me. I was sleeping on the couch. She would have seen me on her way to the kitchen. And yet, I knew she hadn't lied. Hoped, I thought suddenly. Some dark craving for the high wire of catastrophe had made her hope against the impossible: that the name would be mine.

I heard footsteps on the walk alongside the house, and then the porch door opened and Margaret stood in the doorway of the kitchen. "Oh, you're home," she said softly, serenely, as she stepped into the room. "Good. I want to talk to you."

She still wore her wedding band. She still jammed combs at either side of her head to keep her unruly hair in place and still, by the end of the day, those combs would pull loose and her hair would tumble about her face, making it appear

218

smaller. She still appeared to be all long limbs, composed in her freshly starched and ironed dresses, as though she never perspired; always cool, dry between her legs, too, the crotch of her underpants never clotted with the discharge of desire. She did not hold herself in the night, caress her breasts or place her hands over her abdomen just to feel herself being touched. Not Margaret. I am almost certain.

I stood waiting for what she had to say. I resolved to listen and not speak, to not say anything that might signal what I was feeling or thinking.

"Amy," she said, "I have finally come to understand that there's something terribly wrong here."

My heart lurched with unreasonable hope. At last, I thought, we're going to talk. Our eyes met and I saw grief and longing in hers; over our alienation, I thought, and I felt my own longing for reconciliation rise. For a brief moment I believed this was going to turn out all right.

"We've been praying for you," Margaret said. "And what we've just come to realize is that it's possible you have a demon. It explains so much, your behaviour, how I've always sensed the striving of two spirits here."

"A what?"

"A demon. An evil spirit. I see it sometimes, in your eyes."

It was night time. I stood inside a telephone booth downtown, on the corner across from the White Rose gas station, and I couldn't stop crying. My throat ached with the effort not to cry but each time I lifted the telephone receiver to get the operator my throat would open up and I would begin weeping again, bitterly, for having hoped. Why had Margaret said that to me? To drive me away? Or did she really believe it to be the case and seek to have me exorcized and made over into her own image at last? Or was it, as I have since come to speculate, that Margaret herself is possessed with the mind-set, with the heart, of a terrorist? An inclination that I fear I may have inherited.

The night I left Carona for good I didn't know who I was crying for or what about. My chest muscles ached and my raw throat burned. When I was able to stop shaking enough to pick up the receiver, I hoped for Brenda's voice on the other end of the line. When Brenda was working she would sometimes put us through without requesting we deposit a coin. I was relieved to hear the familiar lilt of her voice. "Brenda, this is Amy."

"Amy! Oh gosh, what a day. Isn't it just awful about Shirley?"

"Yes."

"Is it true?" she said. "Were you really supposed to go out with the guy and she went instead?"

I felt a sudden weariness, making me slack-jawed and sluggish, making me want to curl up and close my eyes and fall into a deep sleep. "Brenda, I have to call Victoria."

"B.C.?"

"Yeah, my father."

She groaned. "Amy, don't ask me. I can't. I'll get into trouble with my supervisor."

"Please, just this once. I have to talk to him."

Again she groaned. "Don't do this to me, I can't."

"Put it on my mother's phone bill."

"But what if she questions it? If she does, I'm dead."

"Please."

I heard static on the long-distance line. "Thanks, Brenda."

"Yeah, sure," she whispered. "But only this one time."

"Hello?" A woman's voice, high, cheerful.

The static sounded like water, waves in the Strait of Juan de Fuca, I thought, rolling up onto a beach outside their front door.

"Hello?" Her voice dropped, its tone now wary. My tongue refused to move as I heard a muffled sound, her hand, perhaps, placed over the receiver, and then the line became clear again. "Well, if you've got nothing to say, kiddo, neither do I," Aunt Rita said sharply and hung up.

I didn't know where I was going to go, but I knew that I was leaving Carona for good. All I had were my white bucks, ankle

220

socks, jeans, underwear, tee shirt, and black denim jacket. What I was wearing. Then I felt the bulge in the breast pocket of my jacket. I patted it and it crackled. I also had most of two weeks' pay from Sullie's Drive In. Thank you, Sullivan.

11

She walked for almost four weeks. The balmy weather held
for her, high skies during the day, and warm enveloping
nights, which carried the essence and softness of the night
she swam in the gravel pits, the night she had recognized as
being one of the few when she did not yearn to be moving
towards another place. Her predilection for the melancholy
is evident in how often she recalls the external landscape. A
romantic Amy, remembering with her body and not her
mind.

She walked well into each night, frightened, imagining
what demons look like. Grinning tiny imps with monkey
tails, or bloated gargoyles with steaming, fetid breath! She
would startle at every small sound by the way, and look with
yearning at lights in windows of distant farmhouses. Then,
as those dots of lights winked out one by one and only yard
lights remained lit and churning with a frenzy of moths, this
was where you could find her. In the darkness. Not during
the day, but at night, when there was no one but herself.

Even though she would like you to think so, there is nothing at all romantic about being alone on the road in the dead
of night. It wasn't so much the absence of people but the
presence of absence; not a single loving person at her centre.
And, frankly, who, if they dared to approach, would find

much that was lovable there – a heart as flat and as polished
as her white face.

That first night I walked until past three in the morning, and
then trampled down some grain, making a nest for myself in a
field, and spread my jacket as a pillow and slept. In the morning I awoke feeling damp and stiff but strangely exhilarated as
I stretched and listened to a dog barking in the far distance and
heard, too, the whistling, cawing, the hiss and croak of the
landscape, and thought: I did it. Then the barking was
drowned out by the sound of a machine's engine sputtering to
life and I knew it was time to move on.

During the days I ignored the curious appraisals of the
truckers, farmers, and waitresses I encountered in roadside gas
stations, and I didn't speak more than was necessary to order
what I wanted to eat and to ask directions to the washroom.
After the first day, when I saw myself in one of those washroom mirrors, I noticed that the skin beneath my eyes looked
bruised from smudged mascara and so I dampened a paper
towel and wiped my face clean of cosmetics. By the end of the
first week my skin took on a rosy glow from the sun and my
arms became deeply tanned. As I travelled I tried not to think
of distances, set no goals, just walked, cutting away from the
main highway after the first day to travel along secondary
roads and then roads that were not really roads but rutted
paths crossing open fields, until I saw on the horizon the crawl
of headlights or rows of telephone poles, meaning that I had
come back to the main highway. I would follow it again, perplexed sometimes to find myself passing by a hamlet or town I
had come across several days earlier.

My feet seemed to move independently of my will, so that
even though the rest of my body ached with tiredness, my
brain screamed for sleep, still I could walk.

In the days and nights that followed I did not think about
Shirley's crushed chest or ruptured heart; but I suppose now
that Cam and Gord did. They were among the pall-bearers at
Shirley's funeral and they must have thought about her brok-
en body as they filed past the open casket and saw her too-

223

high, pointy, and obviously fake breasts thrusting out against the dress her mother delivered to the undertaker, one of her own, probably, because Shirley didn't own a dress.

I did not imagine myself as Amy the squirrel, or standing on a book and floating towards a harbour, heading towards Truth and Knowledge. I thought instead about Margaret. If there was one thing I could have changed, I wouldn't have struck her. I reasoned that my mother had told me I was possessed by a demon for revenge. I began to dread the silent telephone calls in my own future.

But gradually thoughts of Margaret vanished in the open air, and during the days I walked I became aware of how large everything was, how tall and wide the sky, how broad the plains of the Midwest, which seemed to breathe and become twitchy with nervous energy during the night. At night I heard the earth's nervousness in the ground as I lay on it, how it quivered with sound.

Once, I squatted beside a water-filled ditch, dropped pebbles into its scummy surface, one by one, and watched the ripples circle outwards, a water insect riding the ridge of energy I had set in motion to the outer limits of its cosmos. In the days as I continued to walk, I believed that the air rippled with sound waves which circled outwards and upwards, and that my breath pushed the noise of the chirping and sawing insects out further and up through the stratosphere and beyond the stars to the place where angels and God abide.

I began to duck out of sight into deep grass beside the road at the sound of an approaching vehicle, desiring to be alone, unseen, and becoming stealthy. I had no one. You would think that I would have felt sad about that, a bereft child, cut off and cut loose. But as I bent over the squashed remains of a gopher lying to the side of the road and studied its insides which heaved with rice-shaped plump maggots, I believed instead that I had been freed.

I felt myself begin to blend in with the landscape, become as much a part of it as the insects, the frogs gliding through still ponds, the Franklin's gulls hovering over freshly tilled fields, the whippoorwills calling out their own names at nightfall, and the need and desire to see Timothy ebbed. I wanted to spend the rest of the summer outdoors but, towards the end of July, when I squatted in a field to empty my bladder, I realized by the spatters of blood on the ground that my body had played its trick and I would need to go into a town.

Spectrail, the town Amy enters the following morning, appears to be similar to the others she has passed, in that the highway skirts around it, and to enter it she must take the service road which passes through the inevitable ugly clutch of buildings on the town's perimeter, corrugated steel sheds, gas stations, farm-implement lots, and car dealers. She worries that she won't find the main street and the hotel or cafe washroom before she leaks through her jeans. Then she sees a half-moon-shaped building which has a sign above the door. COMMUNITY CENTRE, she reads, which probably means a bingo hall and curling rink and likely not open yet. But just as she thinks this the door does open and a young woman wearing a peach-coloured halter top and white shorts steps outside. As the door swings closed behind her, Amy smells the aroma of food cooking and her stomach turns with hunger. The young woman walks over to a bicycle rack where several bikes are parked. She sees Amy and shields her eyes against the sun and stares. This is Marlene. When Amy thinks about Marlene years later, she sees the heavy sausage-shaped ringlets hanging across her forehead, a clear-eyed person with a broad smile revealing almost perfectly shaped teeth and a friendly, even disposition. She will also remember Marlene referring to her elderly father as "the old bugger."

She asks the girl if there's a washroom inside the building and is startled by the sound of her own voice, at how thin and strained it has become.

"Yes." The girl's long curly dark hair sweeps across her shoulders as she pulls her bike free. She walks it over to the door as though she's waiting for Amy. She isn't wearing shoes

225

and her painted toenails shine as though still wet. "The wash-rooms are just inside the door. Men's to the left." She takes a white cap from the wicker basket on the handlebars and jams it onto the back of her head. She glances up as Amy passes by and her eyes go wide with surprise. "Oh sorry! I thought you were a boy." Snorts of laughter shoot from her nostrils. "Great hair, I really like it," she says.

Yeah, sure, Amy thinks, believing the tone of voice is deri-sion. She steps inside the dim interior to the sound of voices and the smell of perspiration mixed with cooking odours. She hears the snap of a ping-pong ball meeting a paddle and strange shuffling and grunting sounds coming from another room. The washrooms are just inside the doorway and beyond them are the raw plywood walls of a hallway and doors which open up on either side of it. She enters the washroom and is relieved to discover that she's alone. The muscles in her abdo-men have become rigid and ache with cramps. She sees in her mind the girl outside, the perky white tilt of her sailor's cap, the painted toenails, and she feels dirty. Her jeans are dirt-encrusted and grass-stained, the white socks now grey. She pulls her shoes off and removes her socks, turns them inside out, and puts them back on. Then she winds toilet paper into several pads and stuffs them into her pockets.

She studies her reflection in the mirror above the sink as she washes her hands and sees how tightly the skin stretches across her cheekbones, making her eyes look hollow. The door opens behind her and two small girls enter and stop dead to stare at her. They sidle around her and then dash into the cubicle and she hears them whispering and stifling giggles. Well, to hell with this tight-ass town, Amy thinks, and her throat constricts without warning. She hears Shirley's words in her own mouth and for one terrible moment she has to grab hold of the sink to keep from pitching forward. She sees her face twist to one side, her mouth crinkling. A stranger looks out from behind her eyes, admonishing her. She instructs herself not to think about Shirley but to think instead about the maggots in the gopher and not to give in to self-pity. The toilet flushes. She sees the little girls' shoes, a pair of red and a

226

pair of navy sneakers, their mosquito-bitten, stem-like ankles, and how their feet seem to waltz as they tug their clothing back into place. She takes several deep breaths. No one must see anything unusual in her face. She checks her reflection in the mirror and, although her eyes are still suspect, the rest of her face has settled back into place. Now she will walk into the town and buy what she needs and move on.

As she enters the hallway, the smell of food once again pulls at her empty stomach. She hesitates, but then is drawn by it down the hall, past a door and a room where several children play ping-pong. They're engrossed and don't look up as she goes by, following her nose to the end of the hallway and the other door.

When Amy walks into the room, she sees a tall man wearing a Stetson standing in the centre of a raised platform: a boxing ring. The two young men standing on either side of him wear leather helmets and boxing gloves. "Okay, you guys, now remember what I said. You fight fair now." Amy recognizes the voice, the slow, thick tongue, and the frizzy hair above his ears. It's the man called Hank, she realizes, the bass guitar player she met in the park years ago with the country and western performer Stu Farmer Junior.

Just then a bell clangs and Hank steps back and the boys begin to weave and bob. Hank looks up and sees her, stares for a second, and then several young boys who have been shouting encouragement to the boxers turn and stare at her as well. As she walks towards the concession stand at the end of the room she feels their eyes on her. A woman works behind the counter at a stove. This is Elaine, Marlene's mother. Amy is aware of the woman's backward glance in her direction, a question forming in her face, but she ignores it as she reads the menu written on a blackboard and thinks about Stu Farmer Junior. She remembers him sitting on a picnic bench in the city, hugging his acoustic guitar, the day Mel almost fell into the river, and it feels like it happened in another world and to another person. She remembers his music and then Hank approaching as she lay stretched out on the grass about to take off and fly. "So who's the dopey kid?" Hank had asked.

227

She senses that Hank is still looking at her, that he leans against the ropes and peers out over the heads of the dancing boxers, checking her out. She calculates what she can afford to eat and for the first time it occurs to her that she might have to stop moving and get a job. The band of muscles in her abdomen tightens sharply. What if I get sick? I don't get sick, she tells herself. She realizes that the strange shuffling sound she'd heard when she first came in had been the sound of the boxers' feet, the grunting their breathing, and although she has studied flies feeding on blood on a car seat, she has no desire to turn and watch fists pounding bodies. Another clang of the bell ends the round. She hears Hank talking to the boys, his diction slow, a slight lisp, and then Marlene is at her side. Wet teeth, Amy thinks as the girl smiles at her, she should really swallow her spit. Her eyes shine with friendliness. Vacuous.

Elaine comes over to the counter and leans into it. A red bandanna holds her hair off her forehead. She swipes at perspiration on her face with a corner of her apron. Hot flashes, the change, Elaine explains several days later to Amy as they sit out on the back step peeling potatoes for a batch of french fries. She'd made a fake stab at Amy with the potato peeler. "I can't be held responsible for my actions," she said. "I'm in the change and women have been known to go batty." She reminds Amy of Bunny North, Margaret's friend.

"I thought you were on your way home," Elaine says to Marlene.

"I was, but I came back."

"He'll be cooked by now."

Marlene points to Amy's head. "I want my hair like that."

Elaine wipes a spot of grease from the counter. "Sure you do. Now get out of my sight."

"I'm serious, Mom, I want that hair."

The woman sighs dramatically and rolls her eyes. "What you really want is the back of my hand," she says with mock sternness. "Kissy, kissy," she says, and makes kissing sounds with her red mouth. "I happen to think you're beautiful just the way you are."

228

Corny, Amy thinks, and wonders if this is a show staged for her benefit. Elaine leans across the counter and winks at Amy. "She takes after me." Despite herself Amy wants to laugh. They couldn't be more opposite, she thinks. Elaine has a meat-and-potatoes face, ordinary, with large pores and a doughy little nose, while Marlene's sharp and clearly defined features are doll-like, perfect, and dance with a certain mischievousness. Several young boys rush past Amy and straddle the stools at the counter. Elaine sends them off to wash their hands.

"You finished?" Marlene says to someone who has just stepped up behind Amy. Amy can smell him. It's the smell of Hank. It's the smell of Lifebuoy soap.

"Yah," Hank says, "that's it till after lunch anyways." He saunters past Amy over to the stools, appearing disinterested in her, but she senses that he's sprung tightly inside, as tight as his bristly curls, and is acutely aware of her. As the woman sets a cup of coffee down in front of him, Amy turns away, reading the blackboard menu once again.

"Well, if you're finished," Marlene says to Hank, "then maybe you'd like to go down to the house and move the old bugger into the shade." Her voice is high and child-like.

"From where?"

"Outside. In the garden. Since nine," Elaine says. "If you don't mind, Hank, he's had enough of the sun. He'll be cooked by now. Just wheel him into the shade of the tree."

"Will do," Hank says.

Steam billows up around Elaine's face as she lifts the lid of a pot on the stove and Amy smells vegetable soup. Yes, she thinks, something hot, but she can't find it on the menu. A hand taps her on the shoulder.

"Where you from?" Marlene asks. Amy turns, about to reply that it's none of their business and walk away, when Marlene disarms her with formal introductions. "Sorry," she says, "here we are talking all around you. I'm Marlene, that's my mom, Elaine, and the funny-looking person over there is Hank, Spectrail's celebrity and most eligible bachelor. Huh, huh, huh." Her breasts jiggle behind the peach halter top as she laughs.

229

"You can be replaced," Hank says.

They all wait for Amy to tell them who she is.

"You want to order something to eat, dear?" Elaine says quickly, filling the gap.

"No."

"Fine!" Elaine smacks the soup ladle against the counter. "Don't eat then. But skinny is not beautiful, honey, not in my books." She pats her ample thigh. "Check this out. *This* is beautiful." She smiles at them, pleased with herself. "Now sit!" she commands, and goes over to the stove and ladles soup into a large bowl.

As Amy sits at the counter eating the soup, which is thick with barley and vegetables, Hank's sleepy eyes tell her that he thinks it is she who is beautiful, right now, skinny and all. Amy feels that he's stealing parts of her face with his eyes. She vows not to tell him that she's the dopey kid he met in the park that day. She doesn't want them to have any history at all.

Spectrail is an odd name for a town, Amy thinks. Main Street isn't where she expected it to be, isn't broad, either, or strung with those prerequisite coloured lights, which in winter are depressing in their feeble attempt at gaiety and which stay up all year round. The town itself isn't where Amy thought it would be, but hidden behind a screen of trees, she discovers, as she hangs onto the seat of Marlene's bicycle and not Marlene's waist as she had instructed her to do. Marlene rides standing up and her bare shoulders dip from side to side as she pedals. The string ties of her halter top shift against her back. Marlene smells like green apples, Amy thinks, like summer.

The bicycle's wheels jar against the wooden planks of a bridge and Amy sucks in her breath, feeling the jiggling motion in her abdomen and the sudden sharp rise of a cramp. Below the bridge she sees an almost dry creek bed, a trickle of water washing bright the smooth river stones. As they cross the bridge and pass through an arch of trees Amy sees Main Street, how it opens up the town, a strip of shiny black asphalt about four blocks long. It ends in a U-turn just as abruptly as it began and Marlene makes that U-turn at the war memorial which has a colourful spattering of flowers planted around the base of it. The town is clean, the stores and houses neat and bright as though freshly painted. It owes its name to the word "spectacular," Elaine explains later, and Amy doesn't question this, given the view, which stretches beyond the end of Main Street where the landscape drops away to miles and miles of tilled soil and fields of flax and sunflowers.

Spectral. Amy changes the name of the town when she later tries to write about it because of the way it appeared so suddenly behind the trees, because the substance of the events in her life while she lived there will remain foggy, illusive, and come to mind when she least expects it.

Marlene is quick to understand Amy's problem and goes with her to the store, then waits outside the washroom at the playground in the town's centre while inside Amy hunches over, gasping through the pain of what have become strong, intermittent contractions. When one subsides she's left shaking and bathed in a cold sweat. Amy grits her teeth as another contraction begins to crawl through her muscles. She can no longer hold back. "Oooooohhhh," she hears herself moan. The door opens and then Marlene hovers over her, wide-eyed with worry. "Gee. I've got some Midol at home if you want."

When Amy opens her eyes she realizes that she's slept for a long time. The light has changed and the air in the room has become suffocatingly heavy with heat. An attic room. She vaguely remembers entering Marlene and Elaine's yard and seeing a patch of red poppies, petals flipping in the air, a tree, and, in the shadow of its branches, the slight figure of a man slouched in a wheelchair. She remembers Marlene calling, "Have you had enough of being outside, you old bugger?" and cheerfully hopping through the swaying poppies towards him, and that the thin elderly man's head wobbled as she moved his wheelchair along the uneven garden path to where Amy sat on the back step, shivering and holding back nausea. "I'll just take the old bugger inside and I'll be back in a jiffy."

"Why do you call him that?" she'd asked.

"Because he is." Marlene laughed. She leaned towards his ear and yelled, "You can't hear a darn thing, can you, you old bugger? Stone deaf." The old man didn't flinch or his bright eyes flicker with any indication that he'd heard.

The room she's in is large and contains the bed she lies in, a washstand, what looks like a kitchen chair in one corner, and a low chest beneath a small window. The walls are unfinished, rough unpainted boards, and hung randomly at waist level are glossy magazine photographs of movie stars. Marlene's room, she supposes. Strange, Amy thinks, that the pictures aren't hung at eye level. The room is surprisingly bare given the colourful and well-kept appearance of Marlene and her mother. She hears whispering behind the door. Marlene's and Elaine's voices. Amy braces herself, believing that she'll be asked to leave. The door opens and Elaine steps inside. Time to get up, Amy thinks.

"Good grief, it's hot in here." The floor creaks as Elaine strides over to the window and pries it open. Then she stands at the foot of the bed, crosses her arms against her chest, and looks down at Amy. "Well. So what is it? Have you run away from home?"

"No." The sanitary napkins between her legs feel sodden and spongy.

"Kicked out, then?"

"No. I left."

"Left where? From where? You do have a name, don't you?"

Because she's lying in Marlene's bed in this woman's house, she thinks it's only fair. She tells Elaine her name; the place: Carona.

The bed dips as Elaine sits down. Amy notices her ears, large, like bread and butter plates lying flat against the sides of her head, and wonders if they are receivers for the news of the world; whether Elaine might be the town snoop and blabbermouth.

"And you do have parents?"

"No."

"Come on! Left in a basket then, on a doorstep?" She slouches, her work-rough hands resting against her thighs. Amy notices that the lines beside her mouth and eyes curve up naturally. Perhaps Elaine is asking questions, Amy thinks, because she is interested and not gathering information to be used later as ammunition. "I have a mother," Amy says. "Kind of."

"Kind of? Well, did your 'kind of' mother know that you were pregnant?"

Amy's heart kicks and she feels the push of anger in her throat. "I am not." Pregnant. She sits up and swings her legs over the bed. She will get the hell out of this place and gain herself back. But when she stands up the room sways and she must grab the bedpost to keep from falling.

Elaine pats the bed. "Come on. Don't be a silly ass. You can't go anywhere today."

Amy feels the room move inside her head. She sits down. She sees her tiny pointy feet and the dirt encrusted in the cracks between her toes.

"You know, of course, what has to happen between a man and a woman for the woman to become pregnant," Elaine speaks quietly.

"Of course." And I'm not pregnant, she thinks. This is a heavy period, that's all.

Elaine's hand slides across the blanket and Amy feels its warm pat against her leg. "You're right. You're not pregnant. Not any more. It's in the toilet downstairs." She sighs as she gets up off the bed. "So it's all over now and you don't have anything to worry about." She stops at the door, pulls the red bandanna free from her hair. "You're welcome to stay with us until you feel better, but I'll have to call your mother and let her know where you are."

"No."

"Listen. I have a daughter and so I know how your mother must be frantic."

"I'm leaving here anyway."

"It's okay," Elaine says and smiles as she opens the door.

"I'm not going to tell your mother about this. What's the point?"

The door closes behind her. There's nothing to tell, Amy thinks.

She falls asleep almost instantly, sleeping through the grainy darkness of nightfall, through the smell of their supper cooking. On she sleeps into the night, no groaning anxious mother-earth sounds to disturb her, no worry in her ear. She doesn't hear when Marlene enters the room and undresses in the light of a flashlight set down on the chair in the corner. "Here we are," Marlene says as she slides in under the sheets. "We're a couple of honeymooners." Amy doesn't hear the bump of feet on the stairs and Hank's voice as he half carries, half drags the invalid man up to his room next door to theirs and separated only by the thin board wall. Hank does it for Elaine; he comes as often as he can.

Amy sleeps through the rasp of a saw-whet owl perched on a telephone pole at the end of the street and through the sound of Hank's feet against the road as he heads home to the room behind the Craft Collective where he lives alone and has since the age of fourteen when his mother died of breast cancer. Hank whistles as he walks, and thinks of the casket-shaped jewel box under his bed which holds his mother's black Alaskan diamond ring, strings of beads, pins and earrings. He whistles the Hank Snow song about being left behind with a brand on his heart and at the same time thinks of his mother's jewellery and imagines that some day he'll give it to the girl he just met at the Community Centre.

Amy dreams of standing beside the war memorial at the end of Main Street, reading the names of the war dead etched into its surface. Private Howard P. Scott, Lieutenant B. Randolph, Timothy Barber, she reads. Then she is standing in a cobblestone street and the damp air smells of fish. She looks up at a tall narrow house where, behind a diamond-shaped leaded-glass window on the top floor, she sees Timothy sitting at a desk. When he swivels in his chair and looks down at her, Amy sees terrible grief in his eyes. "Why didn't you tell me you were dead?" Her voice echoes in the empty street. "Why

234

didn't you tell me that's why you never came to see me?" Timothy walks over to the window and places his palms against it. He's crying. "I'm coming up there." She begins yanking at the wrought-iron gate in front of the door. In the distance a bell rings, its sound echoing through the thick fog. "No. You can't," Timothy says. "Go away." Amy hears foot-steps, high-heel shoes clicking against stone. She turns and sees Margaret step through a swirl of fog. She's dressed smartly in a tailored emerald-green suit and a hat whose veil covers her eyes. She gestures frantically and her bright red mouth turns down at the corners with worry. "Hurry," she pleads, "we'll miss the ship." The bell clangs and a ship's whistle blats, the noise of it vibrating harshly. The sounds envelop Amy like the fog, drift inside her ears. "Go away. Go away," Timothy says. He presses his mouth against the glass and it looks like a fish mouth gaping open, sucking for air. "Hurry, hurry. The Lord is going to leave without us," Margaret pleads. Their voices become a hollow-sounding echo inside Amy's head. "He doesn't want me to come and live with him because he's dead," she hears herself say. Then Amy is standing beside the war memorial again and before her is the spectacular view, the fields which spread for miles, curving over the side of the earth at the horizon.

When Amy awakens the following morning Marlene is already gone. She hears paper rustling and then the soft sound of rubber tires gliding across the floor in the room on the other side of the wall. Resting on the foot of the bed is a mound of clothing and a note. She finds it difficult to read Marlene's back-slanted loopy script. She has gone to the Community Centre with Elaine. Amy can wear whatever she wants. Amy can have a bath, too, and when she comes down to the Centre Elaine will make her something to eat, she reads.

Amy carries the clothing downstairs to the bathroom and runs water into the tub. A bottle of bubble bath rests on the side of it and beneath it is another note in the same strange scrawl. "Be my guest." Amy picks up the bottle. Now they will both smell like green apples, she thinks, as she watches the lime-coloured foam bubble up beneath the rushing water. She sinks down into it, up to her neck, and then slides beneath the surface, entirely submerged, and holds her breath for several seconds. She feels the grit of the road lift and float to the surface and lets her limbs float and her body roll to one side. She's relieved that the bleeding diminished during the night and that the cramps are gone and she can now get back on the road again.

Later, when she looks at herself in the full-length mirror on the bathroom door, she likes what she sees. She likes the way Marlene's tan cotton twill pants fit her, baggy, concealing the fact that she has almost no shape at all. She rolls up the legs and then tucks the shirt down into place. Yes, okay, she thinks and begins to make a list of what she might go looking for. Food in the refrigerator. A heavier jacket for cooler nights ahead. She sees a brush resting on the toilet tank. Yes, a hairbrush too. Her hair is going to grow in eventually. She wonders what colour it will turn out to be. Then she sees the bottle of cherry-red nail polish beside the brush and so she sits down on the toilet seat and paints her toenails, carefully fanning them to make them dry quickly while she listens to the sound of the wheelchair overhead as it rolls across the room, pivots, and rolls back again. When she goes into the kitchen in search of food and a closet where she might find a warmer jacket, she hears a steady dripping sound and then sees her jeans, the black denim jacket, her tee shirt, washed and draped across the backs of chairs, puddles forming on the floor. She realizes she'll have to stay in Spectrail a bit longer. Long enough for her clothes to dry.

Instead of going straight to the Community Centre, she decides to see what the rest of Spectrail has to offer. The houses are more like cottages that have had rooms added to the backs or sides of them. No sign of a new bungalow or split level as there is in Carona. The residential streets are short, sometimes with only three or four houses on either side of them, houses with bright floral plastic curtains in the windows, and some with lawn ornaments, others with plastic roses stuck in the flower-beds. The Craft Collective is something different too. She reads the announcements taped to its windows. It appears that people meet in the building several times a week and make things. There are announcements of play rehearsals coming up and Glee Club practice, which Amy reasons must be music given the treble clef and notes drawn on the poster. The presence of the Community Centre with its summer program of activities for the town's children, the bowling alley she had seen on Main Street when she'd ridden on Marlene's bicycle, are different too. And there is no hotel, Marlene had explained yesterday, which means there isn't a parlour or a lounge so those who want to wet their whistles must drive to another town to do it. The oddest thing of all, though, is the absence of churches. There isn't a single building with a cross or a spire. Amy notes that the streets are as empty as a Sunday afternoon in Carona. Marlene will explain later that this is because most of the people work in other towns.

Amy passes by the playground and sees a woman standing watch over a child riding a swing. As she turns a corner to head back towards Main Street she sees a two-storey house. LIBRARY, she reads on the sign beside the front door. She inches up the walk in order to read the smaller letters beneath. Enter Quietly. Why not? she thinks, and mounts the stairs.

The library is no more than the front hallway of the large house. But she has never been inside one before and it feels strange to be surrounded by books on all sides. She turns, scanning the shelves. She feels as though she's entered a church by mistake. Several rows of books near the top appear to be bound in leather. *Pilgrim's Progress, Gulliver's Travels, Don Quixote*. She reads the names of Dickens, whom she read at school and liked, Chekhov, Tolstoy, Sir Arthur Conan Doyle, Shakespeare, of course. Then she becomes aware of the smell of pipe smoke and hears footsteps. The door at the end of the hall opens a crack and she sees a long thin nose and a white bushy eyebrow.

"If you see something you'd like to read, just put your name and the title of the book in the ledger." The long nose disappears and the door closes.

"Thanks," Amy says to the closed door. Then she sees the ledger lying open on top of an old school desk. There are only a few names written on the open page and it seems that the last person to borrow a book did so several years ago. She slides a volume from the shelf and blows dust from its cover. *The White Company*, a book Mel read in his final year of high school. No thanks, she thinks, as she puts the book back on the shelf and walks out the door. Books are too heavy to carry.

She hears voices as she enters the Community Centre. "Hello, Amy," Hank calls as she passes by the ping-pong room. She's startled by the shape her name takes in his mouth. It's as though she's hearing it for the first time. It doesn't sound like Shorty, or Short Stuff, she thinks. It's a softer, rounder sound. Amy doesn't know that he's practised saying it. That when he got home last night he'd stood in front of the mirror and put his mouth around her name. *Amy*. He'd said it over and over, in the same way he was teaching himself to play his latest favourite, the Hank Snow song, "I'm Movin' On."

The ping-pong table is covered with newspaper and sitting around it with him are several children. "I told Marlene I'd keep my eyes open for you. They're out back," he says and Amy sees colour rise in his neck.

"Look." A little girl sitting beside Hank demands Amy's attention. She holds up a white object for Amy to see. Her sun-browned fingers are tinged with white dust. "I'm making a turtle."

"And I'm making a gopher," the girl across the table from her says loudly. They're the same two girls she'd seen in the washroom the day before. They look up at her and their eyes are inquisitive, their faces shine with intelligence.

"Not bad," Amy says against her will.

238

"Soap carving. We went out first to scout an animal we might carve," Hank explains.

"I didn't, I didn't," the girl interrupts Hank. "I didn't actually *see* a turtle. It was a rock that looked like a turtle."

Cute, Amy thinks.

"Mostly we're making a mess. I'm no good at this." Hank laughs, a nervous little cough.

She's surprised to discover that there's a large vegetable garden behind the Community Centre building. Elaine sits on the back steps with a bucket of peeled potatoes at her side and a basket of unpeeled ones between her legs. Beyond, Marlene stands among the vegetables, hoeing. "Howdy," she calls when she sees Amy. "Man, oh man, were you ever sawing logs when I got up this morning."

"You have two gardens?" Amy asks.

"No," Elaine says. "This is the community garden. We take turns looking after it. Some of the old folks don't have it in them any more." She squints up at Amy, searching her face. "How you feeling? Better, I'll bet."

"Yes."

Elaine moves over on the step, indicating that Amy should sit down. She hands her a peeler and a potato. "We've got fries on the menu every single day." Her voice drops. "Your mother says hello. Talked to her this morning." Amy's hand stiffens around the potato and her stomach tightens.

"And?"

"And that's about it. Here." She takes the peeler from Amy and demonstrates how to use it. "She said, 'Please say hello and tell her'" – Elaine coughs and clears her throat – "'tell her that I'm praying for her.' Is your mother religious?"

Amy watches the wrinkled skin give way to white flesh as she scrapes at the potato. Marlene drops the hoe and walks through the garden towards them.

"You could stay with us," Elaine says quickly. "We'd find something for you to do." Her voice becomes businesslike. "Marlene's always harped about not having a sister. You'd be good for her."

Yeah, sure, fine, Amy thinks. I am a stray dog to be fed,

fattened, my coat brushed until it shines, and in return, of course, I will wag my tail and look up adoringly at every pat, and all for the sake of your darling daughter. What if it isn't good for me, eh? And anyway, this is probably a pretty dull and boring place. She sees Marlene's feet stop in front of her own. "I think Hank's got a crush on you," Marlene says. Amy doesn't notice Elaine's sharp sideways glance, or how her hands have stopped moving for a moment.

Twit, Amy thinks. "How come there aren't any churches in Spectrail?" A diversionary question.

"We've got enough trouble without asking for more," Eliane replies curtly. "There's a Denver sandwich in the oven. You're probably starving."

She is starving. She feels weak with hunger, and her legs are rubbery as she climbs the stairs and goes back inside. She hears the children's low chattering in the ping-pong room as she stands behind the counter, hands trembling as she devours the sandwich, and then sucks bits of egg and butter from her fingers. She senses that she's being watched and turns and sees a girl sitting on a stool. She sees only her head, dark braids trailing down either side of it, brown eyes fixed steadily on Amy's face. Jill, Amy thinks, and wonders what she would look like now. If she had not died, would I be here in this place or still back in Carona?

"What's you name?" the girl lisps.

Amy wants to turn away from that steady gaze and ignore the question. It seems that each time she tells someone her name, a piece of her is given away.

"What's you *name*?" the child insists.

"Alice," Hank says from the doorway, "come on now. You're not finished yet." Alice slides from the stool and walks over to him. "Her won't tell me her name," she complains. Hank laughs. "Amy. Her's Amy," he whispers loudly, taking the child by the hand as they leave the room. Amy hears him whistling a tune between his teeth. And her's getting out of this creepy place, Amy thinks.

Hank was still whistling when he worked at the ping-pong table with the children for the rest of that morning. But even if

Amy had been listening, she wouldn't have recognized the song.

It was a song he'd absentmindedly sing while driving down the road on a Saturday night on his way to play with a pick-up band at an anniversary or wedding social, or when Jerry called and he'd take the bus into the city, or, years later, in bed. Hank would whistle between his teeth, or sing softly under his breath "The Girl That I Marry" – the song a brand or a legacy from his mother.

12

Main Street isn't where I thought it would be, Amy writes in her notebook. *And it goes nowhere. Ends suddenly at a war memorial. No hotel. And no churches either.* Elaine and Marlene have hitched a ride with friends Steve and Laura and have driven to Brandon, a major centre which is known as the wheat city of the west. Steve is a jovial, pot-bellied butcher, who agreed to give Amy a few hours' work on Fridays and Saturdays. And although he winced her first day when he discovered that she'd fed a whole tray of sirloin steaks into the meat grinder for hamburger, he made jokes about it later, saying that his customers kept coming in after that and demanding the grade "A" grind; "A" for Amy. Laura, his stringbean Duchess of Windsor look-alike wife, putters constantly in the four-stool coffee bar set up in one corner of the shop, which is a tilting wood frame building, painted bright green on the outside and coral inside. She makes pathetic-looking gingersnaps and chocolate chip cookies that people refer to as "Laura's hockey pucks" but nonetheless feel obligated to buy. Elaine travels to Brandon with the couple three times a year. In spring for her gardening needs, before Christmas, and now, at the beginning of September, to shop for back-to-school supplies and clothes for Marlene. Amy is at home, babysitting the old bugger.

She glances out the window and sees the old man below in the garden where he likes to sit, and which, except for the cornstalks stripped bare of their cobs and several root vegetables grown too large and pithy to be eaten, is now bare. Earlier in the week Amy had helped Marlene dig the potatoes and carry them basket by basket to the bin beneath the cellar stairs. Elaine also has a root room for storing turnips, parsnips, and carrots. Amy had collected poppy seeds for her, emptying the little brown seed shakers into a jar so Elaine could use them when she baked poppyseed bread during the winter. They were like animals, Amy thought, in a frenzy to store food for the winter. When Elaine proudly pointed out that there wouldn't be the need to buy a single can of anything, Amy felt some of her pride too.

They're poor, she realizes. The old man always wears the same shirt, and his jacket has been mended at the cuffs and elbows many times. He receives a pension from the First War which is not enough for them to live on. Marlene is vague when it comes to answering questions about her father but Amy has learned enough to understand that the old bugger fought for the other side. For a full hour now he has been working over his stamp album. A strand of his hair lifts and flutters. There's a breeze. Perhaps she should go and bring him inside. She closes her notebook and her eyes turn to the page of the dictionary lying open to one side. Love. The word she'd been searching for earlier. "Love is a zero score in tennis." She likes that line. Unlike her mother's journal, Amy's is forceful, witty, and creative. The day it begins to sound snivelly, I will burn it, she thinks. Love. Love could also be a table. The table Elaine rescued from the dump, scrubbed, painted, and set down in front of the window so that Amy can look out from time to time while she reads or writes. She has read almost two full shelves of books from the strange little library in town, and, although she sometimes hears footsteps on the other side of the door and smells pipe smoke, she hasn't seen the long-nosed librarian again.

A movement in the garden draws her attention. The top of a cornstalk dips and sways wildly and then she sees Hank attempting to wrench it loose from the earth and failing. "It's okay," Elaine had said when Hank offered to come over and clean up the corn. "Wait until the first hard frost. It's easier then." But Hank would not be deterred. The cornstalks had to be pulled out. Today. He steps back from it, puts his hands in his pockets, and studies it. His legs are short, most of his length in his trunk, she sees, as she studies him and imagines for a moment that he might make a good back-up musician for her life. Her mind jumps with possibilities; hanging out with Hank the way she'd hung out with Cam and Gord. Leading the way to adventure, and Hank following behind carrying the suitcases, the required male presence to get her through doors and backstage. She does not realize that churning beneath his genial and rather placid expression is the excruciating desire to mate with her and merge.

Hank circles the cornstalk and lunges at it again. He yanks and falls backwards as it comes loose. He turns and looks at the old man, who has spoken. The sound of the man's voice is like a rusty gate in need of oil, Amy thinks. Hank gets up and heads off out of sight and returns moments later carrying the garden fork. Use the proper tool for the job, Amy thinks, remembering how Timothy once took away the rock she was using to pound a nail into a board and replaced it with a hammer.

"Love," she reads in the dictionary, "is an attraction based on physical desire." In the weeks that she's been in Spectrail she's become rounder, though not by much, and her hair is a little longer and two-toned. She can't imagine anyone desiring her. She watches as a cornstalk flies through the air, landing beside the garden. She doesn't see anything particularly sexy about Hank's solid, utilitarian body. But he is unusually kind and thoughtful, and she wonders why she doesn't find that attractive. Oh well, she thinks, he likes to be useful.

At first, her writing and reading had been a covert activity, snatched on the run. Sometimes she would simply disappear for hours into the country outside of town with a book and offer no explanation for her absence. But all that changed in one day. She had been sitting on the edge of the bed too engrossed in what she was reading to hear Elaine come up the stairs. When she looked up for a moment she saw that Elaine was standing, and for God only knew how long, in the doorway with her hands on her wide hips. Oh fart, Amy thought, I guess I should be down there doing something. Elaine strode towards her and in a single movement lifted both of Amy's legs, swung them onto the bed, and heaped pillows behind her head. "You really should be comfortable when you read," she said. It was after this that she'd gone and scrounged the table and a larger bureau, too, and added them to the furnishings of the sparse room. The two bottom drawers are Amy's and are surprisingly full given what she had the day she arrived. In one corner of the bottom drawer is a tobacco tin where she keeps her savings. She feels a bit guilty over the fact that she isn't proving to be the sister Marlene has always wanted. She declined joining the teen bowling league and going down to the Craft Collective with Marlene in the evenings to learn how to make papier mâché bowls.

The old man's eyes follow Amy as she crosses the yard now carrying a TV tray and checker game box. The breeze that dips and sways in the tree's branches in the centre of the garden is full and moist. She stops and turns her face up to the sun. Here I am, she thinks. This is me. She absorbs its light and heat. "I think I was meant to live outdoors," she says to no one. Another cornstalk arcs through the air and shushes down on top of what is now a large heap. Hank leans against the fork watching Amy. "Why don't we go camping one of these weekends?" he asks. "You, me, and Marlene. Before it gets too cold. I've got a tent."

His voice startled her and she feels silly to be caught, mouth open, gaping at the sky. She sets the game down on the ground and struggles to set up the TV tray. Hank is at her side instantly. He takes the tray from her and wrestles it into place. "I'll go and get a chair," he says and rushes off into the house. The old man looks at her. She sees the knot of puzzlement in his forehead give way to a single word, What? And then a whole sentence unravels. What is this?

A reasonable question, she knows. She has never spoken to

him and sees him only at the evening meal when he sits hunched and silent, his chin almost resting against the table-top, looking down at the food on his plate or at his hand grasping the fork. They talk around him as though he's invisible and it seems to Amy that no sooner is he done eating than he's whisked away out of sight.

"I thought you could teach me how to play checkers," she says, though she knows he can't hear her. "It might be useful information. For my future."

His hand tightens around the stamp album in his lap as she reaches for it. Get lost, his expression says.

Hank returns with a chair and positions it on the other side of the TV tray. He's surprised when Amy sits down. "Oh, okay." He backs away. "You know how to play?"

"I'm sure it's no big deal. He can teach me." She knows from having watched the two of them play how to position the checker pieces. The old man frowns and swivels sideways in his chair, cups his chin, and fixes his rheumy eyes on a distant point. It's only his legs and ears that don't work, Marlene has explained. He can talk when he wants to. Amy is aware of his legs beneath the wool pants. Dry twigs. She waits. His face says, If you don't go away I'll just ignore you. She hears Hank grunt as he yanks at a cornstalk. Well, to hell with this, Amy thinks, and watches as a monarch butterfly floats down through the air between them. Then it dips and wavers, coming to rest against the edge of the checkerboard. "Hey, Shorty, you know what happens when a caterpillar spins its cocoon?" Amy remembers her grandfather saying this one summer when she was on the swing. "Yes, it goes to sleep inside the cocoon." "And then what?" he had prompted. "Jill is not a caterpillar," she said.

As she watches the butterfly fan its wings, Amy remembers how she would put cocoons in jars. She'd either take the jar inside the house where she'd store it until the cocoon dried up, or else she'd be too impatient to wait for the metamorphosis to occur and would break open the cocoon and be disappointed in what was revealed: a tangle of strings and ashes, paper-thin unformed wings crumbled beneath her probing. She holds her breath as the sun glazes the mosaic of gold and black panels outlined on its wings; iridescent powder-covered scales, she knows, from having captured them and seen the silvery powder on her fingers. "Pretty." It lifts off suddenly and she watches as it flutters across the yard and away.

The old man turns to the table at his side and places his hand on top of a stack of magazines. He slides a magazine out and hands it to her. On the cover is a photograph of monarch butterflies. She flips through it to the feature article. It's a story about the migration of monarch butterflies with photographs of eucalyptus trees bending beneath the weight of thousands of clustering butterflies. Then the old man straightens in his chair. You can read that later, he indicates, as he nudges a black checker piece forward a square.

The remainder of the afternoon passes swiftly. Amy loses every game of checkers they play. But even though she loses, the games begin to last longer and she learns the necessity of thinking several moves ahead. When Hank finishes clearing away the cornstalks he brings them a plate of sandwiches Elaine had prepared that morning. She feels Hank watching as she begins to nibble at a sandwich and her throat closes when she tries to swallow. She excuses herself and goes up to her room.

Amy sits in front of the attic room window, feet propped up on the small chest beneath the table, paging through the magazine the old bugger has given her. She becomes aware that the light in the room is fading as the sun drops behind the trees at the end of the street. She switches on the lamp in the centre of the table, and the colours of the monarch butterflies, a patchwork quilt covering the branches of a tree, leap to life from the glossy page. She has heard Hank when he's dragged the old man up the stairs to his room on the other side of the wall, and she hears him now, outside, sitting on the steps, she supposes, humming and strumming softly at the strings of his guitar. She sets the magazine aside and listens as he seems to find what he's been looking for and begins singing. It's a whiny sound, and she wonders why country and western singers think they sound great singing through their noses. She recognizes the song. It's about a man pining for a pillow his sweetheart has slept on, wanting to put it beneath his head so that he can dream her dreams. Elaine and Marlene should have returned by now. The breeze flowing through the screened window feels cool against her hot skin and she shivers. She doesn't want to think about Elaine and Marlene being late.

She goes over to the bureau to get a sweater from her bottom drawer. As she leans forward her eyes look directly into the face of James Dean. Strange, she thinks, as she notices a small eruption on his face. The picture has been torn or poked with something, she discovers, as she examines it more closely. Marlene will flip out, she knows. She loosens the strings of Marlene's peach-coloured halter top and lets it drop around her waist. Her breasts are stark white against the deep tan at her throat and shoulders. Perky. She cups a breast. She strokes the nipple until it draws up into a tight bud. She wonders if Marlene ever masturbates. From the way she keeps herself covered most of the time, dressing in a corner with her back turned to the room or undressing in darkness, Amy doubts it. She's tempted to slip her hand down there and press the button which is already swollen. Hank's song becomes a moan. Corny, Amy thinks, and resists the temptation. She pulls the sweater on over her head. He sounds sick. Lovesick, lovelorn. She goes downstairs, following the sound of his singing. When she steps outside and sits down beside him, he grins at her because she's humming the tune, harmonizing under her breath.

When he breaks off singing to tune the guitar strings Amy watches how his tongue flickers at the corner of his mouth as he concentrates and she feels a tightening in that hard nub at her centre. She pushes off the steps and walks down to the gate. When she sees headlights of a car moving through the trees and turning the corner onto the street she's relieved, realizing that it's Elaine and Marlene. The car sways to a halt in front of the house and all four doors open simultaneously. Marlene leaps from the car first, laden down with packages. "Hi! How have you two lovebirds been making out?"

248

"We have not been making out," Amy replies darkly but a great worry has been lifted from her chest at the sight of them.

"Oh! So you *are* lovebirds," she sings. "Huh, huh, huh." Her shoulders jerk with laughter. Hank has followed and steps up behind Amy. He takes packages from Marlene's arms. Amy wonders suddenly, Why not Marlene? Why not Hank and Marlene? She hears Elaine's voice mixed with the sound of big band music blaring from the car radio. "Well, I don't know, Steven," Laura says, her voice uncommonly loud. "It seems to me that if we're going to stop in for a pee, we could stay for a short snort too."

"They're looped," Marlene whispers as they walk towards the house. "We stopped at a hotel for supper and they must of drank a gallon of beer. Each."

"Honey?" Elaine calls.

They both turn. "Yah?" they say in unison. Elaine hates the word "Yah." They tease her with it. Amy has never seen Elaine wearing a dress before. It's a sleeveless white cotton dress with red polka dots, cinched at the waist with a wide red belt which makes Elaine's hips jut out like two shelves. The V-neckline reveals the deep crease between her breasts. Amy thinks that Elaine looks nice wearing a dress. Real. She sees through that full-blown woman to the girl Elaine may have been, daring, impudent, and probably a flirt.

"Go down to the cellar and bring up some of that choke-cherry wine, okay?"

"Okay," they both say and salute.

When Amy remembers that night she recalls Steve sitting beside the fire, the burning cornstalks, which Hank had doused with kerosene and put a match to, going up in a great whoosh of flame, dimming the stars overhead, roaring and crackling, and that they'd had to yell in order to be heard above it. She remembers Steve sitting on an overturned washtub, dabbing perspiration from his face, which shone with the heat of the bonfire. She remembers the story he told about Buddy, a dog he once had. A little fox terrier who could deliver meat. Steve would tie a package of meat to Buddy's collar and off he'd go without a backward glance. "And the little beggar, he'd never think to even take a sniff of that package, never mind eat it," Steve had said, pounding his fist against his hand for emphasis. "By gum and that's a fact," he repeated over and over.

"He'd just pick up the phone," Laura says, "and tell them Buddy was on his way and to watch for him." She crosses her legs and a white high-heeled shoe dangles from her toe as she leans forward, clutching a glass of red wine and laughing uproariously when Steve tells them about an electrician who has a sign in his window that says "Let Us Check Your Shorts." Even Elaine cackles over this one although she's probably heard it several times before. Laura's big square horsey teeth are smudged with lipstick and her white plastic button-earrings dance with the light of the bonfire. Hank stretches out on his chair, full length, feet crossed, and chews on a straw.

And Amy remembers being upstairs later in the attic room after Steve and Laura leave and only Hank remains. He's downstairs in the kitchen playing gin rummy with Elaine and having the last bit of chokecherry wine. The smell of smoke clings to Amy's hair and sweater. She watches Marlene open the packages spread on the bed. She holds up a sweater, a skirt, a blouse. Then she unpacks her new school supplies and the room smells like clean paper. Marlene lists the items out loud: loose-leaf paper, binder, geometry set, pencils, ruler. Amy falls silent. She sits on the edge of the bed and counts the cracks between the floorboards. When the school buses arrive, the town will empty and she'll be alone.

Marlene doesn't notice Amy's silence. She carries the stack of supplies over to the bureau. As she sets them down she sees the hole in James Dean's face. It wasn't there this morning, she thinks. The old bugger, Marlene rages silently. Tears of anger push behind her eyes as she walks along the wall slowly, checking all the other magazine pin-ups for evidence of the holes that her father makes by slipping the tip of his Swiss army knife between cracks in the wall boards in order to spy on her.

Amy lies beside Marlene and wonders if there's any way

possible for her to get on that school bus too. She has earned enough money at the butcher shop to buy supplies. So what if this is a dull and boring place? she thinks, as she curls onto her side to try and sleep. She feels the pull of sadness, though, because she knows she will not be able to bring herself to speak to Elaine about it. She falls asleep then and doesn't stir later when Marlene gets out of bed and feels her way around the room for the flashlight. Or when she tears off a corner of her school paper and tapes it over the hole in James Dean's face.

Amy doesn't hear Elaine and Hank or the slap of cards against the table as they play game after game of gin rummy. Elaine has heard the creak of Marlene's step but it's been quiet upstairs for half an hour. Her hand stops Hank's hand from dealing cards and she says to him with her eyes, Honey, do you want to? She nods in the direction of the maroon floral curtain which divides the living room in half. She sleeps behind that curtain in a bed that is wide enough for two bodies. The chair legs scrape against the floor as Hank pushes away from the table. He stretches, yawns, feigning tiredness, and says he'll take off for home.

Elaine begins to understand at last that the reason why Hank has declined her invitations lately to lie beside her in bed and let his penis grow thick against her leg while they listen for a cough or the sound of a footstep against the stairs, before they begin their hurried, stealthy lovemaking, is the girl Amy.

"I hardly got a wink of sleep last night," Laura complains to Amy the next morning in the shop. "That damned Skinner dog woke me up and I couldn't get back to sleep."

"Oh, too bad," Amy says sympathetically. Probably hung over and that's why she couldn't sleep, she thinks, but she feels generous this morning. She feels like singing, only she wouldn't know what. She stands at the block behind the counter, working. The boning knife's slim blade moves

251

swiftly as she pares fat and sinew from chunks of stewing meat that she'll arrange in a tray for the display counter.

"Second night in a row now," Laura says as she bangs around behind the coffee-bar counter, opening and closing cupboard doors with more force than necessary. "I've got a good mind to call Randolph and give him an earful." Her frown is accentuated by the uneven and heavily pencilled arch of her eyebrows.

Amy's fingers are tinged red and the apron she wears is streaked with animal blood. Laura's hands can no longer take the cold, Steve explained when he'd hired Amy. Or the blood, Amy thinks. Amy dislikes the smell of animal blood. Steve has told her that it's not really blood, but it's red and it's in the sinewy tubes she comes across and rips from the meat.

"What do you mean you didn't sleep a wink?" Steve says. His voice booms out over Amy's head. He works on a counter behind her, making sausages. "Every time I woke up you were sawing logs." His fingers loop and twist the meat-filled sheep gut into clusters of breakfast sausages.

"I beg your pardon," Laura says, in a huff. "I was awake most the night. I know because when I looked at the clock it was two. And then three. It was a quarter to five before I got to sleep."

Steve snorts. "She's as blind as a bat without her glasses," he says under his breath and Amy grins. She knows what's coming. It's a ritual, a volley of shots over who slept the least and therefore who is entitled to be more tired in the morning. Laura slaps a cookie sheet against the counter. Amy looks up. Through the slant in the venetian blinds she sees Hank walk towards the bowling alley and work. He's provided for himself one way or another ever since he was fourteen, Elaine had said to Amy over coffee at breakfast that morning. "I know," Amy said quickly so that Elaine would spare her the recitation of Hank's history. Cleared snow. Delivered papers. Ran errands. Set pins at the alley, babysat kids at the Community Centre, and all the while practising, working hard at becoming a country and western singer. Elaine polishing Hank's halo. When she passed the butter, she looked Amy hard in the face and said, "There's some people in this world you don't treat lightly, you know? You don't fool around with some people's hearts."

"I don't know what you mean," Amy said.

"I mean," Elaine said as Marlene entered the kitchen, "that life's a more serious business for some people. They have a lot more to lose than others. And when you start loving them, then you'd damned well better be prepared to keep on loving them for as long as they live."

When I want a sermon, I'll ask for one, Amy thought.

"She means Hank," Marlene said.

"I never said that," Elaine snapped. "What do you want for breakfast?"

"Nothing," Marlene said. "I need to talk to you. Upstairs. It's about the old bugger."

"Oh," Elaine said, and her expression grew flat and unreadable. "I'll be up in a minute." She turned to Amy once again. "Listen, you'll have to let me know what you plan on doing."

Here it comes, Amy thought, I'm getting the big turf.

"Because if you're going to go to school with Marlene then we'd better get you registered right away."

This is the reason why Steve and Laura can go at it tooth and nail this morning for all Amy cares; this is why she feels like singing.

Steve clears his throat to prepare for another round with Laura. "Now look here," he says energetically, "don't you let on that you never got a wink of sleep past two o'clock because it was you who woke me up. You were snoring. I was up to the bathroom at a ten to four and you were out like a light."

"I heard you get up, Steven. And it wasn't four, either." Laura has become fully engaged now and stands with her hands on her hips and her jaw thrust forward.

"I said a ten to four." Amy watches how his fingers never miss a beat as he threads, loops, and twists the bulging casings into sausages.

"No it wasn't! It was more like one-thirty. The dog was making a racket and you said to me, 'Skinner must of just got home.'"

At one-thirty you were still at Elaine's, Amy wants to interject, but this is their dance. She feels the tickle of laughter inside.

Steve's voice becomes puffed with indignation. "You think I don't know the difference between one-thirty and a ten to four? I was up to the bathroom twice."

"Twice." Laura winks at Amy. "Now he was up twice. Well, I only heard you the once and it must of been one-thirty because –"

"Ahhh!" Steve groans in frustration.

"Because I took a pill before I went to bed. You know how it knocks me out, and then I woke up around two-thirty and you said to me, 'Skinner must be just getting home,' and I remember looking at the clock and saying to you, Steven, 'Not at this hour. Skinner can't be getting in at this hour.' And, Steven, it was two-thirty."

"Can't see past her nose without her glasses," Steve murmurs. "Laura, honey, just what difference does it make?"

"Well, now, it does make a difference," Laura says and Amy hears the quiver of tears in her voice. "You're calling me a liar."

"I did no such thing. And just a darned minute. First you say it was one-thirty and now you say it was two-thirty."

"I did not. You're the one who said it was one-thirty when you got up, not me."

"I give up," Steve says.

Great, Amy thinks. They'll be quiet now as they work until Steve goes over and flips the sign on the door to OPEN and by the time the first customer walks in their grievance will have given way to pleasantries.

"Anyway," Laura says, "I'm so tired I could cry. So I won't be going to Souris with you tonight. You'll have to go alone."

"I wanted to look at shoes. Zack's got that sale on, you know that."

"Well, go and look at shoes. You don't need me," Laura says briskly.

"I've been wanting to go down there all week. But no, we had to go and visit your sister on Tuesday. The grass needed

254

cutting on Wednesday, yesterday I take you to Brandon to do your shopping. Why didn't you say you didn't want to go in the first place? The sale ends today."

"Love, I just can't go," Laura says and Amy hears the smile in her voice. "I'm just too darned tired to go traipsing around after you while you stand there gawking at things for hours. My feet won't take it."

"But the sale ends today."

"You go then."

"But I won't know what colour to buy."

"Oxblood."

"Oxblood?" he asks, astounded. "To go with my blue suit?"

Laura's answer is cut off by the drone of her electric hand-mixer.

"I'll go and get the car gassed up at noon!" Steve yells.

Amy wonders if this is what love is. If this is what it comes down to in the end, these exchanges of conversation centring around the previous night's sleep, white or brown bread, oxblood shoes.

"Turn that danged thing off!" Steve shouts.

The electric mixer stops. Laura is about to protest when the door opens. "We're not open for business yet," Steve calls. Amy looks up and her heart jumps.

"Hi ya, Sis." It's Mel. Garth stands behind him, staring over his shoulder. They don't walk, they strut as they enter the butcher shop. Mel's tan trenchcoat is rumpled and the belt trails down one side. He leans into the showcase and peers across at her. He's unshaven, and the brown fedora tipped back on his head looks like a poor joke.

"Hi, Cuz," Garth says. She smells stale whisky and ciga-rette smoke.

"What're you guys doing here?" She's shocked at how Mel brings with him that other world, the shapes of familiar rooms, an inner landscape that she thought had been erased in leaving. Has Margaret sent him? she wonders.

"I thought it was high time I popped in and said hello to my baby sister."

Stir, Amy thinks. Mel slurs the word and it sounds like

255

"baby stir." Still half-drunk, which accounts for his careless appearance, his bravado. She feels Laura and Steve listening. She wipes her stained hands against her apron as she rounds the showcase. The apron is too long. It reaches down to her ankles. She suddenly realizes this and feels silly and awkward in their presence.

"How did you know where to find me?"

Garth cackles fiendishly. "Oh, we do have our ways."

"Actually we were at a dance last night. About twenty miles from here, so we said, Why the heck not?" For a moment Amy thinks Mel will engulf her in a clumsy brotherly hug, and so she steps back.

"Where can we get some breakfast?" Garth asks and glances at the coffee bar where Laura has busied herself plopping spoonfuls of batter onto a cookie sheet so as not to let on that she's listening.

"You go on," Steve tells Amy. "I'll finish putting the counter in. You go and have a visit."

With a certain stiffness Amy introduces Mel and Garth to Steve and Laura. "Nice place you got here," Garth says, and Amy sees the snicker in his eyes. Then he tiptoes over to Laura's counter and rubs his hands together over a plate of dry-looking cookies. She sees Laura colour and simper as she holds the plate up for him to choose one. Amy goes into the bathroom and unties the apron and throws it into the laundry bag. She washes her hands and looks into the mirror and wishes that she'd put on make-up this morning. When she steps back into the shop she sees that Mel is behind the counter now with Steve, who is demonstrating how he makes the links of sausages, how he twists and threads them into clusters of four. "It's the seasoning," Steve says to explain the difference in colour between the large and the smaller breakfast sausages.

"Interesting," Mel says and scratches his chin. "Pretty good little set-up you've got here."

Steve beams. "Oh, we get by."

"What the hell are you doing in this place?" Mel says under his breath as they leave. "It's a rat-infested hole."

256

As she walks between them heading down towards the town's only cafe, she wants to say she's there because she likes Steve and Laura. "It's a job," she says, and feels herself stepping away from the people of Spectrail. She sees the shop through Mel's eyes and realizes how pitiful it really is with its rippled and worn linoleum floor and the paint-by-number landscape pictures Laura has hung on the walls to cover gaping cracks in the plaster, how the building sags in one corner. When she looks down the four blocks of Main Street, which stops so abruptly at the war memorial, she knows how dead-end the town really is.

In the cafe she sits across from Mel and Garth, watching as they dab egg yolk from their plates with chunks of toast. Mel has told her about the job he got in the city to begin later that fall, and he's brought news of Cam who is about to leave for the navy. Gord was just put in a reform school where he will spend half a year being reformed, Mel says, and Amy sees bits of the old world spill down onto the table, the pieces beginning to lock together. "Dumb shit," Garth says and goes on to tell how Gord was caught red-handed in the office of the town secretary with a batch of birth certificates that he'd planned on selling to others for fake ID's.

"Not bad," Mel says as he pushes the plate to one side. He lights a cigarette. He exhales and looks across at her through its smoke. "So why did you leave?"

Amy watches her hands turn the coffee mug around and how moisture from it leaves half-circles on the tabletop. "Because I couldn't take it any longer." She's aware of the curiosity in the glances of several people at the tables around them. The same curious looks she was subjected to when she first came. She knows that even though they accept her now, she doesn't belong here. Nor does she belong with Mel and her cousin Garth.

"What was there to take?" Mel asks, a sudden edge in his voice. "You know what your problem is, don't you?" He pulls hard on the cigarette. "You were spoiled rotten, that's what. You always got everything you ever wanted without lifting a finger."

Amy resists the desire to leap up and run away from his straight-line reasoning. "There's not much I can do about that, is there?"

"What a loser attitude."

Garth taps his onyx ring against the coffee mug, signalling impatience.

"How's Mom?"

"Okay. She's thinking of going to some creative writing thing. In Saskatchewan."

Does she ever talk about me? she wants to ask.

"She's thinking about writing a book," Mel says, sounding embarrassed.

"A book?" The notion of it makes Amy want to laugh. "What would she write about?"

Mel shrugs and butts his cigarette out. "She's going to call it 'The Angels Among Us.'" His voice drops. "It's supposed to help people who are grieving. So I guess it's about Jill."

"Who's the cowboy?" Garth asks.

Amy turns and sees Hank enter the cafe. He glances over at them and then goes and sits at the counter. It's too early for his break, Amy thinks, and annoyance chews at her. He must have seen them when they passed by the bowling alley. "Oh him," Amy says. "So how long are you guys staying?"

"This is it," Mel says. "We have been up all night, you know."

"But it was worth it." Garth winks at Mel.

As they leave the cafe Amy is aware of Hank's heavy-lidded and sideways glance at them and his presence weighs heavily. When she steps outside she notices how the air seems lighter and easier for her to breathe. She has begun to be able to predict when Hank will appear around the corners she turns.

She walks back to their car parked in front of the butcher shop. "It's my new shagging wagon," Garth says and pats the top of his father's new Chrysler Town and Country. Yuck, is what Amy thinks about sex with Garth, who still wears his greasy hair slicked back at the sides and falling across his forehead. Caught in a time, she thinks. He slides in behind the wheel and turns on the ignition. Mel hestitates beside the

258

open door and Amy feels her throat tighten. The urge to cry wells in her chest. Don't go, she thinks, wanting to hurl herself into him. "So," he says. "You coming with us or not?"

"Longing," "loneliness": words Amy feels but doesn't allow to have a shape because she isn't sure what she longs for or misses. "No."

"I didn't think so, but I thought I'd ask. Let me tell you, though, you sure as hell could have picked a better place than this dump." He reaches over into the back seat for a paper-wrapped package. He hands it to her. "I was supposed to mail this off ages ago." She sees her name and address written in the sprawling flourish of Margaret's hand.

Amy watches as their car sweeps around the U-turn at the war memorial. Garth taps the horn as they pass by. She watches as they cut through the screen of trees, cross the bridge, and disappear. Laura stands behind the venetian blinds, looking out, expecting that Amy will come inside now. Instead, Amy walks back down to the end of Main Street. She looks out over the land and sees that it has become solid and flat. Not at all like an Impressionist painting, as she'd come to think of it after she'd discovered a book on that period in art in the library. Mel's arrival has changed Spectrail.

As she walks back towards the butcher shop Marlene appears on her bicycle in the middle of the street as if by magic. She moves gracefully and effortlessly, as if she were floating. Her hair streams out on both sides of her head and the sausage ringlets part, exposing her clear forehead. "Look at me," she calls and lifts her hands from the handlebars. She glides by, riding free-handed, her arms flung out on either side. "Neat, eh? I finally figured it out." She grins as she passes by and it seems to Amy that Marlene is caught in a photograph, her hair still streaming out behind her, frozen that way, and that her eyes have become a doll's glass eyes looking out across the street at Amy. Eyes that seem to say they know all but will give nothing away. Marlene will go to school until she finishes, Amy knows. Then she'll probably get on another bus and become a nurse or a teacher or a secretary and work in another town and come home to Elaine every weekend and be happy to do it. She will be one of the lucky ones, Amy thinks, content with a meat-and-potatoes life.

"Seems like a nice fella, that brother of yours," Steve says as Amy enters the shop.

"My, yes, wasn't that nice of them to drop by and see you," Laura says.

Well, at least they're agreeing with each other, Amy thinks. "Yes, nice," she says and hurries to the bathroom. She rips the package open. Inside are several items of clothing which are vaguely familiar, but it's Margaret's note that holds her attention. She scans the lines that boil down to, How are you? I am fine. Keeping busy and please keep in touch. Amy sees the word "Shirley" and her eyes drop to the bottom lines. "Shirley's mother wanted you to have these clothes. I don't know if you'll want them but I did promise that I would see you'd get them." The package contains a pair of bell-bottom jeans, an orange sweater, and a bracelet with a mother-of-pearl inlay. Amy was with Shirley when she'd stolen every single item. I wonder if her stepfather misses taking inventory of the fridge every day? she thinks, sliding the bracelet onto her arm. She sits with the clothing on her knee and sees Shirley kneeling beside the bathtub, cooing babytalk to her little stepsister. She knows she should feel remorse over not telling Shirley the real story on Dave, and she could if she tried. But what purpose would it serve? It would only make me feel good about myself, she thinks, because I can feel those things; it wouldn't change a thing. She sets the clothing aside and goes over to the sink and splashes cool water against her face. All right, she tells her reflection in the mirror. You have been raped. I know, the reflection says. But there's no need to slit your throat over that one, is there?

"Oh!" Laura exclaims as Amy enters the shop. "You've changed your clothes. You do look nice, dear. Is it a gift from your brother?"

"Yes."

"Well, you'd better get a clean apron. You wouldn't want to get dirty."

260

Amy walks out of the butcher shop without acknowledging that Laura has spoken. She walks down the street to Elaine's house and goes upstairs where the tobacco can rests in the bureau drawer. She will take only what she has on, Shirley's clothes, what she wore when she arrived and has since bought, and her notebook. She hears movement on the other side of the wall, the sound of wheels gliding across the floorboards. Goodbye, you old bugger, Amy thinks, but he's already gone, a dream forgotten upon awakening. The room, too, disassembles as she walks out into the street and, behind her, the house vanishes entirely.

A week later Amy is sitting in a dark movie theatre in the city watching *The Bridge on the River Kwai*. It's an old movie but a long one and a way to fill time among strangers who by their presence agree to suspend memory of the world outside the theatre and for a short time become as one. Halfway through the movie someone comes in and sits down several seats away. Gradually her attention is drawn from the film by an awareness of a different odour permeating the ever-present smell of popcorn. Lifebuoy soap. "You," she says without looking away from the screen.

"Hi." Hank slides across the space between them and slips his arm over her shoulders. Her eyes stay fixed on the screen for several more minutes. When she chances a quick glance at him she meets his large eyes, which are soft with adoration. As she turns back to the sweaty face of Alec Guinness she can no longer concentrate. She looks at Hank once again and their faces are only inches apart. Clean, she thinks. Safe. Thoughtful. In the enclosing semi-darkness, the soft light that bathes his face, she sees his love, and it's possible for her to believe that she loves him too.

They hold hands as they walk beneath swaying elm trees on Ruby Street towards the furnished room she's rented. When they reach the rooming house they stand outside her door, both hands entwined now, their bodies inches apart. "I don't have any place to stay," Hank says. As the door closes behind them, Hank embraces her, holding her still against him for several moments and she feels the steady thundering of his heart and the growing heat of his body against hers. He sighs and begins rubbing against her. He moans into the top of her head and rotates her body, her back pressing into him now, and she feels his hardness and his hands stroking the length of her from her thighs and up over her breasts in a single sweeping motion. Then he turns her into himself again and heaves against her, wanting to fuck all of her, to get in everywhere he can, she knows. And when he does enter he's gentle, not wanting to hurt her, he says, and he takes the care to use a condom so she won't become pregnant until she wants to. Amy hangs on to his heaving back as he moves inside her. She hangs on because he feels good, warm, and for a moment she's tempted to let go and ride free-handed with her heart. She holds him even more tightly then, so that she will not fall, and is able to think clearly about how he smells and feels, and what she's experiencing during this first time of lovemaking.

When it's over he strokes her hair and pleads with her to sleep in the crook of his arm, head nestled against his heart. "Now you'll have to marry me," he whispers and Amy sends him away then, to the couch across the room, because his body is too hot and she won't be able to sleep and she has to get up early the next morning to go out job-hunting. But she lies sleepless, listening to the sound of Hank's steady, even breathing across the room, and thinks about how his presence is settling, enough so that she could turn her back to the darkness and fall asleep instantly. She imagines being with him, travelling across the country together, earning a bit of money here and there and then moving on.

Hank lies awake, too, thinking that across the room from him is his motivation and his reason to grow up. He is twenty-six years old. He has to face the fact that he doesn't have what Stu Farmer Junior has, doesn't have what it takes to become more than what he is: a second-rate guitar player running at the drop of a hat whenever his so-called friend, Jerry, happens to remember his name and throw some work his way. He will go down to the Manitoba Institute of Technology and get an education. He will register for a course in Major Appliance Repair and become a provider. And he does.

13

Hank and I were married the next month, October, an afternoon wedding held in the United Church in Carona. Timothy sent a set of steak knives and sheets. Mel escorted me down the aisle. He came with one in what would be a string of girlfriends, a tall, thin woman who kept clearing her throat throughout the entire service. Margaret held a small reception for us at the house. She had bought a new dress for the occasion, a violet and grey floral cotton sateen, and she wore pink gloves and a hat. Among the guests were my grandparents, Uncle Reginald and Aunt Emily, and of course their entire family, which included Garth, who kept singing under his breath, "Oh, there'll be a hot time in the old fart sack tonight." Hank's only guest was his best man, Jerry, a sometime promoter of country and western bands and a full-time welder at the CN yards in Transcona. I had written to Elaine and Marlene, inviting them to come, asking Marlene to be my bridesmaid, but they declined. The expense of the dress, Elaine explained, and Carona was too far away.

Only an hour before the ceremony was to take place, I sat in the back booth at Ken's Chinese Food, watching the clock. Ken had greeted me warmly, with a shy smile and nervous little chuckles. He knew I was getting married that day. I imagine everyone in Carona did, supposing, no doubt, that little Amy Barber was up the stump. The cafe was empty, everyone gone, disappeared into their own lives. Then I saw Jerry's car pass by the cafe window; Jerry and Hank arriving for the ceremony. They were heading towards the Sleepy Hollow Motel and the room Hank had reserved in order to dress for the wedding. My stomach dropped when I saw him. There wasn't anyone I could tell what I was thinking: I don't want to do this. "My, my," Ken said as I set change onto the counter. "You very nervous, yes?"

Margaret was already dressed when I entered the house, and looking worried. "You're going to have to hurry," she said. "I bathed early so there would be lots of hot water for you." She'd also decorated the dining room, hung paper bells from the ceiling, twisted and strung streamers, pastel yellow and green, the colours of my wedding, and pinned them to the corners of the dining-room table. In its centre was a two-tiered wedding cake, and I was surprised because we had agreed not to go to the expense of the traditional cake. Around it were plates of food encased in plastic wrap.

"Nice." I meant the cake, the room, and Margaret too, who looked unusually elegant.

"It was Bunny's idea. She came over and gave me a hand. And why not? You only get married once," she said and rushed off to tend to something in the kitchen. This had been the pattern of our encounters since I'd returned several days earlier. Brief, light chatter interrupted by a supposedly just-remembered errand that took her out of the room. We were two billiard balls glancing off one another in passing and veering off into opposite directions. "I'm getting married." I had broken the news on the telephone. I'd expected shock, not her brightness, her immediate acceptance of Hank, her barely concealed relief. I followed her into the kitchen. I knew I couldn't say that I was now doubting my decision to marry Hank because she would only ask, What about the guests, the gifts? What am I to tell everyone? What about Hank? But most of all: Well then, what are you going to do?

I stood in the doorway, watching her work at the counter. I

had an unreasonable desire to touch Margaret. She turned. "What are you doing? It's getting awfully late."

"Mom."

She stood rooted, her eyes going wide. "What is it?"

"I need to talk to you." As I stepped towards her, she moved away from me, but I'd seen the evasive look in her eyes.

"There's no time for that, not now."

"Please." It suddenly became imperative that we talk. If I was going to be married I needed Margaret on my side. "I want to straighten a few things out," I heard myself say.

"I don't know what you're talking about." She dismissed me, impatient to get on with the next item on the list.

"Please." My voice sounded whiny, a child's begging for attention, as she pushed past me and left the kitchen. I followed her through the back porch and outside, down the walk beside the house. She broke into a little run and so I chased my mother until the front gate when I reached and grabbed at the back of her dress. She whirled and lunged at me, features contorted with rage; the fear of a cornered animal.

"Stay away from me." The words were spat as though she'd just bitten into something rotten. I saw clearly the bare face of hatred. "I don't have to talk to you. Not now, or ever. Now go in and get dressed and marry that nice man and consider yourself lucky."

I stood in front of the mirror in my bedroom that day, the room I used to share with Jill, watching my hands set a sequined tiara and its veil onto my head. I stood beside Hank in the musty-smelling church, a bouquet of red roses and white carnations trembling at my waist. All eyes were fixed on the bride, a rodent in a jar held up to the light to be scrutinized. Or perhaps they stared out the window or up at the ceiling, bored and impatient for the fiasco to end.

After the ceremony, Mel stood beside the car Jerry had lent us for our week-long honeymoon to Devil's Lake, North Dakota. "Jesus," Mel said quietly, "you must be nuts." He shook my shoulder as though to jog me awake. "Just make sure that turkey uses a rubber, okay? You can always get out of it as long as he uses a rubber." The tall woman he'd brought to the wedding stepped to his side, and I recall her crimson slash of a mouth moving in a sneer as she said to Mel, "The wheels are going to fall off that one in about six months. Tops. I kid you not."

I was stung by her comment and angry as I slid in beside my brand new husband. Is that what they all thought? Margaret backed away from the car, her duty done. She smiled and waved goodbye. A shower of confetti billowed against the windshield and Bunny North blew a kiss. Goodbye, good luck. There'll be a hot time in the old fart sack tonight. Hank tooted "Shave and a Haircut" on the car's horn as we pulled away. When I turned to look they were all preoccupied, walking back towards the house or their own vehicles. Not one person stood looking after us. It was clear to me then that I was definitely on my own. I moved over into Hank's side and he put his arm around me. I studied the jubilant face of my husband, a stranger, the man with whom I would spend nearly nine years of my life.

Indian summer overtook the entire following week in North Dakota and the weather turned hot. The humid air left me gasping for breath and moving away from Hank in bed, constantly in search of a cool spot. We lounged around the motel room in our bathing suits, drinking beer and feeding quarters into a radio but without getting much more than static. We swam in the community pool and ate chips and gravy in crowded, smoky bars and toured the Aylmer's soup factory. At night my dreams were fragments of different places and people. In one dream I walked down Main Street in Spectrail holding Timothy in my arms. He was ill and neither Margaret nor Aunt Rita wanted to care for him and so I snatched him away from them and carried him to Spectrail and promised to nurse him until he got better. But the most vivid dream I had and recorded in my notebook was of lying on my stomach on the floor beside the bed. I was naked beneath the cape that I was wearing and had spread all around me. I had just bathed and my hair was still wet and my body cool. Hank lay on the bed watching me. I closed my eyes and my fear was great as I commanded myself to fly. Fly, I repeated over and over, and just when it seemed possible, just as I felt the lightness infuse my limbs, Hank got out of bed and stood above me. Then he knelt beside me and flipped me over onto my back. His stiff cock swayed above my belly. "You promised, not without a rubber, not until I'm ready," I said. "Don't worry, I won't penetrate you," Hank said. Then he groaned and his milky stream spurted down the length of my body, falling between my breasts and against my belly. "Fuck you! Fuck you!" I yelled and wiped his semen away with the cape. Now I would have to begin the process all over again. Scrub the cape, cleanse my body, wash my hair, try again.

It was to be the last of my flying dreams for too many years.

She doesn't write about Hank very much. He's a nice man, she tells herself, therefore not interesting enough to record at great length. Insipid, she would tell you, but clean. Lifebuoy soap. A man to hang on to. A lie.

During the first few years of our marriage Hank's hair turned completely grey and he relished making jokes about that. On Sundays I would wind my legs around his waist and sing to him about finding silver threads, and growing old, while I squeezed blackheads on his back and popped the tops off pearl-shaped pimples that grew there because he was allergic to the synthetic fabric in the uniform that Eaton's required he wear. Synthetic fibres and the city made him perspire. He was uneasy all the time now, complaining that he had less freedom and rights in the city. This seemed to him to be confirmed from the first day when he made a bonfire in the backyard out of his packing boxes and, minutes later, a firetruck came to a screaming halt outside our yard and then the police arrived and gave him a ticket for parking on the boulevard. He would never feel comfortable in the city.

In our first year Hank bought a used Chrysler 450, maroon, a gas guzzler, nine miles long and nine miles to the gallon; for protection, he said. Hank took personally any traffic infraction against him, and while he wasn't one to threaten to dim anyone's lights, he did fume about the incident for days afterwards. He grew quieter, defensive, his fluttering eyelashes often the only betrayal of his frustration or anger. I discovered that Hank had a streak of stinginess in him and that he mistrusted information to be found in newspapers and books; he mistrusted anything he himself had not experienced. I discovered, too, that Hank could barely read.

We didn't gain any friends from the neighbourhood we lived in, the neighbourhood Shirley Cutting had once taken me to. U-hauls loaded down with furniture, as people moved in and out, and traffic were among the few constant things. The traffic and Mrs. Pozinski, our immediate neighbour, who had a well-tended yard, and who had lived there twenty years, she told me over the fence; the young woman across the street, Selena, for ten, Mrs. Pozinski informed me. A single mother on welfare with three kids, she said, in such a way that I knew she didn't approve. Our house was second from a busy corner. The occasional accident there and the ensuing scream of an ambulance's siren were but brief respite from the steady flow of traffic. But then, in the early years of our marriage, my real neighbourhood was just Hank, Pete the grocer, Stanley Knowles, and, later, my son, Richard.

The first year Hank showed me many wonderful and magical things such as how to make a cat's cradle with butcher string and the way his testicles revolved all on their own, two floating worlds turning slowly inside their wrinkled sacks. He wanted to see all of me, too, and persuaded me to climb up onto the kitchen table and park my behind over the edge of it while he took a peek inside me, hoping to see the tip of my uterus and being disappointed when he was unable to. Was it true, he wondered, the saying he'd heard, that it would stretch a mile before it would tear an inch? It, meaning the opening to my vagina and a baby's head passing through. I will allow now for the fact that he was curious. I said I didn't know and didn't want to find out. Then he unzipped his pants and entered me and picked me up and carried me from room to room until he came. Often we slept connected like that, or, rather, Hank slept. I would wait for him to grow limp and then move away in order to sleep. On cool nights he slept with his hairy leg

269

draped over mine and I would feel his testicles turning, those two watery worlds, two prickly wild cucumbers turning, the motion a ticklish crawl against my leg, which I liked.

We lived then on unemployment insurance while Hank attended M.I.T. to learn how to repair major household appliances. What should have been a six-month course turned into a full year because he needed to upgrade his reading and math skills. He didn't want me to take a job, and I felt at loose ends, a pebble ricocheting off water or an echo among the concrete buildings of the city. When I passed the day in my front yard or in the neighbourhood park, a tiny green space beside a main traffic artery, sitting on a bench reading or watching children building up and smashing down castles in the sandbox, I felt myself come up hard against these things: the constant sound of the city, the smell of dust on pavement, the potato chip wrappers caught along the bottom of my fence, the flow of strangers driving by my yard as I sat on the steps watching the going-home rush-hour traffic. What had started as a way of passing the time became a compulsion, to see Hank's car turning at the corner. I was glad and then not glad to see him. When he was away at work I felt parts of me were missing. When he came home I was dissatisfied and wondered why I had missed him. I felt I had no direction or substance at all until his car pulled into the driveway at the end of the day, and I suppose I resented him for that.

Sometimes we visited Jerry in Transcona, and after his kids were put to bed and we'd drunk a few beers, we'd go down into his sound studio in the basement. Jerry played the steel guitar and Estelle, his wife, sang. One night after several beers my throat opened up and I began to harmonize with Estelle. Jerry was impressed and recorded us, and Hank, even though he didn't say so, was irritated, as I could tell by the nervous flutter of his eyelids. Our trips to Transcona grew fewer and farther between after that. For a while Hank also took me downtown on Saturdays to the Country and Western Jamboree. On one occasion the Elvis Presley impersonator, whom I had seen along with Stu Farmer Junior and Hank years ago, was playing. He performed as himself now although he still sounded like Elvis. We went backstage and I waited in a corner while Hank caught up on the news of Stu, who had changed his name, gone to New York, and was about to cut a record down there. Jazz, blues, the singer said. "Oh yah?" Hank kept saying. "Oh yah?" as though he was working hard to be interested. He called me over and introduced us and the entertainer winked at me and gave me an autographed photo of himself. He was still pimply-faced, I noticed, even through the heavy make-up.

In our first year, Hank told me about himself and all that he had learned about life. He told me in a matter-of-fact tone about nursing his dying mother and in the same manner presented me with her casket of costume jewellery, which we set in the centre of our bureau, on a doily. If when I moved it to dust I hadn't put it back where it had been, the exact centre, the next time I'd look, as if by magic, it was back in its place.

Hank nursed me, too, the one time I can remember being sick with a cold and fever. He rubbed my chest and back with camphor, made a tent with blankets and chairs, and set the electric kettle on the floor inside it. I crouched under the blanket tent, shivering with fever in the hot steam while Hank played his guitar and sang the song his mother had taught him. He sang in a sentimental drippy way, then put the guitar down, stripped naked, and crawled beneath the tent, and, because I was too weak and sick, I didn't have the energy to protest that he wasn't wearing a condom. Later I became angry. Cold steam when there's a fever present, not hot, I had read, and you don't fuck someone's brains out when they're sick either.

Early on I gave up my notion of leading Hank the country and western musician from adventure to adventure, and instead I learned how to bake whole-wheat bread. To reward me Hank brought home two hamsters, a male and a female, who would, he hoped, copulate and multiply. I named them Simon and Garfunkel. Several months later he brought home a skinny, half-frozen ginger cat, which he'd found parked on the hood of his car at work. I was careful, but what happened was inevitable. I had thought the cat was outside when I took

271

Simon and Garfunkel out of their cage so that I could clean it. But the cat wasn't outside and, in the blink of an eye, it leapt from the couch in the living room, bounced across the hallway and into the kitchen, up onto the counter, and, with two quick slashes of its paw, it opened up the tiny bellies of the hamsters. The cat could not be blamed, Hank said, and didn't say that he blamed me.

Shortly after that the cat went into heat and kept backing into the toe of Hank's boot and he'd rub her and laugh when she yowled and tipped her bum into the air in front of him. When he was away she kept backing into my foot, too, and yowling for me to let her outside and out of her misery and so I did. She didn't return, and neither Hank nor I spoke about Judy the cat again.

On the weekends we often drove out to Carona so that Hank could take care of Margaret's odd jobs. In the first year he had replaced the dead or partially working elements in her stove, adjusted the oven door hinge so that she no longer had to prop a chair against it. Over the years he continued to be her weekend handyman, repairing, painting, rewiring the lamps with loose connections that had plagued her for years, she said, looking pathetically grateful and forcing him to take five-dollar bills. She never inquired how I was doing. That is, until I became pregnant. Then, both of them wanted to know night and day how I was doing. Margaret grew solicitous, almost tender, even went so far as to place her hand against my ripe belly. How're you feeling? they both asked continuously as they fussed over me, brought a stool to put my feet up on, a pillow to support the small of my back. But that concern for my well-being vanished, of course, the day Richard was born.

On the weekends when Hank wasn't compelled to drive out to Carona to help Margaret, he took me camping. Once we took a week-long vacation, rented a canoe, and paddled through the chain of lakes in the Whiteshell. As my heart and lungs opened wide to the picture-book red sunsets reflected in still water, the smell of pine, and the rushing sound of poplar leaves filling the tent at night, I felt centred and grateful to

272

him. I would return to that little house near a busy intersection and resolve to try harder. And I did.

When, in our second year, Hank brought home a portable sewing machine from a scratch-and-dent sale, I said thank you, went to the library for the appropriate books, and taught myself how to sew. Simple things at first, tablecloths and curtains, but by the end of the year I had sewn him a polo shirt that looked as though it had come from the store. It was that good, Hank said, but his praise meant nothing to me; it hadn't been difficult to make a polo shirt. He wore it to work the following day and returned with orders for six more, twenty dollars apiece, matching polo shirts for the winter bowling-league team he belonged to. I said I would be too nervous to sew for anyone else and I put the machine away into a closet. He hid his disappointment but did make a point of bringing home odd things the other wives had made, Christmas-tree decorations and crocheted peter-heaters.

The last thing Hank brought home was a dozen eggs. This was in our third year. We'd been out to Carona, and on the way back Hank stopped at the town's dump. He did this often and I'd wait for him in the car while he put on a pair of coveralls and rubber boots and went rummaging through the garbage. He looked for cast-off stoves and would unscrew the still-good fuses in them, their knobs, elements. He stripped washing machines for their clutches, belts, and pulleys, which he lined up on shelves in the garage and catalogued for the time when he was ready to break away from Eaton's and start his own repair shop.

He was only gone several minutes when he came running back to the car, upset and wanting a box. I followed him down into the smouldering, foul-smelling pit. Bouncing about among the stew of decaying garbage were fluffy yellow balls: chicks, peeping noisily. The egg hatchery in Carona had dumped a load of eggs and the heat of the fire had begun to hatch them. "Oh," I said. "Oh, Hank." Then I saw the darting movement of a rat, its long tail trailing across a mound of garbage as it headed down towards the chicks. Hank saw it, too, and swore and threw a stone at it. We quickly realized the futility of the act, however, as rats began moving en masse, a grey cloud floating across the rubble towards the chicks. They attacked swiftly, silencing the chicks one by one and dragging their yellow bodies away through the stench and the smoke.

Hank pushed the speed limit getting back to the city. He carefully set the dozen eggs he'd rescued from the edge of the fire into muffin tins and into my warm oven. Then we sat in front of the stove, holding hands, waiting. We cheered when the first egg began to wobble and crack apart. An hour later half the eggs had hatched and there were six chicks peeping and running around the bottom of the cardboard box, already drying and their feathers beginning to fluff out. "Now what?" I asked Hank. "What do we do now?" "We'll raise them," he said. I told him that I didn't think I could raise six chickens in my oven. Only at first, he explained, until they were older, and then he'd make a patch for them outside in the corner of the garden and enclose it with chicken-wire. I said I didn't think we were allowed to raise chickens in the city, any more than we were allowed to light fires in backyards or park the car on the boulevard, no matter now convenient it might be. Hank kept putting the box in my arms and I kept shoving it back at him. I had had enough of Hank bringing home little projects for me and so when he shoved the box under my nose once again, I grabbed his arm and bit it. Hard. The top of my head went tight with tension. He didn't jerk away or cry out, just stood still while I bit him. When I opened my eyes and saw the crescent-shaped imprint of my teeth and the bruise already spreading at the edges of it, I felt foolish. It was a rash, stupid thing to do. "If I wanted to raise chickens I would have married a farmer."

"You couldn't raise anything to save your life," Hank said, anger pulling the cords in his neck taut.

He drove to Carona alone with the box of chicks and found a farmer Margaret knew of who kept chickens. In fall the farmer brought Margaret two gutted chickens, one for her and one for us. I stuffed and roasted the chicken for Thanksgiving, and as I watched Hank wolf it down I wondered if it would occur to him that the chicken could have been one of ours.

When Hank takes the chicks to Carona he doesn't return for three days. Amy stands in front of the window for an hour past the time it should have taken him to return and then she telephones Jerry, who says he hasn't seen Hank. She wants to call Margaret and ask, "Did Hank mention anything about where he might be going?" But she doesn't want Margaret to think there are things she might not know about her husband. Amy sits up late at the window, waiting, counting the number of times in an hour the traffic light changes from green to red. Her stomach grows tense and begins to ache.

Around midnight she walks through the rooms of their one-storey house. Lit up like a Christmas tree, she thinks, as she turns off lights and sees that all around her in the neighbourhood the houses are solid blocks of darkness. One last light burns in the house, in the bathroom, and she stands with her back to it, looking into the bedroom. The double bed almost fills the room. At its foot is a maple bureau. This is the furniture Hank inherited and brought to their marriage. Did his mother die there, in that bed? Amy thinks, and wonders why she never thought to ask Hank. The mattress, now spotted with the stains of their lovemaking and Amy's menstruation, had been spotless, absolutely free of the dead woman's presence. Amy goes into the bathroom to wash up. Hanging on the wall above the toilet are a pair of pink swan plaques. It's what everyone hangs in their bathrooms, she thinks, as she brushes her teeth. This is in style. In Woolworth's. But she wonders if she actually likes the swan plaques. She winces as the sweet, cool toothpaste meets cavities and crumbling fillings.

She leaves the bathroom light on, the door partly opened. Except for the weeks wandering in the countryside, and the nights in her rented room on Ruby Street spent lying awake and listening to the sounds of other people around her, since she has left Carona she has not spent a night alone. Margaret, she thinks. By herself. In that large house. She marches into

275

the bedroom, sweeps the blankets aside, but fear clutches at her stomach. Where is he? she wonders, as she crawls under the covers. Where is Hank sleeping? Curled up in the back seat of his huge car, pulled off beside a country road? Asleep on the ground in a trampled down grainfield or wide awake and frozen with fear of the invisible manifesting itself suddenly, a dark presence, a demon with a huge mouth, bulging eyes and genitals? The last bit of water rises in the toilet tank, the sound a faint hiss. The sound a demon might make.

She gets up and tries to read her new book on becoming a fascinating woman. Then she turns on the lights in all the rooms, goes into the kitchen, and makes a graham-cracker lemon square. She feels better with the lights on. She wraps a blanket around her and huddles into the couch and writes in her journal, not about the dark things that lie under cover at the bottom of night, but about day things.

She continues to write until she grows aware of the press of grey light dawning in the windows and realizes that the night has passed. She feels safe now and, as she reads what she's written in her journal, strangely satisfied. Rain begins falling against the roof, a soft enclosing sound, and she is able to go to bed. She feels the house come in around her.

She sleeps for several hours and then goes outside and sits on the front steps and sips at cold coffee and waits for him. The pain in her stomach grows sharp and radiates through her torso. The sun has not yet climbed above the peak of Mrs. Pozinski's house and she sits in the shadows shivering and hugging herself against the pain and the dampness. A pleasant cooking odour rises up from inside Mrs. Pozinski's house. Chicken soup, Amy thinks. Often the tiny round woman cools things on newspapers inside her immaculately clean back porch. Bits of doughy things that have been deep fried until they look like dried shoe leather and then rolled in icing sugar. She sees in her mind the graham-cracker lemon square congealing in the fridge, the crackers sodden, the lemon filling rubbery. The smell of cooking, the profusion of colour in the sweetpea vines climbing up Mrs. Pozinski's fence and beyond it, the thick rows of vegetation in the garden which she planted both in the front and back yards, make Amy nervous. Hank planted a small square of a garden out in their backyard but the front is a tumble of hollyhocks growing out of control, quack grass, and a dense patch of yellow heads, the dandelions that Mrs. Pozinski spoke to Hank about in hushed, dismayed tones. Amy had said to Hank, "To hell with what she wants. I like the dandelions. A little wildness in a lawn adds interest to life. It's our *right* to be able to grow dandelions," she told Hank and he agreed.

The traffic leaps forward once again as the light changes at the corner. She sits through thirty-eight light changes. Useless exercise, she thinks, and spills the remainder of her coffee over the stair railing and gets up. Fear batters at the edge of the day and when she goes around into the backyard, the absence of Hank's car hits her and her stomach tightens around the cold coffee as she thinks of the possibility of another night alone.

Try harder, she thinks, as she goes into the garage in search of the hoe to weed the vegetable garden. If she does this, if she tries harder, she reasons, he'll somehow sense her spirit of good intentions. She can will him to return. She cuts through the hairy thick stems of weeds, which spurt their juices, and soon the hoe's blade is wet and glistening. She likes the sound and feel of the blade severing weeds from their stems. I shouldn't have bitten him, she thinks. I disturbed the natural order of things. The devil made me do it. But Amy knows she has cast the devil that Margaret said she possesses into the basement of her psychic night, where it sits in a corner listening to the fcotsteps above, waiting for the silence that says she's alone.

In minutes she finishes weeding the garden and the paths between the rows of vegetables are strewn with weeds already wilting beneath the sun. The garden appears to be diminished, scraggly, the tomatoes no more than stunted green baby fists. She only likes the garden when it first comes up. She enjoys sitting out on the clothesline stoop each spring, looking at the different colours of green, the wavy lines of new growth set against the black earth, the pattern like that on a babushka Mrs. Pozinski might tie onto her head as she goes off to mass early Sunday morning. Above, a clumsy shaped airplane with a fat belly hangs for a moment as though skewered by the grain-elevator shape of a nearby brewery and its smokestack. The plane hovers for a moment, then it climbs, veers west, and is gone.

She goes into the house and sits down in the kitchen nook and stares at the telephone on the wall; white, to go with the pale decoration of the room. The kitchen is small, its space allowing for only the breakfast nook, fridge, and stove, and, later, Richard's high chair. But Hank had upgraded it, recovered the breakfast nook in a blue vinyl and installed a countertop stove. They'd papered the walls in a pale blue-and-white vertical stripe, which is supposed to give a feeling of height and space, Amy had read. She begins to cry, the sounds going nowhere in the confines of the kitchen. Then she thinks about Margaret sniffling her heart out upstairs on a bed and remembers how this always filled her with scorn. Useless, she thinks, and then is startled into silence by the sound of the telephone ringing. Hank. She waits, answering on the third ring, her voice full, she knows, but controlled, cheerful-sounding, as though he had just gone around the corner to the store and is calling to ask what else she needs. But it's Hank's supervisor, wondering with a little laugh whether Hank has got tangled up in his wife's pyjamas today. "He's in bed with the flu," Amy says. "I was just about to call."

Keep busy, she thinks, and opens her new cookbook, *Foods of the Nations*. She riffles through it and decides that she will make an African stew when Hank returns home. She bathes and dresses to go to Pete's for the ingredients. She looks like Sandra Dee with her medium-length permed hair. She has dabbed lemon juice on it and sat out in the sun and the tips of her light brown hair glint gold. She rubs Vaseline into the ends to make them sparkle. She has a bright face now, pink mouth, blue mascara. Bright. Ordinary. Her jeans hold her stomach flat and she knows that she could be taken for any one of the sleepy-eyed girls who pass by her fence on the way to Sisler High School.

The sun is high in the sky and the sound of traffic vibrates in the windows of the stores as she walks down McPhillips Street towards Pete's. She mounts the steps and the eyes of Stanley Knowles greet her from the election poster in Pete's window. Mr. Knowles has a long, gentle face and she anticipates seeing him whenever she goes into the store. He's like a grandfather the way he smiles at her with affection. He loves the people, she's told Hank, just look at his eyes if you don't believe me. He cares about the rights of individual people, the worker, she'd tried. He's a socialist, Hank said. Vote for him and soon you won't have any rights at all.

Pete is busy grinding meat when she steps inside. The smell of too-ripe produce hangs in the air. Selena is shopping. Must be welfare payday, Amy thinks, since Selena's cart contains more groceries than usual. The status symbol of that neighbourhood: a full cart of groceries and lots of instant foods and treats. Clearly Selena's not wearing a bra beneath her sweatshirt, Amy sees in the way her pendulous breasts sway when she moves.

"And what can I do for you beautiful ladies this morning?" Pete sings over the hum of the meat grinder.

"Use your imagination," Selena says.

Pete hides his reaction behind his meat-stained hand. He's a tall, square-shouldered man, about forty years old, blond and single. Pete the grocer lives behind the store with his arthritically crippled mother. Amy looks at his feet. His shoes are coated with animal fat and covered in sawdust. He wears pointed-toe shoes with cardboard heels. The laces are frayed. Feet turn her off.

Amy tells Pete she will have a pound of lean stew meat when he's ready for her and he becomes all business then. She notices the line of his underwear pressing into his flesh as he bends over the sink behind the meat counter to wash his hands. Hank insists on wearing boxer shorts so that his balls can hang free. Very nice behind, she thinks, and catches herself. But she needn't worry about lusting after Pete, he has eyes for Selena only. A mark, Shirley Cutting had said of him, and Amy wonders how much Selena has taken him for.

"By the way," Pete says as he slides the parcel of meat across to her. "My Weed-Ex came in yesterday if you want some."

Amy says her budget doesn't include money for weed-killer, any more than it did last spring or the one before that. He laughs and says he'd promised Mrs. Pozinski he'd take a stab at it. Selena snorts. "Why don't you just tell the old babe to take a hike?" Amy laughs but she's uneasy around Selena, whose mercurial personality is unsettling. One minute she's beating her kids with broom handles, the next she is roaring across the street to shake her fists at other kids in the neighbourhood who may have slighted them. As unpredictable as a mother bear.

Amy leaves the store and instead of going down to the intersection and the lights she dashes across McPhillips Street and cuts through a yard, passing between two houses. Moisture drips from the eaves down onto a carpet of lily-of-the-valley growing in the shade. The sprinkling of those white blossoms against dark leaves snatches her breath away. They look so new, so innocent in their tiny bell skirts, Amy thinks; lights in an otherwise bleak neighbourhood. She stops to gather a fistful, a centrepiece for the kitchen table. She hurries down the back lane, anxious, wondering what may have transpired during the brief time she's been away. But her heart drops as she rounds the corner and sees that Hank's car is still not there, parked at its usual angle in the gravel driveway.

As she sits on the couch reading late that night, she smells the sweet scent of the flowers. Comforting, she thinks, and goes to get them, placing them on the Coca Cola crate beside the couch. They seem to glow; waxy, tiny lamps. She's been reading about Joan of Arc and as she returns to the book she wonders what the Maiden of Orleans would do in her position. Pray, likely. She puts the book away. She wouldn't want to hear voices giving her answers, whether they be from God or not. Life is this Coca Cola crate, she thinks; a squashed gopher. Then she takes the jar of flowers with her to the bedroom and sets it beside the casket jewellery box. She lies awake, turning this way and that, smelling Lifebuoy soap in Hank's pillow, fear in her own acrid perspiration odour. The clock says one, then two. She gets up and goes out into the kitchen to the tea-towel drawer, which also contains an assortment of nuts and bolts, fuses, small hand-tools, a calorie counter, and her current Hilroy notebook. She slides in behind the table and spends the remainder of the night writing scenes such as these:

Scene #1

Music and laughter. Dimly lit bar. People burp or slap one another on backs. Women's voices, shrill or coy. Depends on the age. Guys play shuffleboard and pool and cigarettes hang out the corners of their mouths. They squint and scratch. Hank sits at a table with a girl on his knee. She laughs and feeds him a huge piece of garlic sausage and grease trickles down his chin. She laughs again. Hank thinks he's cool. From out of nowhere. Kapow! Amy's fist, dead centre in the babe's chest. Then she grabs the woman's hair and tears loose her wig and throws it across the room. She dumps a glass of draught in Hank's crotch to cool him off, grabs him by the ear, and hauls him home.

Scene #2

There's blood and glass and crumpled metal. Bystanders say, "Oh God, holy shit, serves him right, drunken bum." A man's voice calls out from the wreckage. "Amy, help me," the man says. Amy appears, a tiger fighting and clawing her way through the bystanders. They hold her back to prevent her from reaching her true love. A loud explosion. Flames. The outline of Hank's head growing black and then blacker as it dips like a spent candle and rests on the steering wheel. Hank melts away before Amy's tortured eyes.

Amy stops writing to think. Does Hank have any life insurance?

Scene #3

> *A lovely place in the country. Green. Streams and cows. Two children play in a sandbox under a tree. Margaret, a grandmother type with hair pulled back into a bun, sits on a lawn chair watching the children play. "Isn't it wonderful that the nice man had life insurance," Margaret says to Amy, who is in the swimming pool doing the backstroke. Watching is a handsome man with long hair and a beard, who, whenever Amy presses a remote control button, disappears.*

The following day she decides to leave the house, keep distracted, and so she rides the city transit bus to the end of the line on north Main. She walks across a field towards a thicket of bushes and discovers a narrow path leading through scrub brush and nettles. She follows it and steps out onto the bank of the Red River and faces the slippery-looking grey water, the wild tumble of growth on the opposite bank. The air is heavy here, rank with the odours of rotting fish and raw sewer. As she turns to head back she almost stumbles across the body of a person asleep on the river bank, half-hidden by overhanging willows. He is curled up like a child, head resting on a tattered parka. He doesn't stir as she steps around him, smelling then the sickly sweet odour of cheap wine. Nettles bite at her bare legs as she scrambles back up the path quickly. This is a part of the city she would rather not see.

When the next bus arrives she gets on and rides it as far as Eaton's downtown. She wanders about looking at towels and fake gold soap dishes. One, a mermaid, holds a shell-shaped dish on her head. Not my style, Amy thinks, and neither are the heavy cut-glass decanter and wine glasses or the china dinner sets. There seems to be nothing at all in the store that draws her eye, that says Buy me, she thinks.

Then she crosses over into the annex of the store where she

bumps into one of the men Hank works with in the repair department. He asks how Hank is feeling and so Amy knows he isn't there and hasn't called them. She has listened on the radio for news of accidents. Waited to answer the door to the sight of two policemen bearing bad news. But she knows instinctively that he's safe, waiting, punishing her with his absence.

On the ride home the bus is jammed, full of weary-looking people who stare blankly into the air in front of them, clutching parcels in their laps. Several have their eyes closed, catnapping. Four or five stops along, a pregnant woman gets on carrying a small child on her hip. She searches down the aisle for a vacant seat. A muscle twitches beside her eye and her face is drawn with fatigue. Amy offers her seat and the woman's face lights up with a grateful smile. She looks Spanish, Amy thinks, like someone in a Goya drawing. Amy admires the woman's long, kinky blue-black hair and her quick dark eyes. The child senses Amy studying them and raises her equally dark eyes, smiles shyly, and Amy, against her will, is drawn into a game of peekaboo with the beautiful child. She laughs each time the girl hides her face against her mother's large belly. Believing herself to be invisible, Amy knows. Nice, she thinks, and begins to feel better than she has since Hank left. Yes, I wouldn't mind, she thinks. I wouldn't mind having a little girl. I would love her and protect her. A little girl like that one. She would care for the little baby girl tenderly, delight in the sight of its tiny, female body. She would tell her stories.

A drizzling rain sprinkles against her arms as she walks home from the bus stop, her step lighter, feeling energized by the little Goya child. The overcast sky threatens to hold down the diesel fumes and the rancid grease odours from the nearby potato chip factory which permeate the houses and even the clothing hanging in the closets. Not the best place to raise a child, she thinks. But a child can grow if there's love. Mrs. Pozinski comes puffing across the yard to the fence, carrying a paper bag.

"Yoo hoo, missus." She holds the bag high as she plods through her garden in her bedroom slippers. "I do it my baking this morning," she says almost furtively. She hasn't bothered to put in her dentures and her wrinkled cheeks cave in on either side of her mouth. The bag is dark near the bottom, almost transparent with grease. "Take, take." She pushes the bag towards Amy. Amy is surprised by this sudden overture and notices how the woman rises onto her tiptoes and cranes her neck to look over Amy's shoulder. Amy follows her gaze to the dandelion patch. The yellow heads have gathered themselves into tight brown nubs tucked in close to the earth. The dandelion patch is dying. The leaves look like cooked spinach. Before she knows it, she is clutching the bag of food, and the round woman, after smiling a toothless, satisfied smile, waddles back through her garden and enters her house.

Amy bends over the decimated dandelion patch. Mrs. Pozinski has obviously poisoned it. She wonders if there isn't a law against entering other people's yards and sprinkling weed-killer on their lawns. She marches with purpose into the house to change her clothes and then comes back out again. She works for the remainder of the day in the front yard, cutting the tall grass with a grass whip and raking it to the back of the yard. She stakes and ties up the sagging hollyhocks, and is rewarded with a bee sting for her efforts. When she's finished, she walks about the yard with a cardboard box and gathers up the cigarette- and gum-wrappers and empty potato chip bags.

Later, Amy walks over to Mrs. Pozinski's fence with a pocketful of dandelion heads. She tears open several and watches as the seeds float beneath their parachutes and across Mrs. Pozinski's obscenely productive garden.

That evening Amy sits on the couch, the lightness gone and in its place the dread of facing another night alone. The couch is a makeshift affair, a box spring and mattress set up on cinder blocks. Above the door hangs a varnished plaque with the words "God Bless This Wee House and All Who Enter." A gift from Grandmother Johnson. The table lamp on top of the Coca

Cola crate is a gift from Mel. The room is bits and pieces of other people. Not her. What do I have to give a child? she wonders.

But even while she asked herself What do I have to give a child? she knew that she must soon give in and have one. She told herself she would love it, wash its tiny body tenderly, and enjoy the feel of its small hand inside hers as they walked down to story time at the library. She told herself these things because she wasn't wise enough to question her real motive for capitulation. Is it right, do you think, to have a child because you're afraid to be alone at night?

Amy is in bed reading when she hears the sound of Hank's car swinging into the driveway and then the engine dying. The waiting, the worry, is over, she thinks, and her heart grows instantly calm. His footsteps put the world back together again. He enters the bedroom, looking none the worse for wear, and flops down beside her, fully clothed and grimly silent. She smells nothing suspicious. No cigarette smoke, no stale beer odours. He wears a Band-Aid, a badge marking the spot where she bit him. She continues reading as though nothing has happened. She knows instinctively that she must never reveal her fear of being alone at night.

"So who was the guy?" Hank asks, staring up at the ceiling. He wants her to tell him whose baby she lost when she stayed with Elaine in Spectrail. Amy, stunned by what she perceives to be betrayal, reluctantly tells him about Dave the rapist. He listens without interrupting, and when she finishes he gets up to find something to eat. She hears him rummaging about in the kitchen. Elaine's place. That's where he's been. So there were strings attached to Elaine's generosity, she thinks, sensing collusion. When he returns he stands in the doorway chewing on a sandwich. "There's no such thing as rape," he says.

"Oh really? And how do you figure that?"

"Because a girl can run faster with her skirt up than a guy can with his pants down."

"I was wearing jeans," Amy says, thinking, Stupid. Asshole. In what lavatory did he hear that one?

He frowns and says that he doesn't want to talk about it any more. Later, her anger softened by relief at having him home, Amy curls around his warm body. Sleep claims her almost instantly and the notion she'd had of having a baby fades in the light of morning.

But something changes after Hank returns. He'd sat on the edge of the bed the following morning, back hunched, arms dangling, listless and reluctant to go to his work. Once, he complained that sex was overrated. A lot of sweating and a big to-do with nothing to show for it later.

They no longer reach for one another beneath the blankets every single night. Their infrequent lovemaking becomes quick, mechanical, and she imagines him in the bathroom, discarding the condom and checking himself for damage. He hits Amy in the chest with the implication that it is not life, his job, his inadequacies, but her, Amy. It is she who takes too much from him.

One morning Amy is lying in bed watching Hank stumble about half asleep, dressing for work. "Honey," she says, "I've been thinking. You know. That if. . . ." She takes a deep breath. "I wouldn't mind trying for a baby. I think I'm ready."

He has one leg in and the other out of his trousers. She can tell by his expression that he's startled by what she's said.

"You sure?"

"Yes, I'm sure."

"Well, let's get started then." He laughs, self-conscious and suddenly shy as he approaches the bed.

"You'll be late for work."

"Who cares?" He sheds his clothing quickly.

His breath fans through Amy's hair as he lies on top of her and she wonders fleetingly, What have I done? She opens her legs to him. Maybe I won't be able to get pregnant, she thinks. She bites his shoulder and he gasps and comes and she becomes pregnant instantly.

14

During the years that followed, she read books on the care and feeding of a child until she knew by heart and could recite the symptoms of croup, whooping cough, mumps, and colic. Once she and Hank with Richard in arms attended a meeting in a neighbourhood church basement filled with anxious parents who had come to hear a children's aid worker speak on how to develop a healthy parent-child relationship. She listened and grew worried and didn't have any questions at the end of the session. Silent for once, Hank had remarked. Amy the Agitator, tongue-tied. They went home and she put Richard to bed. It isn't enough that I have learned how to keep him alive, she thought, as she stood looking at him.

She became determined from that point on to be creative. She required that Richard stamp in rain puddles, for instance, and showed him how. They made mud cakes and, later, kites, climbed the tree in the front yard. Instead of scolding him she'd laughed when once he crawled among the racks of lingerie in Eaton's, emerging wearing a black brassiere. She wrote these things down and at the end of the day would sometimes read them to Hank.

But there were times when she had nothing to write. Or

chose not to write, because she knew she wouldn't be able to bear going back some day and reading what she had written.

FRIDAY, JUNE 18, 1976. MOTHER ARRESTED FOR SHOPLIFTING. Amy pictures the headline as she stands among the shelves of food in Pete's store. Shoplifting: the shortest distance between two points. Which in this case are: twenty-five dollars every Saturday and the presence of food in the refrigerator seven days later. Thank you, Shirley Cutting. She checks the mirror hanging on the wall behind the meat counter. Pete has his back turned to the room as he bends over a box of toilet paper and so Amy drops the jar of peanut butter, crunchy, Richard's favourite, into her jacket pocket. And peaches, too, she thinks, to garnish the leftover bread pudding. Peaches and peanut butter. As she moves down the aisle she imagines the column.

> Mrs. Amy Blank, wife of Hank the Blank and mother of Richard, was carried kicking and screaming from Pete's Grocery and Meats on McPhillips Street. Customers in the store at the time of the theft quote the woman as saying, "This is just cheatstealie. You can't arrest me for making the ends meet."

The brass bell above the door jangles suddenly, startling Amy, and the can of peaches drops to her feet, rolls across the floor, and comes to rest against the cash counter. Selena enters the store wearing a hot-pink jumpsuit and matching platform heels. She pushes a pair of yellow sunglasses up on top of her head. Like a hollyhock, Amy thinks of Selena's new look. They let you buy sunglasses when you're on welfare? she says to herself.

"Hello, doll," Pete calls.

"Hello nothing," Selena says. "We've got to stop meeting like this, it's costing me a fortune."

Pete hurries over to the counter. A roll of pricing stickers dangles from his pocket. "Well, what can I say?" he laughs.

Amy grins as she picks up the can of peaches and sets it back on the shelf. Hilarious. Pete the grocer trying to be cool. She wonders if his dark and brooding mother is crouched somewhere in the dim hallway, listening, and does she approve? "Oranges," Amy says and plunks the bag she'd been carrying onto the counter for him to weigh.

"Is that everything?"

"That's all for now, anyway. Sure as shooting I'll remember something I've forgot the minute I leave here though." She winces inwardly, feeling the bite of frost as she hugs a tray of frozen meat patties against her side underneath her jacket. She will have to return for the peaches later. She likes Pete and his store but since she got her driver's licence she's begun to shop down the street at Safeway where the prices are lower, as Hank had wasted no time in pointing out, but where their surveillance system keeps a beady eye open and they don't let you buy groceries on the cuff. Selena jerks a grocery cart loose and rattles off down an aisle, reaching for items at random and throwing them into her cart. "Say, think it would be okay if I charged this?" Amy asks. She holds her breath.

"Sure." Pete fans the air above the shoebox where he keeps the records of his customers' accounts while his eyes follow Selena's buttocks jiggling in the much too snug jumpsuit. From the centre of the box he pulls a receipt pad with Amy's name on it.

"Neat trick," Amy says. She is using her sparkling personality this morning.

"You haven't been in for a while," he says. "You should try and come in and whittle this bill down some before it gets away on you."

Amy feels Selena listening and her face burns with embarrassment. Hank doesn't even *know* the price of milk or bread. Twenty-five dollars is all he's got and so it's enough. Any more and the system is ripping him off. "Hank gets paid today," Amy says. "I'll come in tomorrow and put something down."

Selena wheels her cart over to the counter and waits. "I'd like something from the meat counter when you're finished," she says.

"For you, darling, just ask."

"That's going to cost a bundle," Amy says, eyeing the pile of groceries in Selena's cart.

"Doesn't it always?" Selena yawns. "I started work so I gotta stock up for the weekend."

"Really?"

"I've been thinking about going back. I used to work there before the kids. Now that my oldest can babysit nights, I figured why the hell not."

"Doing what?" Amy is still in her sparkling mode. Learning how to be interested in other people. The jar of peanut butter lies heavy in her jacket pocket.

"Cocktail waitressing. At the Club Malibu," Selena says, naming one of the city's nightclubs.

Well, that figures, Amy thinks. But when Selena tells her how much she makes in tips on a good night, she does some fast calculating. It's almost as much as Hank allows her for one week's groceries. "You should think about it," Selena says. "I'm in with the boss and I know they're looking for a part-time person."

"Hank would have a fit," Amy says. "And, anyway, Richard's going to start kindergarten in September. I'm taking him down to register this afternoon."

"What?" Selena says. "The little twerp can't be five already!"

It doesn't feel like the time has passed by as quickly as what already, Amy thinks. It feels longer than five years. She's twenty-six years old, heavier now, with a bit of a pot belly, which she hates. The road-map of the world is in stretch marks on her breasts and stomach and she has lost all her teeth. After Richard was born her teeth began to crumble. She would bite into a piece of toast and the top of a molar would come away with it. Eating utensils touching her teeth made her head shiver with shocks. Hank had left Eaton's repair department shortly after Richard was born and was on his own now, building up an appliance repair shop in an eight-by-ten-foot space he'd rented, part of a warehouse in the east end of the city that used to be an airplane hangar. There wasn't any money for a sizeable dentist bill. Today Amy sometimes wants to take a gun and shoot herself – or someone – over that. But then she was convinced that there was no other way and she'd allowed herself to be led by the hand to the chair and put to sleep. When she awakened the dentist's nurse stood before her holding up a mirror so she could admire a mouthful of plastic teeth.

"Well, he is," Amy tells Selena, "and since he'll be going off to school in September, I've been thinking I might take a course."

"What kind of course?" Selena asks, feigning interest.

"At the university." The words feel strange on her tongue.

"No kidding."

"Yeah. Maybe a literature course, or something." "You like reading books," Rhoda, Amy's new friend, had said. "So why not take an intro literature course?" "I haven't really decided yet," Amy says to Selena.

"Sounds exciting," Selena says and raises her eyebrows at Pete. "Here." She hands Amy a card. "If you want some real excitement, that is. And a paycheque. I could get you on, easy."

Amy hears Pete and Selena laughing over a shared joke as she leaves the store. Fart. Face reality, Amy thinks, and wishes she hadn't bragged about taking a course at the university. Wishes that she hadn't telephoned Mel. "Well, far out," Mel had said. "But why literature, for God's sake? A general arts degree is totally useless. Go down to the registrar and get a calendar," Mel advised. She couldn't bring herself to ask what a calendar was.

The jar of peanut butter jostles against her thigh as she walks down the street. She stands still, debating whether to chance the traffic or to walk to the intersection and the lights. Face the reality of Hank, she reminds herself. Tucked away in the tea-towel drawer in the kitchen are her test results, the grade she's been awarded for her High School Equivalency. Rhoda had told her about the General Education Development Tests and loaned her the examination fee. After Amy had received her marks she'd also got a letter from the University of Winnipeg advising her of its Mature Students Program.

291

She'd taken a bus downtown determined to barge into the registrar's office and demand a calendar as though she knew what it was, as though she'd been coming in for years. She'd stood in front of the university, which was an odd combination of old and new buildings, reading the directional map, her mouth dry, heart thudding, and palms too moist. Students rushed back and forth, tense-looking, with self-importance or affected boredom in their faces. Hordes of students, she discovered, as she rode the escalator up and then back down again; students sitting on floors with books spread around them, rummaging through lockers. She felt their energy, their planed-down sense of purpose. Directed, she thought. Driven? Narrow, she concluded, as she left the campus without picking up a calendar. She had felt that all eyes had been turned on her, and she knows now that if she returns she must wear blue jeans and maybe a corduroy jacket and a minimal amount of make-up. She must also look distracted, bored, pale-faced with fatigue. All she needs is the money and the courage. "Blue-collar workers make a bundle," Rhoda had said. "Old whatziz can spring for a course or two."

Amy had met Rhoda in the checkout line in Safeway just after Christmas. Rhoda had been complaining, to anyone around her who would listen, about the cold snap and how she hated shopping. When she spotted a paperback book among Amy's groceries she picked it up. "Junk," she proclaimed, holding it by one corner as though it was something dead.

Amy told her that it put her to sleep.

"Oh, do you have trouble sleeping?" Rhoda peered at Amy through rimless glasses. "Does this happen often? Because, you know, it could be a sign of depression."

Only when Hank works late into the night, Amy couldn't explain, and so she just smiled and wondered what Rhoda would make of the pain she'd begun to experience more frequently since Richard was born. How, without warning, pain would clutch her body from beneath her breastbone to her lower abdomen, and that in spite of the doctor's probing, and the subsequent tests which revealed no reason for it, the pain was very real. When it hit there wasn't much she could do

292

other than bundle herself in a blanket, much the way Hank used to bundle Richard when he had colic, and wait for it to pass.

"This is junk too," Rhoda said and held up a bag of salt-and-vinegar chips. "But what can I do? Bloody TV makes consumers of kids at age two."

Amy told her that she would not be terrorized into buying junk food for her kid, but the truth was she couldn't afford it and Richard had learned to stop asking.

"Really?" she said and Amy felt Rhoda examining her anew, evaluating. Her narrow blonde eyebrows arched above the tops of her glasses. Her face was free of cosmetics and she didn't wear jewellery but there was something distinctly feminine in her tiny hands, white birds fluttering in the air between them as she spoke, and in the soft pastel colours she was wearing. "Well, that's quite smart of you," she said. "Say, would you like to come to my book club? We meet once a month. Of course you would, silly question." She adjusted her glasses with an index finger and looked at Amy hard. "Just what are you, nationality-wise, I mean? No, wait." She held up a palm as if Amy was in danger of speaking. "Let me guess. You're short, but with your colouring and shape you could be Scandinavian. Anyway, looks can be deceiving. You could, for instance, be Serbian. Have you ever read fortunes? You could be psychic, you know."

Amy told her that she was part Irish and part English and Rhoda said, "Yecht! I spit on that." And then Rhoda said, "Trust me. The depression bit? I took bloody drugs for two years before I realized that I was only doing it for my father. By the way, I'm Rhoda," she said, extending a hand.

"Amy."

"God what kind of name is that to saddle a kid with? Some parents should be shot," Rhoda said.

Doing what for her father? Amy wanted to know and so she said yes, she'd come to the book club, which wasn't in her neighbourhood at all but further out in a suburb where the streets had the names of flowers and trees. They were going to read *The Sweet Second Summer of Kitty Malone*, a novel by a

Canadian writer, Matt Cohen. Rhoda wrote the author's name on the back of Amy's grocery receipt.

Amy had felt light-headed and euphoric after meeting Rhoda that day. On the way home from Safeway she stopped at the library and looked up "Serb. Serbian." "Serbo-Croatian," she read from the dictionary: "The Slavic language of the Serbs and Croats consisting of Serbian written in the Cyrillic alphabet and Croatian written in the Roman alphabet."

Amy thought that perhaps she hadn't heard Rhoda correctly and it was not "Serbian" she'd said but rather "acerbic." And so she looked up the word "acerbic" too, and before she realized it an hour had passed and the lettuce and tomatoes sitting in the trunk of the car had frozen. They went without salad that week and she was back to shopping exclusively at Pete's.

Serbo-Croatian. Mr. and Mrs. Hank Blank – only their language hadn't melded into one. They did talk a lot, of course, but over and around one another, she doing most of the talking. She'd spring on him like a cat the second he entered the house, brimming with snippets of information to alarm or amaze him, or to further an argument that had previously gone nowhere. Her voice was a ram battering against his body. He'd withdraw to the garage and into his tinkering to escape it. He had nothing to say. He worried about this. He frowned and his eyelashes fluttered. His thick tongue could barely get around the words when he read bedtime stories to Richard. Sometimes when she talked and talked, he could stand it no longer and he'd pick her up and throw her onto the bed or chase her down into a snowbank and give her a face wash, pushing snow into her mouth until she gagged. He felt happiest when she was quietly working at something in the kitchen and not talking.

Stub your toe on the reality of Hank, Amy thinks. The skin at her rib cage tingles from hugging the frozen patties. Hank, she knows, would not dish out money for a university course or want her to go to work as a cocktail waitress. She decides not to walk to the intersection but to gamble, and she dashes out into the street. Tires scream on pavement as a blue MG

294

screeches to a halt seconds from hitting her. She feels the heat of its engine and smells gasoline. The white-faced driver clutches the steering wheel and stares at her in disbelief. "Jesus Christ! You stupid broad! You blind or just dumb?" the driver shouts and shakes his fist at her.

The gate clicks behind Amy. She's home. Safe inside the yard. Her knees tremble. This cheatstealie thing takes too much from me, she tells herself. She hears the squeal of the clothesline and then sees Richard's jacket, which is pinned to it, move slowly across the yard. "Richard?"

The jacket sways, empty arms flailing air and dripping water. "Richard?"

He rounds the corner of the house, leans against its grey siding, and stares at her.

"I thought I told you to stay in and play with your toys until I got back."

"I had to hang up my jacket." His voice is rough-sounding, ripe with a summer cold. She was up most of the night steaming him in the bathtub. The top of his head looks ragged, his thick brown hair falling in ropes across his forehead in large C-shaped curls. His eyes are wide, dark, and always questioning.

"Why is your jacket wet?" she asks with a sinking feeling. She imagines water running beneath the bathroom door because in the past he has poked a washcloth in the drain, locked the door, and turned on the taps.

"I washed it. It was dirty."

"Well, that wasn't very smart, what will you wear now when we go to register you for kindergarten this afternoon?"

"I'm not going to kindergarten."

Amy sighs. "You'll like it, you'll see. Now in you go." She raises her arm and the meat patties drop to the ground.

"Hey, you dropped them," he says in an accusing tone. He picks up the tray of patties and carries it into the house. He pushes a stool over to the sink and washes the dirt from the package. Amy believes that a mother's role is not to do things for her children but to teach children how to do for themselves. When he was a baby she would not go to him the second he began to cry. And no matter how red-faced and

295

angry he became, *la-laaing* and punching the air with his baby fists, she would not be intimidated and would close his door and return only when she was ready, when it was the hour of his feeding, for example, or if he needed changing, his bath, a cuddle, or a walk. On her terms, her time. She has "discussed" this at length with Hank. Hank believes that Richard should be allowed to lie on the floor and count the fly specks on the ceiling while she wrestles him into his clothing. What are mothers for anyway? Hank asks, and insinuates that she isn't worth the amount of money he spends if she isn't doing things for Richard.

"Sweetheart," Amy says, "I thought I told you to stay inside and watch television until I got back."

"I can't."

"Why not?"

"Because it's broken."

When she investigates she discovers that every knob has been screwed right around. She has told him repeatedly not to play with the dials but he does every time her back is turned. Anything with moving parts is a target for his tampering. He stands in the doorway watching. "It's broken. Cheap junk," he says, using the phrase Hank uses often to dissuade Richard or Amy or himself from buying something they really don't need.

"Cheap junk, nothing. You've been fooling around with the controls again."

"No, I didn't."

"Don't give me that. I can see and I have told you and told you, play with the television and you'll get a smack." She will not be guilty of inconsistency. When she tells Richard he'll get a smack, he gets one. She raises her hand and he doesn't flinch. He fixes his eyes on the wall in front of him and seems to transport himself somewhere else. How did he learn to do that? she asks herself. Her palm smarts as she strikes his hand but he doesn't appear to have felt the blow. What now, Amy wonders? Nothing seems to work any more. This is the part she doesn't understand: is she supposed to smack him again, hard enough to make him cry? Is that the idea? Or does hitting him just cancel the debt and leave him free to start over again? She turns to leave the room and senses movement behind her. When she looks back she sees Richard with his fingers stuck in his ears and his tongue out, expressing, with this universal child sign, his contempt for her.

"Jesus!" Amy hears herself say. She grabs a fistful of his thick hair.

"Ow, ow, ow!" Richard cries. Amy has him now. She feels the satisfaction of getting a response from him. He whimpers as she pulls him by the hair across the hall to his bedroom. She has caught him in the act this time. No worming his way out of this one: I didn't do it. I never had it. I don't know. She nudges him with the tip of her foot and he falls forward onto his knees and then gets up, moving fast, faster than he likes to move for anyone. But he's frightened. He will learn, Amy tells herself, that when he does these things and makes me angry, he will pay for it.

"Get onto the bed and stay there!" she shouts. Her breathing has become hard and quick and her pulse pounds in the top of her skull. She has taught herself to parcel out her anger bit by bit, only small amounts of it at a time, because if she doesn't she will become sick with pain. Careful, Amy cautions herself. Control your breathing. Count. This is not worth two days of pain. She closes the door and crosses the hall into her own room. "Pig," Richards yells and kicks at the wall. "You're a dumb pig."

Forty-three, forty-four, forty-five, forty-six, Amy counts. Yes, that's what I am, she thinks, ignorant, a pig. She begins to cry, softly, seeing him then, her child on his knees, frantic to escape the brunt of her anger. She gets up from the bed and goes to him.

His eyes are large and sad. "I'm sorry," Amy says.

He seems relieved. "Can I come out now?"

"Yes, sure, you can come out now."

He crawls across the length of his bed, climbs up over the metal railing, and drops down onto the floor. Richard seldom does anything the easy way, Amy thinks, as he pushes past her through the hall and outdoors.

"You have to have a bath," she calls. "Get nice and clean to meet the kindergarten teacher."

"I'm not going, I'm not going, I'm not going to kinder garting," Richard sings. The window panes rattle as the door slams shut.

15

The next day began not with the sun rising behind the window shade in her bedroom but behind eyes closed in half-sleep, the memory of the events of the previous day blessedly unreal, still locked away until her eyelashes began fluttering and dream phantoms shrank in the light of consciousness.

This was the day following the one when a child's jacket had been ironed dry and he was reluctantly coaxed from play to be taken by the hand and walked the three blocks to register for kindergarten at a school named after an Arctic explorer. They had walked holding hands and she'd sung a song about rain-drops. But when she remembers that walk home now – as it was golden, bright with warm June sun and the newly minted leaves swaying in the lilac-scented air – she thinks of another song. She hears music that is swollen with longing, desire, and she feels like the two Marys in Pergolesi's "Stabat Mater." She mourns, as much as she knows how to, her own loss, the pouty mouth, the nimble, tanned fingers, her child, her childhood.

When I woke up Saturday morning I was aware that during the night something cataclysmic had occurred. Deep beneath the strata, in the geology of Hank's and my relationship, something had shifted. If Hank and I were two stone plates floating side by side along a fault line, then during the night one had reared up against the other, gouging and scouring its way to the surface. I felt the tension of the impending rupture as I cooked breakfast that morning, cleaned up, and waited for Hank to get into the shower before I picked up the telephone, dialled the number Selena had given me, and made an appointment for Monday to see her boss about a job.

I'd been reading different books lately. Novels. I liked the Matt Cohen novel I'd read for the book club. Especially the part about Kitty Malone having restless eyes: "eyes that couldn't stay still were her whole restless story, refusing anything except whatever she could see in the centre of herself." Yes, that's me, I'd thought when I read those lines, and felt a twinge of panic. Well, if that was me, then what was I doing here, a mother for life? I'd read many other novels Rhoda had recommended. Stories of men who more or less made love to their wives, waited until they fell asleep, and then got into their cars and drove away forever. The way Timothy had done. I had read about women sneaking out of their marriages suitcase by suitcase until one morning a month or year later the husband would suddenly realize that his wife no longer sat across the table from him. More or less. I had decided that the long way of leaving might not be as painful. I would leapfrog out on the back of a job, security, a goal.

But it didn't turn out that way. Circumstances decided for me, and by the end of that summer I would be gone.

Later in the morning Hank came into the kitchen carrying the alarm clock, which was in pieces, back and front removed. Richard had taken it apart earlier, amusing himself when what he was supposed to be doing was playing quietly with books or puzzles as the doctor at the Children's Centre had instructed. "Make certain he takes it easy for a day or two." Hank slid in behind the table, his back to the window, and light shone through his tightly curled and now-grey hair: an Afro. Hank was finally in style.

"I registered Richard for kindergarten yesterday," I said.

Hank asked how it had gone but seemed distracted. Although his stubby fingers could cope with the insides of major household appliances, the minute inner workings of an alarm clock frazzled him and demanded his concentration.

I told him it had gone pretty well, that the tests had shown Richard had above-average intelligence.

"Well, if Richard is so darn smart, then how come he can't put this thing back together again, eh?" I heard pride in his voice.

I saw Richard through the front screen door from where I stood at the kitchen counter. He had climbed halfway up the chainlink fence and hung there by his fingers and toes like a monkey. He had a good full-sized head. Egg-shaped. Thick, dark hair, which he hated for me to wash or comb. Because of the constant battles we had over washing his hair, I often let it go longer than I should, and consequently most of the time he exuded the odour of a squirmy pup, hot and dusty-smelling. I wouldn't attempt to wash his hair for a while now because of the shaved spot at the back of his head and the two sutures that laced up the cut. He had examined those sutures with a curious kind of satisfaction, almost pride. They would make him king of the neighbourhood. An accident. He fell, I told the doctor. He fell off his tricycle.

I had thought of that puppy smell on the way to the Children's Centre the day before as he curled in my lap in the back seat of the cab, clutching up to his face what remained of his comfort blanket, a frayed square of flannel cloth, while I pressed a sanitary napkin against the cut. His sides heaved with energy and life and I remembered the first time I had held him. I had been amazed by the weight of him in the crook of my arms, at how solid that little floating being had become. He had settled into my arms instantly, a slanted-eyed stranger, and claimed the right to my embrace. Sometimes I would coax Richard with the promise of a treat or an adventure, to have a rest with me. We would cuddle, the two of us, beneath a blanket in the middle of an afternoon. Richard, shrimp-like, curled up in front of me, and me lying there, feeling despair, feeling that a burglar had crept into the house to steal my energy, had sat on my heart so that my blood became sluggish. Sometimes I would lie with him for an entire afternoon,

301

listening for the telephone to ring, for the sound of mail thumping into the box. The warmth of him leaning into me as we rode in the cab spread up to my throat. Richard, Richard, I thought, as I held him against me tightly, watching the grey city glide past the cab window. "I fell, didn't I?" he said. "On my bicycle. I fell."

I stood in the centre of the kitchen, hands on my hips to make myself appear larger, as Hank would often do. "Hank," I said, "I want to talk to you."

"Yah?" he said, still concentrating intently on the inner workings of the alarm clock. "Shoot."

The telephone rang, startling both of us. Hank looked up at me and then his eyes shifted away to the hall and front door where Richard peered in at the both of us, his invisible antennae quivering. I reached the telephone before Hank. My friend, Rhoda, had a way of sounding breathless whenever she called, as though the house was burning down around her and she was pouring water on it and making last-minute calls before the firemen arrived. "Hey," I think she may have said, "I'm just checking with you. I can't talk. Would you believe it? Tom's chosen this very moment to come traipsing in the door with six of his friends. Six, Amy. Six fucking boys. I've got to go and barricade the fridge. Just checking about the book club. You still coming?"

"Of course I'm coming to the book club on Monday," I said, loud enough to remind Hank. Because he worked Saturday afternoons he took off a half-day on Mondays and he'd promised to keep Richard for an hour and let me use the car.

"Well, you never know," Rhoda said, and implied with her tone the possibility of mysterious and exotic happenings in my life. Intrigue, gossip, the things Rhoda fed on. When she talked, words spilled like water into the kitchen sink, a bubbling torrent of sentences, seemingly without direction, but then funnelling into prying questions and sucking me in.

Hank cleared his throat to indicate impatience. Whenever the telephone rang and it was for me, Hank suddenly had to use it. To make contacts, appointments to pick up appliances in need of repair. I told Rhoda that I had finished reading the book we were supposed to discuss on Monday but that I didn't understand it. I had found it rather strange.

"Of course it's strange, dummy," Rhoda said. "It isn't a Harlequin, after all." Rhoda insulted all the women in the book club equally. Once she said to me, "You are an anomaly." And another time, "You are an obsequious person." I went out and bought my own dictionary, and more and more since I'd met Rhoda I'd felt compelled to reach for it. I needed a clear definition for the word "victim." We were reading Margaret Atwood's novel *Surfacing*. I enjoyed reading it, I told Rhoda, but I didn't understand the ending, the point that was being made. I didn't tell Rhoda about my dream, though. Of me standing in the bow of a ship and Margaret Atwood standing beside me. Her hair twitched in the wind. She pointed across the watery horizon, off at something in the distance. "I'm trying," I said. "But I can't see what you see." "Open your eyes. Look, it's over there, plain as day," she said, her voice sounding like Rhoda's. Then she disappeared.

"What's to understand?" Rhoda asked. "The woman in the novel begins to take responsibility. She begins to reject the idea of being a victim. Simple. There, it's yours. I give it to you. Use it in the discussion and I'll let everyone think it was your idea. Thomas!" she shouted. "Jesus! Boys! They're so insufferably smug at this age. They make me want to puke. Oh, why couldn't I have had just one girl?"

The alarm buzzed harshly, Hank proving that he'd fixed the clock. I told Rhoda I had to go.

"Oh, I get it. Old whatziz is home."

"Rhoda," I said as I hung up.

"The spinny one," Hank said, and reached around me for the telephone. I held my breath as I waited for him to finish his call. I could hear the telephone ringing at the other end, four, five times. He hung up.

"Hank." I stood there, hands on my hips. "Hank. I registered Richard for kindergarten yesterday."

"Yah, I know, you already told me."

I could not hold it in any longer. "Well, it seems that our

303

financial state of affairs is worse than I thought. So I think it might be a smart move for me to get a job."

"You have a job," Hank said. "But if you're bored" – he shifted, as though embarrassed, his mouth curling in a half-smile, his eyes evading mine – "well, then maybe it's time we got started on another one."

→

It's still early afternoon on Friday when Amy and Richard return from registering him for kindergarten and so Amy takes him to the playground. She sits on a warm bench, basking in the glow of the June sun and the kindergarten teacher's comments about Richard's evaluation tests. Above-average vocabulary; intelligent.

Middle-aged, fat, the woman had bottle-blonde hair and wore a kind of fairy-queen costume. For the children, she explained, and waved her magic wand. It made them feel more at ease when they were brought in. As Amy watched her float around the room in bouffant netting, she thought, Who do you think you're kidding? She came to learn later that the woman was a trained musician. An opera diva who had sung all over Europe but suffered a mental collapse and became a teacher late in life. "Richard is an intelligent and well-adjusted child," she'd said, and Amy thought, Thank God for small mercies. In spite of me, Richard is well-adjusted. She's impatient to tell Hank that Richard has an above-average vocabulary, which includes a few words she wishes he didn't have, the ones he's picked up at the playground where they have spent entire summers, Amy reading, Richard learning how to defend himself. Children's play, Amy discovered, could be awfully bloody and Richard managed to do his fair share of bashing. Does it hurt? Where does it hurt? she'd ask. Show me. But she didn't offer to kiss it better the way other mothers did. She didn't want to use tricks.

Amy already knew her son was intelligent. She'd known it early on from the books she brought home from the library on child development. She realized he was ahead of his age in the way he stacked blocks or arranged them in patterns. She watched him in the kindergarten room as he explored, going back and forth between the Activity Centre and the Learning Centre, fingers lifting, examining, deftly fitting pieces of puzzles together; fingers never, never still.

She watches now, his thin legs scissoring through the sun as he dashes between the water fountain and the sandbox carrying a soup can. On the bench beside her, unopened, is the latest book she has borrowed from the library: *Your Gifted Child*. Richard waits patiently for the narrow stream of water to fill the tin can and then he races back to the sandbox and empties the water in one corner, his spot. His tongue follows the direction of the road he's constructing.

"Can I? Can I?" Richard stands in front of her now, his sand-encrusted fingers drumming against her knee.

"Sure." She watches him dart off to the refuse barrel to rummage through it for a larger container.

Later, Amy feels the tug of his hand in hers as he drags his feet, tired from the excitement of the visit to the school and an afternoon in the bright sun. She feels the flush of it in her own cheeks too. Amy sings a song about raindrops, and he joins in now and then with his ragged voice, a bit off-key. He wants to go to school again, tomorrow, he says, and Amy will take him to the calendar when they get home and try to explain how many days, weeks, months before this will happen. "When the leaves on the trees are gold and start to fall off," she explains and he seems satisfied by this and turns his face up to the trees as they walk away from the park, heading down towards Pete's Grocery to pick up the can of peaches she didn't manage to get that morning. "Not gold yet," Amy says. He nods solemnly. Her heart twists.

"Hi, hi, hi," Richard says as he scrambles up the stairs in front of her. "Stanley Knowles," he says, and points to the poster.

"What? You here again?" Pete says as she enters the store and then he kicks an empty box down a narrow aisle and disappears behind a shelf. She hears a knife slicing open a carton.

"Milk," she says. "I told you I was bound to forget something. Any specials?" she asks, more to hear the sound of his voice, so that she can determine where he is at all times.

"There's a special on canned ham," Pete says. "I got a good buy."

Richard kneels in front of the bins of potatoes and begins sorting through them, dumping red potatoes in with the white and white in with the red. Amy moves down the aisle. MOTHER AND CHILD ARRESTED FOR SHOPLIFTING. I beg your pardon, ma'am, would you spread your legs, put your hands above your head. Don't move. Careful, she's got a can of peaches in her jacket pocket. Look, I only take what I need. This is just a temporary solution.

"Been a busy day today?" she asks.

"Not any more than usual," Pete says.

Her hand jumps. He's moved. His voice comes from – she looks in the mirror. Where in hell is he? Suddenly, he's standing beside her, leaning against the shelf. He crosses his pointed-toed shoes. "You want to buy tickets for a social?"

She picks up a can of devilled ham and pretends to read its label. "I haven't been to a dance for ages. I don't think I'd know how," she says.

"Go 'way. You and Hank go to socials, don't you?"

"Oh, we used to. But he can't stand the smoke," Amy says. "It's terrible in those halls. It makes his eyes swell."

Pete laughs. "He's pulling your leg. I've seen that man of yours in the Lincoln Motor Inn often enough. The smoke's so thick in that place you could cut it with a knife. I'll bet he doesn't take you because he's afraid he'd never get a chance to dance with you."

No weather talk, this, Amy thinks. She feels the heat of blood rising in her face, feels flustered, confused. "I'll have half a pound of bacon," she says so that they will fall back into their familiar roles. She doesn't need bacon but is relieved as Pete becomes businesslike again. He hurries away behind the meat counter. She's irritated and set off balance by this information. When Hank is away she always assumes it's work, an estimate or a pick-up or delivery. She's never doubted that his absence was due to work.

Mrs. Pozinski is waiting for them at the fence as they enter the yard. "Yoo hoo, missus," she calls. "I don't like it to bother you, but I find glass on my sidewalk. Your boy, he throw drink bottle into my yard yesterday."

"Uh uh, no I didn't," Richard says and backs away from the woman's accusing finger.

"I'll come over and clean it up," Amy says wearily. No peaches for dessert, a half a pound of bacon she doesn't really need, and an irate neighbour. What next?

"Good, good," Mrs. Pozinski says. "Boy oh boy, broken glass, big trouble."

"I'm sure he didn't do it on purpose," Amy says. "I'll speak to him." She sends Richard into the house with the bacon and then follows the woman down the walk to the broken pop bottle. As she bends and gingerly picks at the thin slivers of glass, she winces with pain. A bubble of blood rises on her finger.

They keep the Band-Aids on the top shelf in the bedroom closet and out of reach or else they'd find them plastered on Richard's toys or on cracks in the walls, his attempts to "fix" things. She jumps and makes a grab for the box on the shelf and a clear plastic bag falls to the floor at her feet. Inside it are dozens of plastic monkeys, amber, green, red, the kind used to decorate fancy cocktails. But something else captures her attention. A bank passbook. She opens it and the figures jump from the page. Two thousand and eight hundred dollars. She sits down on the bed. Each entry, the precise accounting of deposits, interest payments, each figure a hammer blow. Bitterness fills her mouth. Here I am, she thinks, a juggler trying to keep all the balls in the air and he's hoarding money in a savings account. The unfairness of this settles heavily in her chest. Her hands shake as she slips the passbook back into its plastic sleeve.

Richard lies on his stomach under the kitchen table shielding something with his arm. "I'm making a surprise," he says. "You're going to like it."

"I sure hope it's not the kind of surprise you gave Mrs. Pozinski," Amy says drily. Damn him, Amy thinks, the cheap bastard.

"I didn't do it."

"I'm going outside for a while. I'll be out in the backyard if you need me, okay?"

"I'll call you when my surprise is finished." He bends over his work, scribbling furiously.

Amy lies back in the chaise lounge facing the garden. She looks up at the latticework of wires crisscrossing the sky above her yard, at the chokecherry bush growing wild beside the battered garbage cans, thinking: Almost three thousand dollars. Thinking of his meagre gifts in the past, a roasting pot for Christmas, a second-hand synthetic Persian lamb jacket, the cheap Woolworth's nightgowns. Thinking: Here I am, twenty-six years old, with a mouthful of plastic teeth. It isn't fair. But it's his secretiveness that unnerves her. What else, she wonders, has he concealed? She sees Selena across the street, closing her gate and teetering off on very high heels to the corner and the bus. To work, Amy thinks, and realizes that she envies Selena. Amy isn't at all certain what courses she would take even if she did go to unversity. Three thousand dollars is a lot of courses. But she doesn't want Hank's money. She wants to be like Selena, to have the freedom a job allows, to weigh possibilities and make decisions. Maybe she should take a course in psychology. She would like to try and learn how to understand herself better. Or perhaps she could become a teacher; or a medical lab technician who tracks down the insufficiencies of human fluids or the presence of abnormal cells, records the hot and cold of the body's climate zones. She would like to be in a position of saving people. Whatever, she would not study what Mel had and become a snob who gets her kicks being recognized by waiters. I want to do something, she thinks, and feels the pressing urge just to *do*. Then she hears a scream inside the house. It

308

yanks her to her feet. Richard meets her at the door, his face gone pale, his mouth open, and his words jumble together. "Mommy, Mommy, oh, oh, oh."

"What is it?"

"Fire." He points towards the kitchen.

As Amy bounds up the stairs two at a time she can see in the kitchen doorway the reflection of orange light dancing on the refrigerator door and as she enters, then the fire itself, shooting up the wall from the garbage can. She grabs a pot of leftover coffee from the counter and sloshes it onto the flames. The coffee sizzles and the fire draws back under cover of a sheet of smoke. Then she flings water from the dishpan, quenching the flames. The smoke rises and billows throughout the room, dark and thick, making her eyes and throat smart. Pieces of burnt paper swirl up near the ceiling and then softly float down onto the table, the countertop, her head and shoulders. Amy opens the window as wide as it will go and both the front and back doors. Her canvas running shoes are tinged black with soot and the wallpaper and ceiling around the garbage can glisten silky black.

"Richard! What the hell happened?" He enters the kitchen rubbing his eyes against the sting of smoke. "You almost burned the house down! What were you doing?" She's an inch from hysteria.

"I was baking a cake," he says. "I was baking you a cake." He points and she sees the broiler element in the oven glowing red.

She forces herself to lower her voice so that he will not retreat into stubborn silence. "What do you mean, baking a cake?"

His eyes shift to a pie plate lying on the floor and a tea-towel beside it, slightly singed. Amy squats in front of him and looks into his fear-filled eyes. "It's okay, Richard, everything's okay. Just tell me the whole story, all right?"

"I put the cake in the oven," he says, blinking the way Hank does and twisting a corner of his tee shirt around one finger.

"And then what?"

"It started on fire and so I put it in the garbage."

309

"Put what, Richard? I don't see anything here."

"It burned. It was a paper cake."

The evidence of this lies under the kitchen table, the crayons, scissors, and brown paper. Her surprise.

She draws him into herself, holding him against her tightly. She feels the sticky warmth of his hands sliding about her neck in a hug and the tickle of his moist lashes against her face. "It's okay, honey," she hears herself say. Positive reinforcement, she has read somewhere, for telling the truth. "I'm glad you told me. Would you like to make a real cake some time?"

He nods and leans heavily into her breasts, clinging, wanting to stay.

She pats his back, draws his hands from her neck, and moves away. "Well, that's what we'll do then. Not now, but another day. Soon, okay?"

An hour later the kitchen is back to normal except for the lingering burnt odour and a scorch mark on the wallpaper beside the garbage can. She looks at the clock and realizes that Hank is late. Her joyful anticipation of telling him that their son will do well has faded and in its place is the sour taste of his secret: the bank passbook. His withholding. She thinks she will use it as ammunition to put him on the offensive, off balance, and then she'll tell him flat out that she's going to get a job. "It stinks in here," Richard says. She agrees and so they go out into the backyard where they'll wait for Hank.

Richard plays in a corner of the yard where Hank has set down a piece of indoor-outdoor carpeting. He moves vehicles through streets in the town he has constructed out of pieces of wood, bits of broken cement, anything he can find. The rush-hour traffic has thinned to a trickle of cars passing through the intersection on the corner. The day has lost its brightness and the sharp edges of the neighbourhood begin to soften. She watches as Richard gets up and tiptoes to the back of the garden and over to the chokecherry bush. He carries a stone, she knows, and watches as he bends and places it among the others he has laid there. A tiny pile of stones, which they were not to touch or ever disturb because they are "very, very magic," Richard had said rather vehemently. He cups his mouth and leans forward and whispers into the tree's branches. Then he turns his ear as though he's listening to something. He walks towards Amy, carrying a twig that he's pulled from the bush. "Daddy's coming soon," he says and offers no explanation. Hank, you bastard, where are you? Amy thinks.

She watches as Richard climbs up onto the clothesline stoop and begins to strip the branch of its leaves. His tongue flicks from side to side as he concentrates. Then he twists the twig until it breaks into two pieces and he sets the pieces one against the other. He lifts the crossed sticks and swings them across the sky, making the *ssshh ssshh* sound of a powerful jet engine as he pushes his airplane up over the roofs of the houses, over the stingy, gritty neighbourhood, high above and on to other worlds. Yes, Amy thinks. Yes, she will confront Hank about the passbook and ask, Why do I have a mouth full of plastic teeth when we have all this money? She will demand the right to get a job, to make decisions, the freedom to choose.

Later, Amy runs water for Richard's bath and then goes out into the kitchen and calls Hank's shop. The setting sun glares through the bedroom windows at the other side of the house but the kitchen is already dim. She sits at the table in the kitchen nook and listens to the ring of the telephone. Richard stands in the doorway, eyes bright, fixed on her. She hangs up. He doesn't wait for her to ask, What is it?

"It's broken again," he says. "Can you fix it? I want to watch 'The Brady Bunch.'"

The world outside the house rushes inside. A shrill ambulance siren, the waspy whine of a motorbike passing by colliding against the sound of water running into the bathtub – she must constantly be on guard that it won't overflow. The stink of the scorched wall, Hank's absence, his duplicity, eat at her. She crosses the hall into the living room and she sees

311

the flickering roll of the television set. "By Jesus, you little bugger!" she hears herself scream, and sees herself grab Richard by the arm, swing him around, and let go. She sees him slide and slide across the living-room floor. She hears the horrible crack of his head meeting the edge of the coffee table.

The shift that had occurred overnight *was* cataclysmic, I realized, because I knew I couldn't be deflected or driven away from my resolution to make changes. I held my ground in the kitchen with Hank. "Another baby? You must have rocks in your head. Number one," I said, "with the miserly bit you've been giving me to run this house we can barely afford the one we have. No matter what you say I won't continue trying to feed the three of us on twenty-five dollars a week. Period." I told him that I had been forced to buy groceries on the cuff at Pete's. "Fact number two," I said, "it's a job I want, not another kid. Selena, across the street, just started cocktail waitressing, and she says she makes as much in tips in one night as you give me for an entire week's groceries."

"Number one," Hank countered, "there's something pretty screwy about the system if it takes two incomes to run a family. And, number two, it stinks if a waitress can earn as much as a skilled worker. It just plain well stinks. And that's what happens because of socialism," he said, jabbing at the tabletop. "That's what comes from voting for the likes of Stanley Knowles."

I said I didn't quite get the connection and he ground to a halt, throat knotting with words that refused to be born. He managed to say, "Richard needs his mother. A full-time mother, and not one with her nose in a book all day either, not watching properly. No wonder accidents happen," he said, his voice accusing.

I could see Richard from where I stood in the centre of the kitchen, opening the front gate to let one of Selena's children into the yard. The cut on his head would need a fresh bandage at bedtime.

Hank's voice grew quieter as he turned the alarm clock around and around in his hands, and I listened once again as he recited the litany of his hard life – about being the illegitimate child of a single working mother, her early death, and his consequent vow that if he ever had children they would have their mother at home, full time. I said that I would try to get a night job, be at work while Richard slept, and he pointed out that he couldn't be expected to babysit, not while he was sweating blood to increase his clientele and needed the freedom to be able to get up and go at a moment's notice.

"What, to the Lincoln Motor Inn?" I asked. "Is that where you find your customers?"

He began to blink and his face became a mask I couldn't read. "I work all day," he said. "I need to go out once in a while."

"And I don't?"

"You do, almost every day," he said, sounding genuinely surprised by my question. I wanted to hear glass shattering, feel the pain of it cutting my knuckles as I put my fist through the window beside his head. Put fear into his flat, smug expression. "And what about this?" I pulled his bank passbook from my jeans pocket. "What about all this money sitting in a bank while I've been short for food, worrying myself sick about how to make the money you give me stretch? What about the fact that we couldn't afford to get my teeth fixed?"

"You've been snooping through my things," he said and then he lunged, snatched the book from me, and jammed it into his shirt pocket. His face grew scarlet.

"So what about it?" I said, unwilling to back down.

"A person's entitled to save ten per cent of what they earn," he said. "It's a smart practice. And, anyway, if you'd known about it, do you think it would still be there?"

"Fuck your money," I said and saw him flinch. "I'll get my own." I told him then I had made an appointment for a job interview on Monday and that if I got the job I would find

313

someone to look after Richard on the nights he had to be out, "working" at the Lincoln Motor Inn.

"Like who?" Hank asked, with a slight mocking smile, implying I didn't have a single friend who might help me out.

"Like Rhoda," I said, and that's when he attacked me.

No way would that "bra-burning bitch" get near Richard, Hank said. What I needed was to come to my senses, to cool off, he said, as he grabbed my arm and twisted it behind my back. He brought his knee up and bumped me across the room to the sink. He turned on the water tap and pushed me under it. I gasped with the shock of cold water against my scalp as he forced my head down and down until my nose squashed flat against the bottom of the sink. "So what do you think of that?" Hank said, me rearing up, gasping and sputtering, unable to say what I thought of it because the moment I tried to open my mouth and talk, he'd push my head down again to the bottom of the sink and the rising water. "You think you're so goddamned smart. You think you know everything about everything. You think I'm an asshole, don't you? You think I don't know that? You with your stupid smirk and big nose always in the air. Big nose stuck in a book all day. Well, let me tell you, life is not in books," he said, the words spat out as he released me then plunged me under again. "Life is out there. Ten hours a day. One week off a year. How would you like being jerked around by guys at work? Locked in the washroom, ha, ha, big joke. Turds in my tool box. Hank the Tank. Big dumb Hank. Did you ever stop to think that maybe I can't stand you? That maybe I hate the sight of your nose? I try to do something. I get my own place. Now I'm being jerked around by salesmen, the sales tax people, income tax, business tax, accountants. And what for? Because I want something better for myself and they don't want me to have it. They see that I'm trying and they don't want me to make it."

Once again he released me and I lifted my head. Water streamed down my face, the front of my shirt. "No, Hank," I said. "I don't think that's the case – " and then he shoved me under again.

"If you want to work so darn bad then why not come and work for me, eh? All that stupid paperwork. You think I wanted Richard to have to say at school, 'My dad works as a repairman at Eaton's'? That's why I'm doing this! I'm a businessman! I'm trying to run a business so that I, I, I. . . . " He couldn't find the words to continue. Red-faced, the cords in his neck still jumping, he turned away, freeing me, half-drowned, dripping and wheezing. I was stunned by his anger.

Hank sat down at the table and covered his face with his hands.

I stood at the sink twisting water from my hair and then sponged my sodden shirt with a tea towel. I saw my reflection in the tiny mirror above the sink. Eyes large, looking black with fully dilated pupils. When I touched my nose it hurt. I was shocked by what he'd said about it. I wondered how it was possible to live twenty-six years and never realize that your face is off kilter, your nose too large.

"What do you mean, big?" I asked. "I don't have a big nose."

I heard the front door open and close. Richard stood in the hallway staring at us. "I'm not going to play with the TV," he said. "I promise I won't play with the TV and I won't ride my bike too far. I'm not going to be bad any more."

"Okay, okay, true," my friend Rhoda said to me Monday afternoon after the others had left the book club meeting. "When a person is a victim they don't have to take the responsibility for the things that happen to them. But when you think of it, doing nothing is actually making a decision too, you know." She curled into a quilted floral chair and her fine blonde hair became a puff ball as the sun slanted though the vertical blinds behind her. In the street beyond I saw the last of the book club women, Sara, get into her car and drive away.

"By the way," Rhoda said, following my gaze, "Sara is fucking someone."

I saw in my mind's eye Sara. Tall, thin, with raw hands, a

315

harried mother of four children, who still managed to donate several hours of her week to UNICEF. I said I didn't believe it.

Rhoda laughed. "The trouble with you," she said, "is that you don't look past the surface. I'd say the guy she's fucking is about fifty-five, grey, and a little on the heavy side." She leaned back into the chair and swirled orange juice around in her glass. "She's fucking her father, if you get what I mean. Have you?"

What Rhoda had "done for her father" was two years in engineering, she'd explained after one of the book club meetings, when what she really should have been doing was throwing pots and drawing. "What makes you think Sara is having an affair?"

"Affair?" Again the trill of laughter. "Quaint word. Well, for one thing, she's so mysterious. She's asked me to take her kids after school three times this week and she never tells me where she's been. Listen," she said, "when you get home, write this down somewhere so you don't forget I said it. I predict that Sara will split within a year. It's the pattern."

The muscles in my neck still hurt from the force of Hank's hand and my nose was sore to touch. I had added little to the discussion around the book *Surfacing* and allowed Rhoda ownership of the idea that the protagonist rejected the label "victim." I looked at the clay pots hanging crooked in Rhoda's front window. Like my head, I thought. "What I like about clay," Rhoda had said to me, "is that no two pieces are ever the same." Wrong, I thought, they're all lopsided.

When she'd asked me to stay on after the others had left so we could talk, I needed to talk but was reluctant. Sometimes I suspected that Rhoda had taken me on as a project of some kind, as though she were building a coil vase to ward off her own depression. She wanted to see if she could make something from nothing.

"Well, so, have you?" She said the words slowly, articulating each one dramatically. "Have you had an affair?"

Most of the women we'd read about had had affairs. They lay on their backs at the bottom of coal mines, on blankets in parks, or in empty or borrowed apartments. They seemed driven to give away little pieces of their hearts here and there for short amounts of time. I wanted to try and get mine back. I wanted to know the process.

"Don't tell me," Rhoda said when I didn't answer. Her eyes went wide behind her glasses. "You're not going to tell me that you married your first love and that there's never been anyone else! Wow, what a can of worms," she said. She tapped me on the knee. "Look, I don't know whatziz very well, but from what I've seen I do know that you're totally unsuited for each other. How in hell do you manage, that's what I'd like to know? Hey," she said, when I didn't answer, "I'll help you any way I can. Just tell me how."

"I've got a job. This morning," I said. "It's just part-time but I may need someone to take Richard at night off and on." Now that it had finally happened I was terrified, uncertain whether I could carry through what I had set in motion.

"Well, good for you! It's a start, anyway. And you can count on me. He can spend the night here any time. Listen, people who stay in unhappy marriages, and who don't do anything to get out, wind up choosing either alcohol or religion to cope." This a quote, no doubt, from one of the many "survival" books she read constantly.

"Or art," I said, and smiled.

"Yeah, art," she said drily. She started at a noise and her hands flew up around her face. "You hear that?"

I'd heard it, too, a crash in the room above our heads. "Something fell."

"Well, of *course* something fell. But *what* fell? And why?" She stared up at the ceiling. "You have to come up with me."

I climbed the stairs ahead of Rhoda and entered her work-room at the far end of the hall. Beneath the window was a door set up on trestles as a work table and strewn across it were curled sheets of drawing paper covered with scraggly lines and smudges of charcoal. All along the window sills sat lumpy shapes of fired clay. Books overflowed from shelves and were piled in stacks about the room, and I ached with envy. Rhoda tiptoed through the clutter. "Look." She pointed to a painting

317

lying face down on the floor. I laughed and felt the release of tension as she bent and righted it, leaning it against the wall.

"What am I going to do?"

"Hang it back up," I said.

"But you don't understand. It's an omen. A picture falling like that means something terrible is going to happen."

I drove home through the residential streets, slowly, carefully, mindful of a group of children standing between a couple of parked cars. I slowed down as I approached them. There was a church on the corner and recorded church-bell music chimed a hymn I thought I recognized. I watched in the mirror as the children crossed the street safely behind me. When I pulled into our driveway I saw Richard rise up from his play corner in the garden. I saw the bald spot and the bandage on the back of his head. Something terrible has already happened, I thought. I saw my eyes reflected in the rear-view mirror. Sharp, blue, hard.

16

The Lounge: the light-hearted room in the Club Malibu where she worked for years, where everything was relax and sip your fears or tears away, until last call and the money was counted and in the bag and her tips in her wallet. People were given the bum's rush then, and the lights came on, revealing the place for what it really was: one great big smouldering ashtray. There were walnut tables, the tops scarred with burns and alcohol and deep gouges, souvenirs from some of the less than light-hearted patrons. A perfect place for her to work, at night, when her scars were less visible, too, and she could be Amiable Amy; friendly, without suggesting anything more than good service. A good time to be had by all in the light-hearted room.

She embraced them with her generic smile. There was the Texan trucker, who graced them with his presence at the end of his haul and who calculated how many people were in the room before he magnanimously ordered a round for the house. He insisted that while he mingled with the people, back-slapping, shaking hands, saying "Howdy, you all," to his Canadian friends, she use an adding machine so he could check the tape later, be certain that she had accounted correctly for the exact number of drinks.

She protected the Indian Prince, whose appearances at the Lounge were unpredictable. He might come twice in a week, or not for several months, always in native dress, white beaded doeskin shirt, eagle-feather bonnet. She collected the twenty-dollar bills that sometimes dropped to the floor beneath his table and stuffed them into his pocket when he left. When he didn't sit in her section, she watched, ready to pounce on the vulture Selena, who might rinse her tray and set it down on his table while she pretended to fuss over him and then walk away with several bills stuck to the tray's wet bottom. He seemed to her a bewildered silent child, and she wished he wouldn't come.

Every so often the man in drag came in, and by the end of the evening, after he'd been sufficiently plied with drinks, he'd get up onto the stage and do his Marilyn Monroe impersonation, which always made her laugh. He was so outrageous, uninhibited. Lucky, she thought.

At first she really lived, to catch up for lost time. She slept with men whose names she can't remember now, including the first one, a man who looked like a weasel and who used to be a drummer in Freddy Fender's band. But he wasn't special; he had no rhythm, she liked to say, honing the art of flippancy and accepting the gratuity of Selena's ensuing laughter. And a lineman for the Blue Bombers, too, who liked to wear women's corsets. There was a man who wore a silver suit and whose movements and hairless body reminded her of an iguana. But she knew she'd finally caught up on lost time when the South American tourist, a dark, anxious man, asked her through an embarrassed interpreter, "How much?"

She became close friends with the bartender, Lee, a Chinese immigrant who was working to bring his family to Canada. He encouraged her to study and so she took day courses at the University of Winnipeg. She moved from her dingy apartment on Stradbrook into Lee's apartment and he taught her how to write essays. In return, she did his laundry.

Then she dated a certified general accountant whose name was Robert and who, one night, brought his entire family into the Lounge to meet her. He proposed in their presence, asking her to marry him and have a baby and call the baby John, after John Diefenbaker, "The greatest living Canadian," he said. He *was crushed by her revelation that she was already married and had a child and he fled the Lounge in tears leaving behind his embarrassed and angry family. She never saw him again.*

Eventually she became floor manager of the Lounge, scheduling the waitresses' hours, handling the payroll, and accounting for the bar inventory and the nightly receipts. She shed her short shorts and knee-high boots for soft jersey-knit dresses, and during the day she took a camera operator's course at the Public Cable Vision and eventually became a producer of a weekly half-hour program on local artists and their work.

She was well into writing scripts when her job at the Lounge ended. She was leaving Toots, a booze can on Selkirk Avenue, where she had taken the current talent for after-hour drinks, when she'd heard sirens echoing in the smoke-filled sky above city centre. Amy learned that the Club Malibu had burned to the ground. Later she would not be able to remember precisely where it had stood.

Oh, this two-faced place had been perfect for her. She had chosen its night side where she could stay undercover in the dimmed lights, watching the maimed and the sick and the beautiful people, receiving the best or the worst of them without any real involvement, without having to know the in-between.

As the cab speeds on towards the Club Malibu, where Amy now works, a metallic taste is thick on her tongue and a dull ache centres in her stomach. The cab passes by Central Park, where the grass appears to be greener, a lush carpet bordered by buff-coloured stone apartment buildings. She tries to imagine living in one of those apartments but she can't. Her life at present makes no allowance for imaginings. Okay, Hank had said the day he tried to drown her, if that's what you want, then go. See if you can keep this place going on your own. And then he walked out of the house. It has been two weeks and she hasn't seen or heard from him.

She feels him, though. She moves through the nights at work as though he's looking over her shoulder, proving to him, she thinks, by her unapproachable behaviour towards the male patrons, with her swiftness and efficiency, the harmless intent of wanting to work. She believes he watches when she returns home late to the empty house and showers the smell of cigarette smoke from her skin, soaks aching feet, and then, bone tired, sets the alarm for nine o'clock, when she will get up, skip breakfast, and ride the bus to collect Richard from Rhoda's house. She is managing the three nights a week alone, which are only six hours long, she reasons, because it's usually three in the morning when her head hits the pillow.

Trees sway gently against the backdrop of stone in Central Park, sheltering a group of young people who gather on the grass around a wasted-looking man playing a guitar. The musician wears all black, a beret worn to the side of his head, and a goatee. The curves and angles of the people's bodies – they are her age, she knows – seem perfect as they lie, chins cradled in hands or hands clutching knees, faces all turned to the man's music and the setting sun.

When she reaches the Club Malibu, the heavy door swings closed behind her, shutting out the soft glow of twilight, and gooseflesh rises on her arms and legs as she steps into the air-conditioned interior. Her footsteps are muffled by thick red carpet as she passes by the coat check, the foyer, and she sees herself in passing in a large gilt-framed mirror. She's twisted her hair up on top of her head and looks younger, wide-eyed, much like Richard. As she passes through the coffee shop, the spicy scent of carnations on the tables greets her. It's been only two weeks, but already the smell is expected, familiar; like the people she works with, who are casual, accepting, as though they have known one another for years. She pushes through the doors into the fluorescent-lit kitchen and slides her card into the time clock. Fifteen minutes early. Rhoda had come by with the car to pick up Richard and so Amy has time for coffee before her shift begins. Cold air slams against her knees as the pastry chef steps from the walk-in cooler and closes the door.

"Well, hello," Giorgio says. "Must be Thursday again. Here's my girl with the big eyes." He tickles the back of her neck in passing. "I've been telling the boss, 'You make her come in every night. I think I'm in love.'"

She smiles. She knows that Selena would have a snappy comeback but she's being careful. She feels as though she's still on trial, that eyes are watching and evaluating. "Any coffee on?"

"Oh, I almost forgot." He grunts slightly as he leans across the bulletin board for a scrap of paper. "Lee left a message. Said to tell you to come up the minute you're in."

She walks back through the darkened coffee shop, across the foyer, to the back stairs. The hired help, she learned her first night, are not supposed to use the front entrance. This is in the event that MacDonald from MacDonald Carpets, or a member of the Blue Bombers football team, or Allsopp from Allsopp, Bamburk and Howard, should arrive at the same time and be offended. She's learned since that none of the employees heed this restriction, and on the second night she worked she used the front entrance, too.

Soft music floats down from the Cabaret. In another hour it will give way to music of "The Four Fendermen," a loud combo of sax, electric guitar, and piano, which blares down into the Lounge every time the door opens and closes. They're an American group whose claim to fame is that two of the band members once played for Freddy Fender.

Lee isn't behind the large horseshoe-shaped bar, although there are several customers there, men in suits. One stands resting his foot on the brass railing in a studied casual pose and at the far end of the bar, as usual, the hippie is there, a man with long blond hair parted in the centre. As she sets up her tray Lee crosses the floor and goes down the three steps that separate the table area from the bar. "Boy, I'm glad to see you," he says. "I got hung up back there. A cruddy wedding party. Ten of them."

"I see our flower child is with us again tonight," Amy says and laughs. The hippie raises his head and turns to face her and she can see the reflection of the chandelier in his dark glasses. A biker in disguise, she thinks.

"It's a free country," Lee says, "as long as he's drinking

and paying and as long as he stays down here." The Lounge allows for casual dress, the Cabaret upstairs is jacket and tie only.

She steps up into the room. Whoever designed the place with its multi-level floors, stairs leading to more stairs, hadn't thought about the people who would work there. The people in the wedding party sit at two tables pushed together at the back of the room. Amy goes from table to table, lighting candles, satisfied with the look of soft red light spilling across dark walnut. Then she adjusts the overhead lighting until it balances with the glowing candles and the wedding party seems to come alive, their conversation more animated.

The room is supposed to be friendly, a light-hearted room, Mr. Broosier, the owner, had explained. One big friendly family, united by the gentle music and bantering of Patrick, head rooster for Patrick's Trio, folk singers. Mr. Broosier had discovered them in Thunder Bay and signed them on for the summer and so far they have filled the Lounge almost every night. Two couples enter the room, seating themselves at a table directly in front of the stage. She waits for them to settle in and places coasters in front of them. Smile, she remembers, even through the persistent ache in the pit of her stomach. She stands poised with her pencil so they'll get the message.

"What's the bar rye?" one of the men asks.

She tells him.

"Better make it C.C.," he says. "I can't drink that crap."

She stifles the urge to smile. They play big shot for twenty-five cents extra. After two or three rounds they don't know what they're drinking anyway and then she pockets the extra twenty-five cents. Selena had warned her, though, against doing it too often. One of the women asks to see a cocktail list, and when Amy returns with it several other people have entered the Lounge, and for the next thirty minutes she works non-stop.

The three musicians enter the Lounge through the back corridor. Patrick squats, and fiddles with the amplifiers. The two others in the trio tune their instruments. They look casual in their open-neck striped shirts, cotton vests, and

324

pants. The people at the table in front of the stage lean forward expectantly, waiting to be acknowledged.

"What kind of crowd we got tonight?" Patrick asks Amy in passing.

"Loud. Especially the wedding party." One of the men at the table in front of the stage signals to Amy for another round.

"Good evening, good evening," Patrick says, plucking at the strings of his guitar. His voice is smooth, soothing, and people stop talking to listen.

"It's so very nice to see so many of you beautiful people here tonight. Welcome to the Lounge. We've got three sets lined up for you this evening. We'll take requests, too, anything your heart desires. . . . "

"How about 'Cotton Fields Back Home'?" a chubby man in the wedding party calls out. He begins to sing the song loudly and is shushed by the woman sitting next to him. "You know the one I mean," he says.

"Sure do. But we always dedicate our first song to the little gals who work so hard to keep your drinks coming, and tonight, gals, here it is, just for you!" Patrick dips his guitar in Selena and Amy's direction. Selena turns on the spotlights, and the three singers are enclosed in a warm yellow circle as they begin to sing "If I Were a Carpenter."

Amy serves the two couples their drinks and waits to collect. Patrick sounds good tonight, she thinks, as she goes over to the wedding party table and begins clearing away empty glasses. It's easier to work to music. "Hey, you," the fat man says. "So what's wrong with singing? Is there a law against it or something?" The woman at his side looks mortified. "I'm as good as those guys."

"I think we've had enough," the woman says.

"Come on," he objects. "It's early."

"Hey, Fred," someone down the table calls, "you going to buy this round or what?"

"Sure, watch me. Think I won't buy a round?"

Lee works swiftly, darting back and forth behind the bar, hands always doing two things at once. Amy sets the tab down and waits for him to fill her order. Glasses clink sharply as Lee slides the drinks across the bar to her, one after another. Amy senses that she's being watched. She glances up. The hippie raises a glass of beer in a toast to her. She nods and smiles, forced and stiff-looking, she knows.

As she serves the wedding party their round, the man drinking C.C. signals for her to come over. He nudges his drink. "I said I wanted C.C.," he says.

"I beg your pardon, but you are drinking C.C." She hasn't switched. Not yet.

"I know my rye. And this isn't Canadian Club."

Amy feels the pain in her stomach swell along with her anger. "Would you like to see your tab?" She shows him where she's written "C.C."

"What does that tell me?" The woman beside him smiles knowingly. The other couple sitting at the table ignore him and appear unconcerned.

"It tells you that you ordered Canadian Club and that's what you've got."

"How do I know the bartender didn't pour something else? I know what goes on in these places." As she looks down at the top of his shiny bald head she imagines herself bringing the tray down against it. Hard.

She smiles. "I would suggest then that you go down and speak to the bartender."

"Ahh, it's not worth the trouble," he says.

"Do you want the drink or not?"

"Not this shit," he says, "I want C.C."

Good, good, Amy thinks as she walks away, still trembling with anger. The jerk obviously doesn't know the difference. She will order the bar rye and make the twenty-five cents this round.

When Amy returns, the wedding party begins to leave, pushing back chairs and gathering up handbags and shawls.

"So sorry you folks have to leave us," Patrick says from the stage.

"Piss on you," the fat man says. "Why didn't you just say you didn't know that song?" The woman he's with pushes him hard in the small of the back with her clutch bag, causing him to stumble on the stairs. He turns and swears at her.

"I wonder if they're the bride and groom," Patrick says. People laugh. "Anyway," he continues, "I want to say welcome to an old buddy of mine. Used to live here in Winnipeg. Come all the way up from New York. I want you to meet one of the finest jazz guitarists in North America. Stu Farmer Junior!" The man sits at a table in Selena's section. Amy recognizes him, it's the same man she saw playing his guitar in Central Park earlier on. The same goatee and beret. He sucks deeply on a cigarette and smiles and nods.

"I want to wait on him," Amy whispers to Selena later. "I'll trade you a table."

She shrugs. "Doesn't drink much," she says.

He doesn't look up as Amy replaces his overflowing ashtray with a clean one. "Would you care for a little porch-climber?"

"Could do."

She can barely hear his voice. "Just what *is* a porch-climber?"

He touches the empty wine glass with a tobacco-stained finger. No more than a bag of bones inside his black clothing. Of course he doesn't recognize me, Amy thinks, but she desperately wants him to. "I married your back-up player," Amy says. "Hank."

His black wing-shaped eyebrows shoot up. "Oh yeah, I remember him. What's he at?" he asks, but from the slouch of his body and the way he avoids looking directly at her, Amy realizes that he isn't really interested in her answer.

"You say hello to him," he says when Amy returns with a glass of wine.

Whatever connection she'd felt she had with him is severed by the reality that she is Amy, a cocktail waitress, a failed parent and wife, who hasn't really progressed at all since the day she'd met him. His presence is a sad reminder of another time when her limbs were infused with energy, with a brash hope, and as light as air.

She stands at the end of the bar, back turned to the room, facing her work area. The ache in her stomach has grown

327

sharper. A lipstick-tinged cigarette burns in a full ashtray. One of Selena's, smoked on the run. Amy picks it up, sucks at it, sets it back down, turns, and meets the image of herself in the hippie's sunglasses. He nods at her and his mouth twitches into a crooked grin and she feels the hair on the back of her neck tingle. She ignores him as Selena steps to her side, plucking up clean glasses, stopping to drag on the cigarette. "Feels like someone has lit a campfire in my stomach," Amy complains and Selena suggests that Amy should take a break from the floor. "I can handle things," she says.

She takes Selena's suggestion and goes into the employees' restroom which is also used as a dressing room for the entertainers. She clears a spot in the clutter on the counter and pulls herself up onto it. Harsh shadows under her eyes show through the cover-up she applies in an attempt to hide her fatigue. Haggard, she thinks. Ugly. I have a big nose. She presses her hand against her stomach and hunches over her knees. She knows where she made her mistake. She'd been too busy reading books and forgot to think about the gopher and the maggots.

Just then the door swings open and the noise and smoke of the Lounge rush into the room. Lee blinks in the bright light. "What's keeping you? Selena says you're sick or something. You okay?"

"Not sick," Amy says, "I'm or something."

He pulls a face. "Look, I'm sorry. I don't know what your problem is, but you'd better get back on the floor. The boss is looking for you."

Amy feels giddy and her stomach becomes a flaming torch.

"What in God's name is going on," the boss snarls as she approaches. The hippie at the bar swivels around and watches from behind his sunglasses. Selena watches. The whole united family of the light-hearted Lounge watches.

"Where were you?"

Amy feels like vomiting down the front of his crumpled grey suit. I beg your pardon, sir, it just kind of slipped out. "Things dropped off and so I took a break."

"That's why I want you to go upstairs," he says. "They're

going out of their minds up there. We're opening up the over-flow room."

"Upstairs?"

"Look, honey," he says. "Look, sweetie, if you want to work here then you'd better be prepared to go where I send you. You've got five minutes. And I want to see you tonight before you leave. I'd like you to consider coming on full time."

Amy mounts the stairs to the Cabaret. Teddy, a young man in his mid-twenties, who acts as both bouncer and doorman, rocks on his heels as he looks down at her through the plate-glass wall.

"I don't think I'm going to like this," she says as she pushes past him and into the plush foyer with its cosy arrangement of velvet sofas and easy chairs. He follows. The room vibrates with the sound of subdued chatter rising above recorded piano music and the tinkle of silverware. She enters the room to the sight of a wall-to-wall mirror lined with glass shelving and bottles of amber, red, and green liquid glowing in the recessed lighting. She likes the white linen on tables, the clean lines of long-stemmed wine glasses.

Teddy steps up to her side. "Better get a move on." He indicates that she's to go to the very back to another room where busboys rush about setting up tables. A pudgy hand pats her buttocks lightly. She turns and glares at him. "Watch it," she says. "I've got teeth down there."

He frowns, his attention diverted by something in the Lounge below. He thinks he's the shop cop, Amy thinks, and looks to see what's going on downstairs. The hippie stands at the bottom of the stairs, looking up at them, as though debating whether to come up.

"I dare you," Teddy says and grins. "Come on."

She sets up her tray and watches as three go-go girls prance through the dark hall and into the room, each going into her own cage. They stand in the dark, poised, as the band, men in pale-blue tuxedos and white ruffled shirts, move like headless ghosts across the stage. Then the pleasant ambience of the room vanishes as a harsh spotlight cuts through the smoke at the first crashing sound of the drum announcing the band's presence. Their music is deafening and reverberates in her ears.

This is crazy, Amy thinks. She leaves her tray at the bar and goes out into the foyer. Amy senses the tension, hears the grunting and scuffling, before she actually sees Teddy and the hippie, whose head is pinned fast against Teddy's side. "Say good night to the folks, pal," Teddy says, clearly enjoying himself. The hippie struggles, and they move back and forth in front of the velvet furniture in a strained kind of dance. As they shuffle towards the door of the Cabaret, Amy sees the hippie's face more clearly in the light of the chandelier hanging above the stairs. His skin is blotchy with what looks like make-up that has rubbed off here and there.

"I'm not going anywhere without her!" he shouts, turning towards Amy. Teddy is surprised by this and caught off guard and the hippie jerks free from the headlock and swings wildly. His sunglasses drop to the floor. Amy stands rooted, shocked. She realizes it is Hank.

"That's my wife and I'm not leaving without her!"

Hank, dressed up. Spying on her. "Get him out of here," she says to Teddy, and flees back through the Cabaret, down a narrow corridor, down several flights of stairs, until she's in the basement and can go no further.

All around her pipes drip with condensation, machines groan and vibrate as cold air churns upwards, rattling in tin ducts. She sits down on the bottom step, panting, and leans into the damp wall hugging herself. Every night she's been at work, he's been there too, sitting at the bar keeping tabs on her while Richard has been asking for him, wanting him. She thinks of Hank's contorted features, the fake yellow hair parted down the centre, and she shivers. Sick, she thinks. She gets up and heads towards an exit sign at the end of a hallway, pushes the release bar on the door, and steps outside into warm, moist air.

A car door slams. Hank's maroon Chrysler is parked in the alley, and inside it she sees his silhouette against the harsh light of the street lamp, his tight curly hair creating a perfect circle. She crosses her arms against her chest as she walks towards the car. He hears the tap of her heels against pavement and his head dips as he looks into the rear-view mirror. The car window glides down.

"Hi," he says softly.

Sick or desperate, it doesn't matter. Either way, he's a stranger. She vows to herself to never again assume that she can know all there is about any person.

"What I want. . . . " he says, his voice trailing off. He swipes at his eyes with the back of his hand, an angry gesture. Desperate, Amy concludes, and despises him. "What I want is for us to have a normal life," he says, his voice stronger now.

"I'm sorry. But I don't think that's possible," Amy says, calmly, coolly. "You see, I'm not normal." She turns and walks away quickly.

"You said it!" Hank shouts. "You just said it! You're not normal. You're . . . you're a. . . . "

Will he give up trying? Amy wonders as she walks around to the front of the building to return to her shift.

"You're a bastard!" Hank screams after her.

"What do you think of this idea?" Amy had once asked Piotr. "Why don't I write a scene where the guy puts on a disguise so he can follow his wife around?" They were in California, in the J. Paul Getty Museum wandering through a dimly lit room where people walked slowly and spoke in muted voices. A sacrosanct room, Amy thought, the room that held a collection of illuminated manuscripts. But they could have been on the Columbia icefields in Alberta or at home sitting across the table from one another, the present script was always uppermost in their minds and open for discussion at every breath, even in bed after lovemaking.

Piotr had stopped in front of a glowing block of plexiglass, inside it a page of a manuscript, *The Adoration of the Seven-Headed Beast*. "I like your idea," he said. "It's dark, quirky, but I don't think we'd be able to slip it past the infantile minds at the CBC."

Amy wandered among the display of Byzantine manuscripts, awed by the intricate colourings, the use of real gold, the handwritten texts, by the pleading and sorrow-filled faces of the figures. I could write a scene, she thought, about a man arranging a wig on a pillow in a bed. Arranging along with it his wife's pink chenille bathrobe, which he plumps with a blanket so that when she flicks on the light switch and enters the room she sees herself in bed, already asleep, or dead, and feels that she is standing outside the world looking in at herself. For another fearful second she believes that she doesn't exist. And then she thinks that she does exist, but only in her husband's careful arrangement of her body upon the bed.

It is late in August and Richard is outside, pressing his hands and mouth against the screen of the back door, peering in at Amy as she squats, dabbing on the wall the last bit of paint from the can. He squashes his tongue flat against the screen, rubbing it back and forth. "Don't," she says, "there's fly spray on that screen. You'll get a sick stomach."

"The pool died."

Amy groans inwardly. He's chewed another hole in his plastic pool, she knows. "Never mind. It's almost supper time. Rhoda is going to pick you up today."

"I think Daddy's coming home tomorrow," he says as his lips move against the screen.

Amy feels an ache of sadness for Richard. His pile of "magic" stones has grown considerably over the past two months but she knows that Hank will not return as long as she continues to work at the Lounge. She steps back to view the kitchen wall. Pale blue semi-gloss enamel, to give the room the suggestion of ethereal airiness, of floating, of space. And to get her ass out of the sling with the landlord. She had stripped the scorched wallpaper off and now she's run out of paint so that a two-foot strip is left at the bottom. Her hands sting and have turned white and rough from turpentine. "Get your things together and come in," she tells Richard. His narrow silhouette drops away from the screen. She doesn't have the energy to go out and buy more paint or search for holes in his pool to mend them.

Richard enters the kitchen trailing a wet bath towel and bits of grass. "It smells funny in here," he says and pinches his nose.

"Yeah, well, this is pretty much your doing. Remember? So don't complain."

Richard goes off into the living room. She hears wheezy music and Popeye stating "I duz what I can. . . . " The refrigerator clunks, and hums to life, vibrating at a pitch that always makes her feel weary. She decides that what she needs is to soak in the tub.

She trickles rose-scented bath oil into the rushing water and watches it become a puff of crimson smoke turning the water pink. She lies back in the pink froth, sinking down until she feels it climb up the back of her neck, and she closes her eyes. "When is Daddy coming home?" he asks constantly. The bubbles pop, the sound an irritating one that makes her clench her teeth. She stays in the tub only minutes and then leaps up, suds sliding down her legs and belly as she reaches for a towel. She tries not to think about Hank spying on her. Creepy. Weird. She thinks instead what to make Richard for supper.

At five past six, Amy is in the kitchen slamming cupboard doors. She smacks a plate down on the table, hoping it will shatter. "Supper's ready," she calls. "Come and get it. Now."

Richard enters the kitchen looking downcast as he slides in behind the table. "Yuck," he says. "I would rather eat dirt than french fries. I hate french fries."

They go through this "I hate" routine each night she works.

"You liked them before."

"But I don't now." His cheeks are flushed – too much sun? A fever? She touches his forehead. Then she rubs his arms and discovers that they too are warm. Don't be sick, she pleads silently. She looks at their meal: swollen waterlogged wieners, overcooked fries, brown and tough. Her stomach closes down and, like Richard, she nibbles halfheartedly at her food.

Several times a car passes by in the lane, and, unable to stop herself, she turns to the window, her movement only a slight shift; imperceptible, she thinks, but Richard notices it every time.

"I want Daddy," he says. "Why isn't Daddy at home?"

"I have told you," Amy says sharply, "I don't know." She hears herself in his question, Margaret in her answer. Hank's absence is a separation in Richard's chest, she knows, a wrenching open of the ribs. She pats his hand. She loves her son's hands, his long, narrow fingers, which shift and slide across the table, touch, move away, return, tap, jiggle, poke, investigate. "You like it at Rhoda's," she says and squeezes his hand.

"No, I don't."

She kisses the pout of his wet mouth and says he doesn't need to finish his supper and she sends him into the bedroom to undress for his bath while she rinses off their dishes. Richard is only five years old, she thinks, he needs an answer to his question, "When is Daddy coming home?" No more evasions or lies. It is time to confront it, she thinks, to break the news and make it real. She shakes her hands over the kitchen sink, reaches for the telephone, and dials her mother's number.

Margaret sounds cheerful and surprised. "Hello, dear. It's nice to hear from you," she says as though she's reading lines from a script. "How have you been?"

Amy's heart thuds. "I'm okay. What have you been up to?"

Margaret lists her week's activities. The visits she's made to the sick, the lame, the elderly, and the broken-hearted. She has delivered talks to "Women Aglow" clubs, speaking to women about the message in the booklet she has written, *The Angels Among Us*, which, she says, is selling out faster than it can be printed. She blesses these women with her presence. She teaches them how to study passages of scripture that will give them hope and courage or enlighten. She explains how the gifts of the Holy Spirit are still for this time and this day. She encourages all whom she can to be born again, only this time "in the spirit"; to raise their hands and

334

pray with their new language, the tongues of angels. At healing services, she lays hands on the supplicant and too-short legs grow longer, arthritic aches and pains vanish, and nervous bladders become calm. What she does for Amy is pray. Every day.

"Where's Richard?" she breaks off the recitation to ask. "Is he enjoying this warm weather? Is he getting lots of the sun?" Richard stands at Amy's side, naked, waiting for his bath.

"Oh, he's great," Amy says, then leaps in with a bright voice, "I was just calling to see if you've seen Hank. Talked to him. That's all."

"Why would he be here?"

"I thought he might have come by. To tell you the news."

"Oh? What news?" Margaret asks, wary, but at the same time Amy hears a hopeful tone.

"He's left me. Us." There, that's done, she thinks.

Margaret doesn't speak for several moments. Amy hears her sigh. "I've been praying and praying ever since you got married. I was afraid this might happen."

Have you been praying for Mel too? Amy wants to ask. Mel, who has lived with three different women. Mel, who, whenever Amy speaks to him on the telephone or meets him for lunch down at the Grain Exchange, is more often drunk than sober. What about Mel? she wants to ask.

"Hank is against your working, isn't he?" Margaret asks, her voice taking on an accusing tone.

"*You* worked."

"That was different. It was only one day a week and, besides, your father wasn't against it. You kids never suffered."

No, Amy thinks, that's true. But it might have been better if you had worked full-time.

"What about Richard?"

"A friend babysits for me."

"A friend? Just what kind of person is this friend?"

"My friend Rhoda is just great," Amy tells Margaret.

Kids should be kept off balance, Rhoda once remarked. Go out without telling them where you're going. A little uncertainty breeds creativity. Otherwise they'll turn out to become lawyers, doctors, actuaries: boring people. Amy wanted to – but didn't – point out to Rhoda that it was her boring accountant husband whose income provided her with the time and freedom to doodle and throw pots. But it was Rhoda who talked and Amy who listened. "I know," Rhoda had said when Amy told her Hank had left, "how do you explain it, eh? He doesn't beat you, he doesn't drink, he isn't a womanizer. People will think you've chucked out a perfectly good husband. You've got to make up something."

"I don't care how *great* she is," Margaret says, "a babysitter is no substitute for a mother. Why do you want to work? Hank is a good provider. Just think of the women who *have* to work. You should be grateful."

The word "grateful" explodes in Amy's head.

"Hank's a good person," Margaret says. "I'll pray for you. You know, it could be the Lord's way of speaking to you, Amy. Think about it. And if it's His will that Hank comes back, you should consider whether the job's worth it."

"If Hank has the guts to show his ugly face around here, I'll kick him in the knackers, that's what I'll do." Amy hangs up.

She turns away from the telephone, seething. She's vaguely aware of Richard kneeling as though in prayer in front of the freshly painted wall. She's puzzled by this. Then she sees him place his palms against it. "Richard!" He turns, startled. His face is smudged here and there with pale blue paint and his bare stomach is covered with hand prints.

"Richard!"

Richard rears up from his knees, his eyes jumping with fear. She raises a clenched fist, and he scrambles around her, across the hallway, heading for the bathroom. "Don't you run away from me!" she screams, and chases after him. She grabs him by the arm, catching him before he can close the door, and swings him around so that she can spank his buttocks. "Don't," he pleads. Her hand stings as it meets his naked backside. "Don't." She slaps him again and again with her open hand. "Don't," he cries as they move in a circle, Amy slapping, feeling the heat of the blows in her palm. "Don't," Richard says, and she sees the flesh of his buttock jerk as her hand meets it and he twists away, one hand clutching his penis, holding it tightly as she slaps. "Don't," he gasps. "It's going to fall off, it's going to fall off!"

But Amy is strong when anger flows in her body. She picks Richard up, sits down on the toilet seat, and flings him across her knee. She grabs the hairbrush. It smacks sharply against his body and he begins to scream. He keeps squirming and so sometimes the brush hits the back of his legs, his shoulders. Her scalp feels tight and the blood pounds into the top of her skull. *Richard, Richard*. She can't believe that it's her hand holding the brush, her voice saying, "You little bastard. It's all your fault." The brush snaps then and the end of it flies across the room. She cannot stop now. She looks around, her rage careening wildly through the sound of his screams. As she looks for something else to hit him with he twists loose and falls to the floor, writhing at her feet, still clutching his penis, his pale child's body set against the brown tiles. A severed earthworm, Amy will think later. She will remember always her son's silent mouth, the impotent O-shape of it as he struggled to breathe. But, then, her only thought was to find something else to hit him with.

The telephone rings sharply, several times; the sound penetrates and stops her dead. Hank, she thinks.

"Amy? That was an awful thing to say!" It is Margaret. "Amy? Why is Richard crying?"

The anger begins to ebb and then flow from Amy's body, away through her limbs, making her suddenly weak and shaky. She slides down onto the floor beside the kitchen table still cupping the telephone receiver to her mouth.

"Say something. Talk to me," Margaret says.

Amy tries to speak, but the words won't come.

"When your father left I thought I would die," Margaret says, her voice becoming thin and pinched-sounding. "But let me tell you, there's nothing worse than losing a child. Absolutely nothing. But I made it. Me and the Lord, we managed. And you can, too, if you'd just –"

"Why don't you give up," Amy says. She leaves the receiver dangling and crawls through the living room and down the hall to her bedroom. She kneels, face pressed into the bed-spread to muffle the sound of her crying. After a few moments she hears Richard gasping and goes into the bathroom where he huddles in a corner wedged between the clothes hamper and the door, his knees drawn up against his stomach, his hands covering his face. Amy sees the marks of her hand and the hairbrush, angry red welts rising on her son's shoulders. She sees the half-moon shape where her fingernails have gouged into his arm. She kneels beside him and encircles him in her arms. "Baby, baby, baby," she croons and rocks him against her. She scoops him up in her arms and carries him into his room and gently sets him down onto the bed. She brings ointment and rubs it into his skin. "I got paint on me," he says through his sobbing. "I got paint on me. I got paint on me."

Amy lies down beside him and gathers him into herself. "It's okay," she says. "It's okay. You're not bad. It's Mommy. Mommy's bad." She pulls his square of flannel from beneath his pillow and he grabs at it, bringing it up against his nose. She holds him tightly against her body to still his shuddering, and waits for his breathing to become normal. "I'm sorry, so sorry," she whispers into his hair.

"I don't want you to go to work," Richard says.

She kisses the nape of his sweaty neck. "I'm not going to go, don't you worry. Not tonight." She leaves him to call Rhoda and the Lounge and then returns to help him into his pyjamas. "Stay," he says as he climbs beneath the blankets.

"I'll stay," she says and lies back down beside him.

Amy falls asleep before Richard does. They lie curled together, asleep for several hours, and the darkness of the night is complete. At one point she hears a noise and wants to rise to it but fatigue pulls her under again. Later she hears something else and thinks vaguely that she should open her eyes. She dreams that she is getting up, but she's lying pinned to the bed by sleep, unable to move. Suddenly, she's gripped by terror. She feels the pressure of sleep holding her fast to the bed, and yet she's stumbling around the room, crashing into walls, floating down to the floor, tumbling over and over. Her eyes fly open in darkness. She's bathed in cold sweat. *Richard*, she thinks wildly. Richard is not in bed beside her. Freed from sleep now she dashes through the house, calling his name. The light is different. The light in the hall. The front door is wide open and moonlight shines in through the screen. The front gate gapes open, too, and Richard's tricycle and the wagon hitched to it are no longer on the sidewalk. She begins to whimper with fear as she runs outside, down to the busy intersection in the dead of night, looking for her son, Richard.

I'm going to Grandma's, I'm going to Grandma's, I'm going to Grandma's, Richard's feet said as the pedals turned and turned and his "magic" stones rattled about in the wagon behind him, wheels jolting against cracks and holes in the sidewalk. He'd taken the stones, his toothbrush, and a candle from a drawer in the kitchen; to keep him warm, he said. But no matches, he was not allowed to play with matches. I'm going to Grandma's, I'm going to Grandma's. Around and around his feet went, pushing the pedals. He knew the way to Grandma's, he said. A garage and then he would turn onto another street. He was going fast, a hundred miles an hour. The streetlights were spread far apart and he had to rush through the darkness between them. Ahead, the road ducked down under a bridge, on which a train creaked slowly along the tracks. I'm going to Grandma's, I'm going to Grandma's. A dog barked. A dog might bite me, Richard thought. I have to hurry and get to Grandma's. Richard, Richard, he heard his mother's faint calling. I'm going to Grandma's, his feet said on the pedals. Hurry. Richard! Richard! she called, closer now. Richard! I know the way, I know the way. Hurry. Richard! she cried. His feet on the pedals began to slow down. The stones stopped rattling. He turned and saw her running towards him, barefoot. His terrible, beautiful mother.

Amy hears the tinny rattling of Richard's wagon in the distance as she rounds the corner at the intersection, the street empty now in the middle of the night and seeming to be a dark tunnel which opens at the other end to the lights of the city centre.

And then she sees Richard, the flash of his teddy-bear pyjamas, as he passes beneath a streetlight several blocks away.

"I'm going to visit Grandma," he says, scowling over his shoulder at her. She cannot pry his hands from the handlebars or make him turn his tricycle around. "I'm going," he says.

"Yes," Amy says. The city's lights smudge together in a blur of colours. "Yes, yes. Tomorrow. Tomorrow you can go to Grandma's."

And he agrees to return home then and watches while she packs his clothing and toys into boxes and piles them beside the front door so that he will know that it is true and go to sleep.

The following morning she finds a seat for him beside a matronly white-haired woman who says she'd be delighted to keep her eye on the "little man," and, as the bus turns the corner onto Portage Avenue, Amy goes back inside the depot and calls Margaret to tell her that Richard is on his way.

Two months later I stood outside the wire fence surrounding the school and watched children lining up before the bell rang. A little girl called Richard's name for what had to be the hundredth time, wanting him to come and take his place in the line. He frowned his annoyance. The kindergarten teacher came out and stood on the top step looking down at them. The wind tugged at her long blonde hair. "All right, children, patience, patience, it's almost time now," she said and immediately they fell silent. Dry curled leaves swished across the schoolyard over to the fence where I stood watching in the chilly October air.

I knew that I couldn't continue to haunt the school yard for a glimpse of my son, wondering was he warm enough, and, if I didn't see him, worrying that he was ill. I became jealous at the sight of his new winter parka, which someone else had chosen for him. I knew that it was time to stop riding the bus from the apartment I had rented on Stradbrook, into the north end and past the house, hungry for details of his life, continuing to reassure myself with the presence of Hank's maroon Chrysler parked beside the garage at the end of the day. Once I had seen Elaine at the front door, shaking dust from the mop, and I wanted to get off the bus, march into what had been my yard, and shout, "Don't blame me!" That it was her fault, too, for having essentially told Hank that I had not been a virgin. Everything had changed following that. But sadness, resignation, overcame the urge. I saw Marlene as well. Twice. She had been out on the clothesline stoop bringing in the wash and, another time, on the bus, wearing a Victorian Order of Nurses' uniform. When she got on, our eyes met and I saw the flicker of recognition in her face, but she walked past without acknowledging me and sat several seats away. Later, when she stood up to get off, green-apple cologne emanated from the skirt of her uniform as she swished by, her blue cape swinging smartly. And in a low voice, almost a whisper, she uttered a single word at my shoulder: "Bitch." Hank, the single parent of a child abandoned by his mother, rescued, by women inflamed with pity.

Richard went to the back of the line of children waiting for the school bell to ring and began jostling the boy in front of him. Then, as though he had received a signal of some sort, he broke rank and his broad knees pumped as he ran. He reached the stone steps, climbed the iron hand-railing, and straddled it. "Charge!" he commanded, an imaginary sword held high. The three straight rows of children became scraggly, sparrows bobbing and tittering.

Richard, don't, I wanted to say. Fit in. Don't try to be different. You get back into that line with the others, I almost called. But this was no longer my territory. I was surprised at how much that hurt. It belonged to the fairy-queen kindergarten teacher, who had told me that Richard was smart. He will do well. Did you know that my son has an above-average vocabulary? I gave it to him. These are words I would repeat to soften the realization that even though other people would now have all the say in my son's life, I had left something of me behind. Resilient, I thought, as I looked at Richard's triumphant grin, his ruddy wind-burned cheeks. Happy.

The teacher let him show off for a moment longer and then she reached for him and put her arms around him, peeling him loose from his iron horse. He laughed and wound his legs around her, clinging to her with his soft hands. He pressed his nose into her cheek.

It would be a kindness, I thought, not to appear in his life again. And I was to keep that resolution. The teacher untangled herself from Richard and set him back into place at the end of the line. The October wind carried grit, which stung my eyes. As I walked away from the school, the wind lifted and carried with it all the debris of summer.

When she went to parties sometimes she would drink too much, loosening the tongue of her youth, and she would drop the "f" word in the middle of a sentence and watch how people eyed her with curiosity or nervousness, wondering back and forth with their eyes who this was they'd allowed in their midst. She used the word for effect, but it expressed what she thought they were doing to one another. They talked and talked, doing talking to one another and never speaking the truth with their hearts.

For instance: the dinner party conversations with other single women where they discussed their splintered, fractured, and worn-out relationships, their histories. They said, more or less, "I left my husband because he kept change for the parking meter in a pie-shaped Tupperware container." Or, "I could no longer tolerate the way he rolled up his jeans and so I ditched him." These women, you understand, did not see themselves as being sad-looking, nondescript or pathetic, scrawny or poorly dressed, or as women who evoked pity as they spoke about rape, revealed their bruises – on the streets, on radio talk shows – or traded healing tips with one another amidst the shelves of books in women's bookstores. No, these women were women who described themselves as "feeling powerful," "having power." These were independent, successful women like she believed she had become, television journalists,

342

producers, writers, politicians, doctors, professors. Of course, they must lie: "I grew out of him," which, translated, meant, "I was more intelligent than he was," a sexy thing to say.

"He smelled like Lifebuoy soap."

But when she attended one of those dinners and they began to "f" one another with their wine-induced chatter, she was careful never to drink too much and drop a stinky bomb onto the white tablecloth. I left because I was afraid I might kill my son, Richard.

17

I wish, Amy thinks, as she watches Piotr study the map spread across the hood of the car. She wishes that she hadn't taken the time to bathe this morning. She would have liked, as in the past when they had to be apart, to keep the evidence of their lovemaking, the odour and moist stickiness of it inside her thighs for the remainder of the day.

She leans against the car, warming the backs of her legs. Beyond, the Trans-Canada Highway curves sharply, disappearing into the trees, and in the far distance she sees the glimmer of Lake Superior and a band of grey mist above it, rimming the almost clear sky of Northern Ontario.

Because it may be his last trip through this area, Piotr is determining whether they can afford to spend an hour or two in Lake Superior Provincial Park with a side trip to Agawa Rock and the pictographs, which they have in the past neglected to visit. Afterwards they would drive straight through to Thunder Bay. Home by Wednesday.

Amy notices the bone-white limbs of a single birch splayed against the deep green backdrop of spruce and pine, the spattering of camomile and blue aster beside the road. Where does he leave off and I begin? she wonders, as she hears the sharp crack of a rifle shot in the distance and then its faint echo. "I thought guns weren't allowed in a provincial park," she says.

The Savage single shot .22 rifle cracked once again and its echo reverberated among the trees beside the highway. It was a clean, distinctive sound, but for the hitchhiker it was muffled by the cotton wads in his ears. He lowered the barrel and watched as blue-black wings clutched at the air and a raven climbed awkwardly up and away into the forest. The rifle's sights were just slightly off, high. A branch swayed under the bird's weight. Winged it, he thought, and headed down into the ditch to investigate.

"A native person probably," Piotr says.

"Why native?" Amy asks, and thinks how not too long ago they both would have said Indian and not native.

"They have the right, don't they, to hunt and fish wherever they want?" he says.

She leans over him as he looks at the map and he feels her heat and the hope she so stubbornly clings to. They had bathed together that morning, she straddling him and rising to her knees to sponge her neck, raising one arm then the other, the sponge following the hollow of her armpit, the contour of a full breast, giving him an image to keep and perhaps use later in a scene, he realized, as he lay back in the sudsy water and studied her.

She twisted the sponge and soap trickled down her belly and into her thick mound of pubic hair. "I'm leaving you," Piotr had said. She closed her eyes and saw them old. Older, perhaps already grey. They carried ice-cream pails and walked among the scrub of the inter-lake in search of blueberries. On the way home they would discuss at length whether the berries would be best put into a pie or eaten with cream and sugar. She hummed and sponged her body for him and saw them old. "My flight's on Friday. Friday morning," Piotr said. "Yes, I know," she answered, still watching her hands pluck blueberries.

He slips the binoculars from his neck and hands them to her. The highway leaps towards her, its surface shimmering with heat waves. She scans the forest on either side of it but there's

345

nothing, no one. The rifle cracks once again, to the north, farther away this time. As she loops the binoculars back around his neck she drinks in the sight of him, his youthful unlined face, small hands spreading the map flat against the car. She believes that he has told her everything there is about himself, while she has told him virtually nothing. He doesn't know, for instance, that she has a son, Richard, who is twenty years old now and lives in Fort Saskatchewan, Alberta, with his father in a house trailer outside of town. That Hank drives a school bus and is the icemaker at the skating and curling rink. He'd wanted flexible hours so that he could care for Richard. He explained this to Margaret when he and Richard used to make infrequent trips back to Manitoba to see her. They did not come to see Amy. Too painful for the boy, Hank told Margaret. Painful for which boy? Amy asked her mother. Not remarried yet, Margaret reported from time to time, and just as good-looking as ever. But many years have passed since their last visit. Margaret has written several times and was rewarded recently with a photograph of a cocky-looking Richard, hair too long and kneecaps shining through threadbare jeans, a bottle of beer raised towards the camera.

When Amy and Piotr return to Winnipeg, she'll go up to the closet that holds the trunk. She will say, See? This is me at age three and four. She will read to him from her journals. But she will not show him the baby pictures she has of Richard. She knows that he would never understand. He would never understand how she could have left him.

"So what do you think?" Piotr asks, the sun glinting off his glasses as he looks up from the map. "Do you think it would be worth to go and see the pictographs?"

The pictographs didn't really interest her. This was the reason why they hadn't gone to see them before. But she said yes because she wanted to be with him for a longer time and it's possible she will forever in her mind see the question in his eyes, his uncertainty, his hesitance, his desire to please her, and not knowing which would please, to go or not to go. Do you think it would be worth to go? It would have been better if she'd said no, she didn't particularly want to go. But she didn't. She said yes.

"Indians have been in the Lake Superior region since around 9000 B.C.," the guide tells Piotr, who wants to chance the gusty wind and venture out onto the narrow ledge worn into the side of a thirty-metre-high rock cliff to take a closer look at the paintings: a caribou, lynx, and fish, totems of the Ojibway Nations. "Ochre," the guide says in answer to his question. "Careful," she tells Amy, offering her hand, "it's slippery." The guide is a small woman, deeply tanned and muscular, and although Amy resents the outstretched hand she takes it anyway and steps out onto the ledge. The turquoise lake flashes light, and waves slap against the base of the cliff. Far below, slabs of submerged rock appear to circle the cliff, resembling giant fish or whales.

"Windy up here today," the guide says. The drawings, she explains to them, commemorate the canoe-crossing of Lake Superior by chief Myeengun and many others from the Carp River to Agawa Rock. "They believed that the great lynx, Misshepezhieu, helped them to survive the trip." She traces the shape of the lynx with her finger. Piotr appears to be captivated by the story and wants to learn more. They've been the only visitors all day, the guide tells them; she's eager to answer Piotr's questions at length. Amy stands behind them, one hand flat on the rock face to steady herself against a sudden gust, which could sweep her off the ledge and down onto the encircling rocks below.

After several moments of not being able to hear what the guide is saying, she leaves them with their heads together, and she climbs down from the ledge and begins to wander along the road. A narrow path winds through the dense growth of trees along the lake's edge and she decides to walk it and search for early raspberries. She finds instead a mushroom and stoops to pick it, twirling the stem. She tears it open and smells its ruffled gills. It's the mingling smell of both of them earlier that morning. She continues to walk for several minutes, and then the path becomes narrower still, the shadows

347

deep. The moist forest floor crawls with moss and fungus. Her breath quickens and she begins to feel that she's being watched. The feeling grows stronger the further she goes. Intruder, trespasser, she thinks, and turns back. No raspberries, she'll tell Piotr, but the forest is littered with mushrooms. I heard a large animal; porcupine, I think. She can barely keep from running back down the path to the road.

When she emerges, the guide has returned to a trailer set off to one side of the rock and sits on a lawn chair in the shade of an awning, reading a newspaper. Piotr has gone down to the shoreline at the base of the cliff, climbed among the tumble of sandstone boulders until he reached the rock farthest out in the water. He sits there cradled in a wedge-shaped groove, legs extended straight out in front of him, hands jammed down between his knees like a small child. His tanned face glows in the sun. He sees her and beckons.

It takes her several minutes to reach him as she climbs up and over sharp stones, skirting around the largest boulders, looking for an easier, safer way. Piotr watches her progress towards him. He has noticed the change from when he first met her. No more of the careless leaping before she proceeds, no more night-long tirades over suggestions of the slightest change to a scene. No more using her advantage of the language. She's quieter now, easily won over. She has given him many, many things. He has grown heavier and sluggish in the face of her largesse. Too many things, he thinks.

She asks for his hand and he pulls her up and makes space for her beside him. She leans into the rock, eyes closed against the sun. "Have you ever wondered why you do this?" she asks. "It never fails."

"What?" he asks. "Do what?"

"This rock," she says. "It's the farthest out into the water. Or else the highest. Or the biggest."

He laughs and shrugs. He knows it's true but it hasn't occurred to him to question why he's compelled to do it.

"How will you manage without French in Belgium?" Amy says, eyes still closed to shut out the bright sun on water. The waves lap and gurgle among the rocks.

"Elizabeth."

"Oh, I see." She both wants and doesn't want him to say more. Her heart lies tightly bound in her chest.

"She speaks many languages."

"You know it's not really necessary for you to move your things before you go," she says. "You could always –"

He reaches for her hand, squeezes it, strokes the backs of her fingers, lifts her hand to his mouth and kisses it. "You know that I care about you very much."

She pulls her hand away. "That means nothing to me."

"Amy," he pleads.

I will not say what he wants to hear, Amy thinks. I will not write the script for this scene. A dragonfly hovers and lights on the tip of Piotr's running shoe, and then flits away. Love, Amy thinks, diaphanous, elusive. A crock of shit.

"How is it possible?" She speaks quietly, lulled by the heat of the sun and the swish and slap of water rising and falling among the pile of rocks. "Tell me. How is it possible to love me one day and not the next?"

"It's too difficult to explain." He turns his face away from her and speaks out over the lake. "I'm not sure that even I can understand it." That is what he'd said in the hotel room in Toronto. "Maybe I've changed, but it isn't the same any more."

"Well, it seems impractical to try and do everything all at once," Amy says. "You can leave your things and then when you come back –"

"No, Amy. A clean break is better."

Better for who? she thinks. She takes a deep breath. "I want to ask you a question. You won't like it, but I want to know. This Elizabeth person. Does she mean something to you?"

His blurted words surprise her but it's his expression that hurts, the twist of anguish and longing there. "I don't know. I don't think so. But, frankly, Amy, I hope so."

Amy closes her eyes and hears the lap, lap of water, a constant, insidious erosion of the rock. It is her will alone keeping them forever together, whole.

"You hope so."

She feels the warmth of his hand on hers as he takes it again, sets it against his thigh, and covers it with his own.

"In my city there's a cathedral," he says, after a time, "where a bugler plays from a tower. Every day, on the hour, he plays, in all four directions. It is even broadcast live to other cities in my country. Except for short times during the war, a bugler has played for six hundred years. Almost every day. Six hundred years!" He squeezes her hand and becomes caught up in his own story. "Tartars were about to invade the city and a guard sounded an alarm to warn the people. Only he didn't get to finish playing because he was killed. *Zzt!*" he says, and then makes a clicking sound with his tongue. "A Tartar arrow in the throat."

"And so?" Amy asks, impatient because he's circling her question with another of his in-my-country legends, an unauthenticated story.

"It became a tradition. The music is played, then stops suddenly, as though the bugler has been shot."

"A real person?" Amy says. "A real person goes up into a church tower each day, on the hour, and plays – and then pretends to be shot?"

He appears not to have heard as he looks out over the water at the green clumps of islands dotting the horizon. "I got used to hearing the music. I would walk through the square and not even look up."

Amy senses him listening now, the sound a spirit guide, the great lynx, drawing him far across the water. She feels desolate. He's shut her out because he knows that where he's going she has no place.

"Well, I think it's ridiculous. It doesn't make sense," she says, feeling inadequate, like a child wanting to kick over someone's sandcastle because it's bigger and better constructed than her own. "Why don't they just use a bloody tape recording!"

As the car glided swiftly along the Trans-Canada Highway across the undulating escarpment, the face of the lake flashed through the dark trees, giving them fleeting glimpses of light on water. As they drove he began to speak, haltingly at first, not wanting to say more than was necessary, not wanting to hurt her. Canada, he said, had not been kind to him. She seemed calm, almost soft, with what he took to be acceptance at last, resignation, and so he told her that he would not be returning. That from Belgium he would go back to his home country. She listened as he attempted to explain how it was, that in his family he was expected to make a mark, to leave behind something lasting, a legacy. It was not possible to achieve this here. He would return to Poland with the hope that some day he would have children, children who would make a difference in the new period of his country's history.

After that they drove in silence for almost five hours, passing through Wawa and White River, stopping once for food, to spell one another off driving, for gasoline. No wildlife stepped out to greet them as they passed by. No special children, she and Piotr. Just an ordinary man and woman. Piotr, about to be swept aside by the whim of fate, a white arm unfolding in a graceful gesture, space opening up between them.

It is steady, monotonous driving, the highway climbing suddenly, trees pulling back to reveal the face of the sky and thin streamers of clouds scudding across it and then dropping back down again to become a buff corridor cutting through a jagged skyline. The traffic is light, sporadic. Several motorized campers driven by early vacationers, cars towing boats or sporting wind-surf boards, semi-truck trailers hauling from the eastern cities to the prairies and on to the west coast, and a red, older-model half-ton with a homemade wooden sleeper on back, which they had been behind earlier, passed, then met again after stopping for gas and pass now for a second time. The truck is a Chevrolet C10, about 1968 or '69, Amy notes, and the driver has a full grey beard and a ponytail, a throwback to the Sixties.

When she and Piotr stop to eat they speak only to complain about the menu and the usual fare of deep-fried foods, greasy hamburgers. Amy watches as Piotr eats with zest, his appetite an affront, one foot already in Belgium, she knows. She hates the fact that he can eat, the politeness he's assumed, his sudden deference as he opened doors, pulled out her chair in the restaurant. It's as though she had suddenly aged, or become his mother.

When they get back to the car they drive in silence again, half-listening to the woman who broadcasts the news, her voice clear, emotionless. When later that evening she announces their own names it will be in the same way. The newscaster tells them that fires north of Thunder Bay pose no threat to travellers, while in northern Manitoba half of the forest is burning out of control. There has been a death in a boating accident on Lake Ontario involving two crafts. Amy hears the deceased man's name, and then the survivor's, a model named Elsa Miller.

Amy turns the volume up and listens, shocked, as she gradually takes in the information. A woman named Elsa Miller, sailing, out on the lake alone but for her companion, a dog. A collision with a large power boat, its occupant, a man, who was killed instantly on impact. Elsa Miller was thrown into the water and kept afloat by the hero of the story, her pet dog, Jock, a springer spaniel.

A picture instantly flashes into her mind. She, Mel, Elsa, appear now as they are in one of the few remaining photographs taken at Jill's funeral. Amy and Mel stand beside the open grave where the white casket rests, suspended on straps, a mound of dark ferns spread across its lid. Margaret had insisted on a white casket because Jill had died a virgin. The little bride of Christ. A polished gem. Mel wears his first suit and has affected a casual pose, hands in his pockets, turning sideways to the coffin and looking off into the distance as though distracted by something more important. Amy's shoulders slope beneath the navy-blue cape she's wearing. Elsa stands behind her, bending forward at the waist as if she has a stomach-ache. Both hands are pressed against her eyes. It's clear that she's crying hard.

"I know that woman," Amy says to Piotr. "She used to live in Carona." She wonders what she should be feeling.

"Is it a common name?"

"It's her, I know it." Elsa had become a model and Amy had seen her from time to time on billboards, always wearing white, gazing out from a tropical island: the heaven you gained if you invested in a certain insurance package. Amy had seen Elsa at forty looking like thirty, had seen her on television, her long blonde hair streaming in the wind as she walked among the twitching flanks of stallions, turning her sun-drenched face to the camera, or selling automobiles with her nondescript foreign accent and her enigmatic smile.

Amy studies Piotr's profile, how he chews at dry skin on his bottom lip, eyes fixed on the road beyond, mind focused on another country. I was struck by lightning, she wants to say. I used to believe that I had enough power in me to light up a city as large as New York. That I could affect the outcome of other people's lives by just thinking.

She turns off the radio. "I was struck by lightning once," she says. "When I was a kid."

"Amy, you'd probably be dead if that was the case," he says curtly. She feels at this point he is beyond being interested in what to him may be one of her inventions.

"I was." When they reach home, and after they store the canisters that contain their latest film in the cool room in the basement, she will take him by the hand and lead him upstairs to the closet and the trunk where her journals and her childhood films lie. "I think I was about nine or ten years old when it happened. A clear day. Not a cloud in the sky." She will at last view what she filmed that day in the cemetery. Trees appear to fly past the window, white lines flash by. She hears a siren. Its sound rises quickly, and she turns and sees a flashing red light. "Slow down, Piotr."

"I'm not speeding," he says, and she lurches forward as he brakes. Seconds later, the police car is upon them. "Should I pull over?" he asks. But the car swoops around them, engine roaring and siren screaming, then swerves into the lane in front of them, swinging out once again and passing the red half-ton with the wooden sleeper. The police car races around a curve in the road and out of sight, the sound of its siren only a faint echo now bouncing off the rock of the escarpment.

"Whew, scary." She doesn't want to see carnage. There was a time when her stomach was stronger. Now she must close her eyes, even to violence acted out on a screen.

"Where's the camcorder?" Piotr asks.

"You're not serious."

"Why not?" he says and grins.

"It's in the trunk," Amy says, peeved, "where you put it this morning."

"Hey!" he says, and pokes her in the ribs. "You never know, I might get something useful." His eyes shine in expectancy of an adventure.

They travel for several minutes, gaining swiftly on the red truck and the bend in the highway. "Come on, slowpoke," Piotr urges and although the curve in the highway is sharp, he decides to pass the truck. As they get closer to it, Amy sees that there are two people in the cab now. Amy recognizes the driver's grey ponytail and, beside him, the red-plaid jacket, the black shoulder-length hair of the weird man she saw on the ferry, beside the road, in the giftshop. The hitchhiker. Piotr speeds up, is only metres away, when the taillights of the truck glow suddenly.

"Watch!"

He swears and swerves around the vehicle and Amy holds her breath. The highway opens up then as they complete the curve, and directly in front of them they see the OPP car angled across the road, light still flashing. Piotr brakes hard. Beyond the police car Amy sees a school bus turned onto its side. "Shit." Little kids, she thinks. But she notices all at once a front-end loader parked on the shoulder, several derelict vehicles positioned up against rock and trees, making the highway impassable at either side of the overturned bus, and people milling about.

The red half-ton stops behind a group of cars parked on the opposite shoulder and the man with the ponytail and the hitchhiker get out.

"What's going on?" Piotr rolls down the window as one of the police officers approaches.

"You're going to have to pull over, folks," he says. It's a

barricade, he explains cheerfully, as if it were a minor irritation which must be endured for a short time only. His partner has gone over to the barricade and stands beside the school bus, hands on hips, a patient smile as he chats with a native man. It's one of several barricades that have gone up suddenly, a chain reaction of roadblocks in Ontario, and there are threats of similar action in Manitoba and Saskatchewan, they learn. This could last hours, a day, or longer. "These people don't have anything better to do anyway," the officer says.

"This doesn't look good," Piotr says, as he studies the map. The positioning of the barricade is not arbitrary, but cleverly strategic, given that at this point the highway hugs the shore of Nipigon Bay and there are no roads to the north. They would need to backtrack a hundred kilometres to Terrace, then head north, and travel miles on secondary gravel roads through wilderness before they could pick up the No. 11 and cut back south again. A good day's drive. Amy feels mildly elated by the prospect. She sees that solid wall of rusted vehicles, the overturned bus, the silhouettes of two native people sitting on top of it. Below them, sitting in a row of lawn chairs, men, women, and children stare across the distance between them. Good for you, Amy wants to say.

"Let's get the camcorder," Piotr says, and pops the trunk.

So you think it would be worth to go and see the pictographs?
Yes, she said.
Time wasted, when instead they could have passed by the spot on the highway chosen for the barricade.

"Let's get the camcorder," Piotr says, and pops the trunk. They get out of the car. People stand around, clustered near the parked cars across the highway from the barricade.

A young man with the build of a weight lifter approaches their car. SNAKE BITE is printed across his tank top. A set of earphones encircle his muscular neck. "I've got to get to the Peg. They bloody got a lot of nerve," he says, and appears surprised when Amy and Piotr don't readily agree. Piotr bends and opens a carrying case and when the man sees the video camera he grins. "Great," he says.

Amy sees two black and white Japanese girls standing beside the highway looking as though they're waiting for a bus. Black oxford shoes, white socks, black shorts, white tops with black geometric designs, white faces, and black, blunt-cut hair. A father, wearing coveralls, walks past them pushing a baby in a stroller back and forth, back and forth.

Let's get the camcorder, Piotr said, and popped the trunk.

Amy hands him a battery, a tape, and watches as he hefts the camera to his shoulder. They cross the highway to where people are standing, two deep across from the barricade.

Yes, he was cautioned, she told them at the police investigation. But he had to be the farthest out from the shore, or the highest, or on top of the largest rock. Of course he wanted to be in the front of the crowd.

As Piotr walks across the space that separates the spectators and the native people, Amy's eyes caress the image of his squared shoulders beneath the tan shirt, his tan Bermuda shorts, his well-shaped legs. Piotr, walking out the farthest. Snake Bite moves up to Amy's side. She can feel heat radiating from his body. "Good," he says, hawks, and then spits. "Get those suckers on film." The Sixties-looking man with the grey ponytail stands on the other side of her. He says something in a dry, sardonic voice, and Snake Bite guffaws loudly. From the corner of her eye, Amy sees the hitchhiker standing behind the grey-haired man, a tangle of black hair against a red-plaid jacket. Her attention is drawn then by a woman in an Adidas sweatsuit who appears suddenly, heavy breasts bouncing as she jogs past dragging a white toy poodle on a leash. The Japanese girls, who have crossed the highway to where the spectators stand, giggle and lift little disposable cameras to their eyes.

Piotr's camcorder looks into the inquisitive round faces of

the native children sitting on their mothers' and grandmothers' knees. Above them, the two men on top of the school bus rise to their feet, sticks dangling at their sides. Guns? Amy wonders. She hears the high-pitched sound of sirens overlapping, growing louder as police cars, one after another, round the curve in the highway. Their shrill alarm makes her shiver.

As Piotr begins to record the images, the enquiring faces of children, the calm, stoical demeanour of the men and women, the wrinkled, patient faces of the elders, a police officer moves towards him. Piotr records the man's palm raised to cover the camera's lens, his businesslike voice saying over the wail of sirens in the background, "Back off, fella."

Yes, he was cautioned, she tells the members of the investigation.

The sirens of the approaching police cars wind down to a halt one by one, and Amy hears car doors slamming shut.

"Hey!" one of the men on the school bus calls down to Piotr, wanting to play to his camera. He raises his stick over his head in a boastful, rebellious gesture, the stick a baseball bat and not a gun, as Piotr's videotape will prove. "Hey, you!" the man yells, his hand dropping to his crotch in an obscene gesture. "Fuck you all!" he screams at the crowd of spectators.

Amy, do you think it would be worth to go and see the pictographs?
Yes, she said.

Amy stands watching with the others as Piotr holds his ground, ignoring the police officer's admonition to back off. She hears the words "fuck you" again, but this time they are uttered softly, from behind her. The hitchhiker, she realizes, as she sees the barrel of his Savage single shot .22 jut forward at her shoulder. His rifle cracks and she hears the whine of the bullet through the trees at the side of the road. Piotr wheels around at the sound, lowers the camera, a question in his face, hesitating. But as the police officer who had tried to warn him away turns now and strides across the space towards the spectators, his hand placed against his hip holster, Piotr raises the camera again.

The hitchhiker steps in front of Amy then, directly in line with Piotr, blocking him from her view. She sees his gun barrel dip and jerk as he reloads. He raises the rifle to his shoulder, pointing it at the barricade. "Fuck you!" he yells this time, and shoots. The bullet pings sharply against the highway. The Japanese girls shriek and their cameras drop to the pavement. "Whoa!" Snake Bite exclaims and backs away from Amy's side.

Amy sees him and sees him, how the hitchhiker swipes at the strands of dark hair which lie across his forehead obscuring his vision. His voice is a roar inside her head. *Fuck you, fuck you.* She hears him later in her nightmares, his voice raw but emotionless, its tone saying that it was not anger directed against any particular person. *Fuck you.*

And then it is over.

He screams his oath, reloads again, and runs towards the barricade. Piotr records the policeman's back, when he drops to one knee, hand at his hip rising. Amy hears other voices barking strong, terse commands. *Or I'll shoot,* her dreams say.

Then she heard another shot, she told them. Not the metallic crack of a .22 rifle, but the fuller sound of a higher-powered rifle. Two shots. They did not come from the policeman who was down on his knee. They came from behind. Another policeman. Another gun, she was certain.

The video camera tumbles through the air and bounces several times across the cement. Amy sees Piotr in slow motion, again and then again, his arms opening wide to clutch at the air. Falling, again and then again, face down. His head moves, once, twice. And then he is still.

"Fuck you! Fuck you!" she hears and then sees the hitchhiker stumble and roll sideways as she runs past him, runs across the open space towards Piotr. Lawn chairs tumble as people flee, crying and calling out to one another. Amy's leg

358

stings suddenly as she runs towards him. A bee sting. The sting of a bee. A bee sting, she thinks, as she kneels down beside Piotr.

Do you think it would be worth to go and see the pictographs?
   Yes, she said.

One year later:

"On the way over to meet you, I realized," Daria had said to Amy earlier as they sat beside the river at The Forks on blocks hewn from tyndall stone, stone imprinted with the shapes of ancient sea animals for small fingers to discover, trace, exclaim over. "It's June," Daria had said. "You must be thinking about Piotr."

A train enters the trestle bridge over the Assiniboine near its mouth, inching into the CN station. The rumble of it echoes in the steel girders, overpowering all other sounds as Amy and Daria walk along the river, now, towards it. Beyond the train trestle bridge, reflected in the water, are rows of the cement columns of three other bridges that span the shallow water; on them, traffic sweeps across the river, going both ways. Buses, cars, are blocks of colour passing above, soundless in the rumble of the arriving train.

The women Amy knows and whom she has in the past sat with at dinner-table discussions believe that what has happened to her is a tragedy. She knows her presence among them incites pity but, even so, she has said nothing to make them think otherwise. Doing nothing is making a choice, too, you know. She hears Rhoda's voice.

She must speak loudly to be heard above the train. "Piotr was leaving me," she tells Daria. "When Piotr was killed, he was running away from me. He was going to return to Poland. Alone."

361

Daria stops walking and turns her soft face to Amy. "Oh!" she exclaims. "Oh, Amy, I'm so, so, sorry." Tears brim in Daria's heavily pencilled eyes. Don't you cry, Amy thinks. Don't you let any of that sadness get out here. You'll make a wreck of your face. Daria wants to touch her, Amy can tell. Daria wants to be as soft as her face, to put her arms around Amy, for the both of them to weep over their collective, unspoken tragedies.

Separate houses and bank accounts, Amy writes in her notebook later that evening. She leans over her desk in her room; where she has sat for a year, thinking, remembering, writing. *The women had agreed when they sat around the dinner table one night, over a year ago, about what might be the perfect relationship. It was freedom they wanted but intimacy too. A relationship similar to her and Piotr's, where they'd have to be apart for work, sometimes a month, or four, and then would come together again to give and receive the best of one another: tender attention, long walks, gourmet meals, back rubs in the middle of the night, a mickey bottle turned hot-water bottle placed gently against the abdomen to ease menstrual cramps. "Being apart on occasion for long periods of time is the only reason why we have lasted this long," she had told them, rather smugly, she knew. She didn't tell them how she felt when they were apart, that it was like being alone on a beach at night, listening to waves washing in and pulling back. The sound of their separation a melancholy sound. Or, that she had often thought that she would stop breathing if for some reason he didn't return. That, to her, Piotr was Timothy, Richard, the sibling she never had, and the only person she had ever loved.*

Amy goes to the closet and the trunk which holds her journals, the reels of eight-millimetre film. The film, brittle with age, proves difficult to thread into the projector she borrowed from the library. The subject of the first one she chooses to watch is "The Robin," so says Timothy's printing on its box. She turns off the desk lamp and sits in darkness watching scratch marks run across the wall and then, suddenly, tree branches sway, their colour washed out, almost yellow, and among the branches she catches a glimpse of what had motivated the filming, a crimson-breasted robin. A square of light leaps onto the wall as the film breaks and flaps noisily on the reel.

She chooses another film, one she has seen before, and watches herself playing at Grand Beach. She leans back, eyes half-closed, studying the little girl on the wall. A stranger, she thinks, as she notices the child's puzzled expression, the smile often too wide, as though over-anxious to please, the flicker of worry darting into the eyes.

She watches film after film and sees the pattern, sees all of them, marching across the wall for Timothy, waving on command or cajoled into more outrageous acts for the camera. A document of their connection, Amy thinks. Together, but apart. Timothy. Only the eye behind the camera. She shuts off the projector and sits in the soft glow of the desk lamp, thinking. Piotr, like Jill, had left too soon. Like Rilke's "godlike youth," they had ceased to exist. Their absence makes "emptiness vibrate" in ways that do *not* comfort, Amy thinks. That do not help me now.

She picks up the last box of film, the one that is labelled in a child's large-size writing. "In the Cemetery." Her fingers shake as she feeds it into the machine. She flicks on the projector's lamp and sits for several moments staring at the square of light on the wall, finger toying with the toggle switch which will set the film in motion. She wonders what will be revealed. Will she see a slash of lightning, or a sheet of light – or a ball of light becoming wings unfolding, carrying a human-like figure in their centre whose eyes are white, whose feet glow as it ascends up and out of sight? She gets up and goes over to the window to look down into the street. Dappled shadows move across the lawn as trees sway beneath the streetlight. Who *do* we turn to? Not angels.

Barefoot, and wearing her housecoat, she stands on the patio in the dead of night. Fire flares in the gas barbecue. She rips a page from a journal, holds it to the flame until it catches, and then drops it among the lava coals. Snivelling, whiny, she thinks; she would never want anyone to read it. She rips another page loose and then another, until the fire burns strong and bright. Then she makes a teepee over the fire out of all her other journals and watches as pages turn brown and curl in the heat. She reaches for the glass she'd set on the patio table, sips at the Scotch, thinking of Hank building a fire, someone calling the fire department, a truck screaming to a halt outside the house. I'm sorry, ma'am, but you're not allowed to light fires in the city.

She takes the reel from the pocket of her housecoat and unwinds a length of brittle film, still tempted, though she suspects that if she held it up to the light of the fire she would see only holes, holes the size of pinpricks, and the light of the fire passing through them. An undercurrent of cool wind rushes in, feeding the flame, and Amy watches how, for an instant, pages, words, glow white hot, fade, and then disappear. The Scotch tingles in her mouth.

The swollen thing moves behind her rib bone, a slight sliding sideways, a pressure. A reminder.

Also of interest

The fiction of Michèle Roberts

DAUGHTERS OF THE HOUSE

WINNER OF THE 1993 W. H. SMITH LITERARY AWARD
SHORTLISTED FOR THE BOOKER PRIZE

**'Remarkable and beautifully written . . . her best book
yet' – *Hermione Lee, Independent on Sunday***

Secrets and lies linger in the very walls of the solid, old
Normandy house in which Thérèse and Léonie, French and
English cousins of the same age, grow up after the war.
Intrigued by parents' and servants' guilty silences and the
broken shrine they find buried in the woods, the girls weave
their own elaborate fantasies, unwittingly revealing the
village secret and a deep shame that will come to haunt
Thérèse and Léonie in their adult lives . . .

Resonant with the sounds and scents of French provincial
life, this is a richly imagined and sensuous tale from one of
Britain's most exciting contemporary writers.

DURING MOTHER'S ABSENCE

'The writing is English at its very best . . . the prose pulses
with a sense of dangerous energy, only just held in
check . . . compelling . . . incisive and brilliant' – *Independent*

Subversive, sensuous tales, wise and witty fictions; this
collection of short stories from one of Britain's most
acclaimed novelists is by turns shockingly delicious and
soberingly disquieting. When mother is away taboos are
breached, the untouchables embraced and the forbidden
tasted.

In 'Laundry', a poor, plain girl takes devilish pleasure in
outwitting the pious monks and nuns she washes for. In
'Anger' a young woman branded by fire at birth by her
mother is scarred – and blessed – for life. In the highly
sensuous 'Taking it Easy' a mother with writer's block finds
an escape from the slavery of her twin enemies by turning
them into food for thought. In 'Your Shoes', it's the mother,
buried beneath the covers of her runaway daughter's bed, who
pieces together the story of their lives (and their shoes). And
in the beautiful, arresting 'God's House' a young girl faces the
ultimate mother's absence.

The fiction of Sara Maitland

DAUGHTER OF JERUSALEM
WINNER OF THE SOMERSET MAUGHAM AWARD

'A challenging and joyful book by an extraordinarily gifted writer – *Books and Bookmen*

For five years, Elizabeth and her husband Ian have unsuccessfully attempted to have a child. Tests have shown inescapably that it is Elizabeth who is unable to conceive. However, her gynaecologist believes it to be a psychological, not a physical barrier that is preventing her from becoming pregnant . . .

VIRGIN TERRITORY

'A novel full of brilliant observations which seldom fail to hit home' – *Emma Tennant*

The rape of a nun in a South American mission house causes more disturbance among the unharmed sisters – especially in Sister Anna – than in the victim herself. She comes to London to work through her emotional reaction, and to examine her vow of chastity. Is virginity positive or negative? And what is the link between sex and violence?

THREE TIMES TABLE

'Wise, complex and often beautiful' – *Zöe Fairbairns*

Three women – Rachel, her daughter, and her daughter's daughter – share a house, but inhabit different worlds. Sara Maitland's remarkable novel focuses on one strange and wakeful night in which Rachael, Phoebe and Maggie find themselves facing the illusions of their own pasts. This is a powerful, magical novel about the shaping of women's lives – their work, their friendships, their mothers and fathers, the extent of their freedom and the boundaries of their experience.

WOMEN FLY WHEN MEN AREN'T WATCHING

'Fresh with a surreal kick' – *Spectator*

The breadth of Sara Maitland's interests and inspiration are brilliantly displayed in this gathering of tales old and new: from folk-stories in 'True North' to classical mythology in 'Cassandra'; from historical incident in 'Forceps Delivery' to Christian heroines like Perpetua in 'Requiem'. And as she intertwines the everyday and the inexplicable to witty or disquieting effect in 'Greed' and 'The Loveliness of the Long Distance Runner', her wildest flights of fantasy remain anchored in a consciousness of the oppression of women, overlaid with a wickedly ironic humour.

The fiction of Janette Turner Hospital

THE LAST MAGICIAN

'Her prose is lucid, sensuous and hard . . . a first-rate novelist'
– *Independent*

A novel about the private terrors and luminous hopes within
the secrets we collude in keeping. *The Last
Magician* is a *tour de force* by a visionary writer.

CHARADES

**SHORTLISTED FOR THE AUSTRALIAN NATIONAL
BOOK COUNCIL AND MILES FRANKLIN AWARDS**

'Janette Turner Hospital goes from strength to literary
strength – ever brilliant in ideas, graceful in expression,
resourceful in story – and in *Charades* throwing in, for good
measure, a heady eroticism. I loved it!' – *Fay Weldon*.

BORDERLINE

'One of the most elegant prose styles in the business' – *The Times*

Surreal yet utterly credible, *Borderline* is a showcase for Janette Turner Hospital's remarkable talent: a political and metaphysical thriller; a journey via dextrous prose and a terrifying insight, to the borderline where 'as at death and in dreams . . . control is not in the hands of the traveller'.

THE TIGER IN THE TIGER PIT

'This family is familiar, damn familiar . . . finally you have to break down, realise it's probably your own family Janette Turner Hospital is writing about' – *Los Angeles Times*

Janette Turner Hospital unravels the skeins of family life – its hostilities, explosive secrets and its constricting yet enduring love. The result is one of the most haunting and accurate explorations of the family in contemporary fiction.

THE IVORY SWING

'A disturbing meditation on the clash of cultures and the rebellion and rage in each . . . A novel of unusual delicacy and power' – *Washington Post Book World*

Sensuous and disquieting, *The Ivory Swing* won the Canadian Seal Novel Award.

ISOBARS

'A brilliant collection . . . Hospital's extraordinary prose style, a model of elegant compression, is as restrained as it is resonant – *Publishers Weekly*

Internationally acclaimed novelist and short story writer Janette Turner Hospital has earned a reputation as one of the most daring and original fiction writers of today. In this, her latest collection, the themes of desire, memory, loss, and the various guises of damage, are woven into stories that cross time and continents like isobars of the psyche.